The Life Adventurous

OTHER BOOKS BY JAMES T. FARRELL

STUDS LONIGAN

A trilogy comprising "Young Lonigan," "The Young Manhood of Studs Lonigan," and "Judgment Day"

The Danny O'Neill Tetralogy

A WORLD I NEVER MADE

NO STAR IS LOST

FATHER AND SON

MY DAYS OF ANGER

BERNARD CLARE

WHEN BOYHOOD DREAMS COME TRUE

THE SHORT STORIES OF JAMES T. FARRELL

Comprising "Calico Shoes and Other Stories," "Guillotine Party and Other Stories," and "Can All This Grandeur Perish and Other Stories"

TO WHOM IT MAY CONCERN

$1,000 A WEEK

GAS-HOUSE MCGINTY

ELLEN ROGERS

TOMMY GALLAGHER'S CRUSADE

A NOTE ON LITERARY CRITICISM

THE LEAGUE OF FRIGHTENED PHILISTINES

LITERATURE AND MORALITY

The Life Adventurous

and other stories

BY

JAMES T. FARRELL

THE VANGUARD PRESS, INC.

New York

MANUFACTURED IN THE UNITED STATES OF AMERICA
BY H. WOLFF, NEW YORK, N. Y.

*To the memory of Ruth Farmer
and to Arthur Farmer*

Contents

The Life Adventurous

I

"I COULD BE A SUCCESSFUL BABBITT if I wanted to," Lewis Gordon boasted.

"I know you could," Powers Norton answered.

They were smoking cigarettes. The difference in their characters was observable in the way each of them smoked. Lewis, a prepossessing young man in his twenties, was sitting on the park bench, relaxed, smoking casually, holding the cigarette between the index and the third finger of his left hand and now and then taking a puff. Powers was a ruddy-faced man with touches of gray around the temples. He was in his late thirties, and there was a harassed look in his brown eyes. He was medium-sized, with light hair. He seemed physically soft. He puffed nervously, taking a few puffs on a cigarette, and then throwing it away and lighting a new one.

Lewis and Powers had met at the Sour Apple, a Bohemian forum on the near North Side, and they had quickly become friends. Now they sat talking on a bench in Lincoln Park, near a path where people passed, and they could see before them a broad sweep of well-kept grass.

"It's easier and it's safer to be a success in business than to live as you do," Powers said.

"And duller. The curse of life is dullness."

Powers didn't answer. He seemed to be reflecting, and Lewis watched him closely.

"Would we have met at the Sour Apple, and would we be

3

friends, if both of us didn't want to free ourselves from dullness, the dullness of the bourgeoisie?" Lewis asked.

"Well, I suppose not. I never could quite understand myself," Powers said.

"Powers, the trouble with you is that you want to blame yourself for the faults of the world. I don't. I blame the world. Come on, old fellow, snap out of it. Be an extrovert. The introvert never has any fun."

"I suppose you're right, Lewis."

"The whole world is run on a series of fictions. It is all as if this were so and that were so. It is as if a man's property were his own. It's his own just as long as I admit that it is. When I no longer admit it, the fiction vanishes like smoke, like a will-o-the-wisp."

"Yes, there's something in what you say, but, then, a policeman and a jail aren't mere fictions," Powers answered.

"Hell, that's the least of my worries, and it should be the least of yours. Nothing can go wrong with my plan. I've worked it out carefully. There's no chance of a slip-up, not unless we lose our heads. And we're not going to lose them. Our heads weren't given to us to be lost. But, there, I'm getting metaphysical. If I say our heads weren't given to us, I recognize that there is a Giver of heads in the universe. If there is a Giver of heads, that Giver is supreme over us. It is in His hands, or Its hands, to control us. And that is impossible. Because we are supreme in ourselves and unto ourselves. Ego is King, if king there need be in the world," Lewis explained.

"You've built up a whole philosophy to justify your kind of life, haven't you?"

"It's merely a recognition of the facts. The facts about ourselves and our nature. And I don't believe in drawing conclusions merely for the sake of drawing them and talking about them. I'm not a Bughouse Square or Sour Apple soapboxer. I want to draw conclusions in order to act on them."

"I have no philosophy. I have nothing."

"You have yourself, your ego. You and I have formed our own League of Egotists."

Powers nervously lit another cigarette. He looked off, troubled.

"Sometimes I can't believe I'm where I am and what I am," he said moodily.

"You taught sociology, didn't you?"

"Yes. I was going along. I was in a rut. I know that. If I hadn't been in a rut I wouldn't have acted the way I did. I have no regrets."

"One of the cardinal principles of conscious egotism is to have no regrets. Regret is folly."

"You know, Kitty was wonderful. I still think of her. My God, I think of her naked body on the bed. I guess I was bored with my wife. After I slept with Kitty I felt like a new man."

"She must have been necessary for your ego."

"We spent a summer at the sand dunes. I came into town for the second half of the summer quarter. And Kitty was a school teacher from the country. But there was nothing school-teacherish about her. She seemed like the sweetest, prettiest thing. She looked so innocent. And she was crazy with lust. No, it wasn't love. It was lust."

"Lust is one of the fine fruits of egotism."

"Anyway, I was bored with teaching and I was even bored with myself. I was seedy and rusty. The first day I took over the class, I noticed her. I couldn't help looking at her. And she didn't seem to mind it. Do you know, within a week I was sleeping with her."

"You had a good time."

"But I ruined my life."

"What's ruined about it?"

"Look at me."

"Your life isn't ruined. You've escaped into freedom."

"I acted like a kid."

"Listen, Powers, I want to act like a kid, in that sense, all of my life. I never want to grow old and smug."

"If you're married, and you have two kids, and you're living quietly, and then suddenly you let go the way I did, you get unhinged. I was. Christ, kid, I couldn't think of anything but

Kitty. I wanted to be in bed with her forever. I'd go to class every day exhausted."

"What better can you want from a woman? Young, beautiful, without shame."

"I used to wish I were twenty-one."

Lewis laughed heartily.

"Where's Kitty now?"

"I guess she's back in Iowa. It's funny you never heard of the mess. The papers carried the story on the front page. University Professor In Love Nest With Student."

"You should have been discreet."

"But what I can't understand is the way I felt toward my wife. When this mess was in the papers, I found out that she had been having little affairs of her own. I was so damned jealous. I knew I had no right to be jealous. Hadn't I done the same? And yet I was."

"What did she do?"

"She took the kids and ran off with a tap dancer. I don't know how she met him, but she did. It broke me up. And Kitty was dismissed from school. I lost my job. Her father came to Chicago to shoot me, and, when he found her, she was in bed with some kid."

"Did the father shoot?"

"No, he didn't. Hell, it was a disgusting mess. My colleagues avoided me like the plague."

"I'll bet they envied you," Lewis said. He continued: "Are you still brooding over it?"

"No, I really am not. I'll tell you, I'm still bewildered. It's almost a year since it happened."

"You never hear from Kitty?"

"No. Nor from my wife and kids. I keep wondering where they are, what the kids are like."

"Hell, you're free. You and I have no responsibilities. You stick with me, and we'll go places."

"I really don't care what I do or what happens to me. What difference does it make?"

"It makes no difference except for your ego."

"Let's get a drink."

"All right. We'll get a bottle of gin."

They got up and left.

II

"Instead of looking so gloomy, why not be glad we have enough dough to eat breakfast with?" Lewis said.

"My gloom is purely physical. I'm not as young as you are. At my age, a man can't drink the way you can and not feel the effects," Powers said.

They sat eating ham and eggs at a marble-topped table in a restaurant on North Clark Street. It was noon, and the restaurant was crowded and noisy.

"I have a headache," Powers said.

"It was an amusing evening, and the two dames weren't so bad either, were they?"

"No, they weren't," Powers said, but he agreed with Lewis because he didn't want to disagree. It would have been too much effort. He had a wretched hangover, and he didn't even want to talk. It was too much of an exertion even to utter the words.

There was no sensible reason in the world why he should be disgusted with himself for getting drunk and sleeping with the girl he'd picked up. In fact, he could feel proud of himself in a way. Here he was, a man who had had little youth, who had worked his way through college, become a sociologist. He had been Puritanical, repressed, timid. And now, look at the way he lived. Why should he seem ridiculous in his own eyes?

"Oh!" he exclaimed, half aloud, without realizing it.

"Come on, snap out of it. Eat. You're going to feel better. We'll sit in the sun in Lincoln Park and philosophize."

Powers looked blankly at his ham and eggs. He ate slowly, with weary motions.

"I always did have a preference for telephone operators. I don't know why, but I do. All of the telephone operators I've known have been dumb. But I don't mind a Dumb Dora if she has looks and knows the tricks."

—What the hell does it all mean? Powers asked himself.

He wanted to get out of this damned rut he was in, and he didn't know how. Every time he resolved to do something about himself, he broke his good resolutions. His self-confidence was gone. He didn't have the will power necessary to get out of his rut. He wanted to be a respectable married man. A smug professor. And he couldn't be. He was afraid he wouldn't even be able to get references, and what else could he do?

"Mine's name was Dora. Well, Dora gave us what we needed to change our luck. I suppose by now she's discovered that I pinched a five from her pocketbook. Poor Dumb Dora."

Powers was disturbed.

"I don't see why I shouldn't have done it," Lewis said.

Powers didn't answer. Yes, arguing was too much of a form of violent exercise for him this morning. It wasn't right to do such things. He was as responsible as Lewis. Wasn't he eating out of the five? God, he was disgusted with himself. But nothing mattered. Nothing mattered. If he only didn't have this hangover.

"In fact, I gave her something. I gave her some of my manhood," Lewis said, enjoying his own witticism.

Yes, he had been a promising professor with a promising and secure academic future ahead of him. Now he was a bum. What was so attractive, so pleasurable in a fly-by-night success with a stupid telephone operator? The lack of consequences and responsibility? But he didn't mind that—that is, he hadn't when he was first married. He had to realize that the past was irrevocable.

"Hell, sex is half a fraud unless you decorate it with logical 'as ifs.' "

"It wouldn't have mattered in my life one way or the other whether I'd met this girl and slept with her, or not," Powers said.

"Now you're showing some healthy cynicism," Lewis said.

Powers smothered his resentment. Think of it—allowing this kid to patronize him.

"Well, Dumb Dora loved it, and that's no boast. But do you know what occurred to me, Powers?"

"What?" Powers asked, wiping up his plate with a piece of bread.

"She wanted to talk about everything we did. And she didn't know who she was with, because suddenly she blushed and asked me if I thought she was awful because of the words she used. The actions didn't seem to give her any qualms of conscience, but the words did. And she wanted to keep using them. Do you know why?"

Powers didn't say anything. He stirred his coffee.

"People have to build ideas and emotions around sex. She had to fill in the gap between desire and fulfillment with talk because she wanted more than she got. Ah, the pitiful damned fools who belong to what is called humanity."

"I kind of felt sorry for them, poor kids."

"They got what they wanted. Weren't they itching for it? But my observation is very good—even if I admit it. I always admit I'm bright, though, when I am. My Dumb Dora wishes that you could have some rousing bedroom sport every minute of your life."

"She was a nymphomaniac."

"They're the best kind of Dumb Dora to get. You know, they generally can't become pregnant either. I like 'em. Give me a bitch every time."

Powers was uneasy because of an acute sense of loss. He wanted to be back with his wife and children. And yet he hadn't really wanted his wife and children. If he had wanted them, would he be here now? Hell, there was no free will. He had not been a free agent. He had done what he couldn't have prevented himself from doing with all the will power, self-restraint, moral sense, and decorum in the whole world.

"I suppose I'd feel the hollowness of it if I weren't an egotist. I have my way of enhancing such mundane details of life. To me, a female is a delectable piece of warm, living, panting property that I can own. And when I do, I score up another triumph for my ego. I look on a woman's body as a violin, and I'm touching all of the strings. I begin with great delicacy, and I like to end in lust, with a few smacks and some bites to finish it off. And my Dumb Doras like it. But, then, they're generally bitches. As I said, give me a bitch every time in the week. It's not merely their experience that I appreciate. They aren't encumbrances. In a way, I guess they have something of the real old ego in them, too."

Powers drank his coffee.

"Have some more. It'll fix you up."

He signaled to the waitress, and she brought him more coffee. He drank it black and without sugar.

"What are we going to do?" he asked.

"Contemplate a blade of grass like Walt Whitman."

"I don't mean immediately. This five isn't going to last forever."

"It's too early in the day to discuss that. We'll see."

Powers gulped his coffee. He didn't seem to feel any better. And, besides his physical condition, there was his deep depression. He was ashamed of himself, filled with self-disgust.

He wanted to get out of the restaurant. He had nothing to do to make him want to hurry anywhere, but he wanted to get out and go to Lincoln Park.

"Let's hurry," he said.

"I want more coffee. And then we'll restore our souls in the sunshine," Lewis answered.

He lit a cigarette and sipped coffee. Powers tried to think of nothing. He imagined a tennis game in his mind, a trick he always used on himself when he had a hangover. He would play tennis games by himself for hours because he found this a means of not having to face himself, to assimilate his sense of shame. He shouldn't be ashamed. What difference did it make? His reputation was ruined anyway. What he did mattered to no one. Why should he be ashamed? He played mental tennis with himself.

"Dumb Dora asked me what I did, and I told her I was the president of the Junior Chamber of Commerce."

Powers nodded.

"Listen, I've got it. We've stalled enough. Let's carry out our plan now. I'm fed up with this burg anyway," Lewis said.

"But . . ." Powers began.

He stopped, shrugged his shoulders, and said: "All right."

III

They waited for the bus at Sixty-third and South Park Avenue. Lewis gazed across the street at White City. He had gone dancing there a week ago, picked up a dame, shot her a line, and she had come across.

"Well, the bus will be in any minute now," he said, turning to Powers.

Powers nodded. He fingered his Masonic pin nervously. Lewis questioned himself about Powers. Would he turn yellow on him? He liked the guy, but he wasn't sure of him. Oh, hell, everything was going to work out all right. It had to. Everything always had to work out all right for L. Gordon. He'd been born under a lucky star. He was destined to get all the luck that was supposed to come to anyone who found a four-leaf clover. He had found one in Lincoln Park this afternoon. For a while, as a boy, he'd even had the nickname of the Four-Leaf-Clover Kid.

A blue bus stopped in front of the curb. Each of them carried two suitcases. They followed others into the bus, put their luggage on the rack overhead, took seats, and lit cigarettes. The day was ending. The sun had gone down, and it was slowly getting dark. Lewis watched a Whiting, Indiana car pull out. Their suitcases were overhead, and they puffed on cigarettes, saying nothing. Lewis watched a girl pass. She wasn't bad. No, she wasn't bad. Just the build he liked, slender but with enough flesh on her so that she wasn't skinny. He would find more girls like that, plenty of them. Hell, he was leaving to get everything in the world that he wanted, everything in the world that the little heart of L. Gordon desired.

Yes, this was a sucker country, and a smart lad like himself could live in clover. There was justice and reason to his boyhood nickname, the Four-Leaf-Clover Kid. He had been born smarter than was good for the world. He smiled, proud of himself and of his mind.

"Well, it'll be off soon. And it's not a bad ride we're going to take, either," Lewis said.

Powers nodded.

"I'll never hear from my wife again," Powers said, almost to himself.

"Listen, Powers, when a dame acts that way, there's only one thing to do—forget her."

Lewis squashed his cigarette and, for want of something to do, lit another one. He glanced about the bus. A few salesmen, a few Hunky workmen, a fat middle-aged woman—a typical conglomeration of dumb human dopes.

"Say, suppose someone asks us what we do—what do we say?" Powers nervously asked in a whisper.

They talked in low voices.

"Salesmen. Hell, the country's full of 'em."

"What do we sell?"

"Anything. Peanuts."

"I'm serious," Powers said, getting more nervous.

Again Lewis had his doubts about Powers.

"I'm worried. I wish the bus would get going."

"Listen, Powers, forget it. Nobody's following you. Hell, the checks are finished, past. What did you say about forgetting? Well, forget the check. Forget the dumb manager of the Warwick Hotel. He won't know where the hell to look for us."

"Strange things happen. Did you ever read Thomas Hardy?"

"It's all right to believe in evil fates in a book, Powers, but that doesn't mean that one is going to pursue you. Listen, we're not dopes. How can we be caught up with? Not if we're smart and clever, and not if we play our cards right. Relax. Take it easy. Worry's bad for the blood pressure."

"Lewis, look at my face."

"It's all right. Nobody would take you for an ex-professor, if that's what you're worrying about."

"No—don't you see any little clusters of red veins around my nose?"

"I never noticed."

"Well, they're there. I've had high blood pressure for six years now. I can't do anything about myself, and so, what can I do about it?"

"Stick with me, and you won't be sorry. We're going to have a good time, Powers. Listen, don't you want to have a good time? Christ, wait until you see what New York's like."

"I wish the bus would get going," Powers said.

He eyed the door nervously. Finally they pulled out, the bus slowly moving off.

They sat back in their seats. Powers relaxed.

"Well, that's finished. I don't think they had anybody watching us at the bus station there, do you?" he asked, very gently.

"Listen, Powers, you're not getting yellow on me, are you?"

"Lewis, what have I got to live for? What do I care what happens to me?" Powers answered, looking sincerely at the young man. His hands twitched.

The bus sped along South Chicago Avenue, past factories, garages, gas stations, shacks, near the steel mills.

"I always pity the poor saps who work in steel mills. You know, I think they're saps, but I sympathize with them."

"I'm glad I'm getting out of Chicago. I never did like it. I never was happy there. You know, once we get to New York, I'm going to pull myself together and do something."

"Now you're talking, Powers. Of course you are. Hell, you're still young yet, aren't you?"

"I'm thirty-eight."

"You don't look it."

"Oh, I think I do."

They lapsed into silence. Lewis stared out of the window, thoughtful, planning the first stage in their journey to New York.

IV

They got off at the bus station in Carmody, Indiana, lugging their suitcases. Powers again looked around nervously, eyeing strangers with apprehension. Lewis noticed him but said nothing. Perhaps he'd have to shake the tail off this fellow. If he did, he'd have to get someone else. It was easier to pull this racket with two than it was with one.

"Let's go to the railroad station to check our luggage."

Powers followed him. He glanced behind him.

"Powers, for once and for all, no federal marshals are on your tail," Lewis said.

"I guess you're right. But there's no use in taking any chances."

Lewis didn't answer. He led the way to the station. He took the grips in which he and Powers had put their belongings and checked them, while Powers waited outside with the other suitcases.

"Well, let's register," Lewis said, handing Powers a baggage check, pocketing one himself, and picking up his grip.

Lewis led the way to the Hotel Metropole, the best hotel in town. A doorman took their grips. Lewis sauntered to the desk, and Powers followed. He was calmer now. They took a double room with bath and registered as John Keen and Thomas Allen. The bell boy led them up to a comfortable room, typical of hotels all over America. Lewis tipped him, and, when they were alone in the room, Powers sighed with relief.

"We'll have to remember the names we used," Powers said.

"That's easy. Listen, Powers, don't think you're palling around with a dope."

Powers sat down on the bed. Over and over again he silently told himself the name under which he had registered and the false one Lewis had signed. Lewis smoked a cigarette and watched Powers with a twinkle in his eye. He enjoyed Powers' nervousness, the man's fears and apprehensions, because these proved how superior he was to the older man.

"I'll remember now," Powers said, relieved, ending his practices in memory.

"Good, I knew you would."

Powers lit a cigarette and asked: "What'll we do now?"

"Wash up and eat. I'm hungry."

"I'm hungry myself."

They washed, went out, and found a restaurant.

"I wouldn't do this if I didn't think it was a sure thing, Powers," Lewis said as they ate.

"I know it. I'm not worried. I was a little nervous, but it's not because of the bad checks I forged at the Warwick. It's my condition. I've really been in bad shape since I was fired from the University."

"Well, you're going to do better with me than you did as an instructor in sociology," Lewis smiled in appreciation of the remark he was going to make. "You're going to practice economics and sociology."

Powers ate rapidly.

"Not bad food for a hick town, is it?"

"No, no it isn't."

"Well, we'll have better grub than this. Don't you worry."

Finishing their meal, they had coffee and smoked. Powers lit one cigarette after another.

"Let's find a place and get a shot," Powers said.

"Oh, hell, forget it. That's bad medicine for us now."

"Yes, I guess you're right," Powers said sheepishly.

v

They had strolled around the town and then come back to their room. At the desk when they'd got their room key, and in the elevator, Powers had made a point of addressing Lewis as Jack. Now they were sprawled out in their B.V.D.'s on different ends of the bed, talking.

"When I get to New York, I'm going to get myself in shape. I've got to. I've been a damned fool these last few years."

Lewis looked up at the ceiling, watching the smoke he blew after inhaling.

"Yes, I've been a damned fool," Powers said.

"I've learned that the best thing in the world to do when you've been a damned fool is to forget it. That's pragmatic; it works. When I was eighteen, I was a damned fool over a dame, and I learned then and there—if you've been a horse's ass there's nothing you can do about it except forget it. So I forgot it," Lewis said.

"If I were eighteen, I'd say the same thing. But I'm not. I'm old enough to know better."

"Powers, you worry too much," Lewis said.

"Maybe I do, I don't know. Lewis, you're a young fellow. You haven't gone through what I have," Powers said.

"My aim in life is to go through only one thing—the other fellow."

"You're different from me. You're an extrovert. I'm an introvert."

"You take life too hard, Powers. Hell, you're busted up with your wife. Forget it."

"I'm forgetting her. It's hard, but I rarely think of her now. But it's hard. Perhaps it is my vanity. But sometimes a sudden bolt out of the blue can hit you, hit you very hard. I was getting along, working on my book, teaching, and I didn't even know that she was betraying me."

"You ought to see that it's an experience that teaches a lesson and then learn the lesson. *Be hard*. Hell, you've got to be hard in this world. It's gyp or be gypped, right from the moment the bell rings until the end of the last round."

"No, I was hit hard. I couldn't understand why it happened. I was happy, but I didn't know what she was doing. She fooled me. She was lying to me all of the time, lying. I'd worked hard for a number of years, and this blow was too much. Well, I won't go to hell. I won't let myself. You know, Lewis, I've thought a lot about what happened to me, what happens to men. I've decided that there's one reason above all others which should lead us to keep ourselves in check, save us from ourselves even when we want to let go and allow ourselves to disintegrate, and that's pride. Pride. It's a matter of pride, isn't it, to keep a firm grip on yourself?"

Lewis nodded philosophically.

"Well, I'm going to get a good start, a new start."

"Of course you are. Now let's get our plans straight. To-morrow morning we ask for mail at the desk. Then, before we do—or, better still, just after we do—as we're going away from the desk, remark about the check, but do it casually."

Powers nodded.

"Then you take the bus back to Chicago and mail the letter. We'll get it the day after, in the morning, and I'll have the letter as proof. I'll do the rest, and we'll get the hick manager of this place to okay it. Then we get our stuff at the railroad station, and we blow."

"But do you think it'll work?" Powers asked skeptically.

"Why won't it?"

"Don't you think that hotel managers come up against such tricks regularly?"

"But they get taken into camp regularly, too. Did we have any trouble at the Warwick?"

Powers shook his head, a dubious expression on his face.

"I tell you, it's easy."

"It makes no difference to me. What makes any difference?" Powers exclaimed, suddenly filled with self-pity.

"Listen, the letter I wrote is damned clever," Lewis bragged.

Powers didn't answer. He brooded.

VI

Powers took a long time shaving and diddled as he dressed.

"Christ sake, let's step on it," Lewis said.

"We haven't got anything to do, why hurry?"

"Hell, you're still worried."

Powers didn't answer. He was still nervous. They finally left. Lewis sauntered up to the desk. Powers came behind him, walking slowly and gazing about as if absorbed in the atmosphere of the hotel lobby.

"Any mail for me?" Lewis asked casually.

"No, Mr. Keen."

They left and walked off to a cheap restaurant. They had ham and eggs and coffee for breakfast. They sat eating.

"I'm going to eat this slowly. I don't know when I'll get as good again," Powers said.

"You can take the bus to Chicago, and mail the letter and get back here this afternoon. Tomorrow we'll have our important documents, and we'll cash the checks and clear out of this hick town. We'll go to South Bend, and I'll write a letter ahead to us care of the hotel there. We'll change our names, though. I'm not so dumb as to use the same name twice running," Lewis said.

"You know, a chap like you could go a long way in life, and without taking chances the way you are," Powers said.

"I am going a long way. Don't worry about that."

"You could, without taking risks."

"It wouldn't be as much fun. The risks add spice, and, hell, I'd have to work. I want my pickings fast and easy, and I'll get them, damned fast, and as easy as water rolls off the proverbial duck's back."

"You know what you want."

"When you go to Chicago, can you raise any jack?"

"I don't know where."

"I was just thinking—we need some dough for our dinner tonight. I don't fancy the prospect of going hungry."

"I don't know where I could raise a cent."

"I'll tell you—I think that I better go, then. I can always grab off a five in Chicago. With a fin, we'll have a good meal tonight and take in a movie to pass the time."

"You'll come back, won't you?"

"Of course I will."

"I meant right away. I don't want to stay here alone, with no money. You know, I don't like to be alone under any circumstances."

They finished eating and, smoking cigarettes, sauntered outside. Powers walked with Lewis to the bus station and waited with him. They talked a little, and Powers kept looking around unobtrusively, as though he were being spied on, followed by detectives. He was relieved when Lewis pulled off, and he turned to go away. He had been fearful of returning to Chicago. He knew that his fears were probably irrational, and that there was no reason why the hotel manager in Chicago should know that he was registered in Carmody, Indiana, under the name of Allen. But despite his explanations to himself he had been fearful.

He didn't know what to do with himself. He returned to the hotel, and was almost shaking as he approached the desk. There were three guests there, and this was a relief for him. The clerk casually pushed his room key across the counter to him. He slunk off and entered the elevator, standing in a corner, avoiding meeting the gaze of the colored elevator boy. He got out of the elevator, unlocked the door of their room, locked it from the inside, sighed, and slumped onto the bed.

He felt suddenly safe. Here, in the room, he did not have to look anyone in the eye. There was no danger that he would give himself away by a nervous gesture, a fearful glance, a mishap.

Safe here. Suppose the management should come up with a detective and ask him his name and address? Suppose he had been followed, and they were merely playing cat-and-mouse with him, waiting for him to try to cash a forged check?

He sat on the bed, pale and perspiring as his fears became intense. He looked out of the window at a dreary inner courtyard. He heard footsteps in the corridor and stood rigid with shock and fear. The footsteps passed. He heard a door closing, a man's voice. With envy, he thought of the sleek, well-dressed men he'd passed in the lobby. They were not worried about jails and detectives. They earned money, spent it, had no fears of any kind. They were within the law.

Why had he let himself in for this wild venture? It couldn't succeed. This boy was young and wild, foolish. Anyone as cocky as Lewis was riding to a fall. There was a Nemesis in this world. Each man was the pawn of Nemesis, and he was coming to his day of reckoning.

He dropped down onto the bed. He brooded a while, and fell asleep.

He awoke perspiring in about half an hour. His heart was pounding violently. His horrible dream had already escaped from his memory. He looked around, and his sense of the present returned. Sun came in the hotel window. The curtains waved slightly. He stiffened as he heard footsteps in the hall. They passed.

He sat up, mopping his brow. He waited in terror for some-one to come and get him. No one came. He waited. If a detective or a city policeman came, what would he say?

He got up and pulled the suitcases from under the bed. They were filled with stolen telephone books and newspapers. They had not been opened. At least they didn't seem to have been. But who could tell? He pushed them back under the bed.

He heard the hotel elevator. He waited.

The sound died.

Nervously, he went to the bathroom and drank a glass of water.

What could he say? How could he get out of it?

Would the judge let him go as a first offender? He was older than the kid. He would be blamed. Lewis might get off. Not he.

Suddenly he decided to leave. He washed his hands and face, tied his tie, and combed his hair. He left the room. He walked to the elevator, his head down, even though no one was in the corridor. He waited for the elevator, perspiring with his grow-ing anxiety. His armpits were wet. His lips were tense. He felt his heart palpitating.

The uniformed elevator boy casually opened the door.

"Hot today," he said.

"Yes," mumbled Powers.

He looked down. The elevator seemed to take a long time to get to the first floor.

Emerging from the elevator, he paused, and took his time

lighting a cigarette. When he saw several guests approach the desk, he hurried out without leaving the key. Once outside, he turned to the right and moved rapidly along the main street. He turned a corner and then he walked on, turning several corners and taking a roundabout way back to the railroad station. He entered it, perspiring, fearful that he would be picked up. He got his suitcase with no trouble and left.

He lugged his suitcase out of town and stood on the main highway, flagging automobiles to get a lift to Indianapolis.

VII

Confident, satisfied with himself, Lewis strode into the hotel. He was smoking a cigarette and whistling a tune. The letter had been mailed, and everything was set. In the morning they'd get the letter at the desk, and he'd give the manager a spiel, and after they got the dough they'd be off. Life was sweet, and he was proud of his cleverness.

An attractive girl passed him, and he turned and looked after her.

In time, he would have many such girls.

He walked up to the desk.

"Good evening," he said in a tone of naiveté and graciousness.

"Oh, good evening, Mr. Keen."

"Is Mr. Allen in?"

The clerk looked into the box and didn't see the key.

"Yes, he is."

The clerk turned and nodded his head, and at that moment the house detective stepped up and grabbed Lewis.

"Don't make any trouble," the house detective said.

"Take your hands off me," Lewis said.

"Don't make any trouble. Come along with me, Bud. I want to ask you some questions."

"All right, but take your hands off me. Who are you?"

The house detective relaxed his grip. Lewis swung with his right at him and started to run. The house detective, a burly man, was rocked, but quickly recovered and ran after Lewis, and, making a flying tackle, caught him before he got outside. Lewis went down, his face hitting the floor. He was pulled to his feet with a bleeding face and dragged to a room by the house detective, while surprised guests looked on.

The police were called, and he was taken to jail.

VIII

The sun was hot. Powers trudged along the side of the concrete road, lugging his suitcase. He set it down and waited. He put out his hand, but the cars whizzed by. He picked up his suitcase and trudged on. He didn't know where he was going, nor why.

The Philosopher

I

DR. EMERSON DWIGHT quietly bid good night to Peter, the elevator man in the main library building, and walked northward across the campus. The scene was tranquil. The grass was neat and trim. The Gothic buildings, arranged in quadrangles, were gray against the blue sky.

He was a tall, sturdily built man. His face was sharp and distinctive; his hair and beard were gray; he had lively gray-green eyes and a prominent forehead. But he was beginning to walk with a tired gait, and his shoulders were beginning to stoop. He was sixty-nine years old.

He had spent two hours in his office, reading Whitehead's *Process and Reality* and making notes. When he had finished reading, he had been disappointed in his notes and had torn them up. One of his major disagreements with Whitehead concerned Whitehead's "ingression of eternal objects" into the process of nature. Here was, in reality, the old, old philosophical problem of the One and the Many. Whitehead's "eternal objects" were the One.

Now, walking across the campus, slowly and like an old man, he reflected that Whitehead, with all his brilliance, with all his wealth of speculation and fluidity of thought, was still a traditionalist, a rationalizing myth-maker. And perhaps one key to the understanding of Whitehead was the fact that the man had come late to philosophy. He had begun with mathematics and logic, and then, at a relatively late date, he had turned to philosophy. He revealed the deficiencies of a late starter. He had had to gobble up large slices of philosophy in haste. He was weak in his historical sense, in his interpretations of the development of ideas from one thinker to another, from one age to the next. He was a mathematician turned philosopher, and this was inherent in the weak side of his thought. And it suggested one reason, probably, why Whitehead had to invent his own language and why he was a traditionalist using the screen of a new language for this traditionalism. He was an interesting figure in the history of modern thought, a genius who was fertile, brilliant, stimulating. A great and original thinker who mingled the most original of modern ideas with a re-expression of traditional ones. Often, his thinking was striking in its lucidity. His respect for Whitehead was enormous. But he could clearly perceive all the holes in Whitehead's system. The man was a victim of his own over-crystallization. He, himself, had been fighting this danger during his entire intellectual career. He wanted a system of explanations of the world as process without eternal objects. But he often feared he might stamp too much finality upon expression. It was always too easy to defend one's verbalizations. One's ideas hardened. One fell unsuspectingly into the traps which had caught the system-makers. He smiled wistfully. Did it all mean anything? Did it mean anything if Whitehead was, or was not, subtly spiritualizing the universe? Did it mean anything if he himself did not complete his life's work?

Whitehead was subtly spiritualizing the universe, and the universe was not spiritual. The effort of philosophers to spiritualize the universe was unscientific—it was myth-making. And in the end, did it matter?

An overpowering rush of feeling came on him. It did matter. It mattered to the man himself. Intellectual adventure was art. All life was. And life gave to man—consummations. It mattered as consummations. Life was joyful. Through consummations man lived fully for himself and for his fellow man. It did matter.

He glanced idly about the familiar campus, the familiar campus where he had spent thirty years studying and teaching.

Familiar and yet ever so new. It was a little miniature of life, full of novelty, ever changing. Always there was some new value, some new impression to be gained. Even the grass seemed never quite the same. The sun would always strike it in some new way. There would always be something fresh, as well as something seemingly eternal, in it. Now the sun, dropping in the west, colored the grass with a kind of opulence. The grass, the sunlight on the buildings, the University towers, the long windows, the sounds of birds in the spring, the presence of young men and women, these formed a pattern, became parts of the ever-freshness, the eternal newness of life. The world seemed to be recreating itself anew every minute. The world, nature, was the great improviser. And it was the effort to handle this element of novelty in the world that paralyzed his writing. It cut the nerve of action in him. This explained why he had written so much less than so many of his colleagues. This campus, the rows of small blades of grass before and behind him, these were full of worlds, and they became a focus for the central problem on his mind.

He walked slowly northward across the campus where he would probably eat supper alone. Again his tiring eyes wandered over the grass; it was so refulgent in the sunlight. When he looked at a field of grass, he systematized it, isolated it. He drew upon past impressions. If he looked away and then looked back, the grass did not seem quite the same. Within him, as within every human being, there was a laziness—Proust had written of it beautifully and perceptively in one of his books when he described a railroad journey. And out of this laziness and inertia one tended to rely upon routine, upon systematized impressions. The mind and the spirit of man were hampered by this inertia. The thinker had constantly to struggle against it in himself. Habit, inertia, was always destroying the wonder of the world. He walked on slowly, his shoulders still bent.

He was lonely, and this pervasive loneliness cast its shadows upon his mind. He had given long and patient years to his study, his thought, his teaching, but required many more years to complete his task. And he would not have these years. He was sixty-nine years old, and his life paradoxically seemed to him to be both long and short. He had the premonition that he would die with his work uncompleted. All men die in a world that moves, and in a world of movement nothing is ever completed. His loneliness seemed to run in an ever-deepening current within him.

His wife was dead. For two months of the academic year now ending, he had gone to the university every day, teaching, working, while she lay dying. He had taught by habit, read by habit, studied by habit, formulated the ideas for his papers and articles by habit. There he had been, alone in his office, writing, tearing up the sheets of paper on which he had written, writing again, again destroying what he had written, struggling intently, sometimes struggling for a whole day or week to express one idea, one formulation, one thought clearly and lucidly, and finding at the end of his effort that there were qualifications he had neglected, so that he had to begin all over again, and still discover that his formulations were not sufficiently precise, not expressed in the proper phraseology. And all that time she had been at home, dying. Each day she had had less strength, less life in her. The process of her dying had gone on before his eyes. The woman he loved, the woman with whom he had lived all the best years of his life, had suffered day after day in a protracted agony of death. And this, too, was a process. For a moment, he thought bitterly of his own philosophical views. Agony, declining strength, death, these, also, were novelties in the process of emergent events. He had seen her die, he had heard the death rattle in her throat, and he had felt her forehead, her hands, after she had died. Something of courage, of scholarly ambition, of interest in life had seemed to leave him, never to return. Before her illness and death he had been much haler, better preserved. He had prided himself in the small and rather excusable vanity that he was something of a marvel on campus, that colleagues younger in years than he were stooped and falling into crochety old age while he remained straight and limber, his beard and hair still partially red. Until her illness and death, he had ridden his bicycle to campus daily, astounding many colleagues with his vigor. After her fatal illness had developed, he had never done this again. Something had gone out of him. He had turned completely gray. He had begun to stoop. He walked less briskly. Perhaps he, also, was now a dying man. Every day there was less strength in him, less energy. His mind alone seemed to resist this process, to function as well as always.

Because of his loneliness, a cynicism, foreign to his spirit and nature, seemed to be growing in him. A severe break in his life had come on this very day. He had written out the formal statement of his resignation as Chairman of the Department of Philosophy, and he had accepted the professorship offered him by a large eastern university. His younger colleagues had resigned with him, almost in a body. Their loyalty had touched him deeply. He had felt tears welling up in his eyes. He had spoken to them, telling them that he had accepted this new post, and his voice had broken, the suggestion of a throb coming into it.

He was leaving the University now after his long dedication and service to it. He would not walk across this campus to an empty home for many more days. When he left the campus, it would be as though he were leaving his life behind him. And yet his life would go on. New classrooms, new students, a new office, a new city, and still that unceasing mental strain and effort to formulate his thought clearly and to put it into lasting shape.

He no longer cared to control his bitterness against the new young president of the University. He had worked for years with and through the thought of many men, great and small. He had traversed and absorbed more fields of knowledge than perhaps any other man in America. He had devoted his life to a study of the basic works of literature and of civilization. He had studiously traced out the history of philosophy and of science. He was at home in the contemplation of the civilizations of Greece and Rome, the middle ages, England, France, Germany, America, and of much of the art and literature of

continental Europe. He was aware of how intellectual and philosophical systems were built, of the patient and humble labor of
many thinkers, scientists, and artists that was necessary to con-
struct a philosophy, a philosophy which would then be expressed
and developed as one of the peaks of human achievement by
some great thinker. This awareness of his had checked in
him any undue pride of achievement, any irrelevantly magni-
fied conception of himself. But still, he was proud. Now he
was a very proud man whose pride had been wounded. His lips
curled ironically as he walked past the campus tennis courts.
He remembered the fanfare and publicity that had greeted the
arrival of the miracle-making young president just a year ago.
The newspapers had been full of this vain and empty publicity concerning "the boy president."

Here he was, a man who had always emphasized newness,
freshness, fluidity in thinking, and he was an old man. But this
fluidity of thought he struggled to achieve was a characteristic
of youth. And he was actually being pushed out of the University by youth. Fresh blood! He sneered again, and with
contempt—a contempt usually foreign to his nature. He was
full of contempt for many of his colleagues, professors in other
departments of the University, men younger than himself. He
was convinced there was a genuine issue involved in the fight
he had just lost. The almost wholesale retirement of his department was not merely a personal tribute; it was not mere
loyalty to him. This struggle had been a test case concerning
who would retain control of the appointments of new members
to the faculty—the boy president or the separate departments
and their various chairmen. Yes, there had been a clear-cut
issue involved. Would those who teach have any voice in university affairs, or would control be completely centered in
administrative hands? He and many of the other men, living
and dead, had not worked at this University in order to make
it the kind of institution the new administration wanted. For
if the boy president gained complete control of appointments,
the results could be foretold easily. The boy president had al-

ready forced through some appointments, and these appointments were a prophecy. The caliber of the new men, yes, the young men, was low; they were a laughing stock. Perhaps in time they would turn the University into a laughing stock. He recalled having recently heard a graduate student remark:

"All the University needs to do now is to appoint Will Durant to its Philosophy Department to make the president's work complete."

The boy president had a sophomore's view of traditional philosophy, and, on the basis of this view, he was going to reform an educational system and revise an established educational theory. And his reform was what? An abandonment of the democratic theory of education for one based on the idea of authority. His struggle with the boy president involved an intellectual issue as much as it involved University politics. And yet many of his colleagues had hedged at the meeting of the faculty senate. They had strangled the issue in compromises and had protested against the new administrative policy only in the weakest and most cowardly way. Men whom he had known for years, men whom he had respected—they all had revealed a lack of backbone.

As he crossed the street to enter the faculty club, he could not resist a rising tide of anger and contempt.

II

He sat alone in the club restaurant. He ate slowly, without interest. There was a steady hum of conversation about him. At the next table a colleague in the History Department sat with his wife and children. The girl had recently graduated from the University and was leaving for the Sorbonne. The boy was getting an appointment in the fall as an instructor in history at a Southern university. He directed his contempt at this historian. He recalled the war, for his attitude on the war had been one of his own major and regrettable mistakes. For years now he had regretted his conduct, even at times stigmatizing himself for it. And this man, this historian, was still preserving the attitudes and even the prejudices of 1918. He had written a book on Woodrow Wilson in which he had shoveled up all the wartime myths. Thanks to his own bitterness, his contempt for the historian was intensified. He smiled a greeting, however, when his eyes met those of the other man. Respect —all, almost all of them, were respectful toward him. Empty respect when they had to face an issue. He did not want that kind of respect. He was, he felt, being driven from this University where he had spent his life. On the other side of the dining room he saw the man who was director of publicity for the University. It would be this man's task to minimize the struggle with the president and to prevent the University from receiving any unfavorable publicity because of it. Here he was, a man who all his life had retained a persistent faith in the principles of democracy and had argued for their application, not only in the broad affairs of government but also in other domains, in university life. He had made contributions to the life, the work, the prestige of the University. And now he was being undemocratically shelved. His bitterness stung him profoundly. Listlessly, he ate a light supper. After eating, he left, and in the hallway he met a colleague from the Department of Sociology.

"Is that new book of yours ready yet?" he asked the colleague, to make conversation.

"No," the colleague answered. "But when it is, Doctor, I'll send you a copy. I'm anxious to know what you'll think of it. You know, Dr. Dwight, I'm profoundly indebted to you for your papers. They've been a great stimulation to me, and they've had a permanent influence on my thinking."

"Bill, I'm indebted to you for your books on statistical method in sociology. They've been very valuable to me."

"Your generosity flatters me. But, say, I was very sorry I couldn't get to that meeting of the faculty senate. I had to go downtown that day. I couldn't get out of an errand. But I want you to understand that my sympathies are with you. I tell you that he is going to ruin the entire University if he has his way."

"Thanks," Dr. Dwight said curtly to his colleague; the man was a coward. He did not want to hear him talk about the matter now, when it was too late for his voice to have any influence.

"Dr. Dwight, how about a game of pool?"

"No, thanks, Bill. I've got to go home to get some work done."

They parted. Dr. Emerson Dwight, the philosopher, felt the smugness of Bill Randolph. Smugness and hypocrisy, he told himself. He walked home. It was a lovely spring night. A fresh breeze was coming off the lake. There was something invigorating in the very air. And here he was, a stooped old man. Well, he had one consolation. With such a man as the new president of the University, it was better that he was leaving. Far better not to have any further association with him. Far better that way than to have constant fights and disputes. This trouble was distracting him too much from his work. With his resignation, and the new post, the greater part of this time-wasting distraction was ended. At sixty-nine, he couldn't expect to live indefinitely, and he was anxious to leave behind him a finished structure of work. His students had come to him with the collected papers he had written, and with steno-graphic notes of classroom lectures, and had proposed that these be published. But he had put them aside on his desk because he had not had the time to work over them and would not have them published in book form without carefully revising and checking them.

The spring night stimulated a sense of his youth in him, of his early days of intellectual struggle, particularly his struggle with and against God and the Absolute. He remembered his student days in Germany and his undergraduate years at the University of Michigan. He remembered that far-off exciting night when he had first opened a book of the great Hegel.

He had traveled a long road intellectually since those days, and yet Hegel's influence on him had been permanent. He was nostalgic, wishful that he could recapture the feeling he had had in those days. He wished he could once again read the works of Hegel for the first time. He had been a clergyman's son, and before Hegel his nonconformity had never amounted to much more than a few Emersonian platitudes. Yes, he had traveled since those days, and the chilly God of his heritage had been left at the wayside long since. And the transcendentalism he had avowed, the dualism he had espoused, these two also had been dropped along the route. At the same time, a major part of his life had been devoted to the preservation of his heritage. He had tried to develop a body of thought where value, ethics, was set inside the framework of nature as intrinsic factors. This ethics was at the core of his thought. And it was his heritage, also.

But on this spring evening he felt like a stranger in the world. Other men, younger men, had come up. Even though he was resigning because of his principles, he was, withal, resigning. And it was because of the new president—*the boy president*. *The boy president* believed there must be new blood in the Philosophy Department. And so *the boy president* had brought from the East a slick, smart chap named Milgram, who was to be one of the fresh infusions of blood. This chap prated and lisped Aquinas and had only a nervous and superficial intellect. All he really had was a snappy and clever manner of expressing himself which would, of course, appeal to the intelligence of *the boy president*. Milgram represented new blood. New blood in the Department of Philosophy was not a question of age. It was a question of ideas. Still, he was considered an old fogy, and a lad who came forward with stale, pretentious, and regressive ideas, a lad expressing a new medievalism and a debased conception of Hegelian dialectics, was youth, was the infuser of new and fresh blood in the faculty. He who had all his life struggled within himself in order not to harden and rigidify his ideas, he who had published so little because of his sense of the dangers of overcrystallization—he was now an old fogy.

III

She was gone. She was a decaying corpse now, and he would never see her again, and she would never see him, not in this or in any other world. He had no hope, no consolation, no belief in any after-life. All that remained of their relationship was its effects in this world. Their children, now grown and living their own lives. The memories he treasured. He had written often on the question of the past. Here, the past affected him in the most intimate sense. And, when he died, the memories he treasured would all be destroyed. When the cerebral cortex in his organism decayed, then all these beloved and precious memories would vanish from this world forever. It was as if worms, maggots would eat these very memories. Worms, maggots would eat the structures and patterns which the associations of these memories had formed in his brain, just as the worms and maggots had eaten the body of the wife he had loved. Nothing else would remain. He quoted the word from Poe's poem . . . *Nevermore.*

Often when he returned home, slowly climbing the stairs to his second-floor apartment, he had the feeling, the illusion, that she would be waiting for him. He had the illusion that when he entered the apartment she would be there and would come to him, kiss him affectionately, and that he would talk with her for a while before he pitched into work for the evening. He had such an illusion now. He felt strongly that he would see her. He found his key, put it in the lock, turned it, opened the door, entered the darkened and lonely apartment. He realized, like a man opening his eyes after having been knocked unconscious by an unexpected blow, that he was entering an empty apartment. He pushed the button to light the entrance. He hung up his hat and topcoat in the closet next to the front door. He went into his large, neat bedroom and study and turned on the light. He stood in the center of the room. He went to the dresser and picked up her picture, a picture taken in her youth. Her hair piled high on her head, her face fresh and lovely; she stood in a long, lacy white dress. A smile was on her lips, a smile he so well remembered. He set down the picture. He hung up his suit coat, put on a pair of slippers, and went to his desk. Although it was piled with papers and books, it was orderly. He carefully sharpened a pencil. He commenced to write slowly. He wrote several long and carefully phrased sentences. He scratched them out, rewrote them. He became absorbed, lost in work. All the rest of life was closed out, as if a door had been closed in his consciousness. He worked steadily until eleven o'clock, producing four neatly and carefully written pages on the character of scientific and perceptual objects. He was satisfied with what he had written. But he still felt that it would be just as it had been so often before. In the morning when he'd wake up these pages would seem utterly inadequate. Tomorrow evening he would work over them again. Writing was this kind of misery for him. He put the papers into the desk and went to bed, falling asleep quickly.

IV

The next day he continued on his usual daily routine. On his way to a morning class he met the vice-president of the University, a sly, corpulent man with shiny jowls. Dr. Dwight nodded coldly.

"How are you feeling this morning, Dr. Dwight?" the vice-president asked with unctuous cordiality, his manner that of a man trying to make pleasant conversation.

"Very well, thank you. How are you?" he replied, wondering at this unctuousness and preparing himself for what was to come.

"What's this I've been hearing, ah . . . about the little difficulty you've been having?"

"You must know about it fully."

"Well, Dr. Dwight, I've never heard your side of the story. And . . . ah . . . I'd like to. I'm very anxious to see that this difficulty, this misunderstanding is, ah . . . patched up. I've been hoping I'd meet you so I could arrange for us to have a talk. I was planning to send you a note, but, now that we've met, let's arrange it directly."

"There's little for me to say, sir."

"Come, come, now, Dr. Dwight. We're old friends, colleagues, and we've been here at the University together for years, two decades. We can discuss this matter like friends. I'm sure that you and Al, that is, President Johnson, can come to some understanding. You know, we all have the good of the University at heart, and we have to settle this difficulty in the best interests of the University, for the future that awaits it. After all, Dr. Dwight, this University is your life's work and mine. We're getting on in years. It developed under us, and no man has contributed more to its development than you have. We all know that and pay you great honor for your work. We want to look ahead. Now, what do you say, Dr. Dwight, about our having lunch some day this week? We can have a long talk and go into this matter properly, and in a friendly spirit. I'm free any day this week."

"I am sorry, sir, but I have nothing more to discuss, and I have other engagements for lunch."

"But, Dr. Dwight, you know this is a very unfortunate occurrence. You know what we in the administrative end of the University think of your work, your distinguished career. We hate to be losing a man like you, and we hate to have an unpleasant end even if you are going to a more remunerative post. We hate to allow unfortunate difficulties and disagreements to intrude in our official relationships with you now, after you have had such a brilliant and distinguished career in our midst. And I can assure you, Dr. Dwight, that there's nothing personal in Al's, ah, President Johnson's, feeling toward you. He is acting in terms of what he considers to be best. You know, Dr. Dwight, we all have to see things in a broad light, in terms of the University as a whole instead of one department or one science. He, President Johnson, has to take into consideration policies and plans for the best effect on the University and its future as a whole, whereas you have only to consider the affairs of your own department. Now, Dr. Dwight, I earnestly believe that if you and I can sit down and thrash over this entire problem calmly, I can clarify certain points on the other side of the argument and act as a go-between to straighten out these unnecessary hard feelings between you and the President. You know, he'll be mortally aggrieved if this difficulty is not straightened out."

"I shall be proud that, following this quarter here, I shall never again have to meet . . . him," Dr. Dwight said heatedly.

"But—"

"Good day, sir."

He walked on toward the library building, where his first class was scheduled, striving to check and control his anger. A passing student nodded a respectful good morning. He nodded. He took the elevator up to his office before going to the class. There was some correspondence on his desk, and he looked through it hastily. One letter was a formal and curt acceptance of his resignation, signed by President Johnson.

It was finished. His affiliation with the University was formally ended. His anger and hatred turned to weariness. He suddenly became a man sapped of purpose. He sat at his desk, listless. This was like a death. There were many deaths in a man's life, and this was one of the deaths in his life. He envisaged the University under this new guiding hand. He saw new streams of thought introduced, regressive streams of thought. He remembered the University in its early days, recalling the program, the ideas, the early idealism of that period. All this was now eliminated. The entire educational theory on which the University was built would be abandoned. A spirit of failure clogged him. He looked vaguely at the papers in his office. He was sixty-nine years old. That was a long time to have lived, long enough to have taught a man to meet failure with equanimity. Whenever you are distressed and likely to lose your temper, look at the stars: Bertrand Russell speaking. Look at the stars, old fogy! Look at the sky, look at the sun, look at the grass! Look at the world! The world which ever creates itself anew, the world which is a thousand, is a million, is an infinitesimal number of acts of recreation and emergence at every second. Look at it! Keep your eyes fixed on it, and not on yourself, not on your sudden inclination to develop a sickness of soul. Look out of yourself, and at the emergent novelty and beauty and ever-recurrent wonder of the world. Value is in process, value is in nature, value is in your own acts, your own doing, and you must go on, you must be and remain a part of the process, you must go on to new scenes, to gain new values. Apply your philosophy, old fogy, apply it!

There was a duality in him, in his formal teaching and thinking, on one hand, and his personal life, on the other. There was now no composure, but neither was there a spirit of adventure in him. He had no adventurous desire to go forth to his new work, the new university, the new surroundings. He wanted to stay here, to go along as he had. While here, he constantly found himself holding the comforting illusion that she was not dead, but just away. As with the character in Proust, dipping the *madeleine* in a cup of tea, so, with him, many scenes revealed a spread in experience, a spread going back into the past and forming into the future—sights, sounds, scenes touched with memories, and these led him to newness in his memories; they preserved in him an ever more keen and poignant sense of his wife and the life he had lived with her. She often seemed to him not to be dead, only half dead at the most. And to go away, that meant to break off these scenes, these lines of reverie and internal discovery; it meant that all the normal familiar sights, sounds, and stimulations to memory and recollection would be gone from his everyday environment. He would be forced to do abruptly what he had been doing slowly and less sadly—to assimilate the irrevocability of her death.

He was proud of himself for not having surrendered one inch to the new president. And yet, deeper than his pride, there was a biting regret. He felt that henceforth he would go on in life an unhappy man. Henceforth he would go on struggling against time and disappointment in order to finish a life's work and to leave behind him a little of worth, of stimulation, a contribution to the continuing process of understanding the world and of organizing experience. His personal life was largely over. His ambitions were all centered in his work, his race against time. And his life, which he felt to have had so much richness and fullness, would be a meager and poor thing. The pleasures of intellectual discovery, the joys of intellectual struggle, the anticipation of completion and consummation of this work—these seemed to be but poor and miserable goods.

Other strains in life ran deeper. He was an old man. His beloved wife, companion of decades, was dead. His habits of working in this city and at this institution were to be broken. He had begun his work here, and here he wanted to finish it. The Department of Philosophy in which he had worked, which he had helped to make renowned and famous, was now being ruined, reduced to a kind of degradation by mediocrities. This was a further disappointment, and it had a forceful impact on him. He whose philosophy emphasized notes of hope and was a call to doing was now himself miserably pessimistic. He whose work was perhaps even open to criticism because of its excessive generosity now felt hopeless as well as bitter. He felt almost as if he were beginning to disintegrate within himself. His discipline was relaxing. He was alone now. Was he falling apart?

v

For the remaining days of the term, Dr. Dwight went his way, struggling harder than ever to retain a hold and a discipline on himself, and adding a page here and there to his work. He spoke to almost no one. He remained within himself. He finished off the work which he had to do as retiring Chairman of the Department of Philosophy. He planned a summer of work in the country, and then a journey east to take up his new post.

Three days after the quarter ended, he was stricken with pneumonia. He lived a week in the hospital, fighting for his life, wanting desperately to live. He died with his life work incomplete.

Young Artist

BOB WHIPPLE WISHED HE HAD FOREGONE EATING. Because he hadn't, he now had to walk to rehearsal in the snow. Every time a streetcar passed, he thought of how comfortable it would be to ride. He moved rapidly, his thin body bent, his eyes blinded by the flurrying snow, his face stung by the icy wind, his toes numbed.

As he hurried along, with four more blocks to go, he tried to think. It was extremely difficult. His feeling of misery, his physical suffering, contributed to the sense of futility that was conquering him. He was afraid of contracting another cold; a cold would incapacitate him again; he would be forced to abandon his singing temporarily . . . and he couldn't afford that.

He recalled how, as a boy, he would sometimes escape from the books his parents said he should read and wander through the snow. He would allow his mind to entertain endless fantasies, glorying in them and in the silence of a world covered with whiteness. He remembered his father, a tall, silent, dignified Methodist clergyman. He thought back over the man's tragic life. How he had struggled in one parish after another, through Arizona, Kansas, and Oklahoma. His father had died penniless, of a ruptured appendix; he'd become a crushed man whose severe physical agonies had been accompanied by the realization that he was leaving a faithful wife almost in poverty. Once his father had been a rising young clergyman. But he had defied the authorities by accepting a parish in Arizona, against their advice and wishes. The Methodist Board never forgot or forgave him. And the years had rolled over the man; he had aged; his family had grown up into a new world full of ideas hostile to his faith. The years had rolled over him, cancelling what had been dear to his heart. His life, his struggle, his faith! Futility! Bob believed his father had been heroic. As he walked on, he suffered for his father. The man had held firmly and nobly to his principles and ideals; he had striven to live by them, to raise his family according to his lights. He had gone on like a patient hero. At fifty, he had looked old. To Bob it had been very sad, terrible to watch. And he suspected that his father had died without hope.

Bob was worried about his family. He had always been their hope. From earliest childhood he had been impressed with a sense of his personal worth and talent. He had been isolated from other children, kept to himself, to his music and his books. He had suffered many a bitter day because other kids had sneered at him, the minister's son, the bookworm, the sissy who sang in church. His father and his mother had always drilled into him a sense of his great future. In their well-intentioned way they had hammered into him the fact of his supposed superiority to others. Again and again they had spoken of the distinguished life he had before him. Now, walking along the cold, drab, snow-covered streets of New York, he saw a hard irony in all this; and he felt a resentment that seemed to sting more than the wind chafing his face and blowing through his thin coat.

And he hurried along to another rehearsal.

Back home they had felt that he was a coming singer. His brothers and sisters, now scattered over the country, believed in him. His sweet mother, running a boarding house for students in Oklahoma, lived in the expectation that some day his fame would bring the family together, lift it to the realization of those early dreams she and her husband had entertained. The come-downs he had met in the city, where he was an unknown, the lonely bitterness of the experiences he had had to meet, had led him to curse his whole past, his education, his very existence. When the trio with which he now sung had gone on the radio for the first time, the station had been flooded with letters,

letters from his brothers, his mother, from old family friends, from forgotten parishioners of his father scattered through Kansas, Arizona, Arkansas, Iowa. They had brought back pathetic recollections of these people, their uneventful, unsung small-town lives, their slow journey on to the degradation of senility. He probably represented a justification of their lives; he was one of their number sent out into the larger world to conquer. Could that radio concert be called conquering? He had sung trashy, popular songs, used his talents for the sale of health-giving sausage. His voice had helped to lull people into a state of enfeebled sales resistance.

He now walked on, sad with the recollections of the life he had lived and known in these distant American small towns. He thought of the good, simple people he had known there. He still had faith in people. He knew that their lives were meager, brutal, and crude; that their cherished religion was barbaric. Yet he recalled them by their generosities, their attempts to live by their lights; deliberately he forgot their meanness, narrowness, smallness, savagery.

Two weeks ago he had talked with an elderly lady, the wife of a famous historian, who had made a difficult fight to sing and who had won a small measure of success, a crumb of compensation for the efforts she had made. She had described it as a "ghastly struggle," and those words had had a significant meaning to both of them. The words were fixed in his mind, as if they had been nailed there. They represented the grim fight, the relentless pace, the worry, the long, intense effort of practice, the merciless going on from day to eventless day, from week to fruitless week, from month to empty month, from year to unsuccessful year, all demanding the sacrifice of pleasures and comforts. This struggle required a terrific concentration, a grueling preparation, an intense straining of one's entire self, and then, when one's chance came, one slip, one false note could damage one's performance, stamp the seal of failure on all that one had done, convince one of one's incapacity, drop one down into the deep and defeated doldrums. Time after time this had happened to him, as it had when he'd sung a solo so badly at the Good Friday services out at the University chapel; this experience had given him an almost abiding sense of incompetency and failure. Now, sensing, convincing himself of his own ineffectuality, he gave way to anger and, requiring an object upon which to vent it, he cursed all those who had told him that he would one day be famous. He had seen singers, writers, other artists, some of them with more, some of them with less, talent than himself, who had grimly gone on into painful and silent defeat; and he felt that their fates were but a forecast of his own. Often he had even hoped and yearned for the insensitivity of a pig, for anything that would erase the black uncertainty of the future and that would endow him with even a slender measure of security. He had reason to hope, because he had talent. Or had he? He had known many persons whose faith in their talents had been illusory, and who had gone through poverty, disease, sorrow, humiliation, nursing hopes that were unfounded, and who, for their straining sacrifices, had earned only ignominious defeat.

He walked on, trying to convince himself that he had more talent than others, that his struggle would not be in vain, that his present failures and defeats were but the necessary preliminaries to success, prestige, power, power over himself and his voice. He tried to convince himself that he was marked for success, a child of destiny; but this seemed to be nothing but a mere acquiescence to his own wishes and dreams. He hastened on, and he drew out his struggles with melodramatic coloring, intensifying the drama, as if it were more vital and important than it seemed, as if his battle meant something in the large, noisy city, as if his fate had some meaning to the millions of strangers who daily struggled for food, clothing, and shelter. It was a battle, he told himself, a battle in which he would have all or nothing, in which he would become an artist or else ruin himself in the effort. Again he envisioned a tomorrow in which all his self-discipline, his sacrifices and stinting, his crushing of impulse, his failures, his hours of miserable practice and even more miserable brooding, would be justified, would be, in fact, a crown of personal glory. And then he thought of fame, and of women. He wanted women; a wife. Others whom he knew had wives, or at least mistresses. But he was still romantic, perhaps foolishly so. For him, sex borrowed all the trappings and conceits of romantic poetry, and he yearned for a soul-mate, a Shelleyan abstraction of a woman. A gust of wind, rustling under his overcoat, restored to him some sense of balance.

He laughed at himself ironically, and with that twisted sentimentality so characteristic of many romantic and oversensitive young men. A streetcar rumbled by. He wished he were in it. But now he had only a block and a half to go. He tried to move more quickly. His feet were numb; his face was red and raw; his ears burned; his eyes watered. He was now almost terrorstricken by the fear of catching cold.

His thoughts rolled on. Fame was, after all, only an abstraction. It was something other than fame which he sought; some balance and harmony within himself, some organization of impulses. Again he damned his parents and his early teachers for befogging him with false words, for confusing his ends with a lot of rotten rhetoric. Music gave him something else, something other than a doorway to money, noteworthiness . . . fame. Without it, he couldn't live. He had learned this when he had sold insurance in Arizona, when he had worked in a department store, when he tried to make himself over into a student of philosophy and anthropology. These had all been periods of restless misery. He crossed a corner. It was his last block. He hastened on, condemning himself for being so much like the moody young men in nineteenth-century Russian novels. Growing melodramatic, he thought of suicide, briefly debating with himself whether it should be by gas, by gun, or by jumping into the river. He knew it would be none of these. He loved life; he feared death. His was an organism attuned not to less, but to more, living. And his singing was what gave him the power to achieve this. It resolved, harmonized, bestowed benedictions on the chaos of his impulses. Repressed, limited as he was in the present, he needed music now even more than he would in the future. It was not a curse, it was a blessing. All his vague aches and confusions, all his sensitive responses to the life around him, to the city whose ugliness was itself a form of beauty, all the mystery of the universe, that sense of similarity and union which he felt when he perceived sunshine falling over the lake, the delicious joy he experienced when spring winds touched his hair, the mystery of budding girls, of life and death—all could be pressed into one song and could leap from one song in an expression of wild joyousness. To be the instrument expressing such joy—this was given only to the artist. It was enough! It justified him. It was a gift for which he was thankful. Now, with the last few steps of his walk before him, he no longer envied the cart horses of humanity who were doomed to live in a squalor like his own; he no longer envied them the compensations and releases they derived from gin, sexual excess, and street brawls. He no longer envied them their insensitivity. Feeling a joy within him, he still shrank from completely envisaging what his future might hold for him, the skimping, suffering, saving, sacrificing, the long hours of practice, the cold, cramped rooms, the frequently unnourishing meals.

He told himself that he was committed to this life whether he liked it or not, whether fortune would smile or frown upon him. It gave its own rewards. Even if it didn't provide one crumb of ulterior compensation, even if it offered him nothing, he was committed. There was nothing else he could do. The thought of his many failures returned to him. He had worked himself up to a certain pitch, time after time, and . . . then he'd failed. Perhaps his ability was limited. Perhaps he was a mediocrity. Perhaps he would never get beyond singing in churches or occasionally over the radio, where standards of accomplishment were dubious. Perhaps . . . but he was committed. He had no alternative. Even though it meant starvation, sickness, tribulation, he had no other choice.

He entered the cold, dreary hall, and the trio practiced. It was a good rehearsal. And their director informed them that he expected something to break at a radio station—perhaps three or four commercial programs that might net fifty dollars for each participating artist. Bob felt good, buoyantly hopeful. If the thing went through, he could save to take lessons from the famous Camelli. And he thought of finding some girl to marry. He left the hall in good spirits. He had borrowed car-fare and money for his meals. A decent dinner helped to change the complexion of his spirits.

The Triumph of Willie Collins

AFTER SUPPER, Willie Collins rode downtown, nervously expectant. What a great and historic day in American history! How wonderful it was merely to be alive on this day! Coolidge's victory was already conceded! There would be a Republican landslide. Why, Coolidge might even win by a greater majority than any other president in history, even greater than that of Harding, the dead Chief. Yes, it was a great day, a day for rejoicing, and there would be great doings in the Loop tonight. There'd be a hot time in the old town tonight—a hot time in the old town tonight, and now let McGinty from the office talk! Why, the bastard was such a damn good Democrat that he hadn't even taken the trouble to vote.

He looked around the car. The other passengers seemed so calm, so casual. He wanted to talk to someone, to tell them that he was a good Republican, and a friend of Eddie Chance, one of the Republican muckety-mucks in Cicero. He wanted to talk. But there these people were, sitting in the car, just as if it was any night in the week. Well, it wasn't. And this showed why Willie Collins was different from most people.

Downtown, something was going to happen to him, too, something damned swell. He hesitated to admit to himself openly what he expected this wonderful event to be and even assured himself that, no, he was a mature man, a responsible one, and not like the punk clerks in the office who ran after tail like stray dogs. No, that wasn't what he was going downtown for. He was going downtown because tonight was a night of

history. Still, that expectancy spurred him on, and the hope
of a romantic adventure, which still he dared not clearly
acknowledge to himself, remained with him, contributed to
his hopeful feeling of being really on the verge of some wonderful and joyful experience. He was impatient to get to the Loop.
The car didn't go fast enough.

He read his newspaper, which already headlined the Coolidge victory. He studied the picture of the cold New Englander,
wondering to what extent his own face showed as much character as Calvin Coolidge's. He shook his head in an inexpressible
thrill of admiration. Yes, Coolidge was a great man, a great
President, a great Chief, a man with a mighty brain.

He got off the car at State and Van Buren. The Loop was
crowded. The electric lights shed a warming glow over State
Street. But there wasn't as much cheering as there ought to
be. People milled back and forth and up and down, while a few
blew horns. But Willie had expected that there would be a big
celebration, as great as or even greater than there had been on
Armistice Day.

"Hurray for Coolish," a drunk yelled, standing at State
and Madison, spitting as he talked and blowing an alcohol
breath into Willie's face.

Willie bought himself a ten-cent cigar in honor of the occasion. He walked down State Street like a strutting little
peacock.

People surged past him. Someone tooted a horn. A fat,
homely woman yelled in a cracked voice:

"Coolidge! Coolidge!"

Willie thought how wonderful it must be to be a man like
Coolidge. Look at how many of his countrymen had voted
for him. His name was talked about all over the country. His
picture was on the front page of every paper. Think of all the
people who were speaking his name tonight, at this very moment.

How close he felt to Coolidge. Of course, compared with
the Chief, the President, he was not very important. And, yet,
wasn't it true that the whole country was able to get on with

its business and be such a wonderful country because of its
Chiefs. And he was a Chief. Yes, Chief Wagon Dispatcher
at the Express Company. And Calvin Coolidge was the Chief of
all the Chiefs. He stared at passing strangers and wondered how
many of them were, like himself, one of the Chiefs who helped
make the wheels go round. Tonight was the night when the
Chiefs like himself could feel mighty proud because of the election of the Big Chief.

His cigar was mellow and mighty fine. He walked along with
a feeling of his place and importance in the world, and he was
right in thinking just this. If he ever met Coolidge, Coolidge
would like and understand him. A Chief could always understand another Chief. Yes, he was a little Chief, and Coolidge
the big one.

Fine cigar. He felt mighty fine, yes, sir, mighty fine.

And now them Europeans don't need to think we'll join their
League of Nations and go over there and fight any more of
their wars for them, Willie reflected.

He strutted on. People stopped to look at him. He continued
on, wondering where to go, what to do.

A drunk stumbled up to him and said:

"What's happened?"

—The goddamn drunken slob! Willie told himself, filled with
contempt and indignation as he strutted on.

He turned to gaze after a flapper. He forgot Coolidge for the
moment and thought about her full young body. He wondered
what to do, and he strutted along with his big cigar in his
mouth. He joined the swirling, shouting crowd in front of the
Republican campaign headquarters.

"Well, I'm glad Coolidge is in, stranger. He's a strong, silent
man. That's what this country needs," a fellow said to him.

"You said it, brother. I'm a Republican myself, a member of
the Cicero Republican Club," Willie boasted.

All around him, men and women, mostly men, however,
yelled loudly and senselessly. The shouting sounded good to his
ears. These shouts were the noises men made in recognition
of the fact that tonight was a night of history. And, yes, stand-

ing here, smoking his cigar, listening, looking, he was a part of history. One of the little Chiefs who made the wheels turn.

Why, damn it, where would the country be if the wheels of the express vehicles stopped turning? And didn't he help make them turn? No one in the Wagon Call Department had ever made them turn better than he did. Damned tooting, no one ever did.

He beamed. His ruddy face glowed with pride and good nature as he listened to the senseless yells swelling into one mighty roar of human gibberish.

"Well, friend, I said it was a-gonna happen," declaimed a mustached man in a ten-gallon hat, as he leaned on a cane behind Willie.

"Say, I'll bet those boys up there ain't drunk a-tall now," a little fellow on Willie's left commented knowingly.

Down the street a band was heard pounding out *There'll Be A Hot Time in the Old Town Tonight*.

"Swept the country," a man said in accents of profundity.

"The people are goddamn fools, votin' for the Republicans," beefed a tall, thin-faced man. Willie stared at him angrily.

"Yeah, boy!" a man yelled.

Willie wanted to join in this yelling but restrained himself. It was not quite in keeping with his dignity, responsibility, and position to yell. Yet he approved of it.

"Coolidge ain't nobody's fool," someone said.

"You said it," someone replied.

Again the senseless yells resounded through the Loop and rose over Randolph Street.

Willie squirmed and strutted in and out among the crowd, first standing to look up at the bannered windows of the Republican campaign headquarters and then crossing the street to join the crowd at the entrance to watch men of importance enter and leave the hotel. He wondered how many of them were men of political influence. Someday he would be able to enter as they did, he dreamed.

"I was in Boston," a man said wisely, "the time Coolidge ended that police strike, an' that's what won him my vote.

Coolidge is a strong man, the kind that don't say much, but when he does he talks with a punch and a wallop."

Willie wanted someone to talk with, and he looked hungrily from face to face as he edged about continuously. Once again he looked up at the bannered windows. What was going on behind them? What words of jubilation and victory were being spoken? Were drinks being passed around? Yes, what was being said? Who was there? How was everyone acting? Were they making as much of a joyful rumpus as the people down here on the streets?

He imagined himself upstairs, moving about among the high muckety-mucks, getting slapped on the back by them, slapping them on the back. But the continuous shouting drowned out his dream; he gazed about in a daze.

He wanted to shout, but he could not break down his barriers of dignity. He again stood dreamily staring up at the bannered windows. With lonesome eyes, he read the sign:

REPUBLICAN CAMPAIGN HEADQUARTERS
VOTE FOR COOLIDGE AND DAWES

He was the kind of man who belonged up there instead of down here with the ordinary mob. And, think of it, there was singing and dancing and a good time all over America tonight, and he stood outside the Republican campaign headquarters, thinking. Gee!

"Got a match, fellah," asked a middle-aged man.

Willie fished out a match and stood there while the fellow cupped his hands and lit his cigarette. Willie observed how carelessly dressed the stranger was. No, he wasn't one of the Chiefs. Out of a need to speak with someone, Willie said in a voice of condescension:

"Some celebration!"

The man puffed at his cigarette, drew it out of his mouth, and emphatically nodded his head in agreement.

"It's a good thing for the country," Willie said. "We know what kind of a leader Coolidge will be and we don't know what Davis would do. You know, we know Coolidge has the stuff."

"He'll give us a cautious business administration," observed the stranger.

Behind them a fellow shouted the name of Davis. He was drowned out with raspberries. Willie turned and looked at the Davis booster as if the latter were a lunatic.

"Well, I gave him my vote," Willie told a stranger.

"Me, too. I believe in lettin' well enough alone. I think this country is going along all right now under a Republican Administration, and I say this— Let well enough alone."

The senseless shouting and milling continued.

The stranger passed on, and Willie thought of what he'd tell McGinty and the rest of them Continental Express Company Democrats tomorrow morning at work.

"EXTRA PIPEE—LANDSLIDE FOR COOLIDGE," a newsboy bawled.

Willie suddenly saw a well-dressed man entering with a slight stagger. He looked pop-eyed; it was Eddie Chance. Willie squirmed forward a little and yelled:

"Eddie."

But Chance did not hear him and immediately disappeared inside the hotel.

"That's Eddie Chance, a friend of mine," Collins told a stranger who paid no attention to him.

Knowing Eddie Chance, who could go up to headquarters, Willie was now bathed in the reflected feeling and pride of influence. He was not just a rank outsider. If Eddie had seen him, he might even have invited him inside. Other well-dressed men entered the hotel, and the noisy mob eyed them closely, half with admiration, half with envy.

Disappointed to have missed catching Eddie Chance's attention, Willie finally crossed the street. He elbowed about, looking at faces, hoping he would find someone he knew, someone in whose eyes there would shine the light of recognition, hoping to find one face he could single out, speak to understandingly— the face of one comrade, one kindred spirit.

He stood behind a group of young fellows who carried books and who were probably students.

He heard one say:

"The triumph of democracy."

He missed the sneer in the voice and shook his head in a gesture of agreement and acknowledgment. It was just that, and watch him spring it on all the Democrats at work.

—The Triumph of Democracy!

He elbowed and moved about the Loop until eleven o'clock, eager to celebrate but not really knowing how to do it. Still anxious to shout and whoop, he couldn't bring himself to let out a yell.

He thought of what he had read in the papers about President Coolidge being a strong, silent man.

—Still waters run deep, he told himself.

Yes, and the still waters of his own soul ran deep. He resolved that from now on in his work, he, too, would be a strong, silent man. He wouldn't barber and gas with the Route Inspectors. He would be quiet, dignified, strongly silent, and he would impress them all, impress Wade Norris, the chief clerk, the assistant superintendents, and Patsy McLaughlin, the superintendent. He walked wearily down to Van Buren Street to get a streetcar home. He nursed his resolution, nursed it as a consolation for the gnawing sense of disappointment within him. Just think—he had almost met Eddie Chance, had almost been taken up to headquarters where he would have met the muckety-mucks. But, then, a strong, silent man in whose soul the still waters ran deep could bear such disappointments. And he would!

Father Timothy Joyce

MRS. JOYCE'S COMMONPLACE and full-cheeked ruddy face broke into a significant expression of inordinate pride when she opened the door of her married daughter's flat and saw her oldest son, Father Timothy Joyce, standing before her. Her maternal exclamations, her almost fierce maternal kisses, embarrassed the tall, boyishly handsome, curly-haired young priest. Smiling defensively, he entered the flat.

"Hello, Tim," exclaimed Bill, his younger brother, as Father Timothy entered the parlor.

"William, you know you shouldn't call your brother that. He is Father Timothy. You should show respect for the cloth he wears," the mother scolded in her characteristic brogue.

With a gentle tone of deprecation in his voice, Father Timothy remarked that, at least in his own family, formalities might be dropped. He sank into a soft chair in the parlor, and his mother plumped down onto the overstuffed couch to face him, her eyes fixed on him devouringly, her face happy with an almost overweening pride. Aware of the way his mother stared at him, Father Timothy flushed in some embarrassment.

The flat was on the first floor of a three-story, brown brick apartment building at Seventy-fourth and Luella Avenue. The deceased father, a police sergeant, had left this building to his wife. The family had lived in a two-story brick building over near Grand Crossing, but when the daughter, Katherine, had married, she and her husband, Jeremiah Duffy, who, like Bill, worked at City Hall, had come to occupy this flat and look after the building.

The mother and two sons sat in the parlor, and the daughter called from the kitchen that she would be right in.

"Well, Tim, how's everything going?" the brother asked.

Both of them noticed the frown Mrs. Joyce flung at her younger son.

"Now, Mother, we needn't carry on such formality. Gee, I even let the kids at school I know well call me Tim and don't make them call me Father," Father Timothy said.

"Your brother, he has no respect for your station in life," Mrs. Joyce said self-righteously.

"Hello, Sis," Father Timothy said, rising and kissing his sister as she entered. She was rather tall and very thin, with a drawn, tight face, circles under her dark, pretty eyes, curly black hair, and a delicate mouth.

"How are my nephews today?" the young priest asked.

"Oh, Tim, they're healthy and happy, and thank the Lord they're taking their nap. They have me done in," Katherine said. "They're simply gorgeous nuisances," she added, with a white-toothed smile.

The mother quickly cast a disappointed glance at her daughter, but she said nothing.

"How is Jerry?" Father Timothy asked.

"Oh, Jerry's all right. A father enjoys his children. A mother takes care of them," the sister said.

"You children were no trouble at all to raise. My son, Father Tim, he had the sweetest disposition of any boy," Mrs. Joyce said.

"Not when he punched me in the nose under the viaduct at Seventy-fifth that summer," Bill cut in.

"You didn't throw a rock at me, of course," joshed Father Timothy.

"Ah, you were just boys, and boys you still are," Mrs. Joyce said.

"The way my two keep me going, Mother, I don't know how you stood it," Katherine said.

"Your father, Lord have mercy on him, how proud he would be to see you in that cloth," exclaimed Mrs. Joyce.

"He does. I am sure, Mother, that he looks down on us from heaven," Father Timothy said, his voice and manner changing from that of the son and brother to the more formal one of the priest.

"He was a good man, and now he has a son to pray for him."

"I say at least one mass a week for Pop," Father Timothy said.

"The Lord be praised that I should live to see this day," the mother exclaimed.

"Well, how's tricks with you, Bill?"

"I'm having my vacation, that is, the vacation I don't enjoy, working in the City Comptroller's office," Bill boasted.

"You don't work hard?" laughed the priest.

"I have to keep my job, don't I?"

"You should have my work, correcting English composition themes of freshmen. And the penmanship!" Father Timothy exclaimed.

"Is is hard, son?"

"Not really, Mother. It's just boring sometimes."

"Bill, are you going to play basketball in the Order of Christopher League this year?" asked the priest, a trifle wistfully.

"Don't know, Tim, I'm getting old," Bill smiled.

"Hey, listen. I still play around the school with the kids, and I'm in condition and find I can still make myself go the limit. Come on, come on," the priest said.

"Well, maybe I'd be the same, Tim, if I was around a gym regularly," Bill said.

"Come on, kid, you're getting lazy, getting lazy," the priest said.

Bill took out a package of cigarettes and offered one to his brother. The mother frowned again and then leaned back with a smile when Father Tim refused. Bill lit his cigarette and took a long, contented puff.

"Well, lazy or not, I can still go with you. Someday we'll have to put on the gloves."

"You certainly are rash about the affairs of the City of Chicago," Father Tim said drily.

"How come?" asked Bill.

"You want to mess up the affairs of state by causing one important cog in the City Comptroller's office to spend two weeks in Mercy Hospital," Father Tim said.

"No, you mean I want to get those kids of yours out of writing those themes while you recover from what I'll do to you," Bill said.

"Bill, have you no respect . . ." the mother started to remark, and the daughter interrupted her with a gesture of annoyance.

"Mother, just because I'm a priest, that's no reason why I must put myself in a glass case. Sure, some day, I'll come around, and Bill and I'll go out in the back yard and put on the gloves."

"That's a go," the younger brother promised.

The two brothers smiled at each other self-confidently. There was a pause in the conversation, and then the priest asked his mother how she was feeling. Beaming, she remarked that she had no complaints and no ailments. He smiled, expressed his pleasure, and added that he offered up daily prayers for her specially, and also prayers for the whole family. Her proud, motherly smile expanded. The sister rose and said that she would make tea. Mrs. Joyce got up, too, and with a bustle of activity waddled out, insisting that she would make tea for her sons. The sister protested, and the mother loudly dismissed her protests as she and her daughter walked out to the kitchen together.

"What kind of a football team you going to have at Mary Our Mother this season?" Bill asked.

"I think we're going to cop again, and I wouldn't be surprised if our kids took the public-high-school champs, too, if they'll play us. As far as the Catholic title goes, Bill, it's in the bag," Father Tim said.

"Well, I hope so, since you're athletic director," Bill said.

"You want to come to the games. Our first game is in two weeks with the Christian Brothers from Joliet," the priest said.

They were still interestedly talking about athletics when the mother returned with a tray of tea and cookies. Her daughter, smiling in a tolerantly apologetic manner, followed her and offered to help, but the mother shook her head and shooed her off, insisting she was going to serve her own sons. She brought the tray to Father Timothy and coaxingly asked if he was taking enough cookies, and then, with less attention, took the tray to her younger son. Sipping tea, they continued a desultory discussion of athletics, and the two women sat, the daughter relaxed and tired, the mother leaning forward with intent and adoring interest.

Suddenly Mrs. Joyce interrupted her sons to remark in a hearty and energetic manner:

"Sure, Tim's boys will beat the Jesuits' boys from your school, Bill. It hasn't a lick against Father Tim's boys."

They smiled with filial indulgence.

"When I was playing, Mother used to come to basketball games and root for us," Bill exclaimed.

"Yes, because you are my son. But now I know that Father Tim's boys, with that fine coach they have, and with Father Timothy as athletic director, they can't be licked, can they, son?" Finishing her remarks, she looked at her priest son.

"Mother's a real fan!" exclaimed the priest.

"And, Father Tim, how is Father Michael? Sure, isn't he the saint of God like yourself!" Mrs. Joyce remarked.

"Yes, he is a fine priest, a fine man, and he's in perfect health yet."

The daughter collected the teacups and, after Father Timothy replied negatively three times to his mother's insistence that he have another cup of tea, she carried them back to the kitchen, and running water from the sink could be heard.

"Timothy, sure, if your father was only alive to see you now!" Mrs. Joyce exclaimed.

"Mother, that reminds me, I'm saying another mass for dad tomorrow," Father Timothy said.

"And won't he be proud! Looking down from heaven on his

son, a priest, a priest remembering him and saying masses for his soul," she said, an exultant note in her voice.

Father Timothy smiled, pleased because his mother seemed happy.

"Dad, Lord have mercy on his soul, many's the time he said to me, 'Ma, I want one of my boys to be a priest,' " she said.

"Well, he knows now that his wish came true," Father Timothy said, just making conversation.

"And if he could see the bouncing grandchildren he has," Mrs. Joyce continued.

Just then there was a baby's cry. The daughter took them out to the cribs, and they looked down at two babies. The daughter exclaimed that they were wet, and Father Timothy flushed, almost imperceptibly. He and Bill went back to the parlor, while the sister and mother each changed the diapers on one of the babies, and they could hear singing and cooing. Bill and Timothy talked of old times when they were boys, of their exploits, stunts, baseball and basketball games. In due time, the babies were brought in. Father Timothy seemed uncomfortable when he was given one of his nephews to hold, and he sat there, holding the baby as if it were a rare and fragile vase, while his mother and sister both smiled at him benignly. They talked some more, and then the priest announced that he had to be leaving. He kissed his mother and sister good-by on the cheeks and shook hands with his brother. He walked out.

II

He walked slowly back toward Seventy-first Street, trying to make up his mind whether he should walk or take the I. C. to Sixty-third Street. Suddenly, and inexplicably, he felt uncertain and gloomy. He was shaken by doubts, not of his faith, which was deeply entrenched in him, not of his faith in God, but of his faith in himself. The balminess of the day, the lazy, casual charm in the quiet street, only caused him to become sadder. Life would be empty if he lost his faith. He was aware, vaguely aware, of fear in himself, fear of even daring to articulate his own thoughts fully in his own mind. And yet, he knew, knew without having ever dared to articulate them, what these thoughts were. Sleeping not too soundly in his consciousness was the conviction that somehow life, the world, even his own mother had done him an injustice. He recalled how, sitting at home there, with his mother so lovingly proud, sitting there for that brief and harmonious period with his own family, that old pride in the cloth he wore and the priestly powers that were given him unto death had stirred up within him, and he had experienced a lulling sense of happiness. And now where was it? How quickly it had been dissipated and shoved into retreat by forces of doubt and wonder, by this lack of faith in himself. He asked himself, had he or had he not a vocation? Had he been pushed into the priesthood by his mother's eagerness? He looked around him at a street mellow and domestic in the afternoon September sunshine, with a sense of impending autumn in the warm and beneficent air, with women out going to the stores, women with their babies, kids coming home from school playing along the street. Several of them, seeing him, became quieter and more orderly, tipped their hats to him, and chanted:

"Good afternoon, Father."

He endeavored to return to them a kindly and warm smile.

He slowed down his pace further, not wanting to reach Seventy-first Street, where the necessity of deciding whether he should ride or walk home would face him as a problem. He became weak with his doubts of himself.

He thought of how his mother took such pride in him, and of how he so frequently felt himself unworthy of that pride and respect. After all, he was only a man, only a human being, and not a saint. Her naturally saintly religious feeling and her love for him, her son, caused her to look at him as if he were—inhumanly holy. The very phrase made him feel as if he had committed a sin.

He thought of the kids at the high school, kids that he taught, knew, saw every day for one, two, three, four years. Then they went out into the world, and he did not and really could not

ever know them and their lives except as an outsider. He saw
them go out to work, to business, and to marriage. Saw them
with girls, pretty young girls, at alumni dances, proms, athletic
games. He was the victim of the old temptation, that temptation
to think of committing the one sin of the flesh he dare not
commit. It came upon him with a surging force, and he compared the force of this temptation to that of winds and waves
pounding a frail shore. As always in these moods, he prayed to
Mary for strength to resist temptation. He flushed, and walked
more rapidly, his eyes cast on another world, the words of the
Hail Mary running through his mind. Crossing Seventy-second
Street, he was calmer, and he slowed down his gait. A thrill
surged in him, the thrill of having been able, with the help of
God and Mary, to conquer temptation. With grace, yes, the
weak sands of his soul could withstand the battering waves of
sin and doubt.

A girl emerged from a building. She was young, bursting
with beauty and life, the life he had forever renounced, the
life he had vowed never to know. She was a seed blooming into
a summer flower, and his eyes, against his will, could not resist
looking at her, at her legs, and at the motion of her body as she
walked with so much ease and girlish grace. And she looked at
him in a peculiar way. Many girls did. He flushed, and gazed
across the street. But without willing his thoughts, he saw himself going out alone into the woods with such a girl in the
springtime, and he saw himself and her . . . committing a sin
of the flesh. Shame filled his mind and he feared that his feelings
were like words printed legibly on his face. He turned his eyes
to the other side of the street again and watched a boy of about
twelve rolling a hoop.

An old lady blessed herself and muttered a Jesus Mary and
Joseph, Good day, Father, and he smiled and told her God bless
her. Pride again welled up in him. He was proud of his office,
of the distinction it gave him, and of the way it marked him
off for respect among simple people.

He dallied along, so that the girl would get way ahead of him.
When she had disappeared on Seventy-first Street, he walked

more rapidly. He had sinned. He strove to convince himself that it had been merely a temptation, a wile of the Devil, a snare cast at him in an unguarded moment. But, no, it had been a sin, a mortal sin. For he had consented to this temptation, enjoyed the vivid images of sin which Satan had flung into his mind. But, then, he was sorry and he had thrust the sin out of his thoughts. He had looked off. He had prayed for grace. He had not given in, given in wholly. But yet. Girls. Girls so young, so fresh, so supple. Their laughter. God had made them not merely to tempt man. No, God had made them to be loved purely, to bring joy into the world, joy that he would never know. He was almost sorry for himself. He would go to his grave never knowing the mystery of girls, girls so lovely to look at. But, no, he must not think this. He was winning salvation for himself, for others. Yet, his doubts returned. His faith in himself once again was shaky. His young, handsome, almost girlish face was torn with suffering. He walked on toward Seventy-first Street, wishing he were old, an old man, an old priest no longer torn by these desires of the flesh.

He was very hungry and, thinking that it would be some time yet until supper, he stopped in at a drugstore fountain on Seventy-first Street and had a chocolate malted milk and a ham sandwich. He ate almost greedily, aware that now and then people in the store stared at him. At times, these stares made him acutely self-conscious. At other times, he was proud, proud to be a priest set off from others, a shepherd who guided poor sinners. But then, was he a good shepherd? These doubts. Oh, God help him, help him in the face of doubts and desires. Terrible Doubt, terrible Desire! Oh God, oh Mary, pour the strength of grace into his frail soul so that it would not be destroyed by these pounding waves of life. He finished eating and paid the pretty girl at the desk, his face frozen. He looked away and caught her smile only out of the corner of his eye.

He left the drugstore and walked hurriedly to the station at Seventy-first and Jeffery and sat waiting for his train. An old man tipped his hat, and Father Timothy acknowledged the salutation. His train came along, and he entered, sat by himself, and read his office, concentrating literally on the words he silently mumbled. Alighting from the train at Sixty-third Street, he realized that he was still hungry and that he had to wait for over an hour before he would eat. He decided to go to the school gymnasium, shoot baskets, perhaps find enough kids around to get up a game. If he played vigorously, he knew he would work all these uneasy feelings out of his system.

Joe Eliot

"WELL, MY BOY, how's it today?" Willie Collins asked Joe Eliot, a route inspector.

Collins fell into step alongside of Joe, walking toward the car line after the day's work.

Joe was tall and loosely built, and looked ruffled and unkempt. Little Collins, with his fire-sale gray broadcloth shirt, his dotted jazzbo, and his brown hat which seemed to float on top of his oversized head, looked neat but bizarre.

Joe shrugged his shoulders and stole a glance of contempt at Collins.

"Well, my boy, it's fine out now," Collins said.

"Yeah," snapped Joe in a withering manner.

A chubby, gum-chewing girl emerged from the entrance of the telephone exchange. She had black hair with bangs, her thick legs were encased in dirty stockings with runs on both insteps, and she wore high-heeled pumps. She had on too much powder and rouge.

"Hmm!" exclaimed Collins. "I'll bet that broad don't wear no pants."

"Maybe not," Eliot said without interest.

"Yeah, you know, the broads are getting worse every day. It seems as if they don't even need no invitation nowadays. It's a little bit different from when we were young, huh, Joe?"

Instead of answering, Joe lit a cigarette.

"I see you smoke a lot of cigarettes, Joe," said Collins.

"Yeah," Joe answered, bored.

"I don't like to smoke too many. I enjoy a cigarette after breakfast, and a good cigar after supper, and I like a chew now and then. I like my tobacco, but I always like to keep fit and give my heart a chance. So I see to it that I don't smoke too much," Collins said.

They walked along.

"It's starting to pick up, and things are getting harder up on the board," Collins continued. "You know, everybody is on my tail for trucks."

Joe Eliot didn't comment.

"Hm!" from Willie, as he shook his head at the sight of a passing flapper. "What do you think of these flappers, Joe?"

"Oh, they're all right. Some of them have more guts than their mothers and grandmothers had."

"Well, my opinion is that they don't come up to snuff in the womanly way their mothers did. You know?" said Collins.

Joe didn't say anything.

"Going home?" asked Collins.

Joe had intended taking a car, but he didn't want to ride with Willie. He decided he might as well stay downtown. It didn't make much difference whether he went home to a rooming house or stayed downtown.

"No, I guess not," he said.

"Well, here's where I get my car," said Collins.

"So long," Joe exclaimed, unable to repress the sudden rise of surly feeling.

"Say, Joe, that tonight's paper?"

"Yeh."

"Finished with it?"

"Here, take it."

"Thanks. Well, so long, Joe," said Collins.

Joe walked off.

II

Joe stopped at a paper stand and bought another newspaper. He went into a cheap restaurant and took a table in a corner, near an electric fan. He waited while a peroxide blonde, with powder packed on a middle-aged face, set a glass of water, a little butter plate, a napkin, knife, fork, and spoon before him. He ordered liver and bacon and spread his newspaper before him.

"Liver an' bacon," she yelled in a harsh, grating voice.

He looked at his paper. Another murder! He read a few lines about it. A pastor had murdered his wife because he loved a choir singer with whom he'd been intimate. He read a little about Mussolini and the black shirts and a headline about the French in the Ruhr. When he had gone into Germany after the Armistice, he had liked the Germans. He read an account of how a rich American boy had drowned himself in the Seine.

He recalled the Seine in the Paris mist and moonlight back in 1918. The mist had hung over the dark waters, and over Notre Dame, so magnificent, standing on the island, half lost in darkness. He remembered walking along the almost deserted quays in an early autumn evening in 1918, when he had been on leave, and he had seen soldiers there with girls, kissing. He recalled tender nights hanging over the Seine, into which the rich young American had thrown himself. He had forgotten the war on those few nights. Then he'd gone back to the front, and the war had soon ended. They had advanced into Germany, and he'd received a letter saying she had died, but without giving the circumstances. The letter had just mentioned an operation, and then a later one had stated that she had died of appendicitis.

He had given up a lot for that woman.

—The goddamn dirty, filthy bitch!

He had given up a lot for her, a career. He thought of the word career and laughed nervously and neurotically. Hell, he had a Harvard degree, and had been all-American halfback on Walter Camp's eleven, first team, too. He could have had something. He could have been a bond salesman. He could have been a business executive. Maybe a sports writer. Sure, he could; perhaps he could even have been something big. Instead he'd come out here to Chicago, started driving an express wagon, and here he was, a route inspector.

He had taken her out of a restaurant, the dirty bitch.

He ate.

He remembered one of those nights, close to dawn, when he had walked along the quays looking at the dark waters of the Seine and he had heard an American doughboy singing:

There's a silver lining through each dark cloud shining,
Turn the dark clouds inside out till the boys come home.

Plenty of doughboys had sung such songs. He remembered some of them singing one night in a Y hut in France. He was drunk another time in Amiens, and he had sung it with several lads who were kicking up the daisies now. Smitty, a boy from Princeton; Bates, a farm kid from Iowa who wanted to be a baseball player. Murphy had been a streetcar conductor and was always talking about his Lithuanian sweetheart.

Turn the dark clouds inside out till the boys come home.

That blonde bitch, too. He had tossed his goddamn old bastard of a father's fortune away, and he'd landed a laborer's job in the express company. He hadn't cared. He'd been young, and he had loved her, and God, Jesus Christ almighty, she'd been beautiful. When he came back he should have killed the bastard. His old man, too! The dirty, old, filthy, bald-headed bastard. And he'd made plenty during the war and was still making it, but Joe wouldn't talk to him. No, and he could keep his money, too. He had had a letter two months ago: Let bygones be bygones. We are all getting along now, and we all know we have made mistakes. It is for God to decide which of us has sinned the most and which of us should be punished. Let him keep his money, and his tin Jesus, too.

Joe glanced back at his newspaper. He read a well-authenticated rumor that Trotsky had been hanged and quartered and that fierce Red barbarism would break loose in Russia. What did he care? He didn't care about it. He hadn't fitted into the world, and he didn't give a good goddamn. The world had been saved for Democracy. Let Democracy have it.

He finished his coffee and pie, lit a fresh cigarette, left a fifteen-cent tip, paid his bill at the cash case, and walked out. The summer sky was deepening, and now the city was quiet. The falling twilight seemed a delicate thing, a thing of peace, softness, and beauty.

A fellow in bell bottoms snapped by him, humming a jazz tune. A blind man tapped his cane and half staggered along. Two sleek businessmen passed.

"And I told him. I told him, hands off! Hands off!"

He smoked, and decided to take a walk.

III

Joe Eliot's mood of sarcasm and cynicism vanished as he walked about, smoking one cigarette after another.

A slattern dragged her creaking bones past him.

Two girls walked from behind him, moved alongside him for an instant, and then forged ahead.

It was about eight o'clock, and the twilight seemed like a thin veil waving and fluttering between night and day. The redness that had burst full-blooded in the western fringe of the sky was now dying.

A boy and a girl walked by, hand-in-hand, engrossed in chatter.

"Tell me! Tell me! Tell me, Harry, because I wanna know."

Joe walked on, lighting another cigarette. He thought of his life, with all the unfulfilled possibilities that lay strewn across its path. He thought of it as a scattered thing now, a shambles. All those dreams and hopes of his youth on which he had drawn expectantly for the future had come back to him—bad checks. He nervously puffed a cigarette and thought inconsolably that he was a failure. He was a failure in more than a merely financial sense. It might have been because his father had been rich that he had never thought much of money, and it might have been a temperamental inclination or propensity. Withal, it was a fact. He was a failure in achieving things, in achieving something valuable—love, knowledge, something that would be significant and personal and worthwhile. He was a mere collection of habits that functioned like an electric system on an automatic telephone. He was a failure. He walked with slow aimlessness about the Chicago Loop, which was popping into life with the coming of night and the theater crowds.

An aging, conservatively dressed couple passed him; their faces were lost in an apparent dreamlessness, a stupefying contentment that was an expressive abnegation of all feeling.

Joe felt that he had grown akin to such people; or to the men at the Continental like Porky Mulroy, Collins, and the Gashouse.

He happened to glance upward, and he saw, as if it were a discovery, a sky streaming with stars that were radiant on the surface of a deep blue. There was a seeming lavishness about them. He felt humble and weak, and like a child lost in the darkness. He fixed his eyes on a nameless blue star and was inwardly inarticulate. Vague impulses, without names or tags in his consciousness, awoke as from a long sleep within him and stirred like an unborn child in a mother's womb.

He walked on. A man couldn't stand on a corner of Dearborn Street and look up at the sky like a country jay-walker who came to town and gawked at tall buildings. But he walked with the happy feeling that he just sucked a flashing moment of significance from the weltering insignificance of human life.

Three lads passed, one of them with a pimply face and a loud voice; he wore a green shirt and a purple tie.

"Yeah, and I told the bastard, fight with yer fists, not yer mouth."

He reflected that the lives of all men were miserable things, and that all men were failures who accomplished only a minimum of the things they dreamed of accomplishing in their youth. Yes, nearly all men failed, failed even to become human beings. Yes, there was almost no love, no honor, no justice, no decency among them. Life was a shambles, and it toppled over, smothering sentiments like love and friendship.

A gaudy young woman passed, wriggling her buttocks as if they were a billboard display.

Life was a promise of anything and everything in youth; it narrowed and was squeezed down to one man's mortal and miserable little life. He thought of this, and he was acutely aware of his loneliness.

"Hell, that nigger Wills never could take Dempsey, not in a thousand years," a passing man exclaimed.

A blind beggar, led by a thin, miserable-looking woman with a shawl over her head, passed. They were like a slow procession of death.

His wife. Again he snarled the word *bitch* to himself, but he knew he didn't mean it. He did not hate her. No, and he hated no man or woman. And even if he did hate her, it made no difference. She was dead. She was nonexistent. She lived only in the effect she had on the lives of other people, on his life—and that was an evil effect. She was dead, and her bones were rotted in a cemetery. She who had blushed with such sly, maidenly innocence, or apparent innocence, in those premarital days, she who had come to his bed, naked, in that sly and innocent way, she was dead. He had loved her then, and he still loved her. He tried to summon up memories of her, but they were thin and tired memories. But thin and insubstantial as they were, they gripped him. He loved her yet, and he painfully recalled her silly but beautiful blonde face, the face for which he had turned his life into such a shambles.

Now everything was too late. Life gave a man no quarter. Mistakes could not be rectified. Once they were made, it was too late. Too late, and nothing else need be said.

He looked about him. He was on Randolph Street, with all the lighted theaters. It was an ugly scene. Big electric advertisements, announcing cheap, sentimental shows and movies, glared at him. Heaped and tumbled store windows ran along the sidewalk. People passed him, crowds of them. They, too, seemed cheap and ugly. They were America, and this street, with its blazing lights and its stupid shows, was America.

He felt that not only he was going to hell but also Chicago and the country were going to hell. And it was not a merry journey, either, but merely a stupid one.

Suddenly he thought of his little girl, Marie. If she had lived, maybe she would have helped him find some purpose in life. Then living would have acquired some meaning. He thought of her blonde hair, of her face so like her mother's, when she had played before him with such serious and concerned childlike naiveté.

He lit a fresh cigarette and thought that she, too, was a rotting corpse.

He recalled how he had been so delighted to watch her growing. And then her death caused by a speeding automobile— it seemed doubly malignant and uncalled-for. In his mind the concept of death took on a loathsome ugliness. He realized how death reduced all men to a rotting and stinking vileness of equality. It was a messy conclusion to a mess.

Holding hands, smiling with absorbed silliness, a brightly dressed lad and a lass in organdy walked by him.

IV

He walked through Grant Park and over by the lake, where the waves came piling in, smashing against the breakwater. The skyline of the city rose behind him. A few lights glittered on the dense stone hulks. The noise of automobiles was audible but echoed as though from far away, and as if they had no meaning. They bore no relationship with the noises of the waves slashing against the breakwater piles.

He sat down and gazed out across the lake. It seemed coldly and inhumanly beautiful, streaked with lines and avenues of moonlight, waving and wrinkling beneath mists. The very air was a delicate breath, shimmering and flashing above the waters. Rolling wave after rolling wave crashed relentlessly against the wooden piles. He was pleased and calmed by the wind and waves. He sat there, looking far out over the waters which seemed so monotonous but held his attention none the less, while his eye sought out small changes in their patterns: shifts of moonlight and starlight, rolling waves, patches of darkness, where the waters were a dense blackness. He listened to the monotonous slapping of the waves. It seemed to echo something important inside himself. He was appalled and soothed alternately by the insensateness of the waters and the inhuman power they displayed in their continuous drive against the piles.

He wanted to make some contact with the waters. He wanted to hold them and feel them, manipulate and control them, put them inside of himself and hold them there as caged and beautiful things. He dipped his hands into the water. A wave broke and splashed over his shirt.

He sat back and glanced out toward the misty horizon. He saw a world of waste, heedless and removed from man and man's destiny, alien, totally unrelated to his human aches and sufferings and maladjustments. Behind him was man's created world. He had come from it bored and frustrated. Here he sat, as if hung between that created world and this mindless world. He listened to the noises of the water and the strain on the soggy piles, caused by the pitiless pressure of the waves. It was beauty. Why, he did not know. He sat there choking for this alien world, feeling that it furnished the objects he needed; again he looked out over a black waste. He wanted to own that waste, possess it in some inarticulate fashion.

The noises of the water changed from a monotony to a terror beating upon his senses. He sat. Waves and more waves came in, and the undertow dragged them out again. He was torn by his own incoherent emotions. He lit a cigarette and scratched his arm where he had been bitten by a mosquito. A sense of time encircled him, and he thought of how this was a century-long process, and he tried to gain some sense of how the waters had come in and gone out, century after century

after century. And they would go on, century after century
after century, until all life had vanished and there was no me-
mento left of man, or of the life from which he had evolved.
This lake preceded human history. It would outlive man. The
stones behind him on Michigan Boulevard would one day tum-
ble in a heap, while the waves of Lake Michigan came slapping
in monotonously, unconsciously, heedless and insensate.

He was struck with terror, and sentimentally he wondered
why men went on, why generation after generation lived and
suffered and died creating what would end in dust. Life became
a horror of monotony. Men stood before his vision as so many
creatures registering impressions, registering endless impressions, trying to build and order them, suffering and aching
and agonizing, blundering, killing one another. He wondered
why the race did not blot itself out. But he knew why. They
loved life. He loved it, empty as it was to him, and he did not
want to die. He feared death, feared and dreaded the day
when he could not come to the water's edge and sit there, listening to its noises and looking out over its shifting surfaces.

A young man and a girl passed him. She giggled and then
said:

"Help me. I'm afraid. Oh, don't let me fall. . . . *Henry*."
Henry helped her over the rocks.

"Oh!" she muttered with admiration, and they moved out of
audible range, so that their voices became mere fading sounds.
Joe saw them sit down on the rocks and embrace one another.

He lit a fresh cigarette. Some spray brushed his face. He took
his coat and, carefully folding it, set it beneath his head. He
lay back and gazed vacantly upward, his hands crossed under
the lower part of his head. He was calm now, and his mood
became one of speechless melancholy. He watched a floating
cloud and then saw a star shoot across the heavens and vanish.
He drew a deep breath. All he could do sitting there was to
try and translate his feelings and sensations into words, and
this was an almost hopeless effort.

He recalled how, when he had been a young man, he had
lost his faith in God. All the world had then been tied to-

gether in a unity, and now it was a chaos; it was a chaos spread inhumanly about man, and there was nothing to explain or to give reason to his efforts and his humiliations. He had walked about on many evenings, contemplating suicide. Now he never thought of suicide. He fumed, and cursed, and drank himself almost into insensibility. But he never thought of suicide. He had lost things more substantial than God, and yet he sometimes felt that the reason for his despair was his loss of a Presbyterian God.

Once, about two years ago, he had gone into a Catholic Church, and he had been tempted and seduced. The singing, the candles, the incense, the Latin had all been suggestively mysterious. But he had quickly departed, thinking that it was sheer barbarism, and that the priest, in gold-cloth vestments, was like a medicine man incanting among a cannibal tribe. And it seemed to him the Catholics were cannibalistic. Swallowing their God, as they claimed to!

Behind him the automobiles purred, and in front of his prone body the waves piled in.

He almost ached for the past. Trivial things that had been long forgotten arose in his mind, odd words he had spoken in France and at college, ball games he had played in as a boy, meals he had grabbed hastily at forgotten restaurants, people he would never again see. He found himself wanting them all back. He sank into a revery, and its course wandered aimlessly. The sky stretched widely above him, and the lake was wide, and the wind that brushed over him and through his hair came from these wide places. Earthly terrors, broken loves, betrayals, death, disease, treachery, failure, these were now all inconsequential and irrelevant. He was at peace. He lay there. Cigarette ashes fell on his shirt, and he carelessly brushed them off. He was at peace, in a womb of calm. He recalled that he had read somewhere the statement of a scientist who declared that man was happiest as an embryo in the mother's womb, and he felt as if he were in a womb. He lay under the wide sky, by the edge of the wide waters, and the wind brushed through his hair. The fierce earth on which he lay, and on which his race had built and would build its many Chicagos, now seemed to him to be that womb. He lay there, opening and closing his eyes, listening and not listening to the waves.

Finally he rose and put on his damp and crumpled coat. He glanced down to his right, and a flash of moonlight exposed the boy lying and moving upon the girl. He started back across Grant Park.

v

Joe Eliot crossed Michigan Boulevard and walked along Madison to Wabash. The Loop was pretty well emptied. An automobile roared down the street, and its noise heightened his loneliness, which he transposed to the objects about him. An elevated train rumbled overhead.

He paused, indecisive, on the corner of Madison and Wabash, wondering what to do. He did not want to go home. He knew what he wanted to do—go to a whorehouse. He lit a cigarette and glanced around him. A kid passed, shouting the newspaper, and he bought a morning paper.

He walked on, glancing at the headlines, and, coming upon a Thompson restaurant, entered it. The place looked dreary and forlorn, and as he took his check the man at the cashier's stand opened his mouth in a wide, toothless yawn. A white-aproned, red-faced fellow casually mopped the floor. At the counter he ordered coffee and pie. Then he sat in a one-armed chair and read the newspaper, not knowing what he read. He was merely wasting time. He drank some coffee and found that he had not put any sugar in it. He took his coffee to the stand and put two spoonfuls of sugar into it. He stirred it overlong. He returned and ate his pie and coffee, and then read more of his newspaper. He read a column written daily by a University of Chicago English professor, Paul Morris Saxon. But he thought it boring.

He glanced around him. A thin-faced, lonesome-looking man to his right vacantly stared about and sipped coffee. In a corner on the other side, two men about forty-five or fifty and dressed in cheap suits were arguing, but Joe could not hear the subject of their argument. A bum was huddled over a cup of coffee in the rear. The aproned employee mopped the floor, swinging his mop back and forth unenthusiastically.

He did not want to go home. He did not want to leave the restaurant. He envied the men working, not knowing why, and wished he might sit here indefinitely. He turned back to his paper. Then he rose and left.

He walked aimlessly about. The night now was very soft and tender, and he, too, felt very soft and tender. The street was a scene of deserted life, with dark buildings whose emptiness seemed to yawn. They seemed to be waiting for the morrow, when their rooms and offices would be full, and the slow midnight tempo of life would give way to a daytime fierceness. He wondered about the people who worked in them—about their tragedies and hopes and plans and dreams. He thought how each office reflected a world that was almost closed within itself, just as the Wagon Department at the Continental was a world almost closed within itself.

He walked around, reflecting on how he was a stranger to all these little worlds of the city, and on how he only touched the edges of a few of them. He had no common bonds with anything, it seemed. It was almost as if he were a member of another species, rather than a man. Perhaps that was why the city appealed to him more now than in the daytime. Its desertion meant that its many little worlds and private universes were only reflected things, and that their life did not unroll before his eyes.

He walked around, and his thoughts welled around and around, tearing over familiar and much-ploughed emotional ground. Finally he clenched his fists and, summoning forth all the disgust and loathing he could command, muttered through his teeth:

"JESUS CHRIST!"

He boarded a streetcar and rode dully home to his rooming house. He felt very tired.

Scrambled Eggs *and* Toast

THE RAW AIR bit and cut to the marrow. A morning mist hung over the Boulevard Montparnasse, and, while it was slowly receding, the sun was still obscure. Tram cars jangled by. Crowded autobusses clattered along. A few taxicabs cruised by. On the sidewalks, merchants were dragging forth their displays of merchandise for the day, and the *garçons* were sweeping the café verandas, moving and stacking and replacing the chairs and tables, restoring them to their regular order after the night and the sweeping. From below, the metro trams could be heard thundering into and out of the station at the Rue Vavin. Pedestrians walked by—workingmen in rough, unpressed clothing; slovenly and poorly dressed lower-class French women of middle age; a Turk wearing a red fez; a trim officer with a small waxed mustache; schoolboys; several lads in blue army uniforms; a sprinkling of Americans, one of them dazed, sleepy-eyed, and showing the effects of drinking as he stumbled along; blue-caped *flics*; a tall, handsome, and seedily genteel blond Russian; a few ragged beggars, soiled half-creatures who seemed to belong to a subsidiary species between man and animal.

The chairs and tables had been rearranged on the veranda of the Café du Dome, and a few customers began to sit down at the tables, breakfasting or having drinks. In one corner, a well-known pro-Soviet Russian writer sat reading a French morning newspaper, occasionally looking up from his paper to glance at the people sitting at the tables or passing along the sidewalk. Over toward the tables near the center aisle leading to the interior of the café, a thin American with baggy eyes, dissipated features, and a sodden expression sat like one in a half-sleep. On the right side, in a corner toward the front, there was a young Frenchman with a mustache and blue beret who sat over coffee and croissants. Several tables behind him, a young American, presumably a student, sipped at a glass of coffee and interrupted a reverie to stare at several plump midinettes who passed.

The morning was starting to run its normal course along this Paris street. A stout American woman walked along the center aisle, carrying a poodle in her arms and attracting attention by her appearance. She was a peroxide blonde, her face was caked with powder. She was obviously over forty, and she wore an expensively tailored black suit with a fluffy white shirtwaist, and a black Princess Eugénie hat tilted over her left eye. As she took a table toward the rear and just off the right side of the aisle, some of the other customers stared at her and then turned away. She made a fuss about getting seated, and she talked to the dog in cooing baby talk as she placed it on a chair beside her. Several times she admonished it to be good, pronouncing the word as "dood."

"Bonjour, Madame!" muttered a corpulent *garçon* with a waxy face and a mustache, bowing obsequiously at the same time.

She turned rudely away from him and stared out at a tram bound for the Porte d'Orléans which had momentarily halted at the corner. Then she ordered in a loud voice:

"Café au lait pour moi, and scrambled eggs and toast for Ruffles." She smiled up at the *garçon* and added, *"Parlez-vous anglais?"*

"Yes, madame," he said slowly, his manner still ingratiating.

He turned from her and disappeared into the interior of the café.

"Little Ruffles, oo is hungry, isn't oo? Well, oo is going to det a nice big man's breakfast, oo is," the woman cooed, and several of the customers gave her brief, questioning glances.

The dog jittered nervously, its tail wagging, its fluffy ears cocked, its hairy, grayish-white body tense. It raised its head toward her with asking black eyes and then, setting its paws against her, attempted to lick her face. She held the dog off, smiled, pointed a warning finger at it, and said maternally,

"Now, Ruffles, oo must have manners and show the French that oo is a polite American dog. Ruffles must be patriotic and act like an American with breeding." She drew the dog against her, and in a lower tone said, "Ruffles, oo is a darling!"

Then the dog laid its front paws in her lap and looked at her, its dark eyes pathetically expressive. She took it in her arms and permitted it briefly to lick her face, smiled at it, and then placed it back on the chair beside her and warned it to be a good dog. She stroked its head and patted it. It sank its wet snout into her lap, and she again waved an index finger at it and mumbled, "Ruffles mustn't!"

More customers had entered, and the stream of pedestrians had grown bigger. The mist had receded rapidly. The sun was bright over the street. A *flic* drew a taxicab to the corner around on the Rue Delambre and began to argue loudly and with gesticulations with the driver, who had violated a traffic regulation.

The American woman looked out onto the street and superciliously regarded this small drama between the policeman and the taxi driver. She was distracted from this scene by the reappearance of the waxy-faced and corpulent *garçon*, who had brought her order on a tray. He set on the table the plate of yellowish and liquid scrambled eggs and beside it a plate of buttered toast. He set a glass of coffee before the woman and from an adjacent table corralled for her a basket of croissants.

"*Garçon!*" she said with sudden officiousness, and the waiter bowed. "*Serviette* for Ruffles, *s'il vous plaît.*"

The dog laid its paws on the table and thrust its nose forward. The woman shoved the plate of eggs out of its reach, and with her index-finger gesture she warned it:

"Ruffles must wait for his little napkin, and he must not show boarding-house manners. Dogs that are bad and eat too fast get indigestion, and then they have to take nasty-tasting castor oil. Does Ruffles want castor oil?"

The dog looked up at her, its eyes beseeching food. She smiled and failed to notice that one of the Americans from a near-by table turned to laugh at her.

The waiter reappeared with a white napkin. The woman almost tortured the dog by tying it around the animal's neck. She broke bits of toast and dropped them on top of the egg. Then she held the dog while it greedily devoured the food. She watched the dog eat, smiled, coaxed it with baby talk, and, when others turned to stare at her, she haughtily elevated her nose. Outside on the sidewalk the policeman had finished lecturing the taxi driver and was writing in a little book. The taxi driver watched him, forlornly answering questions.

Two old French beggars shambled along the sidewalk. The man, in rags, carried a large burlap sack on his shoulders and dragged his run-down shoes over the paving. He had gray hair and a soiled, sloppy mustache. His face was creased and lined, and dirt was ingrained in the wrinkles. His eyes were shifty, beady, and they contributed to the dejected expression of his face. The woman was taller and gaunt, similarly wrinkled, and her gray hair was unkempt. She wore a spotted black dress with an uneven hem, and a rip along the side revealed underwear so dirty that it was the color of a sidewalk. She had a shawl thrown over her head.

Looking dully at the people around the tables, they spotted the American woman who was holding the dog while it consumed scrambled eggs and toast. The man laid down his burlap bag, and both of them stared at her meekly. They held out greasy palms.

They stood, statuesque for a moment, the almost subhuman products of poverty. The American woman, cooing over her dog, did not see them, and she dotingly watched her dog lapping over the plate.

Failing to attract her attention, the two beggars commenced

to sing in cracked, tuneless voices, the street noises intermit-
tently drowning their song.

Sous les toits de Paris
Dans ma chambre ma Nini . . .

A small, wiry *garçon*, serving a table toward the front,
curtly pointed a finger at them, indicating that they should
move along. Ignoring him, they sang on. The woman held her
palm outward. The man hunched his shoulders more pro-
nouncedly. Both of them eyed the American woman, their
begging gestures and expressions as craven as had been her
dog's before she had started to feed it.

Finishing the plate, the dog turned and twisted to look
again at its mistress, its melancholy eyes asking for more food.
She removed the napkin from its neck. Its ears were cocked.
The woman squeezed the dog against her and in baby talk told
it that it was a hungry rascal with a hole in its stomach. Stimulated by the cooing voice of its mistress, the dog became more
lively and strained in her arms.

Oui l'amour . . .

The American woman noticed the beggars. At the sight of
their silent, accusing glances, her middle-aged face, with powder
caked in its wrinkles, toughened into an annoyed frown. The
waxy, corpulent *garçon* emerged from the interior of the café.
He spotted the beggars; his lips curled. She looked up at him
petulantly and said, in heavily accented and ungrammatical
French, that she was being annoyed. She pointed a disdainful
finger at the beggars. Their song completed, they groveled, and
the man held out his crumpled gray cap, its lining sweat-
stained.

Her waiter moved quickly and asthmatically down the café
aisle. After he had curtly told the beggars to move, they looked
at him and said nothing, but pointed at the American woman,
and seemed to annoy and distress her with their glances. With
the dog down against her bosom and her head elevated in self-

righteousness, she met their stare and then turned away. The *garçon* spoke volubly to the beggars and pointed down the street. A policeman appeared as the man, with calculated slowness, commenced to lift his bulky burlap sack. The conversation became loud and operatic, and the policeman shoved the two beggars. They turned from the café and started to drag themselves slowly along. Unperturbed by the sneers she received from other tables, the American woman watched the scene with pleasure, and in a half whisper she was heard to exclaim:

"*Merde!*"

The beggars crossed the street to proceed on along the Boulevard Montparnasse in the direction of Saint Michel. The *garçon* returned to the American woman and offered bowing apologies. She set her poodle in the chair beside her and, since her coffee was cold, ordered more. The *garçon* returned with a hot glass of coffee. She daintily dipped pieces of croissant into it and ate them, occasionally feeding her dog with fragments.

The tables began to fill up. The sun was now warm and soothing, and its rays turned the streetcar rails into gleaming and dazzling bars. The sidewalks were crowded with pedestrians. The traffic was heavier, and the policeman regulating it barked and gestured almost like a character in a comic opera. Another policeman halted a German in front of the café and, after conversation, the German extracted papers from his jacket pocket and handed them to the policeman. The policeman read the papers and returned them, and the German rejoined the procession of people. The American woman slowly finished her small breakfast. She signaled the *garçon* for the bill, paid him, and handed him a one-franc tip. He scornfully bounced the franc piece on the table, and it rolled off. He breathed rapidly in insulted protest.

"Why, the idea," the American woman exclaimed, tossing back her head, looking about the café for sympathy from those who watched, enjoying the scene.

The *garçon* pointed to his left palm with his index finger and shouted at the woman.

"*Je ne vous comprends pas,*" she kept repeating loudly, quickly shaking her head from right to left.

While the waiter persisted, she gathered up her poodle and stalked away from him, her head tossing in flushed indignation, her crumbling, lifted face taut and angry.

Watching her enter a taxicab, the *garçon* exclaimed, "*Américaine! Vache! Merde!*"

After she had departed, he searched for the one-franc piece, pocketed it, shrugged his shoulders, sneered, and waited for new customers.

The sun was now hot and strong. Traffic swept along in increased volume. Pedestrians strolled by. The *garçon* stood looking out onto the street with folded arms. A lone, wizened beggar paused and stared at the customers with extended palm. The *garçon* caught his eye. He turned and moved away rapidly at a shuffling gait.

Saturday Night

I

DOPEY slouched into the dining room and sat down carelessly at the foot of the table. Listlessly, he laid a nicotine-stained hand, with its bony protuberance of wrist, on the white table-cloth and smiled when his sisters, Kate and Beatrice, greeted him. Kate glanced at Aunt Anna, a large woman with a full, milk-fed face and a mass of light auburn hair. Aunt Anna glowered at Dopey. She filled their plates with steak, carrots, and peas. Kate, noticing the expression on her aunt's face, fidgeted and remarked that it had been thrilling to listen to the radio broadcast of the Notre Dame football game this afternoon. Uncle Mike, seated opposite his nieces, plunged into his supper.

Dopey sat slumped inertly. He was a tubercular-looking young man in his mid-twenties, with thick, sensuous lips, sunken cheeks, and a bony face. His hair was dark brown and curly, like that of his two sisters. His dark eyes were sunken.

With an irritated expression on her face, Aunt Anna handed the plate to Kate, who in turn passed it on to her brother. The family ate in an atmosphere of tension and constraint. Aunt Anna frowned constantly. Kate suddenly laughed at some unexpressed thought. Beatrice glanced at her, slightly annoyed. Dopey looked at the older of his sisters, his lips curling. Kate was plump, with a round, fat face, dark eyes, and black curly hair, and she looked like a school girl in her blue serge dress. Dopey cynically reflected that Kate giggled nervously, like a virgin.

Kate explained why she had just laughed. At the school where she was now teaching, they had received eight dozen potato peelers. Uncle Mike asked what they were for. Kate answered that no one at the school knew. Mike screwed up his lips and ponderously explained that in a large city you had to expect graft and that, anyway, graft meant sales, and sales meant more production, and that lessened unemployment. Kate said it was awfully funny, but all the teachers were angry because of the difficulties they had in getting necessary supplies and because the city was behind in paying them their salaries. Aunt Anna proclaimed it an outrage. Dopey said that everything was a racket anyway, so what difference did it make. Aunt Anna forked a piece of steak, but, seeing her nephew bolt his food, she held it in midair, glared at him, and said angrily:

"You eat like a pig!"

Dopey twisted in his chair, bored; he hoped she wouldn't start all over again, at the beginning.

Kate hurriedly intervened to remark that she hoped she would be transferred to a school in a better neighborhood, because now she had to teach dirty Polacks who would never be any good for anything except possibly to become thugs and bolsheviks and go on causing trouble all their lives, just as they did now in the classroom. Beatrice, after a nudge from Kate, joined in to say she was tired of having to work in the office at Carter School and that she only got a chance to teach when a substitute was needed. And the regular teachers were disgustingly healthy, so she didn't get much chance. She was fed up. And the pupils at her school were worse than Polacks; they were niggers. UGH! Uncle Mike said it was only because he had known Barney McCormack, the politician, and had some pull that Beatrice had gotten any kind of job in the schools, for there were still girls who had finished Normal a year ahead of her who were waiting for appointments. She should be glad she had an appointment instead of complaining.

"You might at least show some manners when you eat," Aunt Anna said to her nephew in a loud, rasping voice. "You'll have no stomach left, and if you get ulcers of the stomach, who's going to pay your doctor bill?"

"Uncle Mike, do you think business will improve soon?" Kate hastily asked to make conversation.

Before Uncle Mike could answer, Aunt Anna burst out at Dopey:

"You have the habits of a ditch digger. To see you eat one would imagine you didn't even know what the inside of a decent, refined home looked like!"

"Aunt Anna, please!" Kate pleaded, while Dopey grinned weakly.

"Katherine, don't interrupt me! Those who live in my house without even making the effort to pay one cent of board are going to listen to what I say. It's just about time somebody spoke seriously to you, young man, yes, *it's just about time*."

She glanced toward Mike.

"I'm disgusted with him," she went on. "He's nothing but a bum, despite all we've done for him. I'd like to know what he thinks we all are—morons? If he does, he's mighty mistaken. He shan't continue living under my roof and go on as he has been. We've all gotten him job after job, but he's quit them. All he's interested in is horse races and getting drunk. Tell me who your friends are, and I'll tell you what you are. His friends are all bums, and birds of a feather flock together. Well, I won't tolerate him any longer."

"But Joseph is going back to his new job on Monday, aren't you, Joseph?" Kate said conciliatingly, turning to her aunt, whose face was flushed.

Dopey wasn't even listening. Instead, he thought how he would have gotten the gravy, rich and thick and brown, this afternoon, if he'd only had two bucks to lay on Red Pepper after Len had come around the corner with that hot tip. But it was always his lousy luck to be stony when he got a real tip. . . . Red Pepper had paid forty to one. Two bucks would have paid him eighty; five, two hundred; and he could have blown town for New Orleans, and then maybe he could have shipped out to Europe or Asia, or at least for the West Coast through the Canal Zone. But it was just his horse luck to be stony when he got a tip right out of the feed bag. . . . And, Jesus Christ, his aunt became a bigger and broader pain in the rump to him all the time. She'd been teaching sixth-grade Polacks and Hunkies so long that she thought she could treat everybody as if they were one of her sixth-grade pupils. And all that old crap about work and save, and grow old to be like Aunt Anna or Mike. Become a carbon copy of Michael J. McGuire, have a few bucks salted away in a bank that was liable to go bust any day, and be an old fox with your hair turning gray, telling your nieces and nephews how to be a Puritan while you had your bonded liquor and your women on the side. That crap had never gone with him. He remembered the one time he had shipped out of New Orleans and gone to Liverpool, and he wished he'd stuck it instead of coming back home because his Aunt Mary wrote him those letters. They could jam their work and save and pray just where it all damn well belonged.

He watched Aunt Anna eat with a vengeance; he hoped she was all talked out now.

"Joe, don't you think you could find some kind of work to stick at and make a future for yourself?" Mike said to him.

Dopey sighed. Mike got a self-righteous kick out of talking this way. Let him talk!

"Yes, you're starting to get old now; soon you'll be sloping down the years quicker than you imagine. Yes, sir, the slope down the years is a little quicker than we'd all like it to be, and before a young fellow knows it, he wakes up one morning and finds out he isn't as young as he wishes he was. You ought to have some thoughts of settling down, some plans for a future. Pretty soon you're going to have to take care of yourself. Your father is married again and he has other children beside you and your sisters. He has a baby. And his business is going very badly at present. And your Aunt Anna and I aren't so young any more, and what with taxes and the mortgage on this building, we can't go on taking care of you, much as we wish to help you. Yes, Joe, speaking straight from the shoulder, don't you think it's time you started thinking seriously about your future?"

Mike hadn't noticed Aunt Anna's frown when he said she was not so young any more. Finishing his steak, he went on to remark that a young fellow should have enough pride and ambition to want to win himself a place in the world, and that anyway he had to or else he'd be scratched, because the race for success wasn't for the slow or the shiftless, and every man in this world sooner or later had to take care of himself.

"Yes, Joseph, you really ought to listen to Uncle Mike and think of the advice he gives you," Kate said in the manner of a school-teacher.

"Mike, you're only wasting words on him," Aunt Anna said, and as she talked on her voice assumed a tone of exaggerated despair. "In all my livelong days, I never saw a boy as worthless as he is. He's always been the same. He wouldn't study and finish high school so he could go to college and study law or engineering, like his father wanted him to. His father said only the other night, after getting him this last job, that he couldn't do any more. It's no use. We've helped him, fed him, clothed him, waited on him, coddled him, tried to point the right way out to him, but it's just not in his bones. If it was, he'd have amounted to something by now."

"Every good job I ever had, I got myself," Dopey said.

"Joseph! Please!" Kate pleaded.

"You see, Mike! He hasn't even the decency to appreciate what was done to help him. After all his shiftlessness, his father last week got him another job, and this is what he says. And he works at it for only three days and then goes out drinking with his bum friends and can't get up in the morning to go to work. And he didn't even have the sense of fairness to telephone his employer and say he wasn't coming to work."

"But what kind of a job was it?" Dopey asked.

"Yes, I know what you want. A banker's job from twelve to one, with an hour for lunch," Aunt Anna said.

"Since your friend Pete Flanagan's bank failed, I don't think I'd care to be a banker."

"Joseph, you know that Pete was honest, and his failure was an honest one. That indictment against him is the work of soreheads and politicians who want scapegoats so they can make demagogic appeals," Mike said.

"Sure!" Dopey said ironically.

"He even slanders a friend who has been so good to him all his life," Aunt Anna said.

"Oh, Auntie, please!" Beatrice said.

"Well, I said my last word. He wouldn't go to work today. I wash my hands of him," Aunt Anna said.

"What kind of a job was it?" Dopey asked again. "If I'm to be treated like a high-school pupil, I want more than seventeen bucks a week. That wasn't a job. It was a slave factory for dopes. You had to get there at eight-thirty before a bell rang, and if you were a minute late you went to the chief clerk with an excuse, just as if you were in high school. He wrote you out a note permitting you to go to work. And if you had to go to the bathroom, you had to raise your hand, just as in school. And a bell rang for lunch, and after lunch another bell rang, and at five-thirty, a bell rang, and your work was checked, and you were given an average. The average was posted on a bulletin board with grades and letters and colors. If I stuck at the job, I'd be given homework to do next week. I'm no slave."

"Well, all I say is this. I'd never have the patience with you that your father and your Uncle Mike and your Uncle Pete have shown. I'd let you roll in the gutter where you belong."

Beatrice took out the soiled dishes, and Kate served coffee and pie.

"He hasn't one iota of manhood in him, and I shan't go on feeding him. I'm no fool. He worried my sister Mary while she was alive, but he won't worry me!" Aunt Anna said, pouring cream into her coffee.

Dopey did not answer. He drank his coffee and thought of his deceased Aunt Mary. He saw her, gray-haired, sweet, gentle, worrying. She seemed to walk into the room and take her accustomed place next to Mike. She seemed to sit there, quietly and unobtrusively. She seemed to smile at him in anxiety and sadness. She had been like a saint, and even though she had worried about him, she had been understanding. She had known that her nieces and her nephew had their own lives to lead. He remembered the first time he had thrown up a job and bummed to New Orleans. How she had worried and prayed for him and sent him money. And the way she had slipped him a ten-dollar bill the morning he had left. She had raised him and Kate and Beatrice, given her life for them, taking the place of their dead mother. And then she had quietly died. She had been the only one in his family that he gave a good goddamn for, and when she had died he had felt sorry. He remembered her, a nun-like, thin woman, who, now that she was gone, seemed holy. She was his one sentiment, his one cherished memory, the one memory that made him feel, made him sad. She was dead, but he imagined he saw her sitting there at the table. Things had been entirely different in the goddamn menage ever since she had died. He imagined her sitting at Mike's left, and he wished she were alive. He even wished he had caused her less worry during her lifetime.

"I've had enough of him," Aunt Anna said, rising at the end of the meal. "He can go out tonight with those bums, but when he returns the burglar's lock will be on the door. His father and stepmother won't have him. Well, neither will I!"

II

Mike called Dopey into the bedroom they shared. Dopey sat on his own unmade bed and wondered if he would be able to stem his uncle for a loan. His uncle did everything he did, only in a bigger way. He played the ponies, got his tail, smoked cigarettes incessantly, despite his bad lungs, drank, sat up at all-night poker games. Now he was going to sound off like a Y.M.C.A. secretary.

Mike held out a box of cork-tip Egyptian cigarettes. Dopey took one, and they lit up. Mike fingered his black knit necktie and looked his nephew in the eye. He ran his soft hand through

his thinning hair. He crossed and uncrossed his legs, puffing
at his cigarette meditatively. Dopey slumped back on the bed
and waited.

"Joe, I want to speak to you," Mike said dramatically.

Suppressing a smile, Dopey also checked an impulse to exclaim:

—Oop, you're telling me something!

That was the way he and Al Herbert always razzed anybody
who told them dumb stories. Mike inhaled and let the smoke
out his nose. He cleared his throat.

"Yes, Joe, I've been wanting to speak with you for a long
time," Mike said. He paused. "Joe, you see, I feel that somebody should have a man-to-man talk with you. Now, your
Aunt Anna, she loves you very much, and she wants you to do
right and amount to something. But, after all, she's a woman.
She has your best interests at heart, but there are things a
woman can't naturally understand. So I decided I better speak
with you, and I want you to understand that I'm going to
talk with you straight from the shoulder."

Dopey spilled ashes on the rug, and Mike asked him to be
careful. If Aunt Anna saw him doing that, she would go up
like a kite. Mike lit a fresh cigarette with his old one.

"Joe, all the young fellows you pal with are getting somewhere. Take Ike Dugan. He's with the Mid City Utilities making good money, and he has a future there. And Marty has a
good job selling for the Nation Oil Company. And you were
telling me that Al Herbert has gotten himself a good job in a
bond house, and that his employer thinks well of him. And
Phil Garrity is on La Salle Street. Pardon me for saying it,
Joe, but they all seem to be a little bit wiser than you. They have
their fun. They're not goody-goody Willies, but they stick to
their jobs, and they all seem to be getting somewhere. They
use a little bit of common, ordinary, everyday horse sense and
don't let their fun and amusements interfere with their work
and their future. Joe, you're just as intelligent as they are. In
fact, I think you're a damn sight smarter. I remember when
you were in high school. You were smart as a whip in mathe-

matics. If you'd only applied yourself more you would have been a shark in that line. There is no godly reason in this world why you shouldn't go miles farther than they, except that you're lazy. A little bit of get-up to you, Joe, and they couldn't see you for dust. That's straight, the God's truth, because, Joe, I've got faith in you. I'm talking frank, and I don't want you to feel hurt when I say you're a little lazy, because, Joe, I'm only trying to give you constructive criticism, and I believe that we all got to recognize the truth when it is told to us. Joe, I have faith in you, and that's why I'm bothering to tell you that you need a little more get-up to you. Maybe these are hard words to say to your face, but, Joe . . . the truth is always a little bit harder than we'd like it to be."

Dopey, who had been simpering while Mike talked, nodded and exclaimed that he'd never found an interesting job.

"Joe, you always put the cart before the horse. . . . But, here, have another cigarette. . . . Got a light? . . . All right, Joe, you got to realize that you can't go through life waiting for an interesting job to come along. People don't work because they find it interesting. They work because they want to make money, because with money they can be somebody and not be ashamed of themselves. They can do things with money, show the community that they are somebody. Work is a curse, the curse of Adam. Do you think I like to work? Do you think I enjoy the insurance business? Not on your life, not on your life! Nobody likes their work. People work because they've got to, because they want *money*, esteem, the independence that only money can buy. When Shakespeare said that your pocketbook is your best friend, he said one of the truest things any man ever said."

Mike paused. Dopey slouched, wondering how long Mike would go on this time.

"Joe, I've been wondering for a long time why you don't stick to a job. Now I know. You've gone along looking for a job that's interesting. Well, you won't find interesting work, except by a rare piece of good luck. You've got to make yourself like whatever work you get. You got to stick to it, and keep your nose on the grindstone, and say to yourself with determination, 'I won't quit, and no one can make me quit, because I've got courage and brains and faith in myself!' If you want to be somebody, you've got to grit your teeth and stick to your job no matter if it kills you."

"I've had plenty of jobs all over this country," Dopey said in a toneless voice. "I don't go for that stuff. It's the bunk. A lad's fun and his life are worth more than a measly twenty or thirty bucks a week. And nowadays you can't start in as the office boy and work yourself up and become a big shot. Those days are over. There's no one starting on a shoestring and making a wad like John D. Rockefeller did. Now you've got to accept being a clerk and a flunkey for some big corporation. The only way you get rich now is in a racket, or by having a lot to start with, or having some luck on the races, or something like that."

"Joe, that's pessimism. If everybody thought like you, we'd all be communists and anarchists, and then how would the world's work get done?"

"There's plenty of suckers to do the world's work, and, anyway, if the world didn't have so much work for itself, we'd all have a better time. Most of the jobs I've ever had were useless ones. I'd add up figures on a comptometer machine, make out useless reports and forms, and prepare records that would be filed and never looked at. Then they'd be tied up, put in a storeroom or basement. And when there were enough records stored up, they'd be burned. And I'd go on filling up new cabinets all over again."

"Joe, you're damn near talking like a bolshevik. Here's one idea you have to get straight. There isn't any work in a good office that's useless, unless it's in politics. I run an office and I know. I know business and businessmen. They aren't dumb. The fellows who have risen to be heads of corporations have their jobs for one reason only—they're smart as whips. If they weren't, they wouldn't be at the top of the ladder. They know economics because that's their business. And they know that according to economic law everything that isn't useful and profitable is naturally eliminated, because it has to be by the law of supply and demand."

"In most of my jobs, there's always been plenty of demand."

"Joe, I'm talking serious, and it will profit you not to be . . . facetious. You're twenty-five now, and you can't afford to fool any more time away. If you do, what's going to become of you? Did you ever stop to think of where you'll be in five, ten, or fifteen years?"

"Yes."

"Well?" asked Mike as they lit fresh cigarettes.

"I may be in Shanghai."

"That's not a serious way to look at it. You know there isn't anything in a life like that for a fellow as smart as you. That's a life for bums and dumbbells. Don't be a fool! Such a life would mean nothing but hardships, drifting, disgrace, vice, poverty. You'll have no decent friends, no home, nothing that the ordinary civilized person has. You'll be a drifter without a cent in the bank, with no place in the community, nothing. If you work hard and keep straight, you'll have something, and be somebody, and be able to walk out of the house every morning with pride and with the feeling of the honest blacksmith in the great poem who owed no man a penny. You'll be somebody that way. You won't be a failure, a disgrace to yourself and your family, and, yes, to your country, because being a failure is being a disgrace to your country, too."

Dopey drew on his cigarette and let the words drum meaninglessly on his ears.

"Joe, what do you think you'd like to be?"

"I'd like to go back to sea or else be a bookie."

"Joe, can't you see that that will never get you anywhere?" Mike asked emphatically, gazing nonplussed at his nephew. "If you were still nineteen, your attitude would be all right, because at nineteen a young fellow still has a few years to waste. But you've wasted enough of your life. You've had your adventures. You've seen more of America than I have. And you never made a go of that kind of life, either. You've gone away on your own more than once, and you had to telegraph for your fare back to Chicago. You had a good job in a Wall Street brokerage house paying you seventy-five dollars a week, and you were a fool for throwing it up. Joe, you better give up some of your ideas before they land you in a mess, with your life and your health wasted. Get yourself a good job, stick to it, invest a little of your money soundly. Then you can have your good times in the right way. I have my good times, and I always had 'em. But I never was foolish. If you're not foolish, you won't have to sacrifice your fun. If you take my advice, you'll get somewhere, and then you'll have money for good times in the right way. I don't say you shouldn't play around a little with girls, take a drink now and then, or even put a little money on the horses. That's all right in its place, and if it's done with moderation. But you've got to harmonize those things with your work so you'll not be a failure. And if you let yourself become a failure, every friend you have will turn his back on you, and you'll be like an outlaw."

Dopey could see that Mike was enjoying himself.

"Joe, I want you to think about these things, and to remember that life isn't so long, and that time crawls up on you just like death does. Time, as well as death, is a thief in the night."

"Well, I don't see much enticement in success if it's very hard to get."

"Joe, I wish you wouldn't joke, because this is a matter that requires serious thought," Mike said as they again lit cigarettes.

Dopey refrained from smiling. He suddenly decided that he'd better agree with his uncle and hurry up with a good gag to get a loan. Mike had talked himself into a swell mood. They sat smoking, and Dopey said in an insincere but serious voice:

"Maybe I had better start considering things in a new light."

Mike beamed. Dopey told him that Phil Garrity had said something about there being a possible opening where he worked soon, and, since Phil was in good with his boss, Phil might get him the job. Anyway, it sounded like a good proposition.

"If you get that job, I'll guarantee to get you good references, and we'll turn over a new leaf, forgetting the past and its errors. And, Joe, go to work determined to stick at it until hell freezes over, and after it freezes go get ice skates and stick some more. If you do, I'll bet that you'll become a new man. You'll find yourself feeling better, free and independent. You'll buck up and be more chipper and know that you've found your place in the scheme of things."

"Yeah, I guess I better get some sort of a racket where the bucks come in regular."

"Snap up this opportunity if it knocks on your door."

"I think I will."

Mike talked more of inspiration, and Dopey nodded in agreement. Mike took out a bottle of bonded whisky and they had a drink. Dopey told Mike that he owed Phil Garrity three bucks, and that Phil needed it, and that since Phil might help him land that job, he'd like to be able to repay Phil. Mike frowned.

"Do you have to pay him tonight?" Mike asked, scratching his poll.

"I don't exactly have to, but I'd like to because I know he has a heavy date and needs it."

"Well!" Mike exclaimed, screwing up his lips. "Well . . . all right . . . I'll take this last chance on you."

He handed Dopey a five-dollar bill, and Dopey thanked him several times. He asked for another cigarette, and Mike gave him a box half full of cork-tips. Mike patted Dopey's shoulder and said that he had to get dressed to go out. But he was mighty glad to see that his nephew was turning over a new leaf.

Walking into the parlor, Dopey heard Mike telling Aunt Anna that all Joseph needed was a good talking to. He'd given it to him, and Joseph was going to straighten himself out. Dopey felt that Mike wasn't a bad guy. And he was proud of his chiseling. He felt the crisp five-dollar bill in his pocket.

III

Kate and Beatrice sat in the parlor listening to the Gold Dust Twins on the radio. Dopey came in. Kate asked for a cigarette, and he handed her a Lucky Strike. She listened by the hallway. She came back and asked what Aunt Anna was doing, and Dopey said Aunt Anna was talking with Mike in the dining room. Kate lit the cigarette. Noticing the cork-tip in her brother's mouth, she accused him of holding out on her. He said he'd gotten it from Mike and didn't have any more. She listened by the hallway again, returned to the couch, sat down. She got her throat filled with smoke and coughed.

Dopey glanced at Beatrice. She was twenty-one years old, and, he decided, had sex appeal; he sometimes wished to hell she wasn't his own sister. She was a nice touch for some guy, no use kidding himself. Was she or wasn't she a virgin like Kate? She had gone with Al Peppler from around the corner of Sixty-third and Stony, and Al had had the reputation of making every girl he took out. Beatrice had gone heavy with him for a while, and he was dubious about there being any exception to Al's rule. But he didn't know. And when Al had run away with funds from the bank he was clerking in, Beatrice had damned near bawled her eyes out. Al had gotten out of the jam, though. Dopey didn't know what had happened between Beatrice and Al, but he believed Al had given her the air. She hadn't gone out on many dates for a long while after she and Al had stopped seeing each other. Fellows ought to like her, though, because she was a nice enough job. He looked at her trim legs. Well, why not? Maybe this brother-and-sister stuff was just hooey, just like everything else.

He studied Beatrice. She was a little pigeon-toed, and had bad lips, just as Kate did, and her teeth were crooked, too. But, even so, she was still pretty neat, and before she had gone with Al, particularly, she had been paged plenty. She didn't seem to go out on many dates, and he couldn't figure out why she was on the shelf. But even if she was, she wouldn't be on it for long unless she wanted to be.

"I thought you were going out tonight?" Kate said to Beatrice, fidgeting on the couch while she spoke.

"I'd just as soon not," Beatrice answered.

"Well, I thought you were," Kate said archly.

Dopey looked at Kate with annoyance.

"Joseph," Kate said suddenly, "I do wish you would take better care of yourself. You know, we all worry about you."

Yawning, he told her to shut up. She acted hurt and shocked.

"You're mean. When someone tries to tell you something, only because they like you and know it will be for your own good, you won't even listen to them. You get mean and insulting. You're vile, and I hate you!"

"Save it," he said.

Beatrice hummed the tune of a popular song.

"You're horrid!" Kate said to him, wiping away a tear.

Dopey laughed. Beatrice yawned.

"Joseph, I really do wish you wouldn't act like that. People say things to you only because they're interested in your welfare. And, Joseph, you really don't look so well, and you're much thinner than you should be. You really ought to take care of yourself. You look awfully pale and you smoke too many cigarettes, and they're not good for your lungs. I wouldn't be surprised at all if there was something wrong with you. And you don't even go to Mass any more, either."

"Jesus Christ!"

"I don't care! Go ahead, insult me and curse me all you want to. I don't care. I do think that Aunt Anna was perfectly right in bawling you out. You ought to listen to her, or to . . . somebody."

"It seems like I have to, even when I'd rather listen to the radio."

"You needn't get so sarcastic."

"Every minute I'm home I hear it. Some of you ought to try sending your tongues away for a vacation."

"But, then, you're not home so much that you hear very much," Beatrice laughed.

"If I was, they'd drive me into the booby hatch."

"You're just incorrigible. Go ahead and have your own way then. Someday you'll be sorry when it's too late. . . . You're just perfectly incorrigible."

Dopey laughed at her. She pouted.

"But, Joseph, won't you *please* try to take a little better care of yourself . . . for your own good?"

He sneered. The doorbell rang. Kate hastened to answer it. Dopey rose and went over to a corner to turn off the radio.

IV

"Hello, Big Shot!" Kate said, greeting Phil Garrity with affected naiveté, as she let him in.

He returned a silly smile, shot out his hand stiffly from the hip, and pumped hers in a collegiate handshake.

"Put it there, Kid from the Limberlost. I ain't seen you in steen million years. How you was?"

"My, but you're strong," she said, and he manfully patted his chest with his left hand. "Why, Phil, you're all togged out like Joe College. New suit, topcoat, scarf, say, you'll look like a collar ad if you're not careful. I'll bet you're scheduled to sing some place tonight. Or maybe you have a new girl on the string. Do tell, Phil, are you *in love*?"

Phil blushed and faked a cough. He shoved his left foot forward, leaned his weight back on his right foot, placed his left hand inside his double-breasted blue suit coat, and smiled insipidly. Kate looked at him with innocent eyes.

"Say, kid, I get 'em in droves," he hurriedly said, gesturing clumsily to emphasize what he was saying.

Taking his beige topcoat and gray felt hat to hang in the closet, she giggled. Phil walked flat-footedly into the parlor, and Kate followed him, squealing as she glanced at his new tan brogans. He smiled insipidly as his hand shot out to Dopey, who shook hands limply.

"Phil is dressed up like a circus," Kate giggled.

Phil squinted sidewise at her through his gold-rimmed glasses.

"You must have played Red Pepper today," Dopey said.

"Nope. Never play the races. Guess again."

Sitting down, Phil carefully pulled his trousers up at his knees in order to preserve their press.

"Who died and named you in the will, Garrity?" Dopey asked, grinning.

"Wrong again," Phil replied.

"Phil looks like he had a heavy date scheduled," Beatrice said.

"I'm stepping out, high, wide, and fancy with something better than Clara Bow," Phil said.

"He's so cute," Kate tittered, and Phil blushed. She added, "Gee, don't you think he ought to wear a flower in his button-hole?"

"Kate, don't make him blush so," Beatrice said.

"Come on, Phil, what's the lowdown?" Dopey asked.

"Well, kid, I knocked 'em dead," Phil said, sliding his right hand out sidewise in an emphatic slicker gesture.

Dopey scratched his head, puzzled.

"Phil, the girl lucky enough to be dated with you tonight should be proud, and, when she steps out with you in that new outfit, she'll certainly have pride and lovelight in her eyes,' Kate said.

Phil quickly sneezed. He blew his nose.

"I knocked 'em dead, Joseph, and it was on the legit. It was on the legit," Phil said.

"Phil uses such quaint language," Kate said with assumed innocence.

"Razzing doesn't phase me, Kate," Phil said, grinning fool-ishly.

"Cut it, Kate!" Dopey said.

"Phil, do me a favor?" Kate said.

"Katherine, anything to oblige, anything to oblige," Phil said, rising awkwardly to bow before her with mock chivalry.

"Well, keep standing and turn around so we can see how perfect a fit you got," Kate said.

"Teasing him like that will spoil the poor boy's evening, Kate," Beatrice said, winking at her sister.

Phil sat down, grinning foolishly.

"Well, it fits," he said like a sap.

"And it's good goods, too," Kate said.

"For Christ sake, Garrity, spill the dope. What kind of a windfall did you have? You got me going," Dopey said.

"I knocked 'em dead this week. And it was on the legit," Phil said equivocally.

"I'm gaga with curiosity. Tell us," Kate said.

Phil pulled up his trousers at the knee again. He crossed his left leg over his right and fingered his bright blue tie. Kate commented on the clocks on his socks. Phil seemed uncomfortable because of the sudden lapse in the conversation. He mopped his face with his blue-bordered handkerchief.

"Dopey, my ship came in," he said.

"But really, Phil, I mean it. You have a good-looking suit on," Beatrice said.

"Thanks, Bea."

"It's the berries, Phil," Dopey said.

"Quite nobby, I should say," Kate said.

"And it was cash, no budget plan," Phil said.

"It makes you look like the answer to a flapper's prayer," Kate said.

"Here's the answer to a flapper's prayer," Phil said, showing them a wallet fat with money.

"How much?" Dopey eagerly asked.

"Plenty. . . . *Plenty!*"

"How did you make the haul?" Dopey asked.

"That's the secret. But get me straight. It was on the legit."

Laughing, Kate told Phil that he just couldn't do anything that wasn't above-board, and he flushed.

"Come on, Garrity, flash the tale. This ain't a detective story," Dopey said.

"I knocked 'em for a row. And you ain't seen all, either."

"I'll faint if you say you bought the ring," Kate said.

"She's a beauty, a genuine bargain," Phil said, palming his hands outward in a gesture of emphasis.

"You talk as if you bought her at a bargain counter," Kate said, giggling.

Phil went to the window, and they stared at a long, impressive, polished second-hand Lincoln, parked at the curb.

"I'm going buggy riding," Phil said.

"Did the old man break down and blow himself to that tin? Or did you rent it for the night?" Dopey asked.

"I told you I knocked 'em dead. I just peeled three hundred bucks spot cash off the roll. And you should hear that Lincoln motor purr. Smooth as they come, runs just like new. It's a beaut," Phil said.

"Jesus Christ!" Dopey said, amazed, and the two girls laughed.

When they left the window and again asked how he got the money, he preserved his air of mystery.

"Phil, you won't make your girls walk home, will you?" asked Kate.

"Listen, little Nell of the Limberlost, I'll knock 'em for a row now. When I get 'em out in this chassis of mine and step on the gas, their hearts will pop right out of their mouths— they'll cry for more like babies cry for Castoria," Phil said.

"Ooh!" sighed Kate.

"Kate, you ain't cute. Lay down and die," Dopey said.

Kate ignored her brother and asked Phil where he had such luck.

"Well, I sure get 'em off on this. You coming around in new togs and a Lincoln. You must be a magician," Dopey said.

Phil beamed.

"Phil is a real slicker. He's been holding out on us all these years," Beatrice said.

"Phil, did you meet an heiress?" Kate asked.

"Well, me lads and lassies," Phil said, beaming, and he paused.

"Hurry up or I'll faint with suspense," Kate giggled.

"With a mean boat like the one you got, you'll be a menace to public safety. When you get snozzled, it'll be even worse. Instead of being nearsighted, you'll be double-sighted. But, boy, you'll have some buggy rides," Dopey said.

"Oh, do tell, Phil. I'm agog," Kate said.

Phil started to brag of the rides he'd have.

"I'll bet that Phil will start thinking that lampposts are Christmas trees and his car and his friends are ornaments to be hung on them," Kate said, interrupting.

Phil glowed. He and Dopey lit cigarettes, smiling at each other with mutual understanding.

"Will you take me for a ride sometime?" Kate coyly asked.

"If you can take speed. Speed's going to be my middle name."

"Phil will put just a wee bit of zip in the car," Dopey said, and they laughed.

"Phil is so *cute*," Kate said.

"Kate, you always razz me. But just to show you that my heart's bigger than an apple, I'll take you for a ride," Phil said.

"I'd just love it," Kate said.

"Let's barge out of here," Dopey said suddenly.

He put on his hat and coat and walked out without saying good-by. Kate helped Phil on with his coat.

"How about a date next week?" he asked.

"Please tell me how you got the car?" she asked.

"Why not have a date tomorrow night?"

"I won't answer you until you tell me how you got the car."

"I got a hot tip in the office and cleaned up on the market," he said.

"That's grand! Why, someday I'll bet you'll be a real financier," she said laughing.

"How about the date next week?" he asked hoarsely.

"I'm not usually asked that way," she said.

"But, Kate, I would like to come over for you and let you see how the boat runs, and we could do something," he said.

"Well," she said evasively.

"How'd you like me to teach you to drive it?" he asked.

"That would be adorable."

"Let's make it definite," he said.

"Hey, Garrity, shake those flat feet of yours," Dopey impatiently called from the landing below.

"What night?"

"Call me up," she said.

"I'll call, but I suppose it's no use. I don't count anyway. I'm nothing but a chump. It won't be any use to call you up, but I'll do it because I'm a chump," he said.

"Now you're getting sarcastic again."

He slowly went down the stairs.

"Have a good time," Kate called sweetly after him.

v

Dopey asked how Phil had gotten the rake-in, and Phil told him. They got in the car, and Phil started it. He drove silently, brooding, thinking that, after all, he was just No-Soap Garrity and that he'd never be anything else. He had had so many plans and dreams about tonight, he had anticipated so much, he had looked forward to his appearance at the Carberrys and the way he would impress Kate. And he had counted on the date he would make with her. She'd put him off, and he guessed that she wouldn't date him. She hadn't given him a date in six months now, and he believed she laughed at him behind his back. There was a wrong twist in his make-up, and there had been even back in his high-school days. He had been one of the best students in his classes, and from his sophomore year on he had done most of the covers for the school magazine and the annuals. But that hadn't made him a regular fellow with the guys. He hadn't even been able to make any of the teams as a sub. He'd never been a good fighter. When the time came for dances and dates, he couldn't learn to dance decently, and he'd always had poor luck in getting dates. He just had a wrong twist in his make-up somewhere. He knew it. He knew he had always been something of a clown. When Dopey and the fellows had had their frat back in their high-school days, they had never bid him for it, even though he had hung around to get bid. He didn't have the social graces lots of other lads had. He just didn't click.

"For Christ sake! Watch your driving," Dopey said excitedly and angrily, as Phil, nearing Sixty-fourth Street, barely managed to swerve away from a collision with a Dodge.

"It's all right, pal. We won't hit anything, and if we do, it'll be the other mug's fault, and some poor bastard's tough titty. This car is built like a dreadnaught, and I mean *built*. Nothing is going to smash into it."

"Be careful. I'm going on a bender not a funeral," Dopey said.

Still brooding, Phil turned onto Sixty-fourth Street.

"Watch that driving," Dopey said, as a car cut in ahead of them.

"I am. I know how to drive."

"You're so goddamned nearsighted you couldn't see the blind sight of a barn," Dopey said.

Phil winced. Always having to take it. Just a misfit. Couldn't even see to drive. Chump Garrity. Like a fathead, he'd thought his clean-up on the market, his new suit, and his car would give him a new personality. And he was still a misfit. He wasn't a regular fellow like other guys were. He couldn't talk their lingo and make it sound like the real stuff, couldn't get girls, couldn't really feel his oats the way Dopey seemed to. He shouldn't be going around the corner. He hadn't in the old days of Nolan's dance hall, because he'd known he didn't belong. Misfit! Maybe he should have been an artist. In high school he had planned to be one, but most guys thought that artists were goofy, and he couldn't stand being laughed at as an artist. So he gave it up, didn't go to art school, and got himself a job in a brokerage house. He made dough now, too, and he was envied for his salary and the extra dividends he made playing the market on his own. But that didn't make him regular either. Yes, maybe he shouldn't have given up art. The priests in high school had told him he was promising. And he knew he had been. Sometimes now he felt that he was, and he went to the Art Institute with materials, and he looked at pictures, taking a hill from Cézanne, mist from Monet, a few trees from Corot, a sky from Inness, and making it a picture of his own. Doing that, he'd think of Kate. And down at the office he'd think of her, think of her as *Mrs. Katherine Garrity . . . Mrs. Philip Garrity . . .* He had enough money to marry on, and with her teaching, too, they could get on jake, save, have a little apartment, and they ought to be happy. If she only would realize that he loved her and would give him a chance to make her love him. He'd like that better than bouncing around and drinking with the fellows as he did, not having any fun. And they always wanted to go whoring, and he still had his cherry, even though he pretended that he'd lost it. If they knew, they'd give him the horse laugh and a nickname like *Cherry Garrity.* Maybe tonight they'd go to Twenty-second Street. But he didn't have the guts. It was sin. God might punish him with an automobile accident, death, a dose. Most of the fellows hadn't taken their doses seriously, but he was afraid of getting one. He didn't want to be going out to get drunk either, but he had to when he was feeling the way he did tonight. He couldn't have a good time with the guys when he was sober. Sober, he was a clown, not knowing what to say, a dunce before girls. Well, he'd get drunk, goddamn them all, he'd get polluted, maggoty drunk. He didn't like the taste of the stuff, but he'd down it like water. He'd even take pure alcohol. He'd show 'em! If he couldn't do anything else better than other lads, he would put on a better drunk than they did. And let Kate hear about it, let her know that they all went to a whore house, let her know everything! Let her see he could go on living without giving a good goddamn. He could be wild, carefree, dashing, romantic, brave, a guy who didn't care two hoots in hell for anything in the world.

Somehow, he'd go romantically, carelessly to hell . . . But, no, he didn't want to. He wanted Kate. If he could only call her *his Kate,* marry her, build a beautiful life, the two of them together, a life better than he now lived . . . *I'm all alone . . . so alone . . . with no one else but you . . . I'm all alone . . . dancing with tears in my eyes . . . With someone like you, a pal so good and true. . . . I'd like to leave it all behind. . . . And go and find . . . Some place that's known to God alone. . . . Just a little spot to call our own . . . We'll find perfect peace . . .*

VI

The corner of Sixty-third and Stony Island was bustling with Saturday-night activity, crowded with people, noisy with the traffic of automobiles and streetcars. The elevated trains kept rumbling into and out of the station overhead. Fellows, most of them young, were lined in front of the drugstore on the southwest corner by the elevated steps, the bus station near it, and the restaurant, modernistically decorated, which was a few doors farther down. Dopey and Phil entered the drugstore. Phil bought four packages of cigarettes and handed two to Dopey.

"Hello, boys," Slag Stone said, smiling at them.

Dopey asked him how he felt, and he said pretty good, considering.

"Considering what?" Phil asked.

He said that he had been pie-eyed last night and thrown some sugar bowls at people whose faces he didn't like in Sally Carns's restaurant. And, feeling rotten, he had to start to work tonight as bouncer in a new cabaret down on Cottage Grove Avenue. He ambled away, a tall, broad-shouldered, powerful fellow of about thirty.

At the door they met seventeen-year-old Young Evers, who had already been kicked out of three high schools. His forehead was breaking out in a rash, and his face was surly.

"Got a jit? I need a couple more jits to get a bottle," he said.

"You still mooching around here?" Dopey said sarcastically.

"You ain't got a monopoly on the business," Evers snapped back in good humor.

"I don't like competition from amateur chiselers," Dopey said, while Phil handed him a quarter. Dopey added, "Why don't you try working for a change?"

"It doesn't agree with my drinking."

"How they coming, lads?" Eggs Mahoney asked, as they lined up outside by the drugstore window.

"O.K.," Phil said insinuatingly.

"Well, if I'd had the dough to play on Red Pepper this afternoon, I'd be swimming in good nature," Dopey said.

"Me, too. I was flat. Jesus, what a break," Eggs lamented.

They lit cigarettes and moved down the line to say hello to Buddy. His face was battered up, and they asked him what had happened.

"Say, got a drink? I feel scrawny," Buddy said.

"We ain't started yet," Dopey said.

"Well, I got to hustle one. I feel snaky," Buddy said.

"But what's the matter with the lamps?" Phil asked.

"I just got let out of the station. Was there since three this morning," Buddy said.

"Another fight?" asked Dopey.

"Yeah. Say, got a fag?" asked Buddy.

"Here's a coffin nail," Phil said, talking out of the side of his mouth and extending a pack to Buddy.

"Thanks," Buddy said, taking one.

"Keep 'em," Phil said.

"Thanks," Buddy said, pocketing the cigarettes. He lit up and added, "I got snaky last night on Whaley's bum gin, and some big foulball of a dick came along. You boys know how I like dicks, so I hung one on the elephant, getting him square in his goddamn loud Irish mouth. He hauled off on me, and we tangled. I might have handled the bastard, but the bastard got reinforcements, and they hauled me off to the station and beat my pants off. The bastards! I'm laying for that big dick, and, when I get him alone, I got a bill to pay."

"They're plenty tough. But, say, your brother was looking for you this afternoon. He had a tip on Red Pepper, and it paid forty to one," Dopey said.

"That's always my goddamn luck," Buddy said.

"Playing football this year, Buddy?" asked Phil.

"Too old for that now. I'm thirty now, and I already played quarterback for four colleges. Saint Vincent's wanted me back again this year. I was told that all the guys I played against when I was with them six years ago would be through now, or should be, and that I wasn't likely to be recognized. But I'm married with a wife bringing in the dough, and I'm getting too old for that stuff. Let younger lads collect the dough in that racket, and if they can't hire any players, the hell, let them use their regular students," Buddy said.

"I see," Phil exclaimed knowingly.

"I'm crawling along to mooch a drink from Whaley," Buddy said, moving on.

Wils Gillen approached and shook hands all around.

"Say, boys," he said, "I got a date tonight with a really *mean mamma*. I tell you, she's *mean*. All class, and what she hasn't got just ain't worth having. And that includes her papa's Cadillac. The old man's a big shot. He sells things here to the schools."

"Maybe he's the guy who sold potato peelers to my sister Kate's school," Dopey said.

"You boys should see the château they live in out on South Shore Drive. It's as grand as a church, and the parlor's so big you got to megaphone to be heard from one end to the other. She's red hot. I'll tell you who her old man is. Connolly, he's big stuff, a ward committeeman who's somebody in the Democratic organization in this country."

"Gettin' up in the world, huh, Gillen?" Phil said, hiding his envy with a smile.

"And, boys, I'm not seeing Maureen Connolly for nix," Wils said proudly, strutting off.

Jean Fournier and his wife came up to them, and Dopey asked Jean what he was doing these days.

"I'm in one of Al Capone's rackets," Jean said.

"Bootlegging or gambling, Jean?" asked Dopey.

"It's another of the Scarface's rackets. I'm driving a wagon for a cleaning and dyein' outfit. It's a pretty good job, considering hard times, and I ain't complaining," Jean said.

Joey White joined them and said he'd lost his job, but that he had a little dough set aside and was going to a school to study aviation, and Jean's wife stood smiling as they talked.

"Well, look who the hell is here!" said Phil, laughing, pointing to a smiling, puffy young man who approached.

"Careful, there's ladies around," Joey whispered to Phil.

Dressed in expensive clothes, and weighing close to two hundred pounds, Marty shook hands with everyone. They kidded Marty about his weight, saying he was guzzling too much beer.

"What's the matter with Lillian tonight?" asked Dopey.

"I had a row with her, and she gave me the ring back," Marty said with a good-natured smile.

"You've been going with her for six or seven years, and you've frozen away all competition. You ought to marry her, at least for charity if for no other reason," Joey White said.

"What the hell, she gave me the ring back," said Marty.

"You'll be back with her," Dopey said knowingly.

"Nope, I'm free, and I got a date tonight with the niftiest polack. She's . . ." he noticed Mrs. Fournier and seemed embarrassed. He added flatly, "She's plenty on looks."

The Fourniers walked on, and Marty told them how, a few years ago, Jean had been the idol of every bum and pig in Woodlawn. It was damn funny that he should have ended up marrying such a sweet and nice girl, like he did.

"Say, changing the subject, I seen a picture down at the show the other day, and do you know who was in one of the mob scenes . . . Slicker Morrie," Joey White said.

"He'll make the grade in Hollywood. He was one guy with a line. He could sell snowballs in hell with his lingo. His tongue was nothing but pure oil," Phil said, to be horning into the conversation.

"If you want my opinion," Joey White said, "I say that not even the Hollywood stars can resist Slicker Morrie. In the old days when Nolan's dance hall was here on the corner, every decent-looking jane who came to the Sunday-afternoon dances was gone on him. Slicker Morrie made more dames and copped more cherries than any lad in the history of Louisa Nolan's dance hall."

They reminisced about Louisa Nolan's dance hall, which had burned down five years previously, about the girls made and not made, the crap games in the can, the fights, the drunken parties, the days that were gone forever. They talked about the lads from those days who had drifted on, and about the girls. There had been Marjorie, broken in by Slicker Morrie, and after his pioneering effort she had laid for every guy in the place. But she hadn't been so dumb, even if she was a pushover. She was married to a guy who had so much dough that he could light his cigars with dollar bills if he felt like it. And there had been sixteen-year-old Myrtle. She'd been well laid before she was out of grammar school, and by the time she was fifteen she had been plain lousy with clap and syph, and she had had gonorrheal rheumatism, and one day she had just jumped into the Jackson Park lagoon and polluted the drinking water for the gold fish. And Esther, poor Esther, the dancing fool, a god-damn swell and decent kid even if she had been a teaser. In those days she used to dance every night in the week, and twice on Sundays, and not even a broad as husky as she was could stand the dancing pace she set. She danced herself right into con-sumption and the grave, poor Esther, and some of the lads had even bawled at her funeral. Poor Esther. And some of the boys, Al Tolan, for instance, who had been in the army with Pershing in Mexico and could drink like a fish without showing it. And where was Al? And Susie, the fag who used to give out bum checks, the dirty fairy. And Three-Star Hennessey, the lousy little cake-eater who used to rob girls' pocketbooks while he danced with them. Ah, those old days, 1920, '21, '22, '23, '24, and '25. Gone forever. And Phil, who had not known them, stood listening, aching with nostalgia for all this vanished splendor.

VII

Phil, Dopey, and Marty went down the street to a speakeasy. Phil ordered a pint of gin. Dopey said he had better make it two. He bought two pints and gave Dopey one, and Marty also bought a pint. They put their liquor in their pockets and left to go and see Jack Kennedy. Phil parked the car in front of a gaudy apartment hotel and followed them to the entranceway under a garishly striped canvas awning. The front showed polished brass, and they passed through a lobby which contained much red plush. They got off the self-service elevator at the fourth floor and walked along a narrow hallway, hearing sounds from behind closed doors, a radio singer crooning *Just A Gigolo,* a woman laughing, a baby bawling. They knocked on the door of Jack's apartment.

"What ho!" they heard Jack shout after they had loudly rapped on the door.

"Open up, chappie!" Dopey said.

"I say, open up, chappie," Phil parroted.

"Jack, I got two bums here," Marty boomed.

Jack opened the door and faced them, a medium-sized, dark-haired fellow wearing a shirt with a soft collar open at the neck. They entered noisily. The apartment consisted of a large room and small kitchen. Most of the space was taken up by a wide in-a-door bed, which was unmade. Glasses, bottles, playing cards, and books were scattered about, and articles of male clothing lay on chairs and the wine-red rug. Jack looked carefully and emphatically at Phil's new clothes, and expressed surprise. Phil smiled at him self-consciously.

"What, ho, the chappie is all togged out and looks like a blighter of ripe intellect," Jack said, drawing back a pace and continuing to eye Phil.

"Yes, Mr. Wodehouse," Dopey cut in.

Carefully taking off his top coat, Phil hung it in the closet, placing his scarf, hat, and gloves on a corner of the disordered shelf.

"Races, Phil?" asked Jack.

"Nope. I made a killing, and it was strictly on the legit," Phil said, emphasizing his words with a slicker gesture.

Dopey crabbed Phil's effect by saying that Garrity had cleaned up some jack playing the market. Phil and Marty handed their bottles to Jack. He went to the kitchen and returned with filled glasses on a tray. Dopey and Marty sat on the bed, and Phil dropped into a cloth-covered chair beside a table where there was a row of books. He looked at the titles— a collection of essays by Emerson, *The Indiscretions of Archie* by P. G. Wodehouse, *Kept Woman* by Vina Delmar, *The Great Gatsby* by F. Scott Fitzgerald, a book of short stories by Irvin Cobb. Phil carefully pulled his trousers up at the knees, and he smiled with gratification while Dopey spoke of his car.

"Better times, friend!" Jack said, holding his glass aloft, and they drank. "What's on the program?" Jack asked then.

"Count me out. I've got a date," Marty said.

"A bender and Twenty-two," Dopey said.

"We're going to get drunk," Phil boasted.

"Sweet words, those, chappies. Your schedule magnetizes me. Let's have more drinks to inaugurate it," Jack said.

He took their glasses, returned with the drinks, and asked if there was anything new.

"My aunt told me that when I come home tonight, the burglar's lock will be on the door. And my uncle had a heart-to-heart talk with me. He nearly wept on my shoulder trying to turn me into a Babbitt," Dopey said.

"Did you chisel anything out of him?" Jack asked.

"All the bastard gave me was one cork-tip cigarette," Dopey said.

"Then you can't pay me the buck you owe me," said Jack.

"Say, if Dopey ever paid his debts, the world would come to an end," Marty said.

"Boys, I'm holding heavy, and tonight's my treat," Phil said.

"Well, Joseph, if you're homeless, you can stay here if you want to, but, of course, if the landlord rudely disturbs your slumbers and unceremoniously shunts you into the street, don't accuse me of a lack of hospitality," Jack said.

"I see you still haven't paid your rent," Dopey said.

"How long have you been living here gratis?" asked Phil.

Jack led them into the kitchen and pointed at the cabinet. It was chuck full of empty liquor bottles. He pointed to additional bottles lined up on the floor.

"I've been here that long," he said, and they laughed. Still pointing at the bottles, he continued, "Gentlemen, a necessity of every modern home."

They drank a toast to the landlord and returned to the other room.

"Listen, Jack, will you do me a favor?" Dopey said.

"Anything if it isn't a request for lucre," Jack answered.

"Would you fix my aunt up for me?" said Dopey, and they laughed.

"Sir, she's over forty, and my age limit is fifteen. I'll have to call on one of my assistants. Marty, you take care of that job for me. If, as a consequence, you are driven to the booby hatch, we'll pray for your soul," Jack said.

Jack changed the subject, razzing Marty because he had put so much of his pay into Nation Oil Company stock and the stock had fallen about seventy-five per cent. Phil started telling them how to play the market with real pleasure. Marty said he wasn't playing the market. He bought the stock because he was selling oil for the company. Phil began again on the stock market, but Dopey interrupted him to say that all he was hoping was that he got a decent broad when they went to a whore house.

"Same old Dopey with his mind in the gutter," Jack said, clucking in mock disgust.

"With my mind in heaven, you mean," Dopey said.

Phil thought of the can house, and of the chance of getting a dose. He thought of going around the corner and casually bragging about it, talking about his condition and his treatments as he had heard so many of the lads talk. He shuddered.

Kate, he said to himself yearningly.

He went to the kitchen and tossed down a drink so quickly that he gagged on it. He heard them greeting Al Herbert. He went back and extravagantly shook hands with Al, a thin and pallid young man whose face seemed unduly flushed.

"Say, Jack, maybe I'll double up with you," Al said, after parking his coat and hat.

"The more the merrier. Only I make a strict rule which absolutely forbids anyone to pay rent," Jack said.

"What happened, Al?" Dopey asked.

"I had another scrap with the old man. He's getting more like an old woman every day. I got sick of hearing him shoot his trap off. I can't help it if he's my old man. He talked too damn much, and so I lost my head and socked him in the mouth. I pay my board, and he has no strings on me, and I'm fed up with his canned advice. Every day since he lost his job he's gotten more crabby. But that ain't my fault."

"So you socked him, huh, Al?" said Phil in a tone of camaraderie.

"That's what my aunt needs, a poke in the kisser," Dopey said.

They had another drink. Al told about how his kid brother was in love with Eloise Flannery, a nice girl who had gone to Saint Paul's. Phil, silent, thought of Kate and wished he could even be kidded about her. Al Jones, a baby-faced, collegiately dressed fellow with wavy hair, came around. He smiled superciliously during the greetings.

"How's the high-school boy?" asked Marty.

"You are in high school again, aren't you, Al?" said Jack.

"And he started at Mary Our Mother just after it was changed from St. Stanislaus, following my own graduation. He played football with Pat McGee. And when he got out he played freshman football at Loyola, and now he's a high-school student playing basketball for Park High," Marty said, and they all laughed.

"Jones is a young Ponce de Leon, the fountain of time," Jack said.

"You fellows can rub it in if it gives you any fun. I'm having my fun. I date the best-looking bims in Sigma at school, and I'm a Kappa, the best frat there, and I'm going to play on the heavyweight basketball team, and we're going to win the city championship," Al said.

"And what a different guy he is from the nice, quiet kid who used to be an altar boy when I was in high school. In those days he wouldn't look twice at a broad. But these young lads, they feel their oats," Marty said in good-natured razzing.

"I was only a kid then," Al protested.

"And now the malted milks you drink put hair on your chest," Jack said.

"Not only malted milks," Al said, his remark a signal for more drinks.

"But what I want to know is how you get away with it? Don't they know you played three years with M.O.M., that you starred there, and then played freshman football in college?" Marty said, a glass in his hand.

"No, and I haven't changed my name, either. A week ago we played a practice game with M.O.M., and I wasn't recognized. We won, twenty to eight," Al said.

"How many baskets you make, Al?" asked Phil.

"Oh, five," Al said nonchalantly.

"You must be the school hero," Marty said.

"We got a good team," Al said modestly.

"With your experience, you ought to have a crack team. But I still don't understand how you get away with it," Marty said.

"Aren't you a bit light for heavyweight basketball?" Phil asked.

"I get by," Al said.

They drank again, and Marty talked about when he was in school with Danny O'Neill. Al said he had heard that Danny had become something cracked, a socialist, and that he was supposed to be trying to write books and stories that were cracked.

"That reminds me. The day after the millennium the socialists will all break their harps," Jack said.

"I heard Father Houlihan talking about socialists in church.

They want to destroy religion. They're chickenshit," Marty said.

"Yeh, the day after the millennium they'll all break their harps in the ensuing riot, and it'll be tough on the Russians because of their beards. Trotsky will be running around yelling, 'My kingdom, my kingdom for a barber shop'" Jack said, and Phil laughed, wishing he could be as witty as Jack.

"Well, I'd hate to be as overworked as a Russian barber must be," Marty said, laughing.

"Al, want to get laid with us tonight?" asked Dopey.

"He's the hero of Park High. Think he has to pay for it?" said Marty.

"I'm getting mine. Tonight I got a date with a Sigma, a keen babe, for a hop at the Shoreland Hotel. I'm hoping pretty strong too, boys," Al said.

"In the old days when Fanny was a girl's name, there used to be plenty of it at Park. Pierre Richard used to go there, and he used to tell me how, after football practice, the football team would get broads up in empty classrooms," Marty said.

"We're not missing anything now," Al said.

"Times have changed a little, Marty. Now they start in grammar school, and the streets are full of jail bait," Jack said.

"I'm gettin' enough, and the only thing I wish is that I could stay at Park for about three more years. I'm having a swell time, better than I had at M.O.M." Al said.

"You were innocent then," Marty said.

Al Herbert drew Dopey aside and asked how about that ten bucks Dopey owed him. Dopey complained that he was stony.

"Al, Dopey's chicken. He doesn't borrow money. He just thinks every day is Christmas and asks for his presents in cash," Marty said.

"He's chicken, all right," Al said.

Dopey smiled in good-humored helplessness.

Phil looked around, slightly bleary already, and Dopey said: "Garrity's drunk already."

They looked at Phil, sweating and nervous in his chair.

"Can't take it like a man," Marty commented.

"All right, go ahead, pick on me, I know I'm a chump," Phil said, his eyes watering.

"He's on a crying jag, boys," Marty laughed.

Hurt by their remarks, Phil thought of Kate. He wouldn't be so affected by them if he could count on her. But, no, she didn't care. He vowed again to show them, to show Kate, to show the world, by getting drunk. Phil took another drink and talked of his new car.

"Born of the moment, built for years," Jack said. He pointed at Phil. "See, men! The Newest Smartest Styled Alden-A Shirts and Shorts for the well-dressed man. Phil, take off your pants to show us your shorts. And look at his hair. He's training for a permanent with Vaseline Hair Tonic."

Al interrupted to brag about the babe he had dated. Marty and he left.

Dopey told Phil to drive back and get more gin, and Phil said they could all go. Dopey dictatorially told Phil to do it. Phil left, sore, but then rapped on the door and asked if one bottle would be enough. Dopey said two would be better, and Jack said Dopey should also bring back some ginger ale.

"And, chappie, now for a facial cocktail," Jack said, going to the bathroom to shave.

Dopey waited until Jack was out of sight. He pulled out his bottle, gulped, and put it back in his pocket. Phil returned, gay and smiling. Jack finished shaving, and they mixed drinks, wondering what to do next.

"I got a bright idea," Jack said.

He explained it was to be a joke on his friend, Al King, but added that he didn't receive credit on his phone calls. Phil was sent down to the desk to pay twenty cents for two calls. Jack called a near-by drugstore and ordered it to send two rolls of toilet paper and a bottle of Pluto Water to Mr. Jones, care of Ellen Thomas, 6191 Woodlawn Avenue. They laughed and drank while waiting for the delivery. Jack telephoned Ellen Thomas and shot her a snappy line of talk. He asked for Al, and both Phil and Dopey could hear her giggling from the other end of the connection. Hearing Al speak at the other end, Jack said:

"Few people realize the seriousness of toilet tissue until it is too late. Tissue that is of a crinkly, sharp-edged texture is apt to . . ."

Al interrupted him in a loud, complaining voice. Jack slammed the receiver on him. They laughed, and drank.

VIII

Red Murphy staggered up to them as they were getting into Phil's car. He sat in the back with Jack and Dopey.

"Boys, I'm drunk, drunk! I'm looking for trouble. Did any of you fellows see any trouble? If you did, where was it? Let me know if you see any of it, because tonight that's what I'm looking for, trouble, and plenty of it," Red Murphy said, as the car went along.

"All that I want to do tonight is get laid," Dopey said.

"Ever want to do anything else?" asked Jack.

"I wouldn't mind that, either, but I'm not holding. And, anyway, I want to find some trouble first," Red Murphy said.

"Phil's holding big," said Dopey.

"Red, I'm with you on finding trouble," Phil called back, talking out of the side of his mouth.

"My old pal, Garrity," Red said.

"Garrity, you goddamn fool! Watch where you're going or it'll be our funeral," Jack said in nervous irritation after Phil had quickly swerved the car to avoid a collision.

"Maybe he put alky in the radiator and the chassis is snozzled," Red Murphy said, laughing in appreciation of his own wit.

It was a fine autumn evening with a gray mist in the air. They drove north to the Midway.

"Say, have you boys any fluid? Another drink, and I'll be just rarin' to go, and any mother's sonofabitch can just try and get tough with me," Red Murphy said.

Jack handed Red a bottle. Red drank. Handing the bottle back, he swung lustily at the air and almost tumbled out of the automobile.

"That proves that nobody better get tough with me tonight," Red said.

Jack drank. He leaned back in his seat and began to recite *Casey at the Bat*. Phil was driving slowly. Red Murphy asked for more speed. Jack said "no" to that because the street was dark, and Phil was nearsighted. Phil said he could drive well, but he did not increase the speed. A chorus of protests and complaints greeted him when he barely missed a safety island. Jack resumed his recitation. Dopey asked for something else. Jack sang:

> *My mother sells hops to the snowbirds,*
> *My father sells barber shop gin,*
> *My sister sells love on the sidewalks,*
> *My God how the money rolls in.*

"Garrity, do me a favor like a pal, will you? Just drive right head on into trouble," Red Murphy said.

Dopey took a drink and told Phil to turn around and go back to Sixty-third. They might find some pickups.

"We're liable to get pinched for mashing on Sixty-third. I heard the Law is watching that pretty close," Phil said, as he laboriously turned the car around.

"Quit singing 'em," Dopey sneered.

They cruised along, up and down Sixty-third Street. Finally they spotted three females in front of a bank building, and Phil was told to pull up. He obeyed, trying to talk and act with foolhardy desperation in order to quiet his fear.

"Get in, girls," he said tremulously.

"Don't wear your shoes out, babies," Dopey called.

"It looks bad, three girls like you there, alone at this time of night," Jack called.

The three girls came toward the car and, as they approached, the fellows within could see that they were not so young. They looked into the car, closely scrutinizing the occupants.

"Boys, better grow up! And you, sonny!" one of them said, finally fastening her gaze on Phil, "you, sonny, you better wipe that milk from behind your funny flap ears."

Laughing hoarsely, the women walked on. All the fellows but Phil laughed. He silently condemned himself and blushed. He drove back to the Midway, turning onto it.

"See them!" Jack said, pointing at the Gothic line of University buildings, "Well, there is many a co-ed around those august halls of learning who learned about life from Jack Kennedy."

"Bull," Dopey said.

"And I suppose you even taught Queen Marie, you liar," laughed Red Murphy.

"I charitably volunteered to, but all she would promise to do in return was make me prime minister. I wanted more than that, so we got no connections," said Jack.

"You mean prime mover, don't you?" Dopey said, and they laughed.

A Ford, with two young lads in it, cut in ahead of them.

"Sonofabitches! Think they own the boulevard," Phil said, in anger.

"Get 'em Phil!" Dopey said.

"They're just the wise bastards I'm lookin' for. Step on it, Garrity, pal!" Red Murphy said.

Protesting that it was no use to go after them, Phil stepped on the gas.

"Catch 'em, Phil! We're behind you, Phil boy. Red Murphy wants trouble, and this is where he finds it. Step on it, Phil boy!" Red encouraged, as Phil stepped on the gas.

The lights at Cottage Grove Avenue held them up. When the lights changed, he shot forward into Washington Park and hummed along through the deserted park. He stopped alongside of the Ford at the exit to Washington Park at Sixtieth and South Park Avenue. Red Murphy was first out of the car, followed by Jack. Dopey watched them.

"You lads want trouble?" Red Murphy asked, jerking open the door of the Ford.

"No," the lad driving it said in a voice of fear and surprise.

"Are you tough?" Red asked.

"We're minding our own business, lad," the other occupant of the Ford said.

"Well, what's the idea of hogging the boulevard then?" Phil said snottily, having joined Red and Jack.

"Are they tough?" Dopey called while the two lads apologized.

"You're getting away lucky this time, but don't try gettin' wise again, or you both might be going home with your teeth left behind to ornament the boulevard," Red said.

"And watch the way you drive, too!" Jack said, slamming the Ford door shut.

They got back into the car and turned around to drive north inside of the park. Under a lamppost along the park driveway, Phil saw many glittering pieces and chunks of broken glass. He stopped and clambered out, followed by his companions. They looked about, curious.

"There's blood on it," Dopey said, holding up a broken chip.

"Must have been a nifty job," Phil said.

"Good business for the mortician," Jack said.

"Too bad we missed seeing it," Dopey said.

"Carberry, you always were morbid," Jack said.

"It must have been a damn neat accident. Look, fellows, there's blood all over the driveway," Red Murphy said.

"And just our luck to miss seeing such a gory show," Jack said.

"It would have been a handsome sight," Phil said huskily.

"Seeing all this blood and glass, my guess is that someone must have been ticketed straight to the morgue," Red said, kicking glass.

"Must have been a drunken driver," Jack said.

"Why?" Phil anxiously asked.

"The remains suggest a thorough accident. A sober driver would not have been in the proper mood to perfect such an accident as this one. Only a drunken driver could have done that," Jack said.

"Drunken drivers don't have accidents. They have a drunkard's luck," Red said, while Phil, swaying near them, wondered if this were really true.

"The best way to stay out of trouble is get drunk. Then nothing happens to you," Phil said with bravado.

"Please take that back, Phil. Please. For Red Murphy is drunk, and he's looking for trouble," Red said.

"Drunk or sober, the guys who sprung this accident were artists. Look at the way they spread around the gore and glass," Jack said lightly.

"Look at this chunk!" Jack said, picking up a hunk of glass over a foot wide. He flung it away, and it shattered on the driveway.

"And here's some rich red gore," Phil said, almost retching at the sight of it.

He staggered to the edge of the grass and gazed off to the east, where the darkness was intercepted by moonlight. In the distance he saw the quiet waters of the lagoon, glassy with the rays of the moon. A feeling of peace entered him. He suddenly wanted to paint, to paint this scene in sombre colors so that he would always have it to look at, so that he could put into it the feelings within him, the feelings of peace, quiet, yearning.

"We're getting bigger and better accidents all the time. Progress!" Jack said, and his words destroyed Phil's mood.

"It's always our damn luck to miss seeing them," Phil said, turning, swaying back toward his companions.

"Don't worry, Garrity. With your new boat and your nearsightedness, you won't miss all the fun," Jack said.

"I know how to drive," Phil said, wincing.

"What the hell, I saw one last week that would have made this one look like a piker," Red said, reeling around. "I was going home about midnight, walking down Stony Island Avenue on the west side of the street, no, the east side. Well, a crazy car crashes through the gates of the I.C. tracks at Seventy-first, misses getting knocked into smithereens by a train, smashes through the gates on the other side of the tracks, shoots down the street for hell and gone, the motor sounding like it was a zeppelin dropping bombs. I said my prayers and nearly pissed in my pants. I knew the guy driving was going to smash over the curb like Joe Savoldi going through the line, and I was ready to fold up and dive. When he passes me, I blesses myself, and down further he jumps the curb like a hurdler, slides off a lamppost like Red Grange evading a tackler, and hits a buildin' that's standin' inconveniently in his way. He was halfway through the windshield, and you should have seen the car. They took the pieces of that poor bastard to Jackson Park Hospital, but they could have saved themselves the trouble and the gas and carted him to the morgue."

"Murphy, that wasn't as good as this accident," Jack said, while Phil was weak with fear, wondering would such be his end.

"How come? You seen neither accidents," Red argued.

"Look at the remains. I deduce that this one must have sent three upstairs to play harps, with others turned in for serious repairs. Why, I'll bet that there wasn't enough left of these cars to interest Warshawsky, the junk dealer," Jack said.

"There's a lot of blood in one person. This blood might mean just one poor sonofabitch killed. And he couldn't have been any more killed than the poor bastard I saw last week," Red said.

"Anyway, it was rummy luck for the bastards in this accident. Maybe they had broads with them and were looking forward to tail, too," Jack said.

They returned to the car. Phil laboriously backed up, skirted the drive, went carefully northward. He was afraid. He had a premonition that something would happen to him tonight. He wished he were sober and out alone on a decent date with Kate.

The fellows in the back seat drank, and Jack began reciting *The Face on the Barroom Floor*.

"Hey, you goddamn fool! Watch your driving!" Dopey yelled after Phil just missed bumping into a car at Forty-seventh Street.

"The boy well nigh filled a mortician's that time," Jack said.

"Phil, I know better ways of dying," Dopey said.

They all insisted that Jack drive. Phil was shaken, but refused to give up the wheel.

IX

They decided to take in the Sour Apple on the near North Side, hoping to find some pickups. Phil parked the car on North Dearborn Street, and they clambered out. Phil was keyed up, excited. There might be girls. And artists were supposed to hang out at the Sour Apple. He asked if they had enough gin. Dopey said he better buy another bottle. He suddenly remembered that back at Whaley's he had given Dopey a bottle. Reminded of this, Dopey slowly remembered that he did have a bottle in his pocket.

"You're not a heel. You wouldn't hold out on your pals," Jack said, masking his irritation with a smile.

Phil defended Dopey as they turned into a narrow and dingy dead-end alley. Halfway down, there was a dim green light, and beneath it the entrance door to the Sour Apple, painted in orange. Beside the door they noticed the bulletin board, with an announcement.

WEDNESDAY FAREWELL PARTY TO MENDEL MARKOWITZ

"Know that guy, Jack?" asked Phil, pointing to the sign.

"He's a crazy Bohemian who gives lectures here sometimes. I heard him speak, but nobody understands him," Jack said.

They read the sign painted in black on the door.

He who enters here leaves his dignity without.

"That means virtue, too, Phil," Red said.

Phil looked at Red, blushing.

"Go ahead, kid me! I'm only a chump," Phil said.

"I was only kidding, pal, and I'll fight the man that says you ain't my buddy," Red said, putting his arm around Phil's shoulder.

They entered, Phil last. Neglecting to duck in the low passageway leading to the ticket window, Phil bumped his forehead. At the end of the narrow passageway, which was walled in between the forum and the tearoom, was the ticket window. Phil shouted that it was his treat. He faced a tall, slatternly, poorly dressed woman at the ticket window and fumbled in his pocket for money. He heard the sounds of many voices within. The anticipation of excitement, a good time, surprises to come, stirred him up with hope. He paid three dollars and was given four tickets, which he handed to an unwashed middle-aged woman who pulled a bar aside and admitted them to the tearoom.

"Who's the hag takin' tickets?" Phil whispered to Jack when they were inside the crowded, noisy, smoke-filled, rectangular tearoom.

"Atmosphere," said Jack.

The crowd, the steady talk, the strangeness of the sight all confused Phil. The walls of the tearoom were plastered with badly drawn murals, the colors largely a combination of weak blues, pale pinks, eye-straining and raucous greens, violets, and oranges. In most of the murals there were graceless, overweight nudes done in bad imitation of Picasso, and Bohemians drawn to look like Apaches. Along both sides of the room there were booths painted in black and Chinese red, with black-topped tables. At the far end there was a small counter. People shuffled from group to group. The jazz band in the adjoining dance hall blared. There was a crush through the narrow entranceway to the hall. The music roused Phil. He told himself that he was raring to go. To the left, there was a wooden stairway leading to the second floor, and they trooped up it to the checkroom, which was tended by a woman with bobbed hair and a wrinkled face.

"Jesus, I hope the floor doesn't cave in on us," Dopey said after they had checked their wraps and were standing indecisively near the stairway, glancing around at the disordered slivery upstairs of a barn.

They pushed into the unswept men's room. The washbowl was filthy, and a gurgling running sound came from the bowl. They drank from their bottle and came out again.

"Hello," said a chubby little fellow in corduroy pants who stood near the stairway. "I remember you. Your name is Kennedy. Mine's Wolcroft."

Jack introduced the others to Wolcroft.

"I'm still on my summer vacation," Jack said.

"When does it end?" asked Wolcroft, smiling.

"Next summer," said Jack.

"Will you get a job then?" asked Phil.

"Well, the golf season will be going full blast then, and after the golf season it will be time for next year's vacation," Jack said, and they laughed.

Wolcroft asked for a drink, and Jack handed him the bottle. Wolcroft thanked them. He turned to Phil and Murphy and asked them how they liked the Sour Apple.

"It doesn't impress me as much as a can house," said Dopey.

"There's girls here, but you got to make the grade with them," said Wolcroft.

"You an artist?" said Phil.

"Yes, I write poetry. I'm reading some of it here at the party next Wednesday. One of the Sour Applers here, a fellow named Markowitz, is going to New York with his wife on his way to Europe. The lucky bastard married a girl at the University, and he's being sent to Paris with her. But we're glad he's going. He talks a lot," Wolcroft said.

"Say, I studied art. I can draw. I can. Sure. I was going to study art some more, but I went into a brokerage house instead. But I know something about art and drew for the school magazine in high school," Phil said.

"Well, come around. We have artists here. I'm a poet," Wolcroft said patronizingly.

"I will," said Phil.

"The hell with art. Biology is our topic tonight, boys," said Jack, and they smiled.

"There isn't a place in Chicago like the Sour Apple. It's unique. It was once the artistic center of Chicago, and all the great writers came around here, Ben Hecht, all of them. And artists, too, like Szukalski," Wolcroft said.

"Ben Hecht? I read his books. Say, he's a radical, isn't he? He doesn't believe in God, does he?" Phil said.

"He writes realism. That's old-fashioned. My poetry, now, it's superrealist. I'm hoping to get some of it published in Paris," said Wolcroft.

"Say, can you spare another drink?" asked Wolcroft.

They went back to the lavatory, and the bottle was passed around.

"As I was saying, there isn't another place in Chicago like the Sour Apple. It's unique. Now, you take Bill Bridges, who runs it, he's unique, too. He's a showman. Here, come along, and I'll show you something," Wolcroft said.

"Who's he?" asked Phil, as they followed Wolcroft toward rafters spun with cobwebs.

"You'll see him downstairs. He's got bobbed hair and needs a bath," said Jack.

"See these?" said Wolcroft, pointing at some loose boards.

"If I had a hammer I could nail them up in a minute," Phil said.

"They show just where Bill Bridges' genius lies," Wolcroft said, and they stared at him, dumbfounded.

"Anyone else would fix them. But not Bill Bridges. He leaves 'em loose. He hasn't touched them for five years. Do you know why? Because it gives atmosphere to the place. It's just that little touch, that little something, which stamps Bill as such an excellent showman. It's just what I'd do, too, if I was Bill," Wolcroft said.

"If you ask me, I'd say that he ought to have an atmosphere around here that includes a little air," Phil said.

Wolcroft looked pityingly at Phil. He smiled.

"Say, one of you fellows got a cigarette?" he asked, and Phil handed him one; he lit it.

"They do have air here, Phil, at their Sunday-night speeches. It's all hot air," said Jack.

"No, we have some good talks here. Markowitz talks on art, and he knows a lot. I'm speaking here on pure poetry and sex three weeks from tomorrow night, and I'll read some of my poetry. Come around," Wolcroft said.

"Let's go downstairs and see what broads they got," Dopey said.

"Well, I hope you like the Apple," said Wolcroft.

"That depends on the fems you got here," said Phil.

"We have intelligent ones, and some of them are poets," said Wolcroft, leading the way.

"Yes, boys, you'll meet the higher brand of hash slingers here," Jack said.

"A lot of sex-suppressed people from Iowa and the colleges come here, particularly on Saturday nights for the dances. The regular Applers come here more on Sunday and Wednesday," said Wolcroft.

They trooped downstairs. Wolcroft walked off toward a group of odd-looking males who were leaning against the wall and smiling superciliously. The others stood indecisively at the foot of the stairway. The air was heavy, almost fetid, thick with cigarette smoke, heavy with alcohol breaths. The orchestra was playing nerve-stimulating jazz. Then it stopped. The dancers emptied into the tearoom, and there was loud conversation and much moving about. Bohemians, many with long hair, leaned wearily against the walls, smiling at the crowd. A tall, handsome man entered, followed by three nondescripts who had the manner and air of sycophants, and the group around Wolcroft greeted him obsequiously. Phil asked who the bloke was.

"John Connolly, King of the Soap Boxers," Jack said.

"Another nut?" asked Phil.

"He's no nut. He's a smart fellow and a goddamn good talker. Don't let him hear you calling him a nut. He's really tough," Jack said.

Phil looked at the man, envied him for his apparent strength and magnificent physique.

"Is he radical?" asked Phil.

"Yes," said Jack.

"Then he doesn't believe in God. Anybody who says there is no God is crack-brained," said Phil.

"Don't argue with him. He knows more than you, and he's tough, too," said Jack.

Phil's sense of humiliation deepened. He regarded the big man with awe and envy. Here, he thought, was a man who could think and fight, who wasn't afraid of anything in the world. He became sensitive about himself. He was afraid his own personality was small. He wished he were an artist, and that he could come here and feel as though he belonged, feel at ease and at home in this place. He glanced around the walls at the murals, thinking that he could do better. Jack pulled at his sleeve, and the group moved over toward the dance hall to wait for the next dance. A stupid-faced, drunken young fellow in a blue suit wavered by them, stopped before a scraggly girl in a stained gray dress, pointed his finger at her, held it under her nose, and proudly said:

"You know, you look just like my suppressed desire."

The girl smiled at the drunk. They moved off, and Phil watched them enviously. Could he get started as easily with one of the broads here? Suddenly there was a commotion and loud talk around the group. The drunk who had moved off with the girl was shouting that he would fight any goddamn Bohemian. Bill Bridges suddenly appeared, wielding a club. He was a rough-looking, wrinkled man, wearing brown corduroy pants and a blue corduroy coat. He crushed through the noisy crowd. The fellows followed him, but could not get close enough to see what was happening. They heard Bill yelling that he would brain anyone for starting a fight. Finally the crowd parted. Bill led the drunk to the exit. The drunk left, protesting. Two fellows followed him outside. Bill walked back, growling.

"What's the matter, Bill?" Phil asked knowingly, ranging himself alongside of Bridges.

"Trying to ruin my business. I'm taking that little bitch off my free list. I got my back to the wall with taxes, and they start fights to ruin my business," Bill said gloomily, and then he walked off grouchily.

The orchestra started to play again. Phil crowded through the narrow entranceway with his companions. The dance hall was a large converted barn, dimly lit; the stone walls were painted with murals similar to those in the tearoom. The floor was of stone and there were many posts spaced around it, supporting the ceiling. Wolcroft danced by with a skinny girl, both of them seeming bored as they danced by like sticks. Then Phil saw Dopey, shimmying. He swayed. He was lonely and felt vacant inside. He wanted a girl. His inferiority clung to him like an inescapable shame, or like something as disfiguring and as permanent as a birthmark. He tried to strike a nonchalant and disinterested pose, as if to tell everyone present that he was not dancing because he didn't feel like it. He covertly glanced about, fixing his eyes on isolated girls he might ask for a dance. An attractive blonde in purple stood to his left. He watched her out of the corner of his eye. He casually, slowly lit a cigarette. He wiped the perspiration from his face. He continued to eye the blonde. He calmly puffed at his cigarette. Passing him, Jack winked. He smiled at Jack. He stepped sidewise, closer to the blonde. He mustn't appear overanxious. He was confused because of his fear that she'd turn down his request for a dance. He was a misfit, and she would know it. He hoped she wouldn't. He must appear calm, interesting. He must have her feel he was accustomed to dancing with pretty girls, taking them out; he must have the air of a lad who knew his way about. He moved closer. He perceived that she had noticed him and knew he was going to ask her for a dance. His foot was in the bucket now. He stood before her, timid, blushing, and choked out his request. She acted as if she had not heard him. He repeated it, humiliation eating inside of him. She thanked him, but said she was sorry because she was not dancing this dance.

He moved away in chagrin. He told himself she was nothing but a goddamn polack anyway, so what the hell? He watched the dancers, aware that he was blushing. Others must be watching. His humiliation must be plain to them. And that dirty blonde polack was quietly, cruelly laughing at him. Girls were that way. They were sadists. She, just a lousy little polack, even she had pierced through him, read the thoughts in his head, saw his inside as if it were a naked body ugly with sores and dirt. His head seemed to be getting more giddy. The dancers seemed to be on a floor turning and whirling by him as if on a rickety wheel. He tried to act normal, nonchalant, as if he were thinking none of the thoughts that were actually burning in his head. He wanted them to see him as someone superior to everything going on about him. He saw Bill Bridges dance by with a girl. He decided that Bill Bridges was as graceful in his movements as an overladen camel, with his body bobbing and jerking, his left arm woodenly extended like a traffic signal. Even a louse like Bridges could get a dance. And he couldn't.

He wandered along the edge of the dancing space, assuming various postures and positions, contorting his face in his effort to appear unconcerned. Two more girls refused to dance with him. He went upstairs for a drink and came down, expecting to be more successful. Another girl refused him. He stood in a corner, murmuring to hell with them. To hell with the world. To hell with them, with Kate . . . *Kate, you go plumb to hell . . . Kate, Kate, I love you . . . be mine . . . my wife . . . Kate, I'm getting goddamn drunk . . . Kate, you go jam bananas up your old tomato* . . . He went back upstairs and poured more gin into himself, fighting to keep it down. He sweated and was uncomfortable under the armpits. His head throbbed. It seemed terribly weighted. He staggered back downstairs, holding onto the rail as he descended.

The dance had ended, and he rejoined his companions. He clung awkwardly to Dopey.

"Dopey, my pal, my old buddy! Stick with me, pal! Carberry, you know me, know me, known me for ages, since Hector was kittens. You know I'm all right, okay, doncha, Dopey? Joe, boy, you know I'm regular, just like other guys, doncha? Ain't I right, regular? Tell me, Dopey, my best, best pal," he said, emitting a foul gin breath, slobbering saliva on Dopey's cheeks as he spoke.

"You're drunk, you bastard!" Dopey said, laughing as he freed himself from Phil.

"All my pals ditch me," Phil sighed, tears coming.

Dopey said sure he was Garrity's friend. Phil wobbled, and his companions seemed vague before his eyes. He frowned. He sneezed. The orchestra started again. He asked a pock-faced girl for a dance, and she nodded. He reeled after her to the dance floor. Taking her in his arms, he tripped. They collided with another couple. They danced, and he stepped on her toes. He talked incoherently and roughly pulled her tightly against him. They hit head on into a twirling, twisting couple. She walked off the floor. He stood bewildered amid the dancing couples. He made his way to the edge of the floor, cursing her. Dopey came up to him.

"What was the matter with the dance you had?" Dopey asked.

"Couldn't stand the pig," Phil said, almost falling on his friend.

He stood there, and crude images of naked girls mobbed his brain. He tried to make himself feel desires, and he could not rouse them, despite the images dancing in his brain. He thought of Kate and silently muttered to himself that he wanted to lay his head in her lap and go to sleep. He staggered aimlessly away from Dopey.

The place was getting noisier, more raucous. Drunks were staggering back and forth. The talk was loud. Couples began to neck publicly. The orchestra played more blatantly. The air was stifling. The cigarette smoke was like a fog. Body odors became so heavy that they seemed almost to possess substance. To Phil, everything was noise and vagueness. He danced with a drunken girl and tried to tell her that he was a student of Notre Dame and a pal of Carideo's and Joe Savoldi, who were stars on this year's Notre Dame's undefeated team. He tried to make her understand that next year he hoped to play on the varsity for Knute Rockne. She didn't understand him and seemed annoyed because he was continually stepping on her toes. As the dance ended, he asked her to go riding with him. She reeled away from him without replying.

"I'm sick of this goddamn joint," he told Dopey back in the tearoom.

The next dance started, and he was alone again. He pushed through the crowd to the dance hall, trying to imagine himself a Notre Dame halfback hitting the line. He asked girls to dance, and they laughed in his face. He tottered back to the wall and stood there in a slumped position. He saw faces dimly, indistinctly, and he imagined himself going through the place like a comet, punching and smashing faces to right and to left, cleaning up this whole damn bunch singlehanded. When the dance ended, he again staggered to his companions.

"Thish is a lousy place," he said.

He staggered away and, passing Bill Bridges, he said hello to him, receiving no answer. The orchestra was now playing a series of college songs: it burst into the Notre Dame *Victory March*. Phil tried to sing:

> *Cheer, cheer for old Notre Dame*
> *Ring out the echoes . . .*

He saw a noisy group, hopping in unison, their ankles twisting and bending, their legs turning into rubber, their buttocks wriggling, their torsos twirling, whirling. It seemed funny to him. The *Victory March* and that dancing. Couldn't dance to it. It wasn't dance music. He staggered toward the group, laughing. He tried to tell them they were trying to dance to the Notre Dame *Victory March* when it wasn't dance music.

"Say, pal, you can't dance to this," he said, tapping a husky redhead on the shoulder.

"What?" the redhead bawled, looking closely at Phil, while his friends, three husky lads, crowded behind him.

The friends asked the redhead what the guy had said.

"He said we can't dance to the Notre Dame *Victory March*."

"We can't, huh?"

"No," Phil said, and he seemed to gag and be unable to utter any additional words.

"We can't, huh?"

"Smack him again, Pat!"

Phil went down from a stiff punch in the jaw. The blow cleared his drunken brain. He was rudely jerked to his feet and punched again. He felt his glasses twist and fly off. Unable to see clearly, he caught another punch in the face, and his head throbbed. A noisy crowd collected about them. Red Murphy piled into the fight, and with a straight right sent one of Phil's attackers stumbling back into the wall. Red was smashed simultaneously from two sides, and the fight quickly became a free-for-all, with many punching and scarcely anyone knowing whom he was punching or why he was fighting. Women and girls began to scream. The milling crowd became larger. The shouts rose.

Jack advanced toward the fight. Dopey disappeared. Bill Bridges went into action with a club, pushing into the center and managing to halt the slugging. Phil and Red were dragged away, Jack following them. The other group was pinioned also. Bill Bridges began to deliver a lecture on his taxes and on how fights ruined his business. Red yelled that he wanted trouble, broke away from the fellows holding him, rushed back toward the other group. He was caught and dragged away more forcibly. Phil loudly declared that he had been hit and had lost his glasses, so that he couldn't see. A girl went to him with the glasses and said that they had caught on her dress. He yelled that he had been hit. Phil and Red were brought to the tearoom and joined by Jack and Dopey. A crowd collected. Phil sat on the lower step of the stairway leading upstairs.

"Look what the bastards did to me," he kept repeating, proudly pointing to his black eye.

"Carberry, they wouldn't let me sock the skunks," Red said.

"I'll get 'em," Phil said, grimacing.

But Bridges passed by and, seeing Wolcroft, asked him if he knew what had started the fight.

"Four drunken Irishmen with liquor, four sober Irishmen with girls," Wolcroft said dryly.

"The goddamn fools, trying to ruin my business," Bill said, walking off in a funk.

The confusion was cleared up, the orchestra started, and most of the customers resumed dancing. The other group, pacified, came to the tearoom and approached Phil and Red.

"What's your name?" Jack said to the redhead.

"O'Connell," he answered.

"Mine's Kennedy."

"We're both Irish."

"And here's Garrity, Murphy, and Carberry."

"Glad to meet you. Sorry we had the rumpus."

"Garrity, my name's Flannagan. We're both turkeys. Shake."

"It's funny, micks like us fighting each other."

The causes of the fight were explained, and they all laughed.

"Micks should battle side by side," O'Connell said.

"All of us lads is Irish, and so's all of you. The fight was wrong, Murphy."

"Yeah, kid, the Irish should be scrapping side by side together, just like the lads from N.D. on the football field," Phil said.

"Say, didn't they win today though!"

"And there's plenty of Polacks and fairies around here that we might have socked instead of turkeys with the name of Murphy and Garrity. But no hard feelin's because it was just a mistake. Sorry I blacked the lamps, Garrity," O'Connell said.

They trooped upstairs and drank gin and sang songs.

x

They could get no pickups at the Sour Apple, and they left for a brothel on Twenty-second Street. But unexpected police raids had closed the brothels. Cursing, they sped on south. They picked up four girls at Sixty-second and Cottage Grove who were leaving the Bourbon Palace dance hall. The girls giggled and said they would like a party. Phil bought gin and drunkenly drove out south to Jeffery Avenue, and then on to Jeffery Road.

They passed houses along the road with cutout open and roared on past country fields. Phil drove one-armed, and the couples crushed in the back pawed one another, breathed heavily, drank. Large shadows raked the road, and the car whipped on. Occasional houses seemed unreal, almost like dream structures. The moon blunted through a heavy mist which lay thickly over the quiet, heavy earth. They roared on. The car smashed head on into a Cadillac which was going as swiftly as Phil's Lincoln. There was a thunderous crash, screams, the sounds of broken glass, and the two cars hooked together and toppled by the roadside. There were more screams, moans, sobs. Drunk and dazed, Phil squirmed out of the wreckage with his newly found girl friend. She was speechless with fear, and neither of them realized what had happened. He staggered into the fields, dragging her with him, heedless of her maniacal sobs, talking deliriously.

A motorcycle policeman found them and said gruffly:

"Come on, you, pull up your britches. And you, too, bitch!" He dragged her to her feet, and she babbled. He looked at Phil's scratched face, flashing a light in Phil's eyes as he socked him. Phil fell. The cop pulled him to his feet and pulled them back to the road, where there was noise and talk as people struggled in the wreckage to get the passengers free.

"You ought to swing for this, you sonofabitch," the cop told Phil.

Automobiles were lined up along both sides of the road. Men and women were crowding around. Injured passengers moaned pitifully. The girl with Phil and the cop screamed, and then she fainted. Two men carried her away. Just as Phil stepped back to the road, whimpering, the dead bodies of Jack and Dopey were pulled out of the wreckage. Phil talked deliriously. He didn't know where he was or what had happened.

A Love Story of Our Time

PETER, a serious and sensitive young poet, came to New York, the mecca, from the Middle West. During his high school days, the depression had blighted his youth and influenced him to become vaguely opposed to the entire capitalist system. He wanted to live in a better world. And he wanted to feel secure. He was a poor boy, and he knew how one can be gnawed into doubt and paralysis of will by a feeling of economic insecurity. He was unsure of himself. He felt that if he did not become a poet—a great poet—his life would be useless. And the social system was against him.

He worked hard in New York, trying to make a living by writing. He wrote book reviews and, in order to add to his income, sold the review copies of the books. He made scenario reports for motion picture companies. He did some ghost-writing. By dint of various kinds of such literary hack work, he eked out a living. He managed now and then to get some of his poems published. They were genuine and sincere, if minor, and they expressed his own doubts and fears. His major theme was doubt, insecurity, anxiety. Now and then he would write a poem of hope, but it would be hollow, inflated; one such was published and heralded in *Mass Action*, but it was his worst poem, an optimistic poem in which the conceit of history was pressed into every line and image. He made friends and came to know some literary people. His doubts infected his rather loosely accepted political attitudes, and many of his friends used to tell him he was a confused liberal. He had a few affairs with girls, but none of these was lasting, and, when they were over, there was no serious heartache on either side.

Then he met Ruth at a party run to raise funds for a new radical literary magazine. This was in the fall of 1936. Many of his friends and acquaintances were excited in those days by the first Moscow trial, but it merely bewildered him. He found it hard to believe that the trial was on the level and not a frame-up, but he avoided making up his mind or taking any stand. At the party there was discussion and argument, and he wearied of it. Bored by the argument, confused, weakly indecisive, he sat looking off vacantly while two Party supporters were telling a writer that opposition to the trial was a way of committing intellectual suicide. It was at such a moment that he saw her. He was drawn to her immediately. She was a pretty chestnut-haired girl, sleek and slender, her girlish figure nicely revealed by a brown dress. She had blue eyes and a very friendly face. He smiled at her. She smiled back. They sat side by side on a couch, sipping drinks.

"This is all over my poor head," she said with a note of irony in her voice.

"I don't know enough about it," he said.

"What importance has it for us over here?"

They talked about poetry and discovered that they shared the same tastes. She told him that she liked those of his poems she had read. He beamed when he heard her praise. They left the party together and walked through the Village and then had coffee in a cafeteria. A quick sympathy seemed to grow between them. Peter found himself able to talk to her without strain or self-consciousness. He told her how he felt about life, what he wanted to do, how he had to be a poet, and how he believed that a poet, too, could help make the world better than it was.

"Of course he can. It's much better to write poetry than to waste time arguing and arguing about that trial in Moscow. Who cares?"

"Of course, I want socialism," he said.

"So do I. But we have to fight fascism now," she said, rather

pensively, looking more beautiful to him than any other girl
he had ever met.

His delight in her, his admiration for her beauty, caused
him to think that anything she said was true. Facing her across
the corner table of the small cafeteria, he found himself wanting to think of things to say with which she would agree. He
tried to present himself to her in a sympathetic light. He wanted
her to fall in love with him. And he suddenly became shy. He
desired her, but he feared to do more than gaze, gaze and talk.
But she did seem interested in him. She called him by his first
name, smiled when he smiled, and by little innuendoes seemed
to suggest that she was one with him in spirit. Their knees
touched under the table, and she didn't withdraw hers. This
slight contact with her flesh made her seem all the more wonderful to him. He felt toward her all the emotions he tried to
express in his poems. As he talked, lines of poetry for her and
and about her traced themselves out in his mind. With her, he
would know love as only a poet could know it. He talked with
her for more than an hour, trying to prolong their conversation because he feared he would blunder when he took her
home. Finally she yawned.

"Gee, it's late," she said.

He picked up her check.

"Please, let me take it."

"Oh, it's nothing."

"But, after all, I think women and men are equal. They
should be comrades and equals," she said.

"They should. That's one of the evils of the system," he
said rather pompously.

Outside, she took his arm crossing a street. She kept hold of
it as they walked on. He gazed, moonstruck, at the sky. Having
nothing else to say, he remarked on the beauty of the night.

"Autumn is my favorite season," she said.

"Mine, too. I love nights like this," he said.

"Isn't it heavenly?"

"I'll have to write a poem about it, and dedicate it to you.
Would you mind?"

"I'd love it. I'd feel flattered," she answered, laughing merrily and squeezing his arm.

She lived alone in a small Village apartment. He stood at the entrance way, not knowing what to do. She looked at him with shining eyes and pursed lips. Her face seemed to melt before him. He knew that he should kiss her. But he was still too shy.

"Peter," she said, paused, and then continued, "Peter, I don't believe in beating around the bush. I can't stand this bourgeois sparring between men and women. Kiss me."

He did. She held him in her arms a long time.

"Come upstairs with me," she said.

They went upstairs. Her apartment was neat and charming.

"I like it with the lights on," she said, immediately beginning to undress.

A vague sense of disappointment troubled him. She was so casual about it. The mystery he had felt sitting with her, touching her knees under the table—this was in danger of being destroyed. But he desired her intensely and forgot everything but his immediate excitement.

"Yes, so do I," he said, confused.

She was quickly undressed and stood before him, smiling.

"Do I pass muster?" she asked gaily.

He nodded his head, almost swooning with desire and confusion.

"Well, you haven't even started to take your clothes off."

He began undressing, still shy. She helped him.

In bed with her, he felt inexperienced and feared he would seem to her like a lout. Then she sank her head onto his moist shoulder without saying anything. He lay back, feeling a consoling fatigue. His mind was blank. He was very happy. She was a wonderful girl.

"Don't go home tonight," she said finally.

She jumped out of bed, turned out the light, and crawled back beside him.

"You're wonderful to sleep with. I'm glad I met you," she said.

"I love you."

"I'm simple, Peter, and I like to call things by their simple names. I don't like bourgeois words like love."

"Whatever words you want to use, you know what I mean," he said.

In the morning they talked about their night together. Ruth said she liked to talk about it, using the four-letter words. These were good words and they weren't dirty, she argued. He agreed with her, but was inwardly disturbed. But she took him back to bed with her, and he lost his disquieting feelings.

He felt as if he had become a different man. A beautiful girl loved him, slept with him. His personality expanded. He had needed a girl like Ruth, a girl who would really stimulate him. Love was the real basis of poetry.

He saw her almost every night and spent many nights at her apartment. At her suggestion they called each other "Comrade" instead of the names lovers usually give to one another. She seemed to him to be frank, direct, realistic. He quickly adapted himself to her tastes and adjusted his ideas to fit hers. He learned that she was a Party member and he respected her, gazed at her in awe. He had, he decided, never had the courage to be a Party member. He began seeing her friends, mostly her comrades, rather than his own.

Although she had said, that night they had first met, that such questions as that of the Moscow trial didn't interest her, he found that she was always talking about politics, about the Popular Front, the war in Spain, the Soviet Union.

Now and then something she said or did seemed mysterious or puzzling to him, but he quickly forgot these little mysteries about her, these little moments of puzzlement that bordered on suspicion. She did not work and said that she lived on an income from her bourgeois family. But, when he asked her about them, she was vague, or didn't want to talk. In general, she didn't like to talk about her past. And on some nights she couldn't see him but said she was at Party meetings.

And now and then he was curious and suspicious of friends of hers, but he reasoned that this was only jealousy.

Gradually she began to talk more and more about Spain.

Peter, disquieted, insecure, was afraid that Franco would win in Spain. Whenever he expressed his fears and doubts, she would tell him that he would have to rise above such petty bourgeois defeatism, and that Franco wouldn't, and couldn't, win. Her confidence and enthusiasm heartened him. She talked often about friends of hers who were going to Spain to fight.

At the same time, she seemed to lose interest in his poetry. When he wanted to talk about poetry, she would change the subject to Spain and politics, and this disturbed Peter. But he was in love with her, and she had made him the slave of her body. The fact that she allowed him to sleep with her seemed to him a privilege of which he was unworthy. He didn't understand how such joy could have come to him.

One night, after their affair had gone on for about a month and a half, he came to see her. When he entered, he embraced her, wanting to kiss her passionately. She was lackadaisical.

She didn't want to go to bed with him, she said, but instead she wanted him to meet some friends. She took him to an apartment on Twelfth Street, where he met a number of couples. It was a party. He was no longer disappointed. She would sleep with him after the party. He compared her with the other girls. None was so beautiful, so intelligent as she. Most of those present were young. But they seemed to be serious young people. Instead of dancing, talking lightly, and holding hands, they discussed Spain.

"Fascism has to be stopped in Spain," Ruth said with an intensity that surprised him.

"The Soviet Union won't let Franco win," another girl said.

"Franco couldn't win if there were enough men in the world with guts. Look at Peter, here!" she said.

He was bewildered. Her voice was hard and cold.

"Peter, here, loves to sleep with me, to eat well, and write poetry while the world is burning up. But will he fight?"

"But I try to fight fascism with my pen," he said in self-defense.

"The world is burning up. The pen isn't enough. While you

are here laying me and writing poems, what's happening in Spain? Aren't you man enough to fight?"

He was shocked. She had so taken him by surprise that he didn't know what to say, what to think. Meekly, he gazed at her. Everyone present was staring at him accusingly. He couldn't meet their eyes. He looked off, troubled.

"But I don't understand you."

"Yes, you do, Peter. You say you are a comrade. Do you know what that means?"

"Why, I think I do."

"It's a sacred word," a young fellow said.

"But what—what should I say?"

"This is no time for words," she said.

"Yes, Ruth, too many fellows love to talk. And write. I love poetry, but the world is burning up," another young man said.

"If I were a man I wouldn't be here," Ruth said.

Peter blushed, ashamed of himself.

"But I don't understand."

"There's no time now for confusion. When the fascist beasts are in New York, what price will you pay for confusion? No, history doesn't allow you to be confused. If you are confused, you aid the common enemy."

"But what should I do?"

"Fight Franco!"

Other girls began to say the same thing to some of the other young men present. Peter was glad now to find he wasn't alone.

But Ruth was persistent. He suggested that they leave and have a talk.

"There's no time for talk. Will you fight?"

Confused, fearful, apologetic, he shook his head affirmatively.

"I knew you were a comrade," she said and, interrupting the others, she shouted:

"Peter is going to Spain."

He gazed blankly about the room as he was congratulated, patted on the back, kissed by the girls. And yet, he wished he hadn't said yes. He didn't know how to fight. He might be killed. He had not had time to think. This was all a surprise.

He didn't really believe he would go to Spain to fight. He remained bewildered. Ruth went home with him and all the way to her apartment she clung to him, praised him.

"I love you. I'm proud of you, comrade," she said, kissing him passionately in her apartment.

In her arms, he forgot all about his predicament. He awoke the next morning, ashamed of himself. Even though he didn't want to go to Spain, he had let himself be pushed into it. But Ruth dominated him. She was very loving to him during the succeeding weeks. And then he left for France with a false passport. He had a heavy heart, but he was proud of himself. His feeling of insecurity had vanished. He was doing something. The ideals with which he had come to New York had crystallized now. He was going to do something greater than writing poetry. He was going to fight, fight for a better world. What could be more poetic than this?

He was smuggled across the Pyrenees. But fighting in Spain was not what he had expected. He was able to withstand the shocks of battle, to conquer fears. But gradually, against his will, he saw many things that disillusioned him. When he expressed doubts or asked questions, he was looked at askance. Unwittingly, he betrayed a comrade who had doubts. He never saw that comrade again. Guilty, disillusioned, feeling betrayed, he wanted to get out, not because of cowardice, but because of his disturbed moral conscience. He didn't know what to do. He considered a bullet that almost caused his death a kindly intervention of Providence. But, after he had recuperated enough to travel and return home, he was kept in Spain for a long time, interrogated, cross-examined, spied on. Finally he was allowed to leave. His health shattered, he returned to New York and was received by the comrades as a hero. He said little. A mass meeting was held in his honor. He got out of making a speech by pleading bad health, but he had to sit on the rostrum and listen to himself described as a hero. He heard speeches about Spain which he knew to be lies. He went home alone, disgusted, ill at heart.

Ruth had been out of New York. He wrote to her. Her letters were breezy, but a little cold. He longed for her. And yet he knew now that she had been an agent of his disaster. Finally he decided that he could not live with himself unless he talked. He wrote two articles trying to tell the truth about what he had seen in Spain. He was denounced as a fascist spy and a coward.

It was then that Ruth came to New York. He heard she was in town. But he didn't see her. His health had waned. He was in a charity ward in a hospital for a while. He got out on a day in spring, pale and thin and penniless. He saw Ruth on the street as he was walking about wondering where to go, what to do.

He stopped as she came toward him. She was as beautiful as ever. He was stirred by memories of his old love for her.

Then he smiled rather ironically.

She called him a fascist dog and walked on. He walked on in the opposite direction, a worn-out, broken young man. He walked the streets until he was almost exhausted, dispirited, sick, and afraid. And he knew that, despite all that had happened, he still loved her. Late at night, he returned to his room in a cheap rooming house on the East Side. He could not sleep. He tossed about in bed and thought of Ruth. He wanted to cry. He told himself that he had lived his life and could only go on now as though he were a human shell.

—Why did this happen to me? he asked himself plaintively as he saw the dawn coming through his bedroom window.

Olsen

WHEN I FIRST heard the stories about Olsen, the crazy Swede, I didn't really believe them. They seemed too exaggerated. But I repeated these stories anyway, because when you tell a story you want it to be a good one so you can get a laugh. Everybody shoots a little bull when he tells a story anyway. Like when my pals talk about the old days when we were nineteen and twenty, we always exaggerate the way we drank, and the fun we had, and everybody gives everybody else something to feel good about when we talk of the old days. Well, I thought these stories were exaggerated and I told them to make them seem funnier and better and I always talked about Olsen as if I knew him. I liked to say:

"Now, Olsen, that crazy Swede."

It made it seem I knew him, was a buddy of his. As if I had some share in what he did and I was like him. Because I wouldn't have the guts, or maybe because I ain't crazy enough, I couldn't be like the crazy Swede. But I wanted to. And damn near every other gas pumper I know did. The big crazy Swede was the most popular supervisor there ever was working for Nation, and all the lads liked him, even those that didn't know him just like I didn't know him for a long time.

All the lads who talked about him always called him crazy, but they said what a regular guy he was, the best one to work under in Nation, and that if all the bosses were like him, pumping gas would be a job no one could beat. But, then, if all the bosses were like the Swede, there wouldn't be no Nation either.

He was a crazy Swede all right, but he was regular. He never came around snooping or sniffing, and didn't give a damn about all the rules, regulations, instructions, and the whole damned rigmarole. Now and then he'd get sore and bawl a lad out, but he never turned you in downtown at the main office. He knew every trick to be known in the stations, and many that nobody else knew, and more than one lad tells of how, when he was short, the Swede would help him make up shortages on the pumps and would pull the pumps more than most gas pumpers. They tell all kinds of stories like these, and, as I say, I always repeated the ones I heard, but I never quite believed them. I always looked forward to meeting the crazy Swede and having him for my boss, too. Hell, you could sit on your can in the station, for all he cared, read the papers or a good adventure story, open up late, close up early, do pretty nearly any damn thing you wanted. He didn't care. He didn't only let you get by with murder. He helped you out on it now and then. The Swede didn't give a damn for anything, most certainly not for Nation. The closest he ever came to giving a damn was about a dame and a bottle. He liked the dames, and he had a cast-iron gut.

One of the stories they always told about Olsen was how there was a lad in one of the stations over near South Shore Drive, and this lad was taking a crack at some tramp that was passing by and that he'd coralled into the station. The lad had her in the little supply room inside of the station and he was taking his crack at her, and it must have been a damn good crack at that, because outside customers were lined up honking at the pumps. Olsen was the lad's supervisor, and he happened to drive into the station, and so he took care of the customers and soft-soaped them, said he was the boss, and the lad was in the can or something, and then he caught the lad taking his crack. So Olsen told him to finish up and, when he did, Olsen took a crack at her himself. That was the kind of a guy he was.

I always used to think of him, long before I worked for him, when it would be dull and slow in the station, and I'd wish a dame would come by, some tramp I could take a crack at, and I'd think, now if I was working for the crazy Swede, maybe he'd just be like a magnet and attract the dames to my station and take care of the trade while I got my crack. When you hang around a station, and it's dull and slow, and there's nothing to do but stand and wait, you think of all kinds of things, and, more than anything else, you think how you'd like to pass the time by taking a crack at a dame. And you can tell a nice story about yourself, how the dame came in, and how you talked her into it, and you took your crack at her.

And of course all the lads talked about how Olsen had been a great gypper when he was pumping gas, and all sorts of things like that. And about how he always warned the lads when spotters were around, or about the City Sealers being out. I felt like I knew him and he was my best friend long before I worked for him. But I always had a hunch I was going to work for him, and then there was some change downtown in the main office, where they ain't got anything else to do but think up changes, and so I drew the Swede. I thought that now I'd begin to like my job. I'd been getting so fed up with it that I was beginning to think I'd let Nation stick its job up the old you-know, although I knew I wouldn't, because where could I get as easy a job as gas pumping, all things considered. Anyway, I liked to think of myself kissing the job good-by. And, anyway, I was glad to get Olsen for my boss.

And I learned he was a crazy Swede all right. He took a liking to me and used to come around often. It was a funny feeling I had, myself actually wanting and hoping the boss would come around. I used to laugh thinking of it, and tell myself I'd like the boss to be coming around to do some of my work for me, because the Swede seemed to like to get at the pumps. It was a damn funny thing. Think of it, your boss likes to come around and wait on the trade for you, and sometimes he'd pull the pumps on a customer and come in and tell you he'd made your lunch money and carfare. I never could dope him out. Maybe it was because he was a Swede. Anyway, he was a nice guy, a swell guy, but the marbles in his head weren't placed the way they are in anybody else's. He didn't give a damn for nothing,

nothing in this damned world, and he gave less of a damn for Nation than he did for anything else on Christ's well-known green earth.

The first time he came around he comes in stern and frowning and says to me:

"Small?"

"Yes, sir," says I.

I guessed it was Olsen, because he came in a Nation Ford coupé, but the picture didn't fit, him coming this way, frowning.

"Isn't there anything you can do, standing around here, doing nothing?" he went on.

I started giving him a line, but he was only kidding and he tells me he's Olsen, my new supervisor.

"Small, we got to get efficient," he says. "Know what efficiency is?"

"Yes, sir," I says, thinking that these stories about him was all crap.

"Well, the Company wants efficiency. Did you ever stop to think what efficiency means to Nation?" he goes on.

So I started saying yes, of course, and so on, and he laughs, and goes on to say something about Nation not making enough money, and it had to make some more, so we had to be efficient, and he sits in the chair, and lights a cigarette.

"You're not allowed to smoke on the premises, are you?" he says.

"No, sir," I says.

"Well, we have to be efficient but, then, what's a cigarette between friends? Here, have one?"

He was always like that, always wanting to help you break the rules, laughing at them. He was the craziest boss I ever had. He was wild, too, let me tell you. He took a liking to me, and used to call me Smallsy, and it wasn't long after he was made supervisor for our district, that he and I was running around, and never before nor since did I ever drink so much beer and home brew, or do so much whoring. He loved to go to beer flats, and he liked the broads, and liked can houses the best, although

I don't know why. Broads always went for him. I guess they always like a lad to be a little bit crazy or screwy.

He used to come around and tell me to close up early and come on out with him.

"But I got orders not to close up early," I'd kid.

"Smallsy, who the hell is your boss?"

"You, sir," I'd go on kidding.

"All right, close the goddamned place. How long have you been earning a living by the sweat of that stupid brow of yours?"

"A long time, sir," I'd kid.

"And not long enough to know you should do what your boss tells you do. Listen, you insubordinate sonofabitch, close the goddamned station up! I know you'll break your arm doing it, because you hate the very idea, but I'm supervisor here. And you—you're just a goddamned gas-pumper. Now do what you're told."

So he'd light a cigarette and sit on his fanny and watch me closing up, and he'd say:

"Shake your goddamned ass. I never saw a lazier attendant. Shake your tail, boy."

"I'm doin' the best I can, sir," I'd say, kidding, you see.

That's the way we'd talk. And then, off we'd go. Of course, he was only supposed to use the coupé the company let him have for work, but he used it all he wanted, and we'd go to some beer flat, or can house, or to pick up some janes he knew in it, and it was like my having my own private car and chauffeur. And the way he drove. The only trouble with going out with him was that he drove so recklessly he always had you with your heart in your mouth. He drove like hell on wheels, and I don't know how he and I are alive as it is. But then he never worried about nothing, and least of all about his job. And he had a drag, after all, so that Prevost and none of the bosses like that in the main office could do anything to him. Boy, it was good to hear him talk about Prevost and the rest of them in the main office, good to my ears. He talked about them like they was just a bunch of punks, that's all.

He was a crazy Swede, and we had one hell of a time for six months. More dames than I can count. I tell you, one way and other, I got mine traveling with the Swede. He never seemed to get enough of it, and yet, it was funny. He really didn't seem to get so much of a kick out of it and he never talked like a guy that loved it, loved all of it he could get. I never really could dope him out. But he was a guy that didn't care. He raised hell because he didn't care, like a guy wanting to forget something. Now most lads get cockeyed in order to make themselves seem like a hell of a lot more than they are, because when you get some shots into you you feel mighty goddamn good and you feel you're hot stuff all right. And the same, when you lay a dame, now, no matter what kind of a tramp she is, still you keep thinking now I laid her, and she wanted me to, and that's one more I laid, and, besides the feeling itself, there's the way it makes you feel about yourself. If the dames want you to lay 'em, why you feel you're hot stuff. But not the Swede. He wanted to forget something.

"Smallsy, I don't give a good goddamn about anything," he always liked to say to me, and I believed him.

I know he came from a rich family, and he hated his old man who lived in Cleveland. He used to talk about his old man.

"Smallsy," he'd say to me, "my old man is a sanctimonious old hypocritical bastard. He did every goddamn thing he wanted to and he probably left kids of his from one end of America to another, and now he's old, and there he is, getting religion. He's no good. Not one of the Olsens in this classification of Olsens called my family—not one of them is any good."

And there was a dame, but he didn't say much about her, a dame that gave him the go-by and, in some way or other, just about left him there in the church. He went to Princeton and got thrown out, and he used to brag about it, and brag about having been thrown out of more places than anybody he knew. You see, he just didn't give a good goddamn. And that was one reason why a lad liked him. Because a lad just doesn't want to give a good goddamn, but he's got to because he has to get one job or another, or do something, and, after all, you liked to think you don't give a good goddamn but put the chips down, and you do. But not Olsen. He didn't, and meant it.

It was a lot of fun traveling with him and being able to kid your own boss and call him a bastard in kidding and be familiar with him, but, at the same time, you were always on tenterhooks and worried. You got nervous running with him. After all, he had friends on top in Nation, but then I didn't, and I didn't want to be no goat. And, still, I never had such a time as I did traveling with him. He was always good company and, as I said, reckless as they come.

Well, I'm going on and on about the Swede, and I better come to an end about him, and all of what I said was merely what they call the prelude to my wanting to tell about that last night.

It was a slow night, and in he comes, staggering, and he was smiling kind of queerly. He planks himself down on a barrel, and he looks at me, and he says, kidding like he always did:

"Come on, Small, shake your tail. Look at that air compressor. The damned thing has two inches, six inches of dust on it."

So I gets out a dust rag and hands it to him, and he laughs. But his eyes were funny, and he looked really drunk, looked really like the crazy Swede he was. I hands him the rag, and he hands it back to me, and he says:

"Throw the godamn rag in the refuse bin."

"I always obey orders, sir," says I, throwing the rag in the bin.

So he lights a cigarette and he says:

"Light up, or I'll turn you in, you insubordinate bastard."

So I lights a cigarette, but I'm kind of nervous. He's really drunk this time, and he doesn't give a good goddamn, but then, after all, I can't afford to lose my job and I'm nervous.

"Smallsy, I'm drunk. Drunk," he says.

"Yeah, I see that," says I.

"Smallsy, I never said this, but I am now. You know, this job I got is a goddamned stool pigeon's job, that's all it is."

I liked that, because, after all, it shows what a regular guy he was, even if his marbles were different from everybody else's.

"You gotta be drunk all the time, or else you won't have no self respec'. Not on this job," he said.

"Yeah, it must be pretty bum to have the job you got, almost as tough as having mine," says I.

"I got to be a rat. Rat Olsen. See. You gotta be a goddamn rat to keep my job. See! See! Say, you know what I wish. Wish the bolsheviks would blow up the goddamn works. Blow it sky high, jus'—blow it—wheesh," says he, throwing his hands up in the air.

"Wait a minute, I got a customer!" says I.

"Tell him to pound cue balls up . . ." says he as I rush out and service a customer.

When I come back, Olsen, he asks:

"Pull the pumps? Huh? Get four for five? But I don't care. Let the bolsheviks come and blow the works up sky high—wheesh!"

"You're drunk," says I.

"Down in the office, Prevost, that sonofabitch, wants to tie the can to me. Ha! Wants to kick me out on my tail in the cruel col' col' world. Can't. Ha! Can't, because I gotta drag. I gotta drag, see, kid, that goes up to the board of directors, you know them sonofabitches. I gotta drag, and Prevost can't give me the gate even if I won't be a sonofabitch and turn you guys in for doing the same goddamn things them guys upstairs do. See! Well, hell with them. See! Let the bolsheviks come, blow 'em to smithereens. Wheesh!"

Then he almost fell over the bowl, and I knew he was drunker than I even thought he was.

"I'm sick of being their stool-pigeon, their goddamn gumshoe rat. Get drunk. Drunk, and save your self-respec'. See!" he goes on.

Then he pulls out a bottle and says:

"Have a drink."

So we drink, but I'm feeling really leary, so he goes on jabbering and then, Holy Christ, he whips out a gat and starts waving it around. I asks him for it, but he won't give it to me. I plead, and even try to snatch it from him, but I can't.

"Let the bolsh. . . . Say, I'm gonna start things for the bolsheviks," he yells.

I don't know what the hell to do. I'm scared, and I mean it. Because he really don't give a good goddamn. And then he aims the gun at a five-gallon can of motor oil on the top shelf. He fires and hits inside the top part of the first N in the Nation lettering. Oil pours out in a little stream. I plead and try again to get the gun from him. He shoots at a second can. People in cars stop and people look in the station, and then they run. And he shoots a third can, another can of oil hit.

"Let the bolsheviks come around and finish the works. Wheesh!" he yells and he shoots again.

So there I am, and the Swede is really out of his head, and he's shooting up the station. I'm shaking at the knees, and I don't know if I'm coming or going, and you can see by his eyes that he don't know what he's doing, and don't care, and, why, how do I know but what he's going to shoot me? And he has the bullets bouncing about, and people are watching across the street, and some are running away, and I don't know what the hell to do, and I run into the supply room, and I think, Holy Christ, he might shoot me. He's nuts, and so nuts he really don't give a good goddamn, and my ears seems numb or something with the shots and the noise they make, and he's out there shooting up the oil cans, and the oil is coming out of them. It was a sight, I tell you, because soon I'm outside again, with cops around, talking, and he doesn't seem to cause them any trouble, and the oil is pouring down off the shelves, and the station is one holy mess. Like what I always wanted to do to the station myself, shoot it up, just like he did, only, after all, enough is enough. Well, the cops, they got him, and they're tough, and he tells them who he is, and I confirm it.

So they don't know what to do, and there's a crowd outside, and it's exciting, and I'm rushing out to wait on customers, and having to tell them what's happened, and more cops come, keeping back the crowd, and they don't know what to do with him.

"Yes," I tells another cop, for I don't know how many times it was, "he's my boss, and he's got a drag with the board of directors. He's just drunk."

And so Prevost comes around, and asks me what's up, after he talks with the cops, and what can I say?

"He just comes around this way, a little drunk, and he shoots at the cans," I say.

And so there it is, and there he is, sitting very calm, and he keeps saying, he says:

"Let the bolsheviks, let Lenin and Trotsky come and shoot the rest of it up."

So they pow-wow, and I'm outside, and I'm still scared, and I keep wondering, will I get canned now, and what can I say or do? So finally the cops and Prevost get him into the paddy wagon, and he waves and yells:

"Small, let the bolsheviks finish it up now."

And Prevost comes back, and he says to me:

"Small, he's just broken down. Now, you don't tell anyone about this and clean the station up. Dump all the oil you can in the barrels and make an audit. I'll have the auditor here as soon as he can come, and you clean up."

So I got to clean the station up, and that's all that happens to me. The crazy Swede shoots the station up because he's drunk and don't give a good goddamn, and I got to clean the shooting mess up, and people come around to ask me what happens, and the auditor comes, but I jockey the figures and the oil a bit before he comes, and make some dough of the shooting, enough for a good date, anyway. And so Olsen, well, he merely gets put in a sanitarium for a while, and they say he had a breakdown, and I don't know what happens after that. I never heard. But I'm still pumping gas.

But I often think of the Swede, and there's more stories about him told by the lads in the station. And if you want to know the truth, every damned one of us in our hearts would like just once in our lives to say we don't care, either, wheesh, and shoot things up that way, if we only could get away with it. Yes, I liked the crazy Swede, only he was a really reckless guy. But then, he could be, and nothing really happened to him that counted because he didn't care if he lost his jobber, and he didn't get put in jail or anything like that, and I'll bet that he's just the same as he ever was, wherever he is. The lads all talk about him, and every one of them talks as if he was their buddy and they did the same things he did. But I was really his buddy. And, nervous as I was running around with him, we sure had a time of it while it lasted. Yes, Olsen sure was a crazy Swede, all right.

A Lesson in History

SCENE: *The large classroom of the second-year class at Saint Stanislaus High School in Chicago. It is a spring afternoon in 1921. The stage is cut into two sections; the large classroom is the dominating one, and on the right is a small portion of the corridor outside. In the classroom, back, left, is a wall with windows, and the back is a long blackboard. The teacher's desk is against the wall, right, set on a dais in the center of the room. To the right of the desk is a wastepaper basket and a map that is rolled up like a shade, and to the left of the desk, lower right front, a swinging door that leads into the corridor. Facing the teacher's desk are the rows of seats, almost all filled except for a few in the back, and except for Danny O'Neill's seat, the fourth from the front in the center aisle.*

FATHER KRANZ (*seated at desk and finishing the roll call*): Zivic?

ZIVIC (*student in rear far row*): Here.

FATHER KRANZ (*as he talks there is a dragging quality in his voice*): Well, now, we'll begin the lesson. Of course, I know you've all recuperated from the effects of Friday. (*They laugh. Various students turn to look at Bart Daly, sitting in the second seat third row, and Marty Mulligan in first seat, fourth row.*) I know that you've all studied and come here prepared, perhaps even prepared to teach me a little history. (*Students all over are noticed trying furtively to steal quick*

157

looks into their textbooks.) I can see Mulligan there suffering the throes of anxiety. Aren't you, Mulligan? (*Laughs.*)

MARTY: No, Father. (*More laughter.*)

FATHER KRANZ: What do you mean, *no*, Father?

MARTY (*smiling*): I mean, yes, Father.

SHEEHAN: Father, he means that he would rather have you ask somebody else.

FATHER KRANZ: All right, Sheehan. Since you're so quick with your tongue, I'll let you answer. (*The class laughs.*)

SHEEHAN: Father, I'd as soon remain silent.

MARTY MULLIGAN: Father, he's already got a charley horse in his tongue from talking.

FATHER KRANZ: Well, we'll exercise the charley horse out of your tongue. (*As Father Kranz says this, Danny O'Neill is first heard, then seen running to the door admitting to the classroom.*) Now, Sheehan. . . .

DANNY O'NEILL (*bursting breathlessly into the classroom*): I see that the cohorts are all here.

FATHER KRANZ: Yes, and the jackass has arrived.

TIM DOOLAN (*as the class laughs*): He's not a jackass, Father. He's a *jumentum*.

FATHER KRANZ: No, he's a jackass in both English and Latin. (*Again the class laughs.*) I think we've had enough humor, and now we'll go on with the lesson. (*Again there are attempts to sneak quick looks into the textbooks.*) And don't do your studying now. You should have done it over the week end.

DANNY: Father, I'm in perfect agreement with you.

FATHER KRANZ: That's such a good start, O'Neill, that I'll give you more opportunity to show how much you agree with me. Don't get too anxious.

DANNY: There's no danger, Father.

FATHER KRANZ: Sheehan, what is the lesson for today?

SHEEHAN: History. (*Laughter.*)

FATHER KRANZ: Sheehan, how did you think up such an answer? Did you listen to me here last Friday?

SHEEHAN: Yes, Father.

FATHER KRANZ: And so you answer my question by saying that the lesson of the day is history.

SHEEHAN: Well, it is, only I was going to go on from there but. . . .

FATHER KRANZ: But what?

SHEEHAN: Well, all this horseplay (*he points around the room*) made me forget. (*Laughter.*)

AD LIB: Yeah!

Try again, that ain't so good.

You talking horseplay.

FATHER KRANZ: Quiet. Now, everybody will be so quiet for thirty seconds that we can hear a pin drop. Quiet. (*A strained quiet of from fifteen to thirty seconds.*) Now, Sheehan, has your memory been restored to you?

SHEEHAN: Well, Father, the lesson is. . . .

FATHER KRANZ (*marking on card before him*): Sheehan, if I could give you a mark lower than zero for your brilliant recitation, I'd do so. You'll have to be satisfied with zero. But to make up for the fact that that is the best mark I can give you, why, you can stay after school at two-thirty and copy the lesson out of the book. Maybe that will help you to remember tomorrow.

SHEEHAN: Gee, Father, I tell you, I did study. I had it all right at the fingertips of my mind, but these distractions made me forget.

FATHER KRANZ: All I'm doing, Sheehan, is giving you something to do that will be an aid to your memory in the future.

SHEEHAN: Aw, gee, Father, I tell you, I did study.

FATHER KRANZ: And I'm going to help you to study more effectively.

SHEEHAN: But, Father. . . .

FATHER KRANZ: You'd better sit down now, Sheehan, before you begin to abuse my patience.

SHEEHAN: But, gee, Father, that's an awful penance to give me.

FATHER KRANZ: Come on, sit down now. (*He looks around the room.*) Mulligan, you look bright today.

MARTY: Looks are often deceiving, Father.

FATHER KRANZ: Well, we'll find out.

MARTY: No, Father.

FATHER KRANZ: What do you mean? No, Father, what?

MARTY: I mean no, Father, I don't feel bright.

FATHER KRANZ: You tell Sheehan and the rest of the class here what is the history lesson for the day.

MARTY: But if I do, Father, they'll know as much as I do.

DANNY O'NEILL: That won't be very much.

MARTY (*turning toward Danny as many laugh*): Wise guy!

FATHER KRANZ: Sit down, Mulligan. You can stay in the jug with Sheehan.

MARTY: But, Father, I got basketball practice this afternoon.

FATHER KRANZ: The team won't miss you. And writing out your lesson might make your hands more limber.

MARTY: I don't think so. And, Father, I don't know what I did to get a penance.

FATHER KRANZ: I'm telling you what you're going to do.

MARTY: But that's not fair, Father.

FATHER KRANZ: Don't talk any more!

MARTY: But listen, Father. . . .

FATHER KRANZ: I told you, Mulligan, to keep still. Now do it, or I'll have to make you! (*He flushes with sudden anger.*) All right, O'Neill, you like to talk. Stand up!

DANNY (*rising*): Yes, Father.

FATHER KRANZ: What is the lesson today?

VOICE (*whispering*): Adrian the Fourth.

FATHER KRANZ: Hurry up!

DANNY: Adrian the Fourth.

FATHER KRANZ: Who was he?

DANNY (*there are whispering voices telling him, but he can't catch what they say*): King.

FATHER KRANZ: King of what?

DANNY: England.

FATHER KRANZ: Tell me, O'Neill, who told you that?

DANNY: The book.

FATHER KRANZ: I heard prompting all the way up here, so tell me who told you that?

DANNY: A lot of them.

FATHER KRANZ: Well, a lot of them are wrong. I think I'll let you keep company with Mulligan and Sheehan after school.

SHEEHAN: Couldn't you let somebody else take his place, Father?

DANNY: Yes, Father, I don't think I should stay with them if they don't want me.

FATHER KRANZ (*as he talks, a student in back seat, far row, is shooting spitballs around the room with the aid of a rubber band*): It's not what they want but what I'm telling you to do when the bell rings at two-thirty and good students like Daly, Shanley, Dawson, and Doylan can all go out.

DANNY: Well, of course, Father, if you insist, then I'll stay. (*Laughter.*)

FATHER KRANZ: I thought you would O'Neill, you are very obliging. (*Laughter.*) Now, let's see. (*He looks around the room.*) We have such a bright bunch here. Doolan, you look as if you were awake this afternoon. Stand up.

MARTY (*as Doolan arises and Danny sits down*): Father, that's a mistake about him being awake.

FATHER KRANZ (*curtly*): Mulligan, if that penance I gave you isn't enough, there are other things I can give you. From now on, you can speak when I speak to you first.

CARRIGAN: I wouldn't let him speak either, Father. He hasn't got a nice voice.

FATHER KRANZ: Carrigan, how are your knees?

CARRIGAN: Well, Father, we had a retreat last week.

FATHER KRANZ: Good, that gave you a chance to practice them. Now we'll test them. For the rest of the class hour, kneel in the hallway outside the doorway. I'm getting tired of some of you fellows. (*Carrigan slowly, sulkily walks to the door.*) All right, Doolan.

TIM DOOLAN: Father, you know, I've been puzzled by a question I wanted to ask you.

FATHER KRANZ: Yes? (*Interrupted by laughter caused by*

Carrigan, who made a face as he went through the door to kneel in the hallway in view of the audience.)

TIM DOOLAN: Yes, Father, I wanted to ask you the derivation of the name Adrian.

FATHER KRANZ: Are you interested in etymology, Doolan?

DOOLAN: Of course. (*Laughter.*) You see, Father, I was reading the lesson, and I got to wondering and asking myself, now where did this name come from?

FATHER KRANZ: You did? Good. Now, I want to ask you a question.

TIM DOOLAN: Honest, I did, Father.

FATHER KRANZ: I know. And, of course, Doolan, I appreciate such curiosity because I know how well most of my students here have studied the day's assignment. So I appreciate the curiosity you have shown. However, before I answer your question, I want to ask you something. Now, Doolan, will you tell the class what you read about Adrian the Fourth?

DOOLAN: Sure I will, Father. But first, could you tell me where the name came from?

FATHER KRANZ: Did the assignment you read for today say anything about the derivation of the name?

DOOLAN: No. It said. . . . (*He pauses.*) It said. . . .

DANNY: Father, I know what it was. He was so concerned worrying over etymology that he forgot everything else.

DOOLAN: Hey, Goof!

FATHER KRANZ: Did it say that too? Hey, Goof! What historical character said that, Doolan?

DOOLAN (*as there is laughter*): Well, Father.

FATHER KRANZ: You told me that about Well, Father. Now, what else? (*Doolan stands in long and nervous silence; students around him furtively look in books; others shoot spitballs; and outside Carrigan gets off his knees and stands against door listening.*) Doolan, you'd better keep your friends company after school. (*Looks around classroom.*) Close your books, everybody!

SHANLEY (*raising his hand*): Father, I know.

FATHER KRANZ (*to Shanley as Marty directs a contemptu-*

ous look at him.) I know you do, Shanley. I want to try to find out if some of the others know. Now, I wonder who else is as interested in etymology as Doolan. (*Catching Marty furtively starting to begin his penance.*) Mulligan, put that pencil and paper away, close your book, and do your penance after school.

SHEEHAN: He can't tell time, Father.

FATHER KRANZ: If you don't like the atmosphere of the room, Sheehan, you can join Carrigan outside.

SHEEHAN: Oh, I do, Father.

FATHER KRANZ: I'm glad you do, Sheehan. Thank you.

SHEEHAN: You're welcome, Father.

FATHER KRANZ: Smilga. (*He rises from his desk on dais.*)

SMILGA (*Rising as Father Kranz stands over Sheehan.*): Yes, Fadder.

FATHER KRANZ (*taking off the black belt he wears around his middle over the brown habit of his order*): What was the Bull Laudabilitor? (*Hands go up and fingers snap from students who know the answer.*)

SHEEHAN: Father, that might hurt.

FATHER KRANZ (*hitting Sheehan several blows on the back as he speaks*): Did you hear the question? (*At this moment Danny O'Neill is hit by a spitball and turns and shakes his fist toward the rear of the room.*)

SMILGA: Yes, Fadder.

FATHER KRANZ: Well, do you know the answer?

SMILGA: Yes, Fadder.

FATHER KRANZ: Why don't you give it to me then?

SMILGA: Is dat what you wanted, Fadder? (*Laughter.*)

FATHER KRANZ: You don't think I wanted you to tell me who won the basketball game last Friday, do you? (*More laughter.*)

SMILGA (*speaking rapidly, and with an accent, and pronouncing his "th's" as "de"*): Well, de Bull Laudabilitor is supposed to have been a bull issued by de Pope, Adrian de Fourth, to de King of England to give the King of England right over Ireland.

FATHER KRANZ: The first one in the class I have called on

who could answer a question. Thank you, Smilga. Now, Doolan, tell Sheehan whether or not this particular bull was really issued by the Pope.

SHEEHAN: Father, the bull was only bull anyway.

FATHER KRANZ: Shut up, Sheehan, unless you want some more wallops. If I didn't give you enough, I'll oblige you more satisfactorily a second time.

DANNY: Father, Sheehan ought to be able to talk all about bull. That's all he knows.

FATHER KRANZ: And O'Neill has spoken his last word of this class hour. (*He aimlessly wanders toward door, and Carrigan slips back to his knees.*) Tell us, Shanley. (*Faces class.*)

SHANLEY: It was a forgery, Father, composed after the death of Pope Adrian the Fourth.

FATHER KRANZ: Suppose it were not a forgery? What was the argument behind the theory that this bull was a true document, and what is the justification for this alleged grant on the part of Pope Adrian the Fourth?

SHANLEY: The Pope, as a feudal overlord over all of Christendom, would have had such a right to grant a fief, like Ireland, to the King of England as his vassal.

FATHER KRANZ: O'Neill, are you listening?

DANNY (*points to his closed lips*): Can I talk, Father? You said I should be silent for the rest of the hour. (*Laughter.*)

FATHER KRANZ: Stop the nonsense and answer my question.

DANNY: Yes, Father.

FATHER KRANZ: Well, thank you for your attention. Now, Daly, tell Mulligan who was the Holy Roman Emperor during the papacy of Pope Adrian the Fourth.

DALY (*rising*): Frederick Barbarossa.

FATHER KRANZ: Can you tell me anything about the relationships between the Pope and the Emperor?

DALY: Yes, Father.

MARTY (*turning to Sheehan and yelling loudly*): Cut it out.

SHEEHAN: Get me a pocket knife and I will.

FATHER KRANZ: What's ailing you scholars? (*Laughter.*)

SHEEHAN (*to Mulligan*): I want to cut it out for you since you asked me to. (*Laughter.*)

FATHER KRANZ: Mulligan, haven't you been assigned a sufficient penance?

MARTY: I didn't do anything. Sheehan was shooting spitballs at me.

SHEEHAN: Father, I wasn't, and he's maligning me.

FATHER KRANZ: Someday, you kids are going to abuse my patience beyond the limits of endurance.

SHEEHAN: And, Father, he's abusing mine. (*Points at Marty.*)

MARTY: Yes, and I'll abuse more than your patience.

FATHER KRANZ: Shut up, both of you! If you're looking for a fight, come and fight me.

DANNY: But, Father, why don't you pick on someone your own size. (*Laughter.*)

FATHER KRANZ: O'Neill, come up here and kneel in the front of the room. (*More laughter.*)

DANNY (*rising and walking forward*): Gee, I don't want to wear my pants out.

FATHER KRANZ (*meeting Danny before his own desk*): You talk too much. (*Slaps Danny's face. Danny tries to cover up and gets a second slap on the side of the face.*) Enough is enough from you kids. (*Turns to Daly, and Danny goes to kneel in a corner.*) All right, Daly.

DALY: Father, Frederick Barbarossa wanted to be coronated by the Pope as the Holy Roman Emperor. When he and the Pope met. . . .

FATHER KRANZ: That's enough, Daly. I see that you know your lesson. I think I shall find out some more from some of my other really bright boys and interested students. Rychewski.

STEVE RYCHEWSKI: Yes, Fadder.

FATHER KRANZ: Tell Mulligan what Daly was trying to say.

STEVE RYCHEWSKI: He was talking about de meeting of de Pope and Frederick Barbarossa.

FATHER KRANZ: Well, what about the meeting?

STEVE RYCHEWSKI (*after a long pause*): Why, Fadder, they met.

FATHER KRANZ: Are you sure they met?

STEVE RYCHEWSKI: Yes, Fadder.

FATHER KRANZ: How do you know? Why are you so sure they met?

STEVE RYCHEWSKI: Because I know dey did.

FATHER KRANZ: How do you know?

STEVE RYCHEWSKI (*after another long pause*): Daly said so, didn't he? (*Laughter.*)

FATHER KRANZ: Did you study your history assignment over the week end?

STEVE RYCHEWSKI: I always study.

FATHER KRANZ: How do you study?

STEVE RYCHEWSKI: I read de lesson you tell us to.

FATHER KRANZ: And what do you learn?

STEVE RYCHEWSKI: Whatever de book says.

FATHER KRANZ: What book? Buffalo Bill, Nick Carter, what book? (*Laughter.*)

STEVE RYCHEWSKI: De history book.

FATHER KRANZ: What history book?

TIM DOOLAN: He doesn't know that one, Father.

FATHER KRANZ: Then he's as bright as you, isn't he?

TIM DOOLAN: He comes from my home town.

DANNY (*turning back toward class*): Father, where they come from, West Pullman, the sidewalks are taken in at nine o'clock.

FATHER KRANZ: Do I hear noises from monkeys or what?

MARTY: No, Father, that's only O'Neill.

FATHER KRANZ: I wonder now, Rychewski, do you really know what a history book is?

STEVE RYCHEWSKI: Yes, Fadder, de textbook.

FATHER KRANZ (*returning to desk and holding before the class the thick, green-bound history textbook*): Tell me honestly, Rychewski, did you ever see this book before?

STEVE RYCHEWSKI: Yes, Fadder.

FATHER KRANZ: Do you know what's inside of it?

SCHAEFFER: Father, it has big words inside of it.

MARTY: And pictures.

FATHER KRANZ: Now, don't you fellows tell him. Rychewski, what is inside this book?

STEVE RYCHEWSKI: History.

FATHER KRANZ: And what is history?

STEVE RYCHEWSKI: Well, Fadder, history is. . . .

FATHER KRANZ: Mulligan, see if you can redeem yourself by telling Rychewski what history is.

MARTY: History is the thing that keeps me in the jug and gives me writer's cramp.

FATHER KRANZ (*glares at Marty and then looks woefully at Steve Rychewski*): I'll tell you, Rychewski, and I'll tell the whole class what history is. Now, listen closely. History is something that I cannot under any circumstances, and no matter what methods I use, manage to teach to you numskulls.

STEVE RYCHEWSKI: Yes, Fadder.

FATHER KRANZ (*irritated*): Sit down and take a load off your brains. You can keep your comrades company after two-thirty.

STEVE RYCHEWSKI (*sitting down, smiling meekly and in a friendly way*): Yes, Fadder.

FATHER KRANZ: How many here studied today's lesson? (*All hands go up.*) How many of you here know the Ten Commandments? (*All hands again go up.*) How many of you know that one of the Ten Commandments forbids lying? (*All hands go up.*) Well, I'll find out. Now, McDonald, answer me, at the risk of your immortal soul.

MCDONALD (*reluctantly rising*): That's a big order, Father.

SCHAEFFER: Father, he spent the week end studying how to comb his hair with vaseline.

FATHER KRANZ: You never studied, did you, Schaeffer?

MCDONALD: Father, he's defaming me. (*Points to Schaeffer.*)

FATHER KRANZ: Well, now, don't you, in turn, go and defame the memory of Pope Adrian the Fourth.

MCDONALD: Father, you can prevent me from doing that.

FATHER KRANZ: How?

MCDONALD: By not asking me any questions.

FATHER KRANZ: Good. Sit down, and stay after school, and do the same penance as the others.

MARTY: We don't want him in our jug, Father.

FATHER KRANZ: What can I do about that?

MARTY: You can let me go, and keep him.

FATHER KRANZ: That would be unfair.

MARTY: But, Father. (*He is laughing and grinning and he looks up at the priest.*) . . .

FATHER KRANZ (*interrupting Mulligan*): Shut up, I'm being too lenient with you kids as it is.

SHEEHAN: Lenient?

FATHER KRANZ: Sheehan, you can speak when you're spoken to.

MARTY: Yeh, Sheehan, freeze your trap.

FATHER KRANZ: Mulligan, you're talking too much. Why didn't you talk when I asked you to recite?

MARTY: I would have, but I didn't want to show the rest of the class up.

DANNY (*turning around from his kneeling position*): Mulligan doesn't think much of himself, does he?

MARTY: Shut up, Dope!

FATHER KRANZ: Mulligan, are you the teacher?

TIM DOOLAN: Thank Caesar's ghost that he isn't.

MARTY: If I was, Father, I wouldn't be so hard on a guy.

FATHER KRANZ: Mulligan, I'm tired of you.

MARTY: Father, you aren't any more tired than my hand will be this afternoon.

FATHER KRANZ (*rising and walking toward Marty's desk*): Do you talk to hear your own voice, or what?

DANNY (*again turning*): To reveal his ignorance.

MARTY: That's enough from you, O'Neill. You're only a goof.

FATHER KRANZ: Shut up, O'Neill. (*Moving more rapidly toward Marty.*) Mulligan, was your opinion of O'Neill asked?

MARTY: You don't expect me to listen to him making cracks like that at me, do you?

FATHER KRANZ: Mulligan, who do you think you're talking to? (*The class, seeing that this time the priest has actually lost his temper, becomes suddenly tense. Marty looks up at the priest, his friendly grin suddenly turning into an expression of surprise.*) Answer me. (*Mulligan's expression becomes one of fear.*)

MARTY: What do you mean, Father? (*Father Kranz punches Marty's face. Marty covers up as the second blow lands.*)

FATHER KRANZ (*punching angrily*): Answer me (*He continues punching as the curtain falls.*)

The Dialectic

I KNEW JAKE AND EDDIE IN COLLEGE, back in the early 1920's. They seemed brilliant then, but my standards were different from what they are now. I have often reflected on what I thought of them in those days, and I am aware that I over-estimated their characters and capacities. However, they were two of the best students of the time at Columbia, and they were unquestionably superior to most of their contemporaries; they were more disinterested, had more intellectual ambition—as contrasted with ambition for success—than the great majority of students. Those of us who knew them expected that they would develop, that they would achieve something, something more humanly important than any mere bank account. Like others in our group, Jake and Eddie were idealistic, and, when they dreamed of careers, they thought of some type of work which would, in some way or another, contribute toward the betterment of mankind. They had both been YPSLs, Eddie in New York, Jake in Brooklyn, while they were still kids in high school. When they began at Columbia, they were outstanding in their class. They were better read and more aware of what the world was like than most of their class. But, combined with their idealism and intelligence, there was also a vein of the cynicism and aggressiveness of the streets. They became intimate friends early in their freshman year. Those of us who knew them fairly well, who often talked with them in bull sessions and went out together to cat houses, who lived the same kind of life as they—we always thought of them together.

They were close friends, and they shared their hopes, their dreams, their feelings about girls with each other. It was a Damon and Pythias friendship.

Jake wanted to be a poet; Eddie planned to become a philosopher. In those days Jake was thin, handsome, charming. He was very witty and had a genuine flair for impromptu characterizations. How often in the dormitory—for two years they roomed together—Jake would have us all rolling off the bed and on the floor at his take-offs of some of our professors. Eddie was quieter, a short and stocky fellow with a moon face. He was outwardly more serious, but he had a quiet and cutting irony. They were both leaders of our group, and they were usually able to dominate the rest of us intellectually. We admired them, looked up to them, found them stimulating as well as buoyant and full of fun. I, at all events, often envied them. They could be so serious and yet so gay. They seemed to know so much and to learn so easily. Yes, they seemed to be so gifted and so promising.

After graduation, Eddie had to find work. He came from a poor family and had to do something. Instead of going on to be a philosopher, he managed to get a job as a newspaper reporter. Jake's father had money; he owned a large hardware store and several buildings. Immediately after his graduation, Jake made a trip to Europe. He used to write wonderful letters, and I've always regretted that somehow or other I lost them. He wrote most often to Eddie, but I saw Eddie fairly often in those days and he'd show me Jake's letters. They were delightful, so full of Jake's charming and ebullient personality. Everything he described seemed to have been felt with such a fresh, such an open, personality. He wrote about the girls he met; his impressions of cities, especially of Paris; amusing little incidents about American tourists; accounts of political news in the French and German papers; and, at times, passages in which he expressed his indignation about the lot of the workers. He was, or seemed to be, growing, gaining new impressions, deepening and widening his sensibilities and experiences, all in preparation to becoming a poet. Eddie believed that Jake would develop into a great American poet. And Eddie wrote frequently to Jake and told of his experiences as a cub reporter. Their friendship was neither sundered nor weakened by distance.

When Jake returned after having spent seven or eight months in Europe, they picked up just where they had left off and once again were inseparable. After graduating, they held to the same views and values they had had in college. At times Jake seemed to throb with idealism. Their expectations concerning their own careers were inseparable from their belief in socialism, their desire to do something for the betterment of mankind.

In those days many of us were stirred by the Russian Revolution and the ability of the Bolsheviks to resist the counter-revolution and the imperialist invasion. We were inspired without having any real practical sense of politics. We were, considering our ages, well read in socialist literature, and most of us had tackled *Das Kapital*. But at the same time our revolutionary enthusiasm and our socialist faith were matters of intellectual ardor; in terms of practical experience we were naive. Our socialist activities in college had been intellectual; in the main we were student and debating socialists. We had no real experience or contact with the working class. But we had great hopes, and because of our hopes we felt superior to other students and different from them. Our feeling of superiority, however, encouraged us to read, to study, to dream more. It helped us to learn from the books we read. We looked to the Soviet Union. We idolized the leaders, and especially the dying Lenin and Trotsky. Jake, I know, identified himself with Trotsky and always talked of him. When he was in Europe, shortly after his graduation, he was able to obtain some of Trotsky's work that was unavailable in America. He attempted to model himself after Trotsky, and for a time—since Trotsky was Soviet War Commissar—he read many military books, and his talk would be a mélange of military words and poetic metaphors. I believe—although this is something he would never have said to me, and I doubt even to Eddie—that Jake dreamed of himself as becoming the American Trotsky, of being a military revolutionist leading the workers in America to the day of final victory.

There was nothing truly preposterous in such dreams. The Bolsheviks had been victorious in Russia. Lenin and Trotsky, unknown a few years before except in revolutionary circles— had risen to shake the foundations of history. We knew that the course of history had been irreversibly altered by the Russian Revolution.

When Jake returned to America, he was bursting with energy, and full of tales of love and life. Eddie had a little room in the Village, Jake one near by. I used to go to one or the other room often. We talked half the night through, as we had done as undergraduates. The future was still before us, and we were confident about it. Eddie and Jake continued to dream the same dreams. Eddie tried to write stories, but none was published. He read them aloud to Jake, who admired them. And Jake—who was now and then getting a romantic poem published—read his poems to Eddie. They admired each other's work. Eddie was getting along better in the newspaper world; he had completely abandoned his plans for a career in philosophy, but he continued to read avidly. He was growing; in fact growing more than Jake. He had not lost his interest in socialism, although his socialism, in the practical sense, was—like Jake's—bohemian. At the same time he hoped to work himself up to the position where he could become a Moscow correspondent, and he believed that in this way he would serve the revolution. John Reed was an idol of his, and, in fact, Eddie had once heard Reed speak. Jake suddenly was able to publish more poems, mainly in radical and liberal magazines. His name began to appear regularly in many places as a book reviewer, and he started to gain a small reputation. He was a promising literary man and poet.

At this time we were receiving fragmentary news of the factional struggle in Russia. This was disturbing. It confused us, and we didn't know what to think. But both Eddie and Jake hoped—especially Jake—that Trotsky would win; they were sure he would. With Lenin gone, he seemed to us in New York to be the greatest and most brilliant man in the world.

Eddie continued slowly to advance as a journalist; Jake proceeded successfully in his career as a poet and critic, and he drifted closer to the Communist Party, finally becoming a member. However, he didn't seem to change his way of life, and he didn't seem to do much Party work. In his middle twenties, he was handsome, charming, witty, slender, and unusually attractive to girls. He had endless love affairs.

But after Jake joined the Party, he and Eddie began to see less of one another even though they retained the same respect and mutual affection of college days. Eddie married a girl from the Midwest, and Jake was his best man in the ceremony, if such it could be called, at City Hall. Then he was out of New York on newspaper work, but I forget where he was. When he returned, I think he and Jake saw each other occasionally. At any rate, I gained that impression whenever I ran into them. In 1927, Trotsky was expelled from the Communist Party of the Soviet Union. Jake was bitter, almost broken-hearted. He and Eddie met me shortly after this, and I sat with them drinking dago red in a Village speakeasy, and they were glum, disconsolate. Jake expressed himself rather violently, condemning, cursing, loathing, denouncing those who had expelled Trotsky. But at the same time he remained in the Party.

As we left that night, Jake was a little drunk. He staggered between Eddie and me toward Washington Square, and I remember him saying:

"They'll have to take him back. He's the Sword of the Revolution, and they need him." Then he seemed to glow with inspiration and he repeated feelingly: "The Sword of the Revolution."

I didn't see them much after this for a while. But I heard that Eddie finally realized his ambition. He was sent to the Soviet Union as a Moscow correspondent. I didn't see him before he left, but Jake told me about it. He went in high hopes, with great enthusiasm. He—and Jake to some extent—had forgotten about Trotsky. He had gone, bound for home, bound for Utopia. Jake envied him, and yet was delighted for Eddie. Eddie wrote Jake for a while, and sent me one boundlessly enthusiastic letter. Then his old friends didn't hear from him. I ran into Jake occasionally. He was the same, except that there was no marked progress in his writing. In his cups, he would speak of Trotsky, and he was convinced that the day would come when Trotsky—already in exile—would come back, or be called back. In all, Eddie spent almost three years in Russia. He then returned to the United States, but disillusioned. I met Jake shortly after Eddie returned. I asked him how Eddie was, and he was curiously aloof, and finally said:

"Eddie's been a capitalist journalist too long. He doesn't understand revolutionary politics."

But from Eddie I learned that Jake had listened to him, avid, enthusiastic, and glum by turn, when Eddie had described his experiences, impressions, and his change of mind as a result of his having spent so much time as a correspondent in the Soviet Union. Shortly after this Jake went to Russia for six months. I didn't hear from him, but when I saw Eddie once or twice on the street I asked if he'd had any news from Jake. Eddie answered negatively, but once he said:

"Jake will learn, too."

Jake sent back a few glowing articles on conditions in Russia, and these were published in the Party press. I showed one to Eddie, but he merely smiled ironically.

On Jake's return I saw him, and he went into a long account of how socialism was triumphing in Russia. He was then writing a series of six articles on conditions in Russia. He had not one criticism to make, and in one of his articles he stated that even the air was different, purer, as one crossed the border from capitalism into the Socialist Soviet Fatherland of the workers.

When he was asked about Eddie, he would answer that Eddie was a bourgeois journalist, but he'd say this in such a way as to suggest that Eddie was much worse than this, and that if he, Jake, wanted to, he could give information to show that Eddie was.

By this time Jake had abandoned writing poetry or, at least, none of it was published. For a while he worked for Soviet agencies in America, and he didn't seem to write anything for publication. He lectured now and then on culture for Party or front groups. And he did a variety of different kinds of contact work for the Party in bourgeois intellectual circles, employing all his charm for such purposes and usually managing to explain away anything that needed to be explained away. And, of course, he had more love affairs, married, and was divorced.

After Eddie's return to America, it seems that the word had come to Jake from higher-ups in the Party that Eddie wasn't to be trusted. In time, I am told, when they met they acted almost like strangers or mere casual acquaintances. Jake seemed uninterested in what Eddie had to say or wanted to say about the Soviet Union, and once Jake flatly told me that Eddie had sold out to bourgeois journalism and was, in the objective sense, a dangerous enemy of the Revolution. Eddie had lost his faith. It was a troubled period for him. He was nervous, bitter, hurt. But once, when they were together and Jake was a little drunk, he was entirely different. He spoke of Trotsky, telling Eddie and me that, of course, Trotsky was a bad politician, but that he was a brilliant writer, a brilliant orator, a brilliant man, and, of course, Jake didn't really think that he was a counter-revolutionist. However, politics was politics, and you had to be realistic in politics, and, of course, that demanded a bitter war against Trotsky because Trotsky was wrong. And then he wistfully lamented on how so brilliant a man could have been so wrong.

Jake's face was a trifle flushed when he talked this way. His eyes were vaguely watery. He leaned drunkenly over the table, pounded it with his fist, and said in a thick voice:

"You've got to have Bolshevik hardness."

I wanted to laugh, but didn't, and Eddie with quiet irony said:

"Someday you'll know something about that hardness."

"If I become like Trotsky, I'll deserve it," he said.

Eddie grinned, but with a touch of bitterness. Eddie was really hurt at this time.

But Jake, drunk and more ebullient than ever, continued to

speak of Trotsky, and suddenly, in genuine and deeply felt and intoxicated admiration, he exclaimed:

"But Trotsky, even wrong—what a man!"

Eddie went back to Europe as a correspondent, but not to Russia. I read his dispatches occasionally, and although they were competent, they usually were merely factual. They revealed that although he had managed now to get a good and a responsible job, he was not realizing any of his dreams of college days. In a sense this proved that Jake was right about Eddie. Eddie had become just another bourgeois journalist. He was recalled to America by his paper and given a desk job as a foreign editor, with a raise in salary. He became their expert on European affairs. The effects of his long journalistic career were more than apparent. All of his early idealism was gone. He was cynical—bitter; his comments on international politics were usually superficial. He took great pride in the fact that he had met, seen, and interviewed many of the statesmen of Western Europe. He looked at events purely from the standpoint of a spectator. In fact, in my random and irregular meetings with him—meetings which were generally accidental and unplanned —I could perceive that he was almost of the opinion that world events happened so that he as a journalist could write about them.

But it was clear that Jake had fared no better. He was getting fat and had become lazy. He was merely a Party writer, and his pieces were no different from most others appearing in the Party press, regardless of the subject. His work showed the same rigidity, the same adherence to formula, the same reliance on character assassination as did that of the other Party hacks. One could frequently take the beginning of an article by someone else, cut it in half, paste it to the conclusion of an article by Jake, and scarcely tell the difference between the two parts of the article. And then he wrote for *Mass Action*, which, while not officially a Party organ, was really Party controlled. In fact, Jake was the Party man on it, for a while, giving Party directions and responsible to the Party for what appeared in *Mass Action*.

At this time, I met him once on the street, accidentally, and he suggested that we have a cup of coffee. We sat in a cafeteria, and I asked Jake if he couldn't write better than he did.

"These dopes won't let me. But don't worry, I will," he said, and he launched into diatribes against many of his comrades.

"Have you seen Eddie, Jake?" I asked.

"There's a tragedy," Jake said, with a glint in his eye.

I waited for him to go on, and he did. Eddie had lost faith. He had sold out. He'd married a bourgeois wife, and she had helped ruin him. Because of her Eddie had bought on the Russian black market, practically taking commodities away from the Russian workers, who were building socialism. And then he hinted, but only hinted, that Eddie was really an agent for foreign governments which were hostile to the Soviet Union and even planning to invade it. When I asked him for proof of this, he said that he couldn't divulge his proof now, and then he let the cat out of the bag. He said that when I read Eddie's forthcoming book on the Soviet Union I would see in it the objective proof showing that Eddie had become an anti-Soviet agent.

From others I met from time to time, I learned that Jake was continually denouncing Eddie, and that he did him considerable harm; in fact, Jake really helped to stigmatize him. Eddie, though he was now merely a journalist, occasionally signed a petition and, as if in expiation of guilt, now and then gave a small contribution to some left-wing but non-Party or anti-Party group. And then Eddie's book came out, an account of his observations and experience in Russia, journalistic in tone, but containing facts we have since learned to know as definitely confirmable. Jake wrote a long and vicious attack on it, in which he went back to their old days as friends, distorted and garbled remembered remarks, even misquoting passages from the book. After this I learned that they didn't talk to one another.

Time passed. I saw neither of them. I occasionally heard about them or saw something one or the other had written. Jake—I could assume from his writings—had become merely a Party wheel horse. He became a kind of cultural godfather of the young writers the Party was attracting to itself. And yet when he was in his cups he spoke of Trotsky in the same old way, or so I was told. When the Moscow trials surprised the world, Eddie wrote analyses of them, denouncing them, and calling them frame-ups; in these articles there were flashing nostalgic traces of his lost idealism, his buried faith in socialist ideas. Jake answered these articles with a counter series in which he denounced Eddie as a Trotskyist, and even a fascist; and he couldn't find words strong enough to denounce his hero, Leon Trotsky.

Eddie was now a truly prominent journalist. He again went to Europe and became more personalized in his reporting, and at the same time wrote collective security, antifascist articles, even though he was bitterly anti-Stalinist. He returned to America for profitable lecture tours, preaching antifascism to ladies' clubs at high stipends. He had abandoned all traces of his college socialism. But now and then he did attack the Party.

Jake's position in the Party never seemed to change one way or the other. But, thanks to his many indiscretions when drinking, he was under suspicion. In due time, and to the general surprise of those aware of these matters, Jake was expelled from the Party and denounced in its press. Among the things that were said about him, the least insulting characterized him as a hack. He was also called a concealed Trotskyist, a concealed bourgeois, an enemy of the people. He wrote no defense of himself, nor did he make any other kind of statement. He began his career writing pretentious novels about the American past. Eddie likewise had taken to writing books regularly, and was a best-seller journalist with an international reputation, one of those of the new crop of journalists alleged to possess inside information about history. Just on the eve of the war, they were both on best-seller lists with current books.

Eddie, recognized as one of the journalistic prophets who had predicted everything, who had called for the antifascist war against Hitler and who had attacked the Munich agreement, was hired as a radio commentator. In no time he became one of the most popular, influential, and highly paid of the com-

mentators. And then, following the German invasion of the
Soviet Union, he changed his views, began to speak differently
of the Soviet Union, and, I heard, was seen with Stalinists and
fellow travelers in night clubs and elsewhere. His name suddenly appeared on the lists of "front" organizations, especially
in connection with sponsored and Party-organized swanky din-
ners. More and more, in his comments and writings, he explained
events in terms of the most favorable light he could cast on the
Soviet Union. And then, suddenly, and without the slightest
reference to past writings, he came out on the radio and made a
statement which in effect amounted to an acceptance of the
official version of the Moscow trials. The Party press exploited
this, and Eddie then flatly defended the official version of the
trials, again, of course, without explaining why he had previously denounced them. Known as a journalist with inside information, his defense of these trials influenced many people.

Jake wrote another novel which was well received, and he
spoke in bond-selling campaigns. He tried to convince people—
I learned—that he had never really been a Communist, or,
rather, a Stalinist.

They were both now in their late thirties, and they had
changed. Each was married for the second time. Each was fat
and successful. Jake was getting bald. Eddie's hair was turning
gray. He also had stomach ulcers. With the progress of the war,
they both came more and more into the public eye. They had
become rich and famous. They owned country houses in Con-
necticut. Jake—it was announced in the papers—was hired to
work in Hollywood at a very good salary and went out there;
in time his name appeared on pretentiously empty films
which were interpreted as revealing the new social consciousness
supposed to be developing in Hollywood. Eddie flew back and
forth to war capitals, to the war fronts, and in the midst of all
this he managed to write an autobiographical book which ended
with an account of himself as a war correspondent and which
became an immediate best seller. The movie columns announced
that it had been bought by a studio at a reported price of one
hundred thousand dollars. And soon after this I saw in some

column that Jake had been assigned to work on the treatment of Eddie's book. And then a note that Eddie was in Hollywood giving advice on the way the book should be made. In the book, of course, Eddie more or less apologetically explained away his college radicalism. And Jake was to take this and to make a film out of it, when Jake knew all about Eddie's views and attitudes in the old days. And then—a note in a gossip column that the two of them were seen together in the Brown Derby in Beverly Hills and elsewhere. And a publicity story about their being old friends.

The gossip columns announced that they were both present at the grand world premiere of the film in New York. The film, too, was a smash hit.

What did they say to each other? How did they sit down together and work out the film? I don't know. But eventually I saw the film, and it was a lie from beginning to end; it so glamorized Eddie that I felt almost ill as I saw it. And Jake's name was signed to it. Jake had written this. There was a touch of Eddie's earlier anti-Stalinism in the film, but it was presented by showing Eddie as the passing victim of a beautiful international spy, a girl vaguely supposed to have something to do with Trotskyism, also.

One day I ran into them. I was walking along Fifth Avenue, when I saw Eddie, and he said:

"Hello."

"Hello," I said.

He was nervous when I said I had seen the picture.

"We were damned fools in the old days," he said, and this was all he said.

And then Jake happened along. He was fat and bald. He and Eddie seemed embarrassed.

"Hello," Jake said.

"Hello," Eddie said.

"Where have you been of late?" asked Jake.

"I've been busy," Eddie replied.

"So have I," Jake said.

They stood there. They both seemed embarrassed. It was an

unpleasant scene. They were uncomfortable in each other's presence. They both knew they had co-operated in a money-making lie, and they were silent and awkward in their guilt. They shook hands, and each went his separate way, after they had vaguely agreed to get together sometime. I walked on. I doubt that they ever see each other. Eddie is still on the radio, and the book columns announce that Jake is writing another historical novel about America's democratic past. I often wonder, however, what really goes on in their minds when they are alone with themselves.

Young Convicts

THEY WERE THE CHILDREN of Slavic immigrants and lived in the manufacturing district around Thirty-fifth and Morgan. Their fathers worked in the factories located in the area. Their sisters, even before they started to bloom and lose their gawky pre-puberty figures, also joined the ranks of those who trooped to the factories at six and seven in the morning. At six, seven, eight o'clock, rain or shine, morning after morning, their fathers, mothers, older brothers, sisters, all became part of the long line plodding to work.

There were six kids in this gang. Tony, the eldest, was a boy of twelve, and Stanley, the youngest, was eight. They all liked candy. They liked to go to the movies, especially on Saturday afternoons, when the serial was shown. They liked serials and movies of that type best because there was danger and adventure, shooting, robbing, train wrecks, bandits, outlaws, Indians, Mexicans, battles. And they scarcely ever had money for candy or for movies.

But they liked candy and they liked movies. And they liked to do dangerous, brave things, to pull off stunts like those pulled off by the older fellows in the neighborhood. They wanted to fight and steal, and then brag about it, just as they heard their older brothers bragging. They could be heroes just like the older boys. And when they could steal, they could have money for candy and the movies.

Home to each of the kids in the gang was much the same. A wooden shack, one or two stories high, with an outside privy that smelled you out every time you wanted to take a leak. Three, four, five rooms, generally dirty, full of rags, papers, the smell of kerosene lamps. Dark bedrooms, old beds, dirty sheets, two, three, four, and five sleeping together in the same bed, and on cold nights there was always a fight for the blankets. A mother and a father who were generally over-tired from work, and from raising a family. And the mother and father didn't speak English. They were greenhorns. And once every week, two weeks, three weeks, the mother and father would get drunk. They would curse and fight, throwing things at one another, shouting, even brandishing knives and cutting one another up, until the police came with a paddy wagon. These kids' homes were alike.

They didn't like school very much. They didn't like their studies, and in the classroom they groaned, twisted, squirmed, itched, dreamed of high deeds like those of the movie heroes and villains in the Saturday-afternoon serials, like those of the older fellows, like those of Al Capone. In school, they waited for the end of class. They were afraid of their teachers, and they neither liked nor trusted them. The teachers, some of them young girls from good families who were waiting until they found a husband, did not like the bad boys much either. Sometimes, in the hallways, the kids would hear one teacher tell another that she wished she would be transferred to another school where there was a better class of pupils than these in-corrigible Polacks and Bohemians.

Often, they didn't learn their lessons. They bummed from school regularly, and went scavenging through vacant lots and streets, keeping their eyes peeled for the overworked truant officers. Or they went to the railroad yards with sacks and wagons for coal that was needed at home. In fact, they learned to steal in the railroad yards. The parents would send them out at night to get coal, and they'd go down to the yards and get it, one kid getting up in a car and throwing chunks down to the others. From the railroad yards they went to the stockyards, going over the fences and leaving with anything removable that could perhaps be sold. They stole everything they could, and finally stealing got to be a nightly occupation.

They knew about hold-ups. They knew that some of the older guys in the district had pulled off hold-ups, and that made them heroes. So they determined that they too would be heroes and pull hold-ups. That would get money for candy and movies. And they would be living like the heroes they saw in the movies. One night, Tony, the gang leader, picked out the Nation Oil filling station on Thirty-fifth Street. They played across the street from the station for two nights. They goofed about, ran, played tag by a closed factory, getting a line on what time the station closed and what time the cop on the beat passed by after it had closed. When they were sure of their time and their layout, they went to work. Young Stanley tossed a house brick through a side window. Tony then stood on a box, put his hand through the broken glass, and unlatched the window. He went in, followed by the others. The money was in the safe, and that could not be touched. So they tore the telephone box from the wall and scooted with it. They broke it open in a vacant lot and divided the nickels that were in it. The loot was three dollars, and, although it was to be divided evenly, Stanley was cheated out of a quarter.

Successful in their raid on the filling station, they made other raids. They robbed every filling station in the district, always running off with the telephone box, and they enjoyed the fruits of their robbery in candy, cigarettes, and movies. Tony liked it. He bossed his gang with an iron hand. Night after night he drove them in raid after raid. If they complained, he kicked them in the pants and slapped their faces. If they talked back to him, he cracked them. He saw himself as a young Al Capone. He dreamed of shootings, gang fights, submachine guns, robberies, money, automobiles, everything the gangsters had in the movies, everything Al Capone had in real life. And he always planned out the raids, instructing each kid in what he should do, going to the place in advance to get the lay of the land. He always had money and gave some of it away to younger kids, to girls whom he would try to bribe in order to get them alone with him in basements. He hung around the corners and the poolrooms late at night, watching the older fellows. He imitated them in walking, talking, gestures, held his cigarettes as they did, borrowed all their remarks. He pushed and pressed his gang constantly, always discovering new places to rob. One night they robbed a chain restaurant. Stanley threw a brick through the back window, and they entered and ran off with the cash in the till. Two nights later, they returned to the Nation Oil Company's filling station and again ran off with the telephone box full of nickels. This time they noticed that the attendant had gone home, leaving his safe open. In it, they saw bills, many of them, dollars and dollars, more money than they had ever seen before. They were so surprised by the sight of the money, so afraid, that they did not take it, satisfying themselves with only the small change in the safe. And on the night after this robbery they returned to the chain restaurant. They were caught by a watchman and a city policeman.

They were brought before Judge Katherine Henderson in the Juvenile Court; she was a woman jurist who was known beyond the city for her good work. The court was crowded with its usual array of young culprits and harassed, shamed parents. The boys had to wait their turn, and they sat with other boys, cowed and meek, and with their shabbily dressed immigrant parents. Nearly all those waiting to be tried were the children of working people, most of them of immigrants. Some were released, some placed on probation, some sentenced to the Juvenile Detention Home. Judge Henderson spoke crisply, hastily, perfunctorily, often in a scolding tone. She hurried through case after case, disposed of it, making instant decisions, bawling out parents, often telling immigrant fathers and mothers that they were responsible for the delinquent conduct of their children.

Judge Henderson just didn't have the time. The cases had to be disposed of. Tomorrow there would be the same number. The juvenile problem was insoluble. There was no settlement of it. The same boys were warned, but they were brought back.

Parents were warned, but they were helpless. There was nothing to do but rush through from case to case, let so many off, put so many on probation, send so many to the Detention Home. Day after day, this must go on. The law must be upheld. There was no time for her to delay, study, probe into the causes of these delinquencies. All she could do was reach out and try, and hope that a few boys would be rescued from crime, and a few girls from the life of a prostitute. That was what she did. Lectures, warnings, scoldings, questions, sentences. Next. Next. Next. All morning. Next. All afternoon. Next. Tomorrow. More. Next.

Tony and the gang were called up. The bailiff rounded them up and prodded them in the back, his language curt and sharp. He shoved them up to the bar of justice. Judge Henderson read the papers on the case, closed her lips as she read, nodded her gray head. She raised her brows. Her benign face showed worry. She seemed to be wondering and thinking. She looked down sharply at the six boys before her. Their heads dropped. They were afraid to look her in the eye, just as they feared looking teachers, or policemen, in the eye. Her gaze shifted. She stared at their parents, who stood silently behind the boys. She asked each of the boys what his name was. The first answered that he was Clement Comorosky. Where was his mother? He shook his head. Again she asked where his mother was. Again he shook his head. More stridently, she asked where his father and mother were. He said that both were working and could not come down. Stanley's mother then spoke in Polish. An interpreter was called, and she spoke to him. He told the judge that the woman had said that the father and mother of the Comorosky boy worked in a factory and were afraid to stay out because they were too poor, and needed the day's wages, and they were afraid that if they didn't report for work they might be laid off. Please, she would take their place.

"All right. Now, do you boys know what you did?" the judge asked.

None of them answered. They stood with averted eyes.

"Can any of you talk? Can you talk?" she asked, sweeping

her eyes from one to another, fixing them on Clement, who
was ten years old.

He nodded his head affirmatively.

"Do you know that it's a crime to break into other peoples'
homes and stores and to take things that don't belong to you?"

"I'm sorry . . . ma'am," Clement said.

"How long have you been doing this?"

"Just this time," Clement said.

She looked through the papers before her and called out
Stanley's name.

"You were here before, and I told you that I didn't want to
see you brought back. And why don't you go to school?"

He looked at her with large-eyed awe.

"Are your parents here?"

A small Slavic woman said that she was his mother; her face
was lined, and an old black shawl covered her head. The judge
asked her if she ever tried to keep her boy in at night. She shook
her head, and said that she tried, but that he went out anyway.
The judge looked down at Stanley, glowering.

"And what did you do?"

"Me? I thrun the brick through de window."

Many who heard him smiled. The judge continued to question them in a brusque manner which inspired fear. Their
answers came slowly. They were evasive. They did not understand all of her questions. She became more brusque. She seemed
annoyed. She listened, with increasing irritation, while the
watchman who caught the boys gave his testimony. Then the
gas station attendant testified that twice the station had been
broken into, and the telephone box had been ripped off the
wall on each occasion. The restaurant manager gave testimony
also.

"You boys have to learn that you can't go on breaking into
places and stealing money. That is not right, and it is not permitted. Do you hear me?"

Six heads nodded.

"Well, why did you do it?"

Her additional questions brought out the fact that Tony was

the leader and inspiration of the gang, that Stevie Lozminski was his lieutenant, and that the raids and burglaries had been committed under their direction. Both had been in the court before for truancy and burglary, and the truant officer testified that all her efforts to do anything that would keep them in the classroom, where they belonged, were fruitless. Their teachers and the principal of the school had turned in written reports describing them as incorrigible. The judge continued her brusque questioning, directing some of it at the parents, who stood in silent awe and fear. She lectured the parents about taking care of their offspring and insisted that the interpreter translate her remarks so that they would surely be understood. Tony, Stevie, and Clement were all sentenced to six months in the Juvenile Detention Home, and the others were put on probation. The mothers cried. They looked with bewildered grief at the judge, their pleading eyes almost like those of sick animals. The boys were pulled from their parents' arms and taken off. Two of the mothers cried.

The next case, that of a colored boy caught stealing, was called.

The mill of the court continued.

Pat McGee

I

IT WAS TOO EARLY FOR PAT TO LEAVE. He sat down in the parlor and opened an early edition of an afternoon paper. He was in a state of restless inner excitement. The old days were gone forever, and yet he wanted to bring them back. It was hard to accept what he knew, to accept the fact that he had passed his athletic prime. The time that had already passed somehow hurt him. He was still too young to be looking backward instead of forward. And these days he was always looking backward, wishing that he had the chance to relive the time of his life that was already gone. Sometimes, for a moment or so, he would believe that he was still living in the old days. He would believe this with ardor, and then he would remind himself that this wasn't so, and he would become gloomy. Yes, the fact that the old days were gone really hurt him.

This afternoon, when he'd made up his mind to go out to Jackson Park, he'd had this feeling about the past. But now it was lost again. He looked moodily at the paper, his mind vague. Turning to the sports pages, he read the football news. He wished that he'd gone to a big university instead of a small college. He might have been an all-American, just as he had been an all-Catholic-High-School football star. That was the biggest mistake of his life. Why had he been afraid of stiff competition, and why had he not thought more about his decision after graduating from high school? It was too late. The best years of his life were gone, and he was only twenty-five. Yes, only twenty-five, and yet he feared that his dreams were over. Now, reading the sports page, he winced.

He read news of the Catholic High School League, but it bored him. He couldn't really work up an interest in the names of kids he didn't know. Of course, he always wanted Mary Our Mother to win, because it was his alma mater. He wanted to see the name of Pat McGee on the sports page. Pat McGee was really a might-have-been, he sadly thought.

He put his paper down and nervously looked at his watch. It was only one-thirty. He wished it were time to go out to Jackson Park; he wondered what he'd do with himself until it was. He could go out, of course, and take a little drive in the park, but he didn't feel like it. Sometimes he liked to drive, merely to drive, to feel his hands on the wheel, to feel himself in control of the car and know that the car was moving because he was in control. Then all thoughts and worries left him. He'd drive aimlessly, looking straight ahead, knowing what he was doing, drawing power from the wheel of the moving automobile. Pleasant, dreamy thoughts would float through his mind, sweetly pleasing thoughts which he'd forget almost as soon as they came into his mind. And he had time to go to the agency and see if Chuck, the Sales Manager, had a prospect for him. But his heart wasn't in selling cars. He'd just sit around here and wait, and let the time pass.

He picked up the newspaper again and read the comics, his mind in a swoon. He wished each strip were longer. He finished with the comics, wishing it were already tomorrow, so he could read new comics. He put his paper down for the second time, rose, and turned on the radio. He listened to jazz music, his face softened by his sentimental thought.

Pat looked like an athlete. He was a clean-cut young man. He weighed one hundred and eighty-two pounds; he was solidly built, muscular, and hard as nails. His calves were thick; his shoulders were broad. His frame was powerful. His light hair was cropped short. His face was broad and genial. His eyes were light blue, eager, and friendly. His skin was fair, reddish. His hands were big, and several fingers on either hand were crooked. He seemed boyish and could have passed for a lad of twenty-one.

At five minutes to two Pat jumped up. He shook his head and blinked his eyes. After listening to the jazz music, he felt just as he often did when waking up after a nap. He got his hat and topcoat, called to his mother in the kitchen that he was leaving, and went out of the apartment. He got into the model Studebaker which belonged to the agency. He stepped on the starter and the car moved away from the curb. That feeling of power came back to him, a feeling of power that was second only to the old thrills he had known in athletics. He drove across the Illinois Central tracks at Seventy-first Street and then on toward Jackson Park. He remembered how, when he was in high school, he'd ridden to school on the Sixty-third Street car, with his lunch and books under his arm. Usually he'd daydream about the next baseball or basketball or football game in which he'd play. And how often hadn't he imagined himself in later life going back around the school just as he was doing today? Yes, today he was doing exactly what he had dreamed of doing back in his high-school days. But his life had not turned out the way he had thought it would.

Next year he'd come back. He tried to convince himself that he would come back, but he had no real confidence in himself. Still, when the kids now at M. O. M. saw him, knew who he was and what he'd done, they'd look at him with respect. He might give Jim McBride a hand with the coaching. Jim was a fine man, and had made him what he was. No, he was a born athlete. But Jim had helped him, taken him in hand as a freshman and taught him. Jim had seen what his possibilities were. He'd developed into an all-Catholic fullback under Jim, and they'd almost won the championship in his senior year.

That seemed to be only yesterday. But it was now seven years ago.

The thought of time having passed this way saddened him. It was, damn it, it was hard to believe that all this had happened seven years ago.

Gosh, he'd be glad to see Jim and to see the kids practicing. Maybe he'd see one of the lads from the old days who might just be coming around as he was. Perhaps he'd see Tom Moss.

Good old Tom. He and Tom had been thick in school. They'd been the two stars. Tom was a regular fellow. Even though his folks were rich, he'd never acted like a snob. He'd been decent and quiet, and damned handsome with his wavy hair. But Tom hadn't ever futzed around like Marty Mulligan, Tim Doolan, O'Neill, and that crowd when they were in school and the star athletes. His crowd had gone farther in sports than they had. His crowd had been much better than their crowd. Think of it, O'Neill used to get the call on him at end. But O'Neill and Tim and Marty had been good. They'd started the pigskin rolling at school, and they could have made the team the year he and Tom and the rest of the boys had almost brought the title to M. O. M. The team in his senior year had been the first of the many really crack teams the school had started turning out. When these new kids saw him, they'd think of this and look at him with awe. He'd feel good. And it would be good to see old Tom or some of his other comrades of those days. It would be great, all right. It would make him feel swell.

His mood became buoyant. He decided that Pat McGee was no mere might-have-been. Yes, he would come back. He was going to lower a bucket into the past, and it was the past that was the best part of his life. High school—high school with Pat McGee a reigning star in Chicago high-school circles. He had been able to do everything in sports, and the future had been bright while the present had been fun. It had been great, wonderful fun to play—to pitch, play basketball, trot out there on the gridiron—to do all this and feel as sure of yourself as he used to feel. He was going back to all this, going back to a day in the past.

He swung the car into Jackson Park at Sixty-seventh and Stony Island.

II

Pat parked his car near the football field in Jackson Park, got out, and walked to the gridiron. It was located on a rectangular strip of ground, running parallel to Stony Island from which it was separated by bushes and a picket fence. Seeing the old field once again, it was just as familiar as it used to be. It hadn't been changed. He thrilled for a moment, and in elation told himself that he couldn't change, either. But he had changed. Still, it was mighty good to come out here and see the good old field. He knew every spot on it. He gazed lovingly at the bushes across the field. A sense of the old days overwhelmed him. He remembered himself in odd moments of the past, looking up at the sky, the bushes, and he recalled how sometimes the laps around the field would be so long that he'd think them endless, and, jogging along with tired muscles, with a charley horse, he'd try to think of something that would take his mind off the distance still to be run. But he had never been able to sidetrack his thoughts, and he would jog slowly and dully, wishing it were the last lap. Those days couldn't be gone. One couldn't lose them. And yet they were lost.

He looked at his watch. It was twenty to three. The squad was not out yet. He stood by himself, gazing about. He was alone with the old days. The field became vaguely peopled with Tom and the other boys of those days.

—It's the same old field, he told himself, moved.

Noticing some park loafers shooting craps, he strolled over to watch them. He was bored, and he turned back and again stood at the edge of the field. He wanted to go out and run the length of it, from goal post to goal post. He imagined himself as he used to run, going like a power house, knees hitting high, head low, his full hard body crashing and smashing forward. Running with the ball, smashing through a hole in the line and breaking out into the open, that had been his biggest football thrill. And he'd gone sixty-five yards like that for a touchdown against St. Rose's in his junior year.

A fellow didn't know how wonderful, how valuable those days were to him until they were all over. He shook his head from side to side, sadly and wistfully. There was a far-off look in his light blue eyes.

III

Pat watched the squad come out. They arrived in groups. Soon there were about thirty-five kids on the field, passing and kicking and running about. They didn't know that one of their alma mater's greatest of the great was watching them. The kids seemed so young. It was hard for him to think of himself as having been as they now were. He could remember the feelings, but not how he might have looked as a high-school freshman, raw and green and young, weighing only one hundred and thirty-five pounds. He watched a lean, tall kid show off by catching passes spectacularly. He had never shown off. But then, he hadn't needed to. Even when he had had a rotten season in his second year, he had always had that confidence in himself. He'd known that he didn't have to show off. He was a natural-born athlete. In football, in baseball, it had been the same. He had always got the hang of things quickly.

He turned and looked at the playground next to the field. On the path running around it, Jim would be appearing any minute, striding along with that burly walk of his. Good old Jim. Gosh, he'd be glad to see Jim. Good old Jim. He owed a lot to Jim. Jim had taught him a lot.

He moved closer to the practicing kids. A skinny lad muffed a ball thrown to him, and a husky redheaded kid razzed him. In his day, it had been just like that.

The skinny kid missed a second pass.

"Better put a catcher's mask on," the redhead yelled at him.

"Skinny, if you sell yourself to a farmer, you'll make dough with all the butter you got in your mitts," another player called, and Pat smiled.

"This is only practice," the skinny player retorted.

"Practice in muffing makes perfect," the redhead shot back.

Yes, just like the old days. These kids were the same as he and his comrades had been. These kids didn't know how lucky they were to be living through the best days of their lives at this very moment.

And there was Jim, rolling like a barrel toward his squad, good old Jim. He was heavier, must weigh about two twenty-five now. The same red, smiling face. Pat drew back a few feet and waited. He wanted to surprise Jim.

"All right, hep into it, everybody," Jim called in the same old barking voice that masked his kindness.

The squad quickly ringed around Jim. Pat watched but he couldn't hear what was said. But he could guess. Jim must be telling them to line up for scrimmage, giving the names of each squad, telling them to shake the lead out of their tails.

He saw a lone football left in midfield.

Several squads lined up. Jim barked at them in the same old way. Pat watched, waited, a sheepish smile on his face. He saw that Jim used the same unbalanced line formation, a variation on the Minnesota shift, that he had in the old days. He approached Jim. A little quarterback barked signals, and the boys ran off an old, familiar play. Jim snapped at them to pep it up.

Pat was deeply excited, but said nothing and went closer to Jim. Jim's face lit up.

"Why, hello, Pat, how are you?"

They shook hands. Jim's hand was bigger than his, and he still had a grip in it.

"You look in shape, Pat," Jim said, giving Pat the once over.

"Oh, I am," Pat said, smiling sheepishly. "You look swell, Jim."

"I feel good, but I'm gettin' old now, Pat," Jim said.

"All right, hep it up, you fellows," he barked.

"Same old Jim," Pat said.

Jim smiled that embarrassed smile he had always shown when one of the kids spoke this way to him. He was watching his squad out of the corner of his eye.

"Lead out of the tail, Sheehan," he bawled. He turned and asked, "What are you doing with yourself, Pat?"

"Oh, I'm selling automobiles."

He noticed the surprise on Jim's face.

"Last month I pitched a few semi-pro games for twenty bucks a game. I think my arm's coming back," Pat said.

"Why—what happened?" asked Jim, a look of surprise on his rough face.

"Didn't you know? I threw my arm out in mid-season at Terre Haute and had to give up. But I'm coming back."

"Say, I'm sorry to hear that. I didn't know it. I'm sorry. What happened? Bursitis?"

"I'm not sure. My arm just went dead on me. One day I just found out that I had a dead arm. But it's coming back. I'll be all right next year," Pat said, trying to sound both casual and convincing.

"You won't be back at Terre Haute?"

Pat shook his head.

"I got my unconditional release. But I think I might manage a tryout with one of the big league teams."

"I hope you do. I always had faith in your ability. Pat, you're a natural-born athlete," Jim said.

The words were soothing to Pat, yet at the same time they didn't really convince him.

He was worried about his dead arm, and, at this moment, a feeling of utter depression came over him. He looked off at the squad running through signals up and down the field, feigning interest. He didn't want accidentally to reveal his depressed spirits to Jim.

"I'm glad I saw you. I had you in mind, Pat. Would you like to play some Sunday games, or aren't you playing any more football?"

"I haven't lined anything up, but I'm in good condition. I'd like to. I'd like the feel of hitting the line again. You know, Jim, once you get it in your blood, you don't lose it," Pat said, while thinking that he could use the money because he wasn't so hot as an automobile salesman, and, with the depression on, how could you be a hot-shot salesman?

Jim's face softened with sympathy and nostalgia. He nodded his head understandingly. Pat sensed how Jim felt. Jim loved the game, too, and had played pro football. But he was too old now. He had never gone as far as Jim, never reached the National Professional Football League. Jim had been a halfback and had played with Paddy Driscoll and against Thorpe, Fritz Pollard, and Red Grange. How he would have liked to have done that, and have brought Thorpe, Pollard, or Grange down in the open field.

"Yes, Pat, I know how it is. Tell me, do you still live at the same place?" asked Jim.

"Yes."

"I'll have this Pullman team get in touch with you. I'm glad I saw you, because I was thinking of you, Pat." Jim smiled wistfully, a smile almost too soft with emotion and friendliness for a man as powerfully built as Jim was. "I miss playing," Jim shyly added.

Then he turned and barked through his hands:

"Hep into it, you fellows. Where's all your ginger?"

Pat tagged along, watching the first strong team snap through signal practice. He recalled that game in fourth year when Loyola had beaten them 7 to 0 and won the title. In the fourth quarter they'd carried the ball to Loyola's eight-yard line. Goal to go, four downs, with a tie for the title at stake. And Morrissey at quarter had called his signal. He'd plunged for about three yards. He'd lined up, confident. His signal was called again, and he'd been so confident that he'd turn the trick. He'd bent down, hands on knees, and decided to dive over the line. But they'd knocked him back a yard. And still he'd been confident. He could do everything in football, and he had determined to do this, but he'd failed. He'd cried after the game, and now he recalled this failure, regretted it, recalled his four plunges to the two-yard line, now imagining himself having made that touchdown. He was sad. He daydreamed that he had made that touchdown by diving over the Loyola line and over the goal line for the touchdown.

IV

Kavanaugh didn't look much changed. But he seemed to be down on his luck. Pat sensed that Al Kavanaugh somehow felt as he did. Things weren't going right for Al. He had been a good end, but hadn't made Notre Dame.

"I thought I'd come out and look at the team. Remember how we used to come out just like these kids every day?" Pat said.

"I wish we were still doing it, Pat."

"I'd give anything if we were," Pat said.

"Cigarette?" Al asked, extending a pack.

Pat shook his head.

"I tried smoking for a while but I gave it up. I can keep in condition easier if I don't smoke. And I'm gonna get myself in good condition this winter. I'm coming back next year. I'm getting back in the game. I'm ready to go up to the big leagues after I get a few games under my belt."

"I'm sure you are. Pat, you're still the greatest athlete M. O. M. ever turned out."

Pat was gratified but thought that while this was possibly true, look where he was! A dead arm. Only able to play semi-pro football.

"What happened to you last year?" Al asked sympathetically.

"I had a bad year. My arm just went back on me. The soup went out of it, and I couldn't pitch. I had to come home. But my arm's getting stronger every day," Pat said.

Longing to be pitching, he went through a pitching motion. As he did, he was gripped with a sudden fear and, instead of the loose, easy motion he intended to make, it was a stiff and un-natural motion, the one he had developed when the pains had first hit him last summer. He winced, thinking that his lame arm had snapped his self-confidence, and he asked himself could he really come back? He looked off at the leafless trees and then up at the gray sky. He watched the kids scrimmaging on the field. They had dreams like his. They didn't know, didn't know what could happen to you.

"Yes, I'm coming back. I pitched a couple of semi-pro games last month and won them."

"Swell, swell. You got what it takes, Pat. We always knew

you had, and so did Jim," Al said, but Pat remembered how he had merely lobbed the ball up in those semi-pro games and had won because of the inexperienced players against whom he was pitching.

"Two years ago I had a good year. And last summer I won sixteen and lost fifteen with a sixth place team, and then, the souper went dead."

"Keep a stiff upper lip, Pat. The good old M. O. M. spirit, and you'll be up there," Al said.

They stood there.

"Seen Tom?" asked Pat.

"I don't see him much. I don't know. I just don't see him," Al said meaningfully.

"Did anything happen between you?" Pat asked, curious about Al's tone of voice.

"No, not at all," Al said, but Pat sensed that something had happened between Tom and Al: they'd been such good friends.

Out on the field, Jim was barking out instructions to two scrimmaging squads.

v

"Hello, Pat," Tom Moss said blandly.

Pat saw that Tom was as handsome as ever. But he was a bit heavy and looked a little soft. He had jowls and, because of his added weight, he wasn't the same good-looking lad he used to be. Moreover, there was an aloofness in the way Tom had said hello.

They stood there facing each other. Pat had been so glad when he'd seen Tom coming along, and now Tom was standing there not saying much. And they had had so much in common in the old days. Was it that Tom looked down on him because Tom had gone to N. D. and been a star in some games and a brilliant second-string man on one of Rockne's undefeated teams?

Tom stood there, looking around with a smirk on his face and an air of condescension. Pat was afraid that it wasn't the same old Tom. His desire for the return of the old days became so painful emotionally that he looked off, unable to control the hurt expression on his face.

"What are you doing?" Pat finally asked him.

Tom acted as if he hadn't heard. After about a minute of silence, he said:

"I'm representing Stebbins and McCreary."

Tom handed Pat an engraved card with his name in the corner and the words *Sales Representative* after it.

"Are you selling bonds?" asked Pat.

The thud of a football being punted echoed across the field.

"Paint materials," Tom said.

Pat realized that it wasn't the same old Tom, and in his present mood this distressed him. He was ill at ease.

Tom said nothing for a moment, and then, with that same note of condescension in his voice, he asked:

"Are you doing anything, Pat?"

"Oh, I'm selling cars, but I'll be back in baseball next year. I'm going to do some semi-pro playing with an eleven out in Pullman, too. I love the old game same as ever, Tom," Pat said, hoping this would restore their bond of high-school days.

"Oh," said Tom.

"Are you going to play any more football, Tom?" asked Pat, regretting now that he hadn't been able to go to N. D. as Tom had.

"No, I wouldn't be a professional athlete. It makes a bum of you," Tom said cuttingly.

He turned, offered a limp hand to Pat, and said:

"Well, old man, it was good seeing you."

He pumped Pat's hand and slouched off. Pat was so bewildered that he didn't get angry until Tom was almost out of sight. But even then he wasn't really angry. He shook his head sadly. He couldn't understand how Tom could have changed so. Tom had practically said that he was a bum and had cut him. He shook a bewildered head, and there was a stupefied expression on his face.

VI

It was dark out. He was driving home through the park. He didn't have that feeling of power with his hands on the wheel. This darkness—he used to return to the showers in such darkness. And all that was gone. Tom was so changed. Tom thought he was a bum, had cut him, insulted him. And the kids hadn't known him. Jim had been friendly but busy. Good old Jim. He had not got the joy and thrill that he'd hoped to get out of this afternoon. They forget you. He, the greatest athlete ever turned out by M. O. M., was forgotten. He was forgotten in the Three Eye League, too.

He drove on, bewildered. He tried to tell himself that he was coming back, but he had no confidence. He was Forgotten Dead-Arm Pat McGee. He sensed that at twenty-five the best years of his life were over, gone with those days that he couldn't bring back by visiting the old scene in Jackson Park.

He drove out of the Park at Sixty-seventh Street. The lights of the street seemed warm and friendly. He drove on.

He shook his head, still bewildered. He didn't know why he had such tough luck. He had never done anything to merit the bad breaks. Again he shook his head in bewilderment. He drove on home for his dinner.

Lunch Hour: 1923

―――――――――――――――

MY SWEETIE *went away, but she didn't say where, she didn't say when, didn't say why,*
   Or bid me good-by . . .

Tom Finnegan and Al Bates rushed into the song shop on West Monroe Street. It was a large store. The floor was of tile, and silver dollars were embedded in it in a regular pattern. On the right of the entrance there were counters, and on the left-hand side, directly down from the doorway, there was a glass case. In the back, there were several glassed-in booths with victrolas and chairs inside them.

"Rain'n', all right," Al Bates said.

Tom nodded.

The female song plugger, a blonde with a slightly bloated face, sang to the crowd in a cracked falsetto.

I know she loves another, but she didn't say who, she didn't say which, she didn't say what her papa has got—that took my sweetie from me.

"Keen, all right," Al said.

Tom nodded. He looked around at the crowd of youths like himself, and at the girls, cake-eaters and flappers who came here almost every lunch hour to listen to the new songs. They were all about the store, singly and in groups, and some of them swayed and kept time to the songs by swinging their shoulders or tapping their feet in fast rhythms.

"I'd like to have all of them on the floor," Al said, pointing at one of the silver dollars.

I know that I'll die—Why don't she hurry back home . . .

Al mumbled the first lines of the song, *My Sweetie Went Away*, and then he said:

"Keen."

Tom, medium-sized, blond, good-looking, gazed around to see if he might spot anyone he knew, or else try and catch the eye of a girl.

"Nice mamas come here," Al said.

"Uh yeah," Tom answered. "If I had dough, though, I wouldn't be coming here."

"That's why I said I wish I had the dollars in the floor, and more of the same," Al said.

The proprietor sang in a broken-voiced tenor.

> *You're the kind of a girl that men forget,*
> *Just a toy to enjoy for a while . . .*

"Sad song," Al said.

His eyes roved here and there and fastened on a thin blonde girl in a raccoon coat. She stood by herself, her face betraying a sentimental absorption in the singer.

"You'd get a lot of mamas if you owned a shop like this," Al said.

> *And you'll soon realize you're not so wise . . .*

"I like the blonde mama in the raccoon coat," Al said.

"Me, too," Tom said.

When they play Here Comes the Bride, you'll stand outside
Just a girl that men forget . . .

Young people came and left continually, and there was a constant noise of shuffling feet. Three cake-eaters lounged by the glass case a foot or so away from Tom and Al and surveyed the scene with an air of sophisticated superiority. Al and Tom looked at them. They were better dressed than Al and Tom, taller, and better built.

"Those cakes are dressed collegiate. Keen. Hot," Al said.

"Uh huh!" Tom exclaimed.

They wore long, loose, beltless coats, and their black hats slanted devilishly over their foreheads. Their shirts looked brand new, and they had on colorful ties. They wore new tan brogans, also.

Tom looked outside. He was not so well dressed. It was raining out, and his clothes were damp and had lost their press. He looked back a bit enviously at the three cakes.

No, no, Nora, nobody but you, dear . . .

Many in the crowd shuffled their feet. Patent-leather toes wiggled, slid on the floor. Bell bottoms flounced, and hips and shoulders swung and swayed.

And would I trade you for kisses?

"Ah, boy. Keen," Al said.

A blond youth began moving and dancing back and forth in a radius of about two square feet, doing what seemed like a combination of the 'frisco and a cake walk, sticking out plump buttocks now and then, shaking and wiggling them, holding his chest erect, his face clouding with an expression of intense absorption in himself and his movements. He snapped his fingers, bent, squatted, rose, swayed, and toe-danced, while others clapped and cheered, and swayed their shoulders in rhythm with him.

"Ummm," exclaimed Al.

No, no, Nora, no, no!

Then there was a bustle of conversation in the store. A girl's giggle rose above the talk. Al and Tom looked outside. It was still raining.

A lad of about seventeen with full, round, red cheeks was

flirting with the girl who had giggled. He wore a blue herring-
bone suit with wide bell bottoms, a belted overcoat, and a
brown felt hat with its crown squared. The girl who had giggled was talking with him and smiled. He noticed Al and Tom.

"Hi!" he exclaimed.

"Hi!" exclaimed Al.

"Hi!" exclaimed Tom.

"Like it?" he asked.

"Nice," Al said.

"Yeh," Tom said.

"Nice mamas here," he said.

"I'll say they are!" Al said.

"The cat's," Tom said.

Tom watched a baby-doll blonde with avid eyes.

"Like her?" asked Al.

"Yeh."

"I'd like to make her on the back porch," Al said.

"I'd like to make her any place, back porch, front porch,
park, on a raft, any place."

"Nice," Al said.

Yes, we have no bananas . . .

Al looked around greedily. Tom rubbed his hand over the
down on his upper lip. He gazed down at the frayed cuff on
his bell-bottom trousers.

"I know that one," he said, nodding in the direction of a
brunette.

"Yeh?"

"Her name is Peggy," Tom said.

"Nice. Peg of my heart," Al said.

"I'd let her be the peg of my heart," Tom said.

> *Monday night, I sat alone,*
> *Tuesday night, you didn't phone,*
> *Wednesday night, you didn't call . . .*

A tall lad, of athletic build, wearing a yellow slicker, was
talking to the girl named Peggy. Tom frowned at him. The lad

took off his gray fedora and held it ostentatiously, exposing his blond, wavy hair.

"Handsome brute," Al said.

"Vain. He gets his hair curled," Tom said.

"Maybe she's the peg of his heart?" Al said.

"He looks like a bum halfback to me," Tom said.

"More like a parlor athlete to me," Al said.

But you brought three girls for companee . . .

Al swung into the rhythm of the song, snapped his fingers, twirled his feet, shook his shoulders. Others did likewise, and soon the store was full of shuffling, swaying, dancing, 'friscoing boys and girls, while an infant-faced songplugger sang with a whine in her voice, and the piano jingled. Eyes met eyes, and smiles were exchanged. With ecstasy and desire shining in his eyes and on his face, Al tapped on the floor and shook. Tom was caught up in the rhythm, and he imitated Al. As he did so, his eyes met those of the girl named Peggy. She smiled at him. He smiled back.

The music stopped. Peggy left the lad in the slicker and came toward Tom and Al. She smiled.

"You don't remember me," she said.

"Peggy, of course I do."

"Do you come here often?" she asked.

"No, I came today because of the rain."

"So did I."

"Yes, it's rainin' out," Al said.

"Say, I'm glad I saw you. How about a date on Saturday night? Saves me the nickel for phoning," Tom said.

"Use a slug," Al said.

"Why, all right, I'm not doing anything," she said.

"Suppose I call at eight-thirty?"

"Okay."

"Oh, excuse me. Peggy Shanahan, this is Al Bates. He works in my office."

"How do you do," she said.

"I do do do doodle de do," Al said.

"I have to dash, but I'll see you Saturday night then, Tom?"

"Be ready 'bout half-past eight," Al sing-songed.

"All right. We'll go dancing," Tom said.

"I'd like that. And I'm glad to have met you, Mr. Bates," she said, and she walked out.

They looked after her, eyeing her slender, young figure.

"Keen. A neat mama you copped off."

"Yes, she'll pass in a crowd."

"Ever take her out before?"

"No, but I've been thinking of trying to date her. She's a decent girl, but a good dancer, and she's good fun."

"Neat, neat and a hot mama."

"She's pretty," Tom said.

"Yeh. Keen."

"She graduated last June from Saint Paul's," Tom bragged.

"Does she rate?"

"Yes, she rates. That's why I dated her."

"So, she rates?" asked Al.

"Yes, she rates," Tom said proudly.

A look of weariness came over the round face of a girl near them, and she exclaimed to another girl:

"If I dance tonight, I'll die-e."

"But, dearie, Jack and Pete are going to be at the Gardens tonight, and you know they're simply divine."

"So are we," Al said.

"What?"

"Divine," Al said.

"What an old line you got," the first girl said.

"Da-dad-dad-da-da deedee da da . . ." Al sang at the girl.

"You sing worse," the second girl said.

"But you don't know what I can do," Al said.

"I don't want to," the first girl said, turning her back on him.

"Tramps," Al said.

"Polacks," Tom said.

"Smarties," Al said.

"You know, Peggy, now—she's different," Tom said.

They heard thunder outside, and some of the lads and girls hurried in, laughing.

"I'm going dancing tonight. Keen. Come along," Al said.

"No, I'll have to save my pennies for Saturday night's date. She rates. I'll have to take her in cabs," Tom said.

"Too bad. It's going to be keen," Al said.

"I'll get enough dancing Saturday night," Tom said boastfully.

"Is that all?"

"She's decent and rates."

"Can't she kiss?"

"Well, I'm not sayin'," Tom said.

"Let's go in and play some records," Al suggested.

They went into an empty booth. Al put a hot jazz piece on the victrola. Tom sat on the couch. His face was thoughtful.

"Thinking of Peggy?" asked Al.

"I'm not sayin'," Tom said.

"She looks worth thinkin' about," Al said.

The music was very fast, and they tapped their feet on the floor.

"Makes you wish you had a piece on the back porch," Al said.

"Or any place," Tom said.

"Hot," Al exclaimed enthusiastically, as a cornet wah-wahed.

Al got up and danced, shaking his abdomen and making eyes at the glass.

"Daddadada," he sing-songed.

He paused, looked at Tom, and said:

"Whoops, Finnegan, where's your pep?"

"I'll save it for Peggy."

"I think you're gone on her already," Al said.

"She rates," Tom said.

Al danced, shook his buttocks, and mumbled to the wild, burning jazz.

"Ummmmmm," he exclaimed as the cornet again wah-wahed.

He stuck his tongue out, slobbered it across his lower lip, and made slobbering noises with his tongue by forcing saliva against the membranes of his mouth. Tom swayed his shoulders and tapped his feet to the music.

The record ended.

"Say, we got to dash or we'll be late," Al said.

"Yeh," Tom said.

They left the booth. The store was still crowded.

My wonderful one . . .

"She's singing about your Peggy," Al said.

"I wish she was mine," Tom said, moodily.

"Maybe she will be. Don't give up the ship," Al said.

"I wish it was Saturday night," Tom said.

"We'll have to run," Al said.

"The damned rain, too," Tom said.

They lit out east on Monroe Street, running in and out among people with umbrellas.

Winded, they entered the building where they worked.

"Well, you achieved something on your lunch hour," Al said.

My wonderful one, whenever I'm dreaming love's love-light, I'm dreaming of you.

"Yes, you're singing about her already," Al said.

"You'd sing, too, if you had a date with her. She rates," Tom said.

They entered the elevator and were whisked up to their office.

Called on the Carpet

I

WADE NORRIS, Patsy McLaughlin's chief clerk, left a letter before Collins, at Willie's end of the call board. Willie read it eagerly, while Wade went down to chat with Heinie Mueller at the other end of the board. There was a lull in the office.

"Hey, Wade what's this?" Willie called anxiously.

"Why it's a committee appointed by Mr. Minton, the new vice-president of the Chicago district, to investigate overtime. The company has appointed a new efficiency expert, and he's studying the whole works. He's going through every department. He is chairman of this committee, and they're going to be working on overtime very soon. Every man in the wagon supervision will be called on to explain why his men are drawing overtime."

"When my men draw overtime," Willie said loudly, pompously, and at the same time defensively, "it's because it's necessary. I watch the overtime like a hawk, you know. You can ask Casey here or look at my records. If any of my chauffeurs get overtime, it's something that's necessary, absolutely."

"I know that, Willie," Wade said reassuringly. "This is something they got cooked up over at main office, and we just got to comply with it. That's all." Wade shrugged his shoulders. "Willie, I don't think anything will come of it."

"Well, I ain't afraid. My expressmanship and record stand for themselves," said Willie.

"I don't believe that anything will come of it," Wade repeated, leaving the office.

"Listen O'Neill," Willie said, "I want you to watch them overtime sheets and let me see the sheet of every driver who gets more than an hour's overtime. There's a big rumpus about it, and I'm getting called on the carpet. Now you watch them."

Danny O'Neill nodded.

"Efficiency expert. Huh. What does a bastard like that know about the express game, huh? Tell me," Collins said to Casey, across from him.

"You know the way it is. Them guys over there have to cook up something to keep themselves busy," Casey said.

"They'll get you, Willie. You won't sound so much like the Chief when they get through with you," McGinty called over from his tractor board.

"Yeah. You think you're wise. Well, they ain't got nothing on me, and they won't. I'll just show them my record, and it will shine for itself," shouted Willie.

"Mr. Collins, here's Pick, regular man for Michelson. He's got a call he can't handle," yelled Stratton, the clerk from the other end of the tables.

"What's he got?"

"Six cases."

"Why can't he handle six cases?"

"He says they're too heavy, and he has regular calls to make."

"Tell him he's got to make it."

"He says he can't."

"Well, I can't either."

"Well, what about it?"

"Tell him to go ahead and make it."

"I did, and he said he can't."

"All right, take the call and give it to Michelson. Mark down on it what he says, and let Michelson handle it. I can't. I'm not going to get called on the carpet to answer for them route inspectors." Willie turned to Casey. "If they think I'm going to be their goat, they got another guess comin' to them."

After a rush of calls, Willie sat back in his chair and bandied back and forth in order to seem calm and unruffled. He shouted,

"Jesus Christ, them wise guys over there. Calling me on the carpet. Well, let 'em. I'll answer for my expressmanship."

He leaned back in his chair. He puffed on his cigarette, trying to calm his attack of worry.

Goddamn it, this was a wise idea! An efficiency expert! Efficiency expert! Yeah, efficiency expert! How did they expect the calls to be made? The company wanted business, all it could get. Well, how did the efficiency expert expect to get it? If the calls came in, they had to be made. If they weren't made, he'd damn soon be hearing from the main office. Goddamn soon. But then, when you did get the calls, you had to go over to the main office to answer damn fool questions about overtime.

He was the best man that Patsy McLaughlin had ever had dispatching up on the board. They couldn't take the ace out of there. If they did, they wouldn't have to take long to find out that they were up the creek. He had done his work to the very best of his ability. You could not ask a man to do more. He could not have done one thing better than he had done it. What did they want him to do? Go out on a truck and see that the men didn't stall? He couldn't watch them all even that way. He couldn't be every place at the same time. What did they expect of him?

The world was always against a good man. When you were too good, they were just jealous bastards, because they knew they weren't as good as you were. Take those route inspectors, all trying to keep piling their work on him. He shook his head and tightened his fists with stern determination. He would go over there. He would go on the carpet and lay his cards right down on the table, flush up, every one of them. He would go with his records and show them!

But suppose they didn't understand him? What did the efficiency experts and the damned muckety-mucks know about expressmanship?

He was so nervous and anxious that he rose and went out to the lavatory to calm himself.

II

Willie sat at home, thinking.

"You look tired," his huge wife said.

"I am. What do you think I do all day, play? I have a job with responsibilities."

"Maybe you'd like to go to a show with me."

"No," he snapped.

"See here now. Don't you talk like that to me. I shan't have none of it. Not a word more out of you," she said like a Brunhilde.

He looked at her like a spoiled and saddened little boy. He complained, "Well, gee whizz, gee! I work hard all day. Can't I have a little peace? You don't know how hard I work or what responsibilities I have, with no one to give me a helping hand. I got to fight all day with the public, and with all them route inspectors and dispatchers. It's fierce."

"I know it is. I know you work, and I only suggested you going to a movie to calm yourself and to forget," she said, patting his head maternally.

He slumped in his chair, nervously restless.

III

Willie knelt upright in the front of St. Peter's Church for the noonday Lenten Mass. He prayed with his hands posed solemnly. Now and then, as he prayed, he was filled with pride and self-righteousness. Anybody seeing him pray would know that here was a man who knew how to pray. He looked at the priest on the altar, clad in purple vestments. He lifted his head to the high ceiling. God was above there, and God was looking down with pleasure at Willie Collins, because Willie Collins served God. It wasn't everbody who would come to the noon-day Lenten services.

Willie prayed to God to help him get out of this overtime mess, to give him strength and fortitude to pull through it with colors flying as he deserved. He prayed that God would give him justice. He wanted that, no more. He wanted justice because his record was clean, as his life was. He did his work well, and he supported his family, and contributed to the support of his pastor, and performed all his religious obligations. He was making the nine first Fridays and attending Mass every day in Lent. He was acting as a good man should. He knew that God would not forget or forsake him, and that He would see that justice was given unto him, and that he would not lose his job or be transferred because of this new efficiency expert.

Willie lowered his head and stroked his breast in a *mea culpa* to the sound of the *Sanctus* bell. . . .

He liked the quiet, too, in the church, the hush, which was pleasingly interrupted by the priest's prayers. Outside the church was the rattle of traffic, noises that now seemed part of another world.

When the collection was taken up, Willie magnificently put a quarter on the plate. He hoped the fellow would remember him. He even felt that he'd like to help by taking up the collection during the Mass. But he guessed parish men did that.

He looked piously at the altar of God who would not, no, never, forsake Willie Collins, and he went on praying. His thoughts twisted and squirmed back to the overtime investigation. He imagined himself before the committee, and thought of what he would say to the committee members and this new efficiency expert. He made a dazzling impression on them all. He knocked them dead with his figures. He showed them he was a businessman. He showed them his record was clean. He showed them he was an ace. He showed them he knew his business. He showed that he was their equal and even their superior. They had no comeback.

Willie looked at the altar and prayed.

IV

After supper, Willie sat in the dining room, with his papers before him, studying the figures on overtime and the record of calls that Danny O'Neill had prepared for him. He was going to have everything down in black and white.

His ten-year-old son started to sing.

"Get out of here," Willie snarled.

"Tommy, your father is busy," Mrs. Collins said, looking up from darning her husband's socks.

"Keep them out of here. This is important. I got to know everything and have it in black and white tomorrow for them wise men and efficiency experts."

He looked at his papers. Suddenly, he glanced up and remarked, "You better go in and light the kerosene lamps. There's no use in wasting electricity. It costs money. They're young and got good eyesight. Let them study under the lamps. It won't hurt them none. And tell them to watch out so they don't start any fires."

Mrs. Collins did this and went into the parlor. Willie was attracted by the rows of figures showing the number of calls he had made from day to day, showing the rise of from eighty in June on up to two hundred and seventy-five and three hundred during the Christmas holiday rush. All that was business he had taken care of and had brought to the company. And it meant plenty of dollars and cents. And, think of it, some damn efficiency expert was coming along to tell him he didn't know his business.

His wife returned to the dining room and resumed darning his socks.

"They're jealous of me down at that office," he complained.

"Don't let them blacken you to your superiors. Don't let them," she said in an embattled manner.

Lighting a cigar, Willie said, "They can't do that. The old man knows I deliver the goods. They can't do that. I'm the old man, Mr. McLaughlin's, ace. He knows I deliver. If they try to blacken me, you know, they'll only blacken themselves. Nobody else could hold down the job as well as I do. It takes brains. That's why Mr. McLaughlin made me the Chief!"

Mrs. Collins nodded her head, continuing her darning.

"That's why they're all jealous of me. But a lot of good it will do them!"

"Small penny it will do them," Mrs. Collins said.

"Well, efficiency expert or no efficiency expert, I'll be staying right up there on the board. They ain't got anybody to take my place and do the thing to perfection like I do it," Willie said, again puffing on his cigar. "When I go out of there it will be to something better, and I don't think I need worry, because I'm delivering the goods, and, when they need somebody to show the stuff at a better job, they'll know where to look for him. Of course some of them other fellows in the supervision, they got more seniority than I got, but they'll find out who's got the stuff up here." Willie proudly pointed at his large head.

"You don't want to let them blacken you in Mr. McLaughlin's eyes. And, Willie, wear your new suit tomorrow for this meeting. I have that new white shirt of yours washed and ironed. And I'll put your new shoes out, and you can wear your new hat. And don't forget that new watch that you got for giving such fine service to those watch people."

"I won't," said Willie, irritated.

"And you just don't let them bluff you."

"My record stands for itself, and I got it all here for them."

Willie again studied the figures, but his mind quickly wandered. He saw himself astounding the committee. Then he was afraid he might not astound them and he feared for his job. He wondered if he could get a job through Eddie Chance if he was fired. He imagined himself getting fired and getting into politics through Eddie Chance and rising to be some kind of Chief . . . COLLINS ELECTED ALDERMAN. . . . Suppose that happened. Then the Express Company and all them bastards would be lumping plenty. But suppose he didn't? Suppose he was taken out of the department. But he wouldn't be. He couldn't be. He wouldn't be. He was a good and an honest man. And tomorrow he was going to go to confession before six o'clock Mass and offer up Holy Communion and a blessed candle or two so that he wouldn't.

"I haven't nothin' to worry about tomorrow. Nothin'. Them fellows won't show me up," he said.

"But, now, don't be insulting. You must be careful and not rouse their anger. You be polite and listen to them, but don't let them accuse you of anything."

"Me! What can they accuse me of? Nothin'. Nothin'. And if they are going to start changing men around and firing, well, there's a lot to go before me, a lot, yes a lot of 'em."

"Now don't you go being a fool for them men—them route inspectors. Don't you do it."

"They should try it. They couldn't with Mr. McLaughlin, and if they try, if they do, I'll just bust their damn jaws in for them."

"Now, Willie, don't you be fighting like a roughneck."

"I won't, but I can see myself letting them put something over on me."

Tomorrow who could tell but he might be out of a job, and he had three mouths to feed, and a wife and two kids to clothe, and he had to keep a roof over their heads. And it would all be because of some damned efficiency expert who wouldn't know what the hell to do if he was put up on the board or in a depot to dispatch.

"I ain't afraid," Willie said.

v

Weary, as much from worry as from his efforts to go over his figures and records, Willie put his papers into a paper folder and yawned. He looked glumly about the small dining room. It was neat and clean. No man had a neater wife than he, no sir.

He looked at her, a huge blonde woman, tenderly. He said, "I wouldn't have it so hard, only them drivers all play for over-time. They are all stallers. They won't play the game right. None of them will. I'm the only expressman in the company. There's not another expressman like me."

He looked out of the window. It was black and lonely out-side. He didn't like the blackness and loneliness. Death. He re-called the tremors and fears he had had at the office before leaving, when Lumbert, the night chief, had happened to men-tion poor Jim O'Neill, Lord have mercy on his soul. Jim was lonely now, too, out in the cemetery. He didn't like to look out of the window. He looked at his hefty wife. Yes, he liked her, and she was a good mother of his kids and a fine wife and manager of his household. But now, well, he had nothing to talk of, he was weary and tired and overworked, and he felt—he didn't know what he felt. It was dark out and pretty cold. He was a man thirty-three, with the hair thinning away in the center of his head, and some day he had to die. There were many things in life he wanted to do. He didn't think of these things specifically. There was just something that had to happen, and, after it did happen, life would be different, and then he would do these many things. He relit his cigar butt. He tried to sink back comfortably in his chair and smoke it. No, he'd come out all right tomorrow.

He rose and paced the room.

"Willie, now you just sit right down here and don't be fret-ting yourself with worry."

He sat down. She knelt and took off his shoes and brought him a pair of slippers. She put a pillow to his back. She gave him his newspaper.

"Now, you forget all about that. You know the Lord will help you tomorrow," she consoled.

Willie shook his head and read his newspaper.

"Say, here's something. The husband of Sallie Morris, the Hollywood star, has committed suicide. It looks funny. You know them movie actors is fast," Willie idly commented.

"Wicked," his wife said.

"Look what that Arbuckle did. And because he has influence, he got out of it. Well, I'd never go to see a picture of his."

"And I wouldn't let little Willie or Tommy go, either."

"There's something funny about this. The paper says that it's a love triangle."

"Wicked," his wife said.

"And here's an old lady who's willed three hundred thousand dollars for a home for pigeons. Pretty nice for the pigeons. Only seems to me she might have left it for the poor."

"I'll see that the children get to bed now," she said, rising.

Willie rose, went to the parlor door, and barked with authority.

"All right, you kids, get to bed now, and good night."

They said they would, and Mrs. Collins left the room. He sat down and picked up his newspaper, but his thoughts drifted, and he worried again about tomorrow. He stared again at the darkness outside.

It was only five after nine. It was a bit early to go to bed. But he felt tired tonight. He wanted to go straight to sleep when he got in bed. She was a big woman, and she could stand a lot. Sometimes she tired him out, and he had to be in the pink for the meeting. He hoped she'd let him sleep. But he could tell by the look in her face tonight that she probably wouldn't. Well, he'd just roll away from her. Goddamn it, why didn't a woman realize that a fellow sometimes got tired, and that there was a limit to certain things, and that a fellow had to keep in the pink to earn a living. Well, tonight he was just going to roll over and go right to sleep.

He was confused. He paced the room. She returned and sat down. He went to her like a timid little boy, sat on her lap, and laid his head against her large breasts. She stroked his head. He felt cozy, warm, protected in her arms this way, against her huge warmth.

"Take me up to bed," he said.

"Yes, my last boy must be put to bed," she said tenderly, and she led him upstairs to their bedroom.

With her, he couldn't lose out, and he wouldn't.

VI

Willie had been on edge all morning, waiting till Mike Mulroney and Porky Mulroy came in. They were the first route inspectors who had been called over to the committee on the overtime. He would go after lunch. He wished this ordeal were over. When they came in, he turned and asked them about it.

"Hell, it's just like I thought. Nothing," said Mike after entering the department.

"Hell, them bastards didn't put nothin' over on us," Porky boasted.

"What did they say?" Willie asked eagerly.

"They didn't put nothin' over on this boy," Porky bragged.

"Huh, Mike?" asked Willie.

"They just ask some questions," said Mike.

"What questions?" Willie asked, leaning forward in his high swivel chair.

"Oh, do you watch your men and check their overtime sheets?"

"Yeah, well I do that . . . Hey, O'Neill, are you watching them overtime sheets?"

O'Neill nodded.

"Listen, every day from now on, you bring me in every overtime sheet on which there is any overtime drawn," said Collins.

O'Neill nodded.

"What else?" asked Willie.

"Oh, they asked us if we watched our men about stalling," Mike said.

"Well, I do that. Say, Casey, you're watching them sheets and keeping tab on all those guys and watching their driving time, aren't you?"

"You know me, Willie," said Casey.

"Well, they haven't anything on me," Willie asserted.

"Hell with them," Mike said.

McGinty winked at Porky Mulroy and Porky waddled over to him. They talked in low voices. Porky rolled back over to

Willie and began speaking with him in low and serious tones.

"Listen, Willie," he said, "I don't want to worry you, but they're tough. They put you through a grill. Jesus Christ, it's awful. They bawl you out for every minute of overtime and they talk to you like you was a dog or a flunkey. Christ, watch yourself and have all the dope you can on hand. The more figures the better. Jesus, they got me worried about my job. I don't like to say this to everyone because you know the way these bastards kid you. But Jesus Christ, Willie."

Fear crossed Willie Collins' face, and he looked suddenly like a very little and scared man.

"Goddamn them, they ain't got nothin' on me. I'll tell them," he said, almost trembling.

VII

Willie sat with a blushing red face. He hoped his new blue suit would impress these muckety-mucks. It fitted him well, but then all suits fit to a T.

Five men faced him across a table in a large office. A girl sat at one end, taking a stenographic report of the proceedings. In the center was Mr. Veltman, the new efficiency expert. He was a thin, tall man with a sharp nose, and although he was scarcely thirty, he was beginning to grow bald. On Veltman's right was the gray-haired new vice-president of the district, Mr. Minton. The three other officials were elderly.

Willie fidgeted, unable to control himself.

"There's all the records of my work," he said, nervously.

"Just a minute, please," said Veltman in a voice of cold and confident authority.

"Yes, sir," said Willie, while he silently cursed the sharp-nosed efficiency expert.

"Mr. Collins, is that it?"

"Yes, sir."

"You're the dispatcher in the Wagon Call Department?"

"Yes, sir, I'm the chief dispatcher in charge of special gas-

car service. I pick up the whole city, taking care of all calls
that the regular pickup men can't handle."

"Just a minute, please," interrupted Veltman.

"Yes, sir."

God would not desert him after he had received Holy Communion this morning, lit five blessed candles, and remained
after Mass to say a decade of the rosary.

"You see, Mr. Collins, there is, we feel, more overtime than
there should be. Now, how many men do you have working
under your supervision?"

"That all depends. Sometimes I have eighty-six, and then on
Mondays I have five extra gas-cars, and some Mondays I have
six. Around Christmas and Thanksgiving, when there is a rush,
I have ten or twelve extra gas-cars, and on Mondays, that is on
Mondays during the Christmas and Thanksgiving rush, I have
maybe fifteen extra gas-cars."

"But on the average, how many?"

"Eighty-five."

"Is that eighty-five men, or trucks?"

"Trucks."

"And how many men?"

"Well, there's a driver and a helper on every car."

"I see. Then, on the average, you have one hundred and
seventy men."

"Yes, and I have the overtime records here."

"Is there any way you could reduce that overtime?" Mr.
Veltman interrupted.

"Well, it's pretty low already, you know. I keep my overtime down as much as I can. It's impossible, you know, to work
without some overtime, because I got the whole city to pick
up. Some nights at a quarter to five, you know, I'll get calls
from the regular man on some route for something he can't
handle. Sometimes it will be at a firm that's payin' its men
overtime, you know, to wait till we get a man there, and if I
don't get a truck there soon, they burn up the wires and write
letters in complaining to Mr. McLaughlin. You know, well, on
such calls I got to send in the first truck that comes up, regard-

less of what time the driver is out, because the calls have to be made. Every night at a quarter to five, and five, and even after, I get calls that got to be made. Then, too, you know, I can't move my trucks around perfect-like. There are always things happening that you don't know about until they've happened, and then it's too late for you to do anything about them. Sometimes I'll count on a car for a call and the car will break down or something else will happen and delay me. I got all kinds of things like that to contend with, you know . . ."

"I understand, Mr. Collins, that there are many practical difficulties to contend with in the course of your daily work, and I sympathize with you. But what we want to do is get together and see if we can't overcome some of these difficulties," Veltman, the efficiency expert, said in a crisp voice.

"Of course, but I can't stop a truck from breaking down and I can't make the public stop giving me calls at a quarter to five."

"We understand that, Mr. Collins," Mr. Veltman said.

"We are going to spend a lot of money in advertising on a campaign to educate the public and to impress the shipper with the advisability of getting his shipments prepared at a regular time, preferably at a stated hour in the early afternoon," Mr. Minton said in a cultivated voice.

"Well, I think that would help us a lot. Now, out at Sloan's Deerfield, they never have their shipments ready at the time they say they will, and, when I send cars out there, over half the time the drivers have to wait. It's things like that that causes overtime."

"I know, Mr. Collins," Mr. Veltman said. "Now what I want to get at is this. We've all got a part to play in the Company and we've got to weld our parts together. We've got to make a synthesis of them. Understand? Now, the reason we are calling you wagon supervisors over here is so that we can effect this synthesis of parts. We know that some of the overtime drawn by wagon men is both justifiable and necessary. But our problem is to keep our necessary overtime down to the minimum without in the least lessening the efficiency of our service and the speed with which we answer all the calls and demands the public makes upon us. Now, do you think it can be done?"

Willie looked lost-eyed at his inquisitor.

"Do you?"

"Do I what?" he asked.

"Do you—Mr. Collins was it?"

"Yes, sir," Collins volunteered.

"Now, do you, Mr. Collins, believe that we can keep our necessary overtime down to as absolute a minimum as possible?"

"Do I? Why, yes."

"Well, have you any suggestions to offer?"

"Well . . ."

"Mr. Collins, that is, do you or do you not think there are any mistakes being made, or that we have any bad express habits, or that carelessness permits the increase of our overtime," asked one of the other members of the committee.

"No, sir. Not in my department. I got my records all up to snuff to show how I run my department."

"Well, do you think you can do anything to lower the overtime drawn by wagonmen in your supervision? Or do you believe that we or anyone could?" Mr. Veltman asked.

"Well, if the route inspectors would watch their men so that I would only get calls to pick up that their route men absolutely cannot handle, and if the shippers would have their goods ready earlier in the afternoon, you know, and if I would get co-operation from checkers at places like Sloan's Deerfield, I might."

"I see," said Veltman.

Willie waited, still fidgeting.

"Well, Mr. Collins," Mr. Veltman said, "it has been a pleasure to have had you over here so that we might mutually gain and educate ourselves in the express business. Now we trust that you will expend your very best efforts to see that the overtime is kept at the absolute minimum for this year."

"Yes, sir," Willie mumbled, nodding his head.

"That's all," Veltman said curtly, and he turned to show Mr. Minton something on a paper he held.

Willie rose and waited.

Veltman, noticing him, paused in his conversation with the vice-president and said in dismissal:

"That's all, Mr. Collins."

"But, pardon me. Didn't you want these records of what I do?" he asked.

"Why, no. We have overtime records from the payroll department."

Willie felt suddenly small. He paused there a moment, picked up his records, and said: "Good-by, Mr. Veltman."

Veltman said good-by and shook hands with him. The other four men shook hands.

Willie left, dazed, with his folder of records under his arm. In the long corridor outside, he was confused. But, then, the vice-president and other muckety-mucks had shaken hands with him. And he had got a clean bill of health. He smiled and strutted to the elevator.

But outside on the street, walking back, he once more felt small and unimportant. He cursed the damned efficiency expert.

—They didn't put nothing over on me, he boasted to himself, but not with great confidence.

VIII

Puffing on a fat ten-cent cigar the next day at noon, Willie boasted to a crowd of route inspectors:

"It was nothing, you know, just formality. They gave me a clean bill of health and said this department was all right, up to snuff, up to snuff. And they're gonna advise the route inspectors, checkers at places like Sloan's Deerfield, and guys like them, to co-operate more with me. You know."

He got the horse laugh and then, flustered, he hurriedly went on in a loud and boastful voice:

"And listen, Mr. Minton, Mr. Minton himself shook hands

with me and asked me to give him suggestions on how to make the service better and cut down the overtime."

Again he got the horse laugh, and the inspectors all talked at once, kidding him insultingly.

Gashouse McGinty, over at his tractor board, immediately called up one of the depot wagon dispatchers, and his booming voice could be heard above those of all the others:

"Say, did you get it? Mr. Minton invited Collins and his old lady to dinner. Yes, they're putting him on the board of directors. Yeh, now it's Collins and Minton."

McGinty heaved with laughter.

"Go ahead, you bums, say what you want. Mr. Minton shook hands with me, and asked my advice. Now stick that wherever you please," Willie shouted in an even louder and more boastful fashion.

They laughed again. Willie rose and, standing on his tip-toes, his five-feet-five of flesh taut, he screamed:

"When Mr. Minton shakes hands with you. . . ."

They laughed so uproariously that he was drowned out.

Comrade Stanley

STANLEY GRADEK was a tall, thin man of thirty-nine, slowly growing bald. He sat in his small, dimly lit apartment, clad in his long, brown monk's robe, the hood thrown back on his shoulders. His hollowed face wore a brooding, reflective expression. His fingers were long, thin, and sensitive, and his well-cared-for hands were soft. The narrow rooms of the apartment were filled with chairs, bric-a-brac, exotic objects, a studio couch, oil paintings by Chicago artists, and a few books.

Stanley suddenly twinged with guilt. The mood casting a spell over him, like his monk's robe, was a residuum of the past. Those days! He remembered how he used to sit in this apartment, wearing this same costume, with the candles, stolen from a Greek Catholic church by friends, flickering just as they were flickering now. Then, he had fancied himself mysterious, exotic, and his fancy had even helped him to become reconciled to growing bald. Baldness went with monkishness. Ah, yes, the pathos of distance! Even though Nietzsche had been a petit-bourgeois aristocrat, he had sometimes happened upon excellent phrases. And what phrase of Nietzsche was better than . . . *the pathos of distance.*

He mixed himself a drink and, sipping it, grew wistful. Holding the glass in his right hand, he glanced about and thought about the days when he had tried to write, aspiring to become the American Huysmans. He stared at the wall. He sipped his drink again, held the glass, and continued to let his eyes rove about his place.

Tonight he was lonely. He reflected on what he called the dialectic of age. From one point of view, thirty-nine was old. From another, it was young. Until a year ago he had been tortured by a pervasive sadness about the weight of his years. But in the last year, since he had joined the Party, he no longer had that pathetic, yes, pinched, petit-bourgeois fear about growing old. Time, the fact of death which lay behind the fact and the fear of time—these no longer seemed so melancholy. At least they didn't very often. Now and then, however, he did have bad moments when hangovers from his petit-bourgeois past troubled him. But he assured himself he was irrevocably done with all that. He cast a thin, sardonic smile at the objects in his apartment. Now, he shouldn't truly blame himself for any pretensions of his past. For even Bohemianism was a premature, primitive, and personalized expression of negative revolt. But why couldn't he have been the son of a South Chicago Polish steel worker? Yes, all that in his past had been a form of groping. And first, before you lost your personality and your individuality in the masses, you had to discover it. There was a pattern and a logic to his past—a dialectic.

Stanley took another drink.

The election was two months off. He flushed with pride. Think of it, here was Stanley Gradek, the standard bearer of the Party in this district. Suppose he should really be elected alderman. It was impossible. The Party was still weak and had to meet the full force of the class enemy. But still, suppose Stanley Gradek should become the first Communist alderman in the city of Chicago. On its face, this supposition seemed ridiculous. But was it so ridiculous? No, it wasn't. Someday he might well be the first Communist alderman in Chicago, or even, when the sleeping giant of the proletariat began to break its chains, the first Communist mayor.

He imagined himself in the City Council, rising to make a speech. How he would flay the other aldermen, the City Administration. Roosevelt would probably defeat Hoover in the election. He'd flay Roosevelt, too. From the President down, he would consign all these bourgeois politicians to the garbage can of history, where they belonged.

Stanley's face grew stern. His lips were drawn tight. He clenched his soft fists. He sat with his torso hunched forward, alert, eager, tense. The speech he dreamed of giving in the City Council swept him along into a mood of emotional exaltation.

But it was getting late, and he ought to be turning in. Tonight he had relaxed and had a few people in. Someone had brought a girl from the University, Charlotte Brand. She was so young, so fresh. Her body was such an invitation. Just at the best period of a female's life, the period of first virginal bloom. When he'd seen her to the door, he had invited her to come again, and she'd seemed pleased and jolly when she'd answered that she would like to. Now, take a girl like Charlotte, alive, healthy, with such a fine young body, take a girl like that and save her from the horrible bourgeois world, win her over to the movement, and you would have achieved something. As for the rest, she had a body, and he had a body, and, despite all the maledictions, curses, horrors, and outworn and outmoded prejudices expressed in bourgeois morality, what was a body for? He would like to make a girl like her his comrade, his co-worker, and his mistress. The two of them would work together, fight together, and after long days devoted to Party service they would come home, tired. Love, sex in all its natural, normal, physical nobility would refresh them, and then, side by side, they would fall asleep.

Stanley began to perspire. He paced the floor nervously.

II

"Got a drink, Stan?" Al asked.

"Gee, Al, I'm sorry. I haven't a thing in the studio," Stanley said.

Fatigued, Stanley sat relaxed in his most comfortable chair. It had been another hard day of conferences. An important New York comrade, Comrade Mortimer, had talked endlessly at the meeting. Stanley was all in. He felt like a drink. But Al never bought his own. He was always bumming drinks from somebody.

"Well, it's too bad you haven't a drink."

"Well, I'm sorry, Al. Are you working?"

"No. I went over to the Employment Bureau at the U again, but they can't give me any help. I went to school there but what good does it do me? I can't get a job."

"Al, I explained why you can't get a job. You're declassed. You're being driven down into the ranks of the proletariat."

"Well, whatever is happening to me, Stan, it's nothing that a drink couldn't remedy."

"Gee, I'm sorry I haven't anything."

"Listen, I got half a dollar. If you chip in, that's a buck. I'll see if Garfield is around. He's always ready to chip in to buy a bottle of booze."

"All right, I'll go in with you," Stanley said.

He handed Al half a dollar.

Al put on his hat and left. Stanley smoked a cigarette and made himself a drink and drank it hastily before Al could get back. Why should he waste bonded whisky on such people?

III

"Look at me. I've never been a plutocrat, have I?" Al asked.

"I didn't say you were a plutocrat. I explained, Al, that you need understanding. With understanding—the understanding of Marx, Engels, Lenin, and Stalin—and the discipline of our Party, we will conquer."

"Garfield, will you have some more of this understanding?" Al asked.

Garfield, a middle-aged, bald-headed man who had once been an architect, nodded. He handed Al his glass. Al made three drinks.

"Al, I don't like your making fun of serious things. I'm with Stanley a hundred per cent," Garfield said.

"I didn't mean it seriously. I'm with you, too."

"Well, you have to understand, Al, that the Party isn't something to joke about in your drinks."

"I wouldn't joke about it. Of course it's serious. Damned serious. I ain't got nothing to lose by being for it. Nothing to lose."

"Nothing to lose but your chains," Garfield said.

"Garfield, got a cigarette?" Al asked.

"Gee, no. Stan, have you got any cigarettes?"

Stanley reluctantly handed Garfield his package of Camels. Garfield and Al each took a cigarette. They lit up and drank.

"How does it feel to be running for office?" Al asked.

"I'm merely running for office as a duty," Stanley said with modesty. "My Party has chosen me. It is my duty. You know, fellows, the great feature of Party life is its discipline."

"That's why I can't join. I'm an individualist," Al said, taking another drink.

"I'm not good enough for the Party. If I were good enough, I'd join," Garfield said, also taking another drink.

"We're not the Kingdom of Heaven. And, fellows, the Party will change your entire life, your entire mental horizon."

"That's what I'm afraid of," Garfield said.

"Why be afraid? I wasn't. I couldn't begin to tell you what the Party has done for me personally. I'm a different man now, a totally different man," Stanley said.

"Maybe you're not like us. You're stronger. I'm too selfish and individualistic. That's why I can only be a fellow traveler, a camp follower," Al said.

"How much Party literature have you read?" Stanley asked.

"Oh, I've read enough. I know what it's all about," Al said.

Stanley got up to get some pamphlets for them. Garfield and Al each mixed another drink for himself.

IV

"Perhaps you ought to go to bed," Charlotte Brand said.

"Oh, no, not at all. We Communists have a sense of life," Stanley said, observing how plump and rosy she was.

He was tired, damned tired. For the last three days he had worked himself until he was ready to collapse. Meetings, conferences, speeches, and then, more meetings, more conferences, more speeches. A meeting about a rent strike at Fifty-fourth and Lake Park Avenue. A meeting with Negro comrades. Another meeting with Mortimer on the West Side for a thorough exploration of the problems of the election, and then a meeting which lasted until five in the morning while Mortimer had explained dialectical materialism. Yes, he was dead tired.

"We Communists have a sense of life," Stanley repeated.

"Yes, it must be so thrilling," she answered.

"Oh, hello," Al said, staggering up to Stanley and Charlotte, glass in hand.

Stanley frowned.

"How are you?" Al asked.

"I'm well. How are you?" Charlotte responded.

"Me? I? Myself? How am I, me, myself?" Again Stanley frowned at Al. "I'm all right, too. Have a drink," Al added.

"Al, we're speaking seriously," Stanley said, irritated.

Al slunk away.

"That's what society does to people. It's one more reason why there is a Party like ours," Stanley said, looking after Al, who was over at a table now, fixing himself another drink.

"I'd be afraid to join the Party," she said.

"Why? We won't eat you," Stanley said.

"Oh, but the work you do, it's so self-sacrificing, so noble."

"Oh, not at all. It's merely in the line of duty," Stanley said.

"Comrade Stanley."

Stanley looked up, disappointed. Comrade Jake Jackson from *The Fist* stood leering at Stanley and Charlotte.

"Miss Brand, this is my comrade, Jake Jackson," Stanley said.

Jackson took a drink, sat down on the couch beside Stanley, and said, eyeing Stanley enigmatically:

"Well, Stanley, this is a nice little party you're having!"

"Yes, but I'm pretty tired from work," Stanley said, disliking the way Jake looked at him, but saying nothing about this.

"Have a drink to the Party," Al said drunkenly, holding up a glass.

V

"I wouldn't even think of saying a word against real proletarian leaders of the workers' advance guard like Eldridge and Johnson. They are great men, and they have in them the making of the American Lenin," Stanley said to his comrade, Abe Goldstein.

Abe Goldstein nodded.

"But I do think there is something about New York that can easily turn even a good comrade into a bureaucrat," Stanley said.

Abe didn't answer. Stanley watched him closely but unobtrusively, cautiously seeking to note any changes in Abe's expression that would signify whether Abe agreed or not.

Stanley held out a package of cigarettes. Abe took one, then Stanley. They lit up.

"Yes," Stanley went on reflectively. "Yes, you see New York is a kind of island removed from America. It's part of America, but, then again, it isn't part of America."

"I know what you mean," Abe said thoughtfully, puffing away on his cigarette.

"Yes, New York does something to people, even to some of our comrades," Stanley said.

"I noticed that. You know, the local comrades are so much more simple than the ones who come from New York."

"That's just what I mean; New York spoils them. It does something to them."

"Stanley, I've been thinking. New York isn't the best place in the world for Party headquarters. Chicago is an industrial town. New York is full of chiselers and litterateurs. Chicago is different. It's the center of America. Someday, Stanley, Chicago is going to be the heart of proletarian America."

Their eyes shone. Stanley got out a bottle of good liquor and fixed drinks. They tipped glasses and drank.

"I was in New York for a few days about five months ago, and I must confess that I left with some bad impressions. Yes, very bad impressions. I wouldn't say this to anyone but a Party comrade. But, I tell you, I didn't like some of the things I saw at all."

"The Party wanted me to go to New York, but I managed to convince them I was needed here."

"I'm glad to know that. We need you here. You're in the streetcar men's union now, aren't you?"

"Yes, I was sent into it."

"That's good. We Communists must stay close to the workers. The hell with these Bohemians, these litterateurs, men who scribble poems, paint pictures, and drink themselves into cirrhosis of the liver."

"Of course, I've never worked on the cars, but then I can give guidance. I'd rather do that than work in an office in New York because—I hate to say it, but damn it, it's true—there are a lot of bureaucrats in the Party in New York."

"Yes, I observed that when I was there."

"I tell you, Stanley, the sight of many of those who call themselves comrades would disillusion me if I didn't realize so fully that the Party is bigger than this or that bureaucrat who worms his way into its ranks."

"Some of them use the Party for all sorts of personal adventures. Why, they even act like petit-bourgeois libertines," Stanley said.

"Yes, they come out here and act like big shots. They give us orders, pose all over the place, and what do they do out here?

They spend their time trying to explain dialectical materialism while they're in bed with a girl. And it doesn't matter if
the girl is some local comrade's sweetheart or wife, either."

"If Eldridge and the Ninth Floor only knew what some of
these walking delegates from Greenwich Village do in Chicago
and other places where we are busy leading and organizing the
workers."

"Yes, if Eldridge only knew."

They had another drink.

VI

It was Saturday night. Stanley was having a little party to
raise funds for the election campaign. Drinks were being sold,
and there was a table at which three girls from the University
were serving them. People were gathered in little groups and
milling about in the small apartment. The air was heavy and
smoke filled.

"Comrade Al, I want you to meet Comrade Gumowski.
Comrade Gumowski is a worker," Clem said, introducing Al
to a tall, blond, horny-handed Pole.

They shook hands, and Al winced at Comrade Gumowski's
grip.

"Comrade Gumowski works in the steel mills. He's a worker."

"I'm glad to meet you. Of course, I'm not technically a comrade, but I'm with you, Comrade Gumowski," Al said.

Comrade Gumowski grinned.

"I won't be on the other side of the barricades. Come on, let's
have a drink," Al said.

He took Comrade Gumowski by the arm and led him to the
table where the drinks were being sold.

"Violet, Irene, Jane, this is Comrade Gumowski. He's a
worker," Al said.

The girls smiled at Comrade Gumowski. He blushed.

"Fix Comrade Gumowski and me up with drinks."

Blonde Irene mixed them a drink, and Al laid half a dollar on the table.

"Comrade Gumowski, to the Revolution," Al said.

They tipped glasses. Comrade Gumowski downed his drink in one gulp.

Al looked at Comrade Gumowski, amazed.

Garfield staggered up to them.

"Comrade Garfield, this Comrade Gumowski. Comrade Gumowski is a worker," Al said.

Garfield and Comrade Gumowski shook hands, and Garfield, too, winced at the husky Pole's clasp.

"Have a drink," Garfield said.

He bought them three drinks.

VII

"Look at him, Charlotte," Stanley said. "He's so simple. You know, it's heartening, inspiring, to talk to a real worker. A real worker is so different from the intellectuals who came over to the movement. Lenin, you know, never trusted most of the intellectuals."

Stanley sat beside Charlotte on a corner of his studio couch, slyly looking down at her dress falling over her thighs, and at her silken legs.

"Yes, one honest worker like Comrade Gumowski is worth a lot of intellectuals from New York, intellectuals who come over to the movement. You know, when I returned from New York, I went out to South Chicago and had a few beers with Comrade Gumowski. I tell you, Charlotte, it was a heartening experience."

Charlotte watched Jake Jackson out of the corner of her eye. She didn't answer Stanley. She tried to catch Jake Jackson's eye. At the other end of the room, Jake was talking with a colored girl. Charlotte bit her lip. Stanley frowned.

VIII

"Stanley, do you know Goldstein very well?" Jake Jackson asked him.

The two were alone in a restaurant near Fifty-seventh Street and Harper Avenue.

Stanley stirred his coffee, took a sip, set his cup down.

"If you mean is he a close friend of mine, no."

"I'm glad to hear that," Jake said. "He's unreliable."

"Well, of course, I always suspected that," Stanley said promptly.

"What do you know about him?" Jake asked.

Stanley didn't like the way Jake was fixing his eyes on him, but he met Jake's gaze without flinching. Stanley knew he must not give Jake any opening. He didn't trust Jake. He didn't want Jake going back to New York and saying anything to the comrades on the Ninth Floor.

"Oh, Jake, nothing in particular. It's just his manner. There's something about his manner," Stanley said.

"Isn't there anything more specific?"

"No, nothing that comes to mind. Except that I have always been guarded and cautious in his presence. I've never conveyed more to him about inner Party affairs than was strictly necessary, and whenever I've had anything to say about such matters I've always kept him off important committees and out of any confidential work."

"Good. I'm glad to hear that, Stanley. You showed real Party instinct. I've always been convinced you are a reliable comrade and have good Bolshevik instincts."

"Well, I'll tell you," Stanley said. "You know my background. You know that I come from Polish nobility. But I was brought up as a little boy in a working-class district out in South Chicago. I think that unconsciously I learned more in those days than I realized."

"That often happens. But, Stanley, I'm not the only comrade who suspects Goldstein of Trotskyism."

Neither of them spoke for a moment.

"Is it that serious?" Stanley asked gravely.

"He's a disrupter, sowing the seeds of discontent in the ranks. He doesn't trust the leadership. I think he has organized a secret faction here. I was supposed to go back to New York but, when I heard that, I got in touch with the comrades back east. I'm staying on to look around here. I think there's an unhealthy condition, a cancer in the party ranks, here in Chicago. Now, Stan, I want you to help me."

Stanley kept his face expressionless.

"Yes, I want you to keep mum on this. It's confidential. I'm telling you because you're reliable, and with your help I'm sure I can cut the cancer out."

"You know, Jake, the Party comes above everything with me."

"Let's have some more coffee."

"George," Stanley called to the Greek waiter in a stiff tone of voice.

George, the Greek, came over.

"Two more coffees," Stanley ordered with authority.

Jake took Stanley's pack of cigarettes, which lay on the table, and lit one. Stanley noticed this, but said nothing. Jake never seemed to smoke his own cigarettes or to pay a check.

"The Ninth Floor's worried about conditions in the Party here," Jake said.

"What's the matter, Jake? You know we're doing some very good work here. My campaign is bringing in good results."

"The recruiting drive seems to have slowed down. Not enough copies of *The Fist* are being sold. And there is this dissension, this crabbing, backbiting, and discontent in some of the units. But I think it's mostly due to the Goldstein faction."

"Are you sure it's that serious?"

"That remains to be seen."

The waiter brought them their coffee. They put in sugar and cream, stirred the coffee, and puffed on their cigarettes.

"Keep your eye on Goldstein and keep your ears open," Jake said.

"Of course, I will."

When they finished their coffee, Jake let Stanley pick up the check. They stood outside the restaurant a moment. Jake then shook hands with Stanley and walked off west, in the direction of the University.

Was he going to meet Charlotte? Stanley was tempted to follow him, but he didn't dare. It would look too suspicious. And what Jake had told him was enough cause for worry. Suppose Goldstein should repeat remarks he'd made about Jake? He stood in his tracks, frightened. He envisaged expulsion from the Party, denunciation. Well, no, he could prevent that. But Charlotte? He went into the drugstore at the corner to telephone her.

IX

"Stanley, you ought to rest more. You do so much, so much for the Party," Barbara Morgan said.

She was a plain-looking, serious comrade who had once been Stanley's mistress.

"Barbara, what am I alongside the workers?"

"What are any of us, Stanley, compared to the workers?"

"Have a drink before we go to dinner," Stanley said.

"All right."

"The drinks are in the cabinet. Mix us two," Stanley said.

He sat and waited while she mixed drinks. He thought of her. She seemed to be such damaged goods, so drab, so ordinary alongside of Charlotte. Charlotte had been home when he'd phoned her this afternoon, but she said she couldn't see him for tea or for dinner. He had asked why. Busy. An engagement. She wouldn't say what it was or whom she was seeing. He knew. And so he had to be content to dine with Barbara. Barbara, good comrade that she was, was something of a bore. He heard her fixing the drinks.

"I'm seeing Abe Goldstein tomorrow night," Barbara said, returning with the drinks.

Stanley frowned.

"What's the matter?" she asked.

"Oh, nothing."

"Abe's a very loyal comrade and a good friend of yours, isn't he, Stanley?"

"Not particularly."

"Stanley, I know you well enough to know there is something on your mind when you act this way."

"I don't think you should see much of Abe."

"Why?"

"Barbara, I don't think Abe can really be trusted."

"Why? Has he done anything? What has he said?"

"He likes to be a general. If he can't be one, he's discontented. And you know, Barbara, that's very bad orientation for any comrade in our Party."

"But, Stanley, are you sure? Why, I always thought Abe was a very loyal and devoted comrade."

Stanley looked at her, annoyed, impatient.

"Stanley, you look at me as if I were a fool not to understand you. But I don't understand. Tell me what Abe has said or done to provoke your suspicion."

He continued to look at her, annoyed and impatient. He took up his glass and slowly took a drink.

"Barbara, you know you are a very good comrade. But you lack a certain kind of political insight."

Barbara watched him, bewildered.

"Yes, you don't see the political meaning in a great many little things. But, you know, in our rotten world of capitalist decay, Barbara, everything, everything has a political meaning."

"Yes, you're right, Stanley. You know, Stanley, I have never seen such development in a man as I have in you during this last year," she said.

Stanley glanced at her, displeased.

"Stanley, don't look at me like that because of what I said.

After all, we all had to come to the movement through various channels."

"I know that. But, Barbara, you know me, and you know me well enough to know that I was always, instinctively, a revolutionist."

Barbara said nothing. She squashed her cigarette and took another sip from her glass.

"But all this is irrelevant. I want to warn you, Barbara, you have to be careful of a man like Abe. He's dissatisfied with the Party. I can tell it from the way he talks. He is always griping, always complaining of comrades, always attacking the leadership in a snide way."

Barbara seemed puzzled. She looked at Stanley, bewildered.

"But, Stanley, I thought Abe had the same views as you," she asked, interrupting him.

"Barbara, devoted comrade that you are, loyal and able Party member that you are, you still lack political insight. There is a distinct difference between my attitude on this question and Abe's. Abe is always griping. He doesn't practice Bolshevik self-criticism. All he does is snipe, snipe, and snipe away subtly in order to sow confusion in the ranks."

"But, Stanley!" Barbara exclaimed.

"Don't say I didn't warn you," Stanley went on, ignoring her exclamation. "Barbara, I know more than I can say. And what little I can reveal is strictly confidential. But listen to me. Abe's days are not long in the Party. Why, I even think he is trying to start a Trotskyite faction here in Chicago in our very ranks."

"Stanley, are you certain of it?"

"Absolutely."

"You mean Abe is really a dirty hypocritical social fascist?"

"Yes, I do. But, of course, I don't want you to quote me."

"You know I wouldn't. But, Stanley, maybe I had better not see him tomorrow night."

"I wouldn't if I were you." Stanley finished his drink and rose. "But, come on, Barbara, finish up your drink, and we'll go out to dinner."

x

Stanley sat with Charlotte in the Coffee Shop at the University. It was only half full. He glanced around. He liked to be in the presence of youth. He noticed that there were a number of fresh-looking girls at the tables. Attractive girl students, wearing trim aprons and caps, were moving back and forth with orders. There was a pleasant feeling to the place, he reflected.

"I don't get a chance to do this often," he said fingering a teacup.

"To do what?"

"Sit and drink tea with you. Sit and act as if I were a *rentier*."

"What's a *rentier*?"

"Charlotte, you should pay more attention to economics. Instead of spending so much time reading dead poets, you must read economics."

"Yes, Stanley, aren't I dumb?"

"Charlotte, you're a very intelligent girl."

"Don't flatter me, Stanley."

"Not at all. I mean what I say. You're an extraordinarily intelligent girl."

"Stanley, please tell that to my professors, won't you?"

"Professors, what do they know?"

"They want to know what I know."

"Say, what's that book you're reading?" he suddenly asked, noticing a red-covered book under her pocketbook on the table.

He reached toward it.

"May I look at it?"

"Of course. You know more about that subject than I do," she answered, still speaking in a casual and disinterested tone of voice.

Stanley reached for the book. It looked familiar. He saw that it was Engels' *Anti-Dühring*, and his eyes lit up as he turned the pages.

"This is a great book," he said.

"Jake asked me to read it. He's going to explain it to me. But, Stanley, I'm not smart enough to understand it all."

"Of course, you are. You're a brilliant girl."

"I only wish I were."

Jake was using Engels as a means of seducing Charlotte. That a Communist would use one of the great books of a founder of Marxism for such ends! What could he do to Jake? He had to watch his step. Had Jake been giving him a subtle and indirect warning the other day when Jake had spoken about Abe Goldstein?

"Tell me, Charlotte, what do you do with yourself all day?" he asked.

She smiled, revealing beautiful white teeth.

"Stanley, I don't know. You know, time just passes, and I don't get anything done. It's the middle of October already, and I don't seem to have gotten anything done yet."

"Time flies for all of us," Stanley said wistfully.

Charlotte toyed with her teacup. She seemed to be complacent, almost bovine, and was prepared to sit and wait and let Stanley talk if he wanted to. If he didn't she seemed to be prepared merely to sit.

"But it is wonderful to be young enough still to feel that you will live to see the great transformation of society under socialism," Stanley said pompously.

Charlotte seemed bored. Stanley wondered what he could say to arouse her interest in him.

"Have you been seeing much of Jake of late?"

"I saw him a couple of times," she answered casually.

He was sure of it. Jake had slept with her already.

"I've been wanting to see him. I was hoping he would come around and see me," Stanley said.

"Why, we can do it tonight. I'm meeting him for supper, and we haven't any plans for after supper," Charlotte said.

The way she had pronounced *we* was suspicious. Flustered, he didn't speak for a moment. He felt that Charlotte saw he was flustered, too.

"Of course, by all means come and see me," he said.

"I'll ask Jake. I'm sure he'll want to."

Yes, from the way she was talking, he could tell.

XI

"Stanley, something I can't understand has been happening to me," Abe said, alone with Stanley in his apartment.

"What's the matter?" Stanley said guardedly, wondering how he could get rid of Abe, hoping Jake wouldn't drop in or any of his other comrades.

"It's strange. Comrades are acting in a peculiar way toward me."

"What do you mean?" Stanley asked. The name Abe had been on the tip of his tongue, but he had checked himself and didn't call his comrade by name.

"Even Barbara acts distant, cold. They act as if they didn't trust me."

"I don't know anything about it," Stanley said.

Stanley wondered—was he being unfair to Abe? Should he stand up for Abe and make a fight against Jake? Should he tell Abe that this was Jake's doing? But if he did, and Jake maneuvered against both of them, then where would he be? If he were expelled from the Party now, or even put on probation, could he stand the blow? He had burned all his bridges behind him. What would life mean to him now, at the age of thirty-nine, if he were expelled from the Party? Go back to trying to write? He had no confidence in himself as a writer. He knew in his own mind that he was glad of his political life because it gave him a reason for not trying to write. Before he had joined the Party, he had really stopped writing. He hadn't written since he left Paris in 1929, and he had done damned little work when he had lived on the Left Bank.

But he had to say something to Abe, and he wasn't sure just what he ought to say.

"Stanley, you're my friend, aren't you?"

"That's a strange question to ask me."

"You've been busy with campaign speeches. Maybe you haven't come in contact with what I mean."

"No, I haven't."

"You seem cold, Stanley. Are you against me, too?"

"What do you mean? Don't get a persecution complex."

"I'm not getting any persecution complex. I know what I'm talking about. Why, the comrades will hardly speak to me. Why? What have I done? What have I said?"

Stanley saw how excited Abe was. He wished Abe would go. He wondered what excuse he could give to get Abe out of his apartment.

"Stanley, I gave up everything for the Party. I left home. My old man and I don't even speak. I sacrificed my education. I broke with all my friends, with my whole past," Abe said.

Stanley waited, embarrassed.

"I was living on fifteen dollars a week I got from the Party. Jake told me today that I'm not going to get that any more. What have I done?"

"Abe, I don't know why you ask me that question. I don't know anything about it. You know, I don't play any role in intra-party disputes. And Jake is here from the Ninth Floor."

"Stanley, as a friend and as a comrade, tell me, have you heard anything about me? Do you know anything about this business?"

Stanley looked at Abe, trying to seem bewildered.

He hadn't heard that Abe had lost his Party job. He knew that he had to get Abe out of the apartment, and do it quickly. If Jake should drop in, Jake would have something to use on him later. Jake was unscrupulous. He wanted to help Abe defend himself, but he didn't dare do it. Party considerations were above all personal matters, all personal feelings.

"Abe, I don't know. I haven't heard a word. I've been campaigning. Yesterday I made four speeches. Today I made another speech. I have to leave now to attend another meeting."

"Will Jake be there? Can I go with you?"

"I'm sorry. It's special Party work. I have to meet some University people, innocents."

"Can't I come?"

"No. It's special Party work. And, besides, these people are Nordics. A comrade named Goldstein wouldn't be the best one to come along with me."

"You're with them. You're against me, too," Abe said heatedly.

"I? Abe, don't get a persecution complex. You know the Party. If the Party disciplines you, it has its reasons. You have to take its orders. We're soldiers in the army of the Revolution, Abe. Our duty is to do what the Party directs. The Party knows better than we. We can't set ourselves up against the Party."

"But what did I do? I was doing good work. I was getting results."

"What orders did you get?"

"I don't know yet."

"Well, go see Jake and have a heart-to-heart talk."

"He won't see me."

"I don't know what to say, Abe. And I'm sorry, but I really have to go."

Abe picked up his hat and glumly left the apartment. He turned at the door.

"So long."

"So long," Stanley said, his voice formal.

He was relieved that Abe was gone. But now he had to go out. Otherwise Abe might be in the neighborhood and see the light on in his apartment. He wondered what to do. He put on his hat and coat and left. He walked about aimlessly, ashamed of himself for not defending Abe. But he was helpless. The Party was bigger than he. And the Party was his life.

XII

Stanley was encouraged by reports of the campaign. Election day was drawing near, and he was hopeful of polling a good vote. The campaign was an avenue of propaganda to reach the workers, and the size of his vote would reveal the success of his work. Of course, there weren't very many real workers in the ward. There were a lot of workers of brain, but, of course, intellectuals were petit bourgeois, too. Still, they had to be won over and used. He was reaching them, reaching key people at the University. If he could poll a relatively big vote, it would be good for him in the Party and show that he was popular and had a following. If he built up a good following, he would be safe from comrades like Jake in a way that Abe wasn't safe. But, more important, yes, more important by far, a good vote would show that the Party was growing, was gaining in influence.

Barbara was busy these days canvassing from house to house, selling copies of *The Fist* and soliciting votes for the Party, and she had reported surprisingly good results. Many families had been cordial to her, had invited her in and talked with her, and Barbara had explained the Party's program for the election. He had tried to line Charlotte up to campaign. She was pretty, young, and came from a good family. A girl like Charlotte would be a wonderful campaigner. She would make a good impression in the homes of University people. But he couldn't convince her, and, also, Jake had vetoed his proposal. Here was an instance of how Jake worked against the best interests of the Party. He had originally interested Charlotte in Marxism. And now, with Jake as her lover, she was not going to join the Party. Jake had said she would be of more use outside the Party. He didn't see it that way, but Charlotte, naive girl that she was, had gone simply gaga on Jake.

But he had to forget all this now and work. He got out paper and pencil and began jotting down notes for a speech he had to deliver tonight.

XIII

Stanley left the meeting hall with Jake, and they went to a restaurant on Fifty-fifth Street. He was disappointed that Charlotte hadn't come to hear him speak. He had been hoping that she would come and see him at his best. Comrades told him he was a fine speaker, and once, after he'd delivered a speech, Abe had said he was the young Lenin of Chicago. Abe was on the way out of the Party. He avoided Abe now.

Stanley wanted to ask Jake why Charlotte hadn't come to the meeting, but he didn't.

"Do you really think my speech went off all right?" Stanley asked.

"Sure. A good speech. But there were a couple of points about it I want to take up."

"Yes?" Stanley asked anxiously.

The waiter brought them the coffee and sandwiches.

"What points?" Stanley asked when the waiter had gone off.

"First of all, you didn't mention how absolutely necessary it is to read *The Fist*."

"I know. I thought about it and decided I wouldn't because of the class composition of the audience."

"That's a mistake. It's not the right tactic," Jake said.

"I don't agree with you there, Jake. I know my audiences in this district, Jake, and I know how to handle them. I've made five converts at the University already."

"Just a minute," Jake interrupted.

Stanley controlled his feelings of resentment.

"I can see that Goldsteinism has had its bad influence through all the South Side cadres of the Party, among all of them except, of course, the Negroes, where all the members in the units are real workers, real stalwart proletarians."

"Goldsteinism?"

"Don't interrupt. I want to tell you about your speech."

"But Goldsteinism?"

"Goldsteinism and Trotskyism are synonymous. But you

made a great mistake. You are talking to a petit-bourgeois audience. What is the political character of a petit-bourgeois audience?" Stanley opened his mouth to speak. Jake raised his hand. "Just a minute, now, and listen. What is the political character of a petit-bourgeois audience? The political character of a petit-bourgeois audience is that it is unreliable, untrustworthy, politically adventurist, and opportunist, not to be trusted."

Stanley waited. He would have to go to New York sometime and go over Jake's head.

"Now, what must you do with a petit-bourgeois audience? You must educate it. How must you educate it? Through the weapon of the Party press."

"Yes, but I think it was best not to push them too fast."

"Stanley, you're not so afraid of the Party press, you're not infected with Goldsteinism, are you, that you are ashamed of our Party press?"

"Jake, you know me better than that," Stanley said.

"Yes, I think it was just a mistake in tactics. And then, point two, Stanley. You didn't discuss social fascism."

"I thought about that. But what I decided was that it was better to make a positive and constructive speech. After all, what is the Socialist Party? Nothing. It doesn't amount to a row of pins. I thought I would point out positively what our Party stands for and not even dignify the Socialist Party and all the other social fascists by mentioning them," Stanley answered.

Jake shook his head slowly from side to side. Stanley waited. He was filled with hatred for the comrade facing him. He wondered how long Jake would remain in Chicago. But his hands were tied. Jake wielded power and authority. The Party was bigger than Jake and he had to serve the Party. It would one day test men like Jake and find them wanting.

Jake waved to the waiter and pointed for another cup of coffee.

"Stanley, I think you ought to lead a picket line," Jake said.

Stanley turned pale.

"What kind?"

"If you got arrested now before election, and got publicity, it would be a great help in our campaign. It would teach the workers of Chicago that the Party is the only one fighting for their demands, and that its standard bearers are out in the front line of the fight."

"What do the other people here think of the idea?"

"I told them. I explained the need to them, and, of course, they agreed."

Stanley waited for Jake to go on.

"Well, what do you think?"

"I just told you. If you lead, say, a rent strike in this district, and we can get publicity, it should be a dramatic example to the workers of this area."

"Yes."

"The idea, then, is to find a place where we can organize a rent strike," Jake said.

Stanley seemed absorbed in thought.

"You know this district. Where can we have a rent strike? How about your landlord?"

"He's pretty good."

"I know, but still he's a landlord. A landlord is always a landlord."

Stanley reflected that he himself was a landlord. He had lost two of his buildings in the depression already. But he still had a building. He couldn't, of course, lead a rent strike against himself. But, then, he hadn't thrown anyone out except one dirty social-fascist Socialist. He had thrown out that fellow Murkson, not because Murkson owed him four months rent; he'd thrown him out because Murkson was a social-fascist Norman-Thomasite Socialist betrayer.

"Yes, a landlord is always a landlord."

Stanley winced inwardly. He consoled himself with the assurance that he was now dedicating his life to the overthrow of the system of landlords.

"Barbara is pretty familiar with this neighborhood, and she's been canvassing. Perhaps she will know of a case," Stanley said.

"Swell. We got to organize this strike right and get a big turnout. We ought to have a mobilization and show the people being evicted that they have something to fall back on, someone on whom they can rely. Our Party."

"Yes."

"Is Barbara home now?"

"She might be."

"Well, we might try to get her and see about it now. We have to work fast."

Jake finished his coffee, and they got up from the table. Jake let Stanley pick up the checks.

XIV

Stanley paced the floor of his apartment. They had seen Barbara, and she was sure she could find a building where a good rent strike could be organized. The die was cast. He was going to cross the Rubicon. He wanted to do this, and he had to do it. It was something he wasn't afraid of doing, either. The only question in his own mind was whether or not it was advisable for him to be risked at this important juncture. If he were hospitalized by the cops because of the demonstration, or if he were put in jail for six months, why, then, yes, he would be a great martyr, but would he be as valuable to the Party? That was the question. And, of course, if he raised that question, Jake would misinterpret it. The point was that a live and free Bolshevik was more valuable to the Party than a dead or jailed or hospitalized Bolshevik.

He continued to pace the floor. He thought of his comrade, Otto Schmoll. Otto had been hit over the head by the cops in a rent strike in the Black Belt, and he had been in the hospital for three weeks with a concussion. Barbara had been in that one. Afterward, he had seen her shaking and in tears, and she had told him about Otto lying in a pool of his own blood.

But what kind of Bolshevik was he? He wasn't afraid. He would face what he would face. But it would be a serious mis-

take for the Party to risk him at this juncture of events, and
if he could only get the Party to see it that way, get Jake to see
it. Jake wasn't the kind of person you could talk to. Jake would
use the most innocent thing you said for his own purpose. He
would distort and twist it if it suited his purposes and his
ambitions.

He paced the floor.

XV

"Stanley, I have to talk with you," Abe said, sitting down
without taking off his hat and coat.

"Abe, you've come in on me just when I have to leave."

"What for?"

"That's confidential," Stanley said sharply.

"Stanley, I've been brought up before the Party on charges."

"Yes? What?"

"Charges of Goldsteinism."

"What do you mean?"

"Goldsteinism, they say, is a species of Trotskyism, and they
accuse me of leading a faction, of backbiting comrades, destroying morale, wrecking Party spirit. I don't know. Stanley, you've
got to stand by me. You know these charges aren't true. I've
got to have worthy and loyal comrades like you defend me,
stand up for me, help me to brand these charges as lies."

"I don't know anything about it."

"You know me, don't you? You've seen me working in the
Party. You're my comrade."

Abe paused, a pleading expression on his face. He was waiting for Stanley to say something. Stanley said nothing but just
looked at Abe impassively.

"Stanley, you can help me defend my honor, my Party honor.
You know I've given everything to the Party and that I'm loyal
to it."

"If you are, what are you worrying about?"

"I'll be expelled."

"What do you mean? If you are innocent, do you think the Party would commit such an injustice?"

"No. But . . ."

"But what?" Stanley asked coldly.

"But I am innocent."

"Well, what's the shooting about then?"

"I don't know. Only it's serious. I don't know what to do."

"Abe, don't set yourself against the Party."

"Stanley, I love the Party. The Party is my life."

"Then what is this little episode? You won't be expelled if you acknowledge what you did and accept Party discipline. They might put you on probation, but you can work yourself back into good standing."

"But what did I do? I tell you, I'm innocent."

"Do you think the Party would make serious charges against you if there wasn't some fire behind this smoke?"

"Are you with them?" Abe asked, glaring at Stanley.

"I'm with the Party, yes. I'm against no comrade. But I'm not a factionalist."

"What are you insinuating?"

"Abe, don't lose your head. You came to me for advice, didn't you?"

"I came to ask you to defend my honor and tell the truth, because you know the truth and can defend my honor. My enemies are using the Party to harm me, to get me expelled."

"Abe, I don't know a thing about this."

Stanley's emotions toward Abe were mixed. He was sorry for him, but he was annoyed with him. He felt a sudden contempt for Abe. Abe seemed weak, undecided, pathetic. He suddenly reflected that, whether or not Jake had done an injustice to Abe, the situation had revealed Abe as being of a weak character. Any man who seemed pathetic and made you feel sorry for him was weak. And if Abe was so weak, then maybe, yes, probably, it would be just as well if he were out of the Party. The Party tested a man's character in many ways. This was one way it was testing Abe's character.

Abe turned toward the door. Stanley wanted to say an encouraging word to him, but he didn't. And Abe walked out without saying good-by. Yes, he was sorry, but why should he stick his neck out? And even though Jake was behind it, Abe couldn't be in trouble with the Party this way if there weren't some basis for it.

Where there is smoke there is fire, Stanley reflected profoundly.

XVI

Stanley led a small group of pickets who marched in front of a gray stone building in the 5400 block on Harper Avenue. He was carrying a sign which read WE DEMAND A MORATORIUM ON RENT FOR THE UNEMPLOYED. Others marched behind him, shouting and making as much noise as they could. A small group of people watched the picket line on the sidewalk, and many people, mainly women, had their heads out of apartment windows, watching.

"We demand a moratorium on rents for the unemployed!" Stanley shouted.

"A rent moratorium for the unemployed," the other demonstrators shouted.

"Go back to Russia where you belong," a fat woman yelled from a window.

"Hands off China," one of the picketers shouted, and the others took up the cry.

The demonstrators were heterogeneous, young and old. Many of them were shabbily dressed. There were two colored men in the line. They marched back and forth in front of the building.

Stanley was nervous. The cops would be here in a moment. Then what would happen? At the same time that he was apprehensive, he felt a sense of unity, almost of losing himself in the group of his comrades who were marching with him. His fate was tied to theirs, and their fate was part of the fate of the Party, and the fate of the Party was part of the fate of the American working class.

"Hands off China!"

"Hands off China!"

The landlord, a small Jewish man, stood on the doorstep watching them, looking sadly from one to the other, his eyes moving as the line moved back and forth.

"You dirty Reds!" a woman yelled from a window.

Suddenly the landlord came forward. Stanley halted the line.

"Here, you give me my rent, and I keep my hands off China," the landlord said.

"Capitalist! Capitalist, landlord bloodsucker," someone yelled.

The landlord drew back.

"The cops! The cops! The cops!" a girl screamed.

The police wagon had come down the street and stopped. The marchers were moving in the same direction as the police auto, and when the policemen dashed out of the vehicle, clubs in hands, most of the marchers had their backs turned on them. As the demonstrators about-faced to meet the police, the first two policemen were on top of them, swinging clubs.

"Cossacks! Cossacks!"

The demonstrators ran in all directions, and the police followed them with swinging clubs. Stanley dropped his sign and ran down the street toward Fifty-third. He heard screams and footsteps behind him, but he didn't dare turn. He lost his wind and ran on out of fright. He turned the corner at Fifty-third and looked behind. Down the street the police were rounding up demonstrators. He saw several persons, male and female, stretched out with policemen bending over them.

A girl came screaming, and, with her, a comrade whose head was bleeding.

They hurried along Fifty-third Street, and pedestrians gazed at them.

XVII

"We have to make it a ringing denunciation. They'll put it on the front page of *The Fist*," Jake said.

"I denounce the Cossack cops of Chicago who battered down the workers defending their elementary rights," Stanley said, and paused a moment. "How's that for an opening sentence for my statement?"

"All right. Now, let's see. You ought to get in the landlords."

"Defending the bloodsucking landlords, the cops of Chicago acted like Cossacks. Wielding their clubs without mercy, they broke up a peaceful demonstration of workers who were defending an unemployed class brother from eviction," Stanley went on.

"That's good. Now I'll add the rest. Vote Communist in order to defend workers' rights and in order to defeat the bloody, hireling cops and the bosses who employ them to beat workers without mercy. Vote Communist to end police brutality in Chicago. . . . I'll go back to my room now and do the piece," Jake said.

He picked up his hat and coat and left.

XVIII

"Stan, how about getting some gin?" Al said when Stanley led him and Garfield into the apartment.

"Gee, Al, I'm sorry, but I don't feel like drinking," Stanley said.

Stanley shook his head. They sat down.

"Stanley, were you hurt in the riot?" asked Garfield.

"The cops rioted," Stanley said.

"All the more reason to have a drink. You must have had your nerves shattered yesterday," Al said.

Stanley thought these fellows were just Bohemian bums. Could they be regenerated by the Party? The Party regenerated worse than they, and it would one day regenerate the entire human race. If the Party could regenerate the entire human race, it ought to be able to regenerate Al and Garfield.

"We ought to do something to train our people," Garfield said.

"Our people. You're not a Party member," Al said.

"Neither are you, Al," Garfield replied.

"We ought to train our people to fight and to know the streets. Now, if the revolution comes, what about fighting out there in Cable Court?" Garfield said.

"The fighting won't be in a little half block," Stanley said.

Garfield thought for a moment.

"No, I guess it won't," he finally said.

"Well, fellows, I have work to do," Stanley said.

"Stan, can you let us take something for a bottle of gin?" Al asked.

"I'm sorry, fellows. I haven't got a cent."

"Well, we got to find someone else then."

"Don't forget to come to the protest meeting tomorrow night," Stanley said.

"We'll be there," Al said.

Garfield and he left.

The International Soviet shall be the human race.

The words of *The Internationale* kept running through Stanley's head. He thought of these words, and of Garfield and Al. Somehow they would never get serious about the Party. Perhaps if he got them to join, then the duties and discipline would regenerate them.

XIX

Comrade Mark Singer, usually called the American Gorky, was the guest of honor at the little gathering at Stanley's after the protest meeting. He was a tall man in his late thirties. He dressed like a worker, and had a charming and pleasant smile. His manner was shy. The comrades all sat grouped around him, with Stanley on his right.

"Gee, it feels good to get away from New York and to come out here among real people," Mark said.

Stanley was tempted to say something, but kept silent. He

thought that perhaps later, alone, he might be able to talk with Mark and sound him out about Jake.

"Well, there's no wasting time with us out here, Comrade Singer. We work hard for the Party," Stanley said.

"Hell, call me Mark. I can't stand these bourgeois formalities," Mark said.

"Isn't he simple for such a great writer?" Barbara whispered to Al.

Al said nothing. He got up and made himself a drink.

"Comrade Singer, what do you think of Sinclair Lewis?" a student from the University asked; she was a thin, ugly girl with bobbed hair.

"A bourgeois defeatist," Mark said.

"So do I. My professor in English talks of him as if he were the greatest living writer."

"What can you expect from bourgeois academicians?" Mark replied.

"That's what I feel like telling him."

Mark Singer seemed to become suddenly shy and embarrassed. He looked around the room, and then his eyes modestly fell to the floor.

"Aw, hell, I don't want to talk about literature. I'm tired of New York intellectuals with all their bourgeois abstractions. Out here you meet real people," he said, still seeming shy and modest.

Stanley grinned.

"We'll try to have you meet real people here, Mark," he said.

Barbara brought Mark a drink.

"We need good proletarian writers, writers who write of the blood and sweat of the workers," Mark said.

"How long are you going to be here, Comrade Singer?" a young fellow named Myers asked.

"Oh, hell, don't call me anything but Mark. I'm a proletarian writer," Mark said.

"That's what I have always felt. Of course, me, I'm an activist and not a writer," Stanley said.

"The party organizers, and the leaders like you—you write

your books with deeds. That's more important. What's important about the books we writers write compared with the deeds you write here in Chicago, in Kokomo, Carmody, in steel, in mines, in factories and sweatshops?" Mark said.

"It's such an inspiration to hear you talk like that, Comrade Sing. . . . Mark," Barbara said.

"Oh, come on, let's all have another drink," Al said.

Barbara took Mark's glass and mixed him another drink.

They raised their glasses and drank to Comrade Singer.

XX

"Jake Jackson, you know, has been here. He's leaving in the morning," Stanley said.

"That guy started writing a short story ten years ago. He's a four-flusher," Mark said.

"I thought he was in with the comrades on the Ninth Floor," Stanley said.

"I know it. You know, Stanley, politics is politics. And in politics for the Party, everyone has his uses, even the petit-bourgeois intellectual," Mark said.

Stanley listened, deciding he would be cautious.

"Yes, even Jake Jackson has his uses for the Party. And he is better as a Party member than he was before he joined the Party. Jake is a sonofabitch, but he's our sonofabitch," Mark said.

"You know, I feel that way. Take that fellow Al who got drunk here tonight. Well, now, if he hadn't come close to the Party, he'd be worse. If we get him to join the Party, perhaps we'll regenerate him," Stanley said.

"Yes, drunkenness is a petit-bourgeois vice. It's because a young fellow doesn't see a way out that he drinks. If we can teach a fellow like Al that the Party points the way out, he'll give up his booze," Mark said.

Stanley thought Mark Singer had very keen insight. It was a pleasure to talk to him, let alone be his host.

But then, Mark Singer was America's greatest proletarian writer. Having Mark here was almost like having Gorky in your home.

"Are you working on a new book?" Stanley asked.

"I'm going to. I'm going to write a novel about a proletarian, a sign painter. Say, have you got any sign painters in the Party here? I'd like to talk to one," Mark said.

"Let's see," Stanley replied. He pondered. "I don't know if we have or not. But I'll ask the comrades."

"Do," Mark said.

Mark began to yawn.

"You had a hard day. You better get yourself some sleep," Stanley said.

XXI

Charlotte came around at night.

"I've been trying to see you all day," she said to Stanley.

"I was out. I just got in. Mark Singer, my comrade, is staying with me, and I expect him in in a minute," Stanley said, hoping she'd be impressed by the name of this guest.

She seemed absorbed, worried.

"Has Jake been here?" she asked anxiously.

"He went back to New York this morning," Stanley said.

"He couldn't! He didn't! He couldn't do that to me," she said.

Stanley didn't say anything. He waited for her to speak.

"He couldn't have gone back without telling me."

Stanley still waited for her to say more.

"Where is he? He left his hotel. Where did he go?"

"Honest, Charlotte, he went to New York."

"What'll I do?"

"What's the matter?"

"Oh!" she exclaimed, suddenly stopping, and then she began to cry.

Stanley was tempted to put his arms around her and comfort

her. He didn't move. It really served her right. But he did feel sorry for her.

"Why did Jake do that to me?"

"What's the matter? Tell me, Charlotte. Perhaps I can help."

"I'm going to have a baby."

Stanley cautioned himself to be careful. Here was something he didn't want to get involved in. How old was she? He wasn't sure. She might be only seventeen. If she were, that was dangerous.

"Stanley, what'll I do?"

Stanley thought for a moment, his face grave.

"What can I do? I can't have a baby. I'll be disgraced."

Stanley again cautioned himself to be careful. He better not suggest anything. She might say he suggested it. And, anyway, he didn't know any doctors to whom to send her.

"I'll be expelled from school. I'll be disgraced. What'll **my** father say?"

"Are you sure about it?" Stanley asked.

She cried. Stanley wanted to comfort her; he didn't know what to do. He was hesitant about taking her in his arms to try to comfort her. He waited and did nothing.

She looked at him, her face pale.

"What kind of a Party is it? You talk about the workers and all the good you're going to do, and so does Jake, and he does this to me," she said.

"But, Charlotte—" Stanley began.

"Where's Jake?" she interrupted.

"I tell you I don't know. He left town this morning."

"What's his address? Give me his address."

"I haven't got it."

Stanley suddenly wondered—would she make all this public —wouldn't it be terrible to drag the name of the Party through the gutter press? She would have to be prevented from doing anything like that.

"Charlotte, what do you intend to do?"

She looked at him, blank-faced, helpless.

And suppose his name were dragged in? Jake met her at his apartment. Well, it wasn't his fault.

"Charlotte, this would be no tragedy for you if we had a decent form of society. If America were as civilized as the Soviet Union, why, this would be no problem."

"Where's Jake?"

"I don't know."

She suddenly put on her coat.

"Good-by," she said.

Stanley walked to the door with her.

"Brace up and be a brave girl," Stanley said.

"Yes!" she said absently.

Stanley squeezed her arm at the elbow. She walked off, and he closed the door.

XXII

"I have the report on the votes," Stanley said.

"How many did you get, Stanley?" Barbara asked.

"Forty."

"The robbers."

"That's capitalist politics for you. I know more than forty votes were cast for me."

"What'll we do? Let's have a demonstration," she said.

"I have to see what the Party decides. I already gave a statement for *The Fist* charging capitalist robbery."

"The Wall Street bandits," Barbara said.

"I made a good showing. And, of course, it's juridical cretinism to expect anything from the ballot," Stanley added.

He didn't say anything for a moment.

"Barbara, is there any news of Charlotte?"

"Oh, yes, she got fixed up. She'll be all right."

"I'm glad."

Stanley seemed reflective.

"Stanley, you weren't at the meeting when Abe was brought up on charges."

"I know it. I couldn't come. I gave an affidavit on his wrecking and factional activity," Stanley said.

"He was broken up. But, then, he should be—a renegade."

"He didn't defend himself well, did he?"

"How could he, the traitor."

"Barbara, the Party always tests your character, and if you're found wanting there's no place in the Party for you. The trouble with Abe was that he wanted to be a general instead of a humble worker in the ranks. That's what you have to expect from a petit-bourgeois college student," Stanley said.

"You took the words right out of my mouth," Barbara said.

"Say, I recruited Al for the Party. You know, the Party will regenerate him," Stanley said.

"Swell work," Barbara said.

"We're gaining. That's why they stole votes on me. They are afraid of us. We have a new president now, Barbara. Let me tell you, before Roosevelt, the agent of Wall Street, is finished with his first term, we'll be on the march," Stanley said.

"And our comrades will be on the march in Germany, Stanley, just think of it—the Revolution can happen in Germany now any day."

"Yes, after Hitler has his turn, ours will come. And Hitler's not going to last if the social-fascist Social-Democrats do put him in as Chancellor," Stanley said.

Barbara's face was shining.

"Oh, Stanley, we're really living history," she exclaimed in exaltation.

Barbara left. Stanley picked up Volume One of *Capital*. He read for a few minutes and then set the book down. He walked up and down the room in a reflective mood. Idly, he glanced at the manuscript of his unpublished novel. It might not be an important work of literature. And yet he remembered when he had written it out at the sand dunes. Finishing, he had had such an extraordinary sense of freedom. He missed this feeling. And yet, did he? He was not sure of his own emotions.

He paced the floor nervously, trying to think. Thoughts evaded him. He sat down again to work on his speech. He worked for a few moments and then put his papers away. He turned out the lights, lit his candles, and sat there in a dark corner. He was lonely.

Episode in a Dentist's Office

THE TWO YOUNG NUNS entered the anteroom of the dentist's office, sat down side by side, and waited. One was very beautiful; her cheeks were fresh and rosy, her skin was very fair, and her eyes blue and sparkling. The other nun was very plain, with a pointed nose and a sallow complexion. They did not speak.

The little girl went close to them. She was an attractive little child of about four or five. Her hair was blonde and curly, and she had an impishly charming face. She wore short socks and a blue dress with a light sweater over it.

"Hello," the plain nun said, a repressed smile on her face.

"I'm waiting for my mommy. She's in there," the girl said.

The plain nun stroked her hair. The beautiful nun smiled warmly.

"Are you ladies?" the little girl asked.

Both nuns smiled, through tense lips.

"Why do you dress so funny?" the girl asked.

"We don't dress funny," the plain nun said in a low and energetic tone of voice. It seemed that she was saying something she didn't want to say, and that she was holding back each syllable a moment before letting it escape from her throat.

"Yes, you are. You don't dress like me."

"What's your name?" the plain nun asked in an evasive manner and obviously with the intent of changing the subject of the conversation with the child.

"I have no name," the child said.

"But you must have a name," the beautiful nun said.

"I have no name. My mommy has no name. I have no name. Only my daddy has a name. What's your name?"

"You must have a name," the plain nun said.

"I have no name. My mommy has no name. I have no name. I have a daddy. My daddy has a name. Only my daddy has a name."

"What's your daddy's name?" the plain nun asked.

"I have no name. My daddy's name is Thomas."

"Thomas what?" asked the beautiful nun.

"Thomas Rucker. My daddy's name is Thomas Rucker. What's your daddy's name?"

"The same," the plain nun said in a restrained voice.

"What's your daddy's name?" the girl asked.

"Thomas Rucker," the plain nun answered.

"No, it isn't. That's my daddy's name. What's your daddy's name?"

"Thomas Rucker."

"What's your daddy's name?" the girl asked, this time more insistently.

"Thomas Rucker," the plain nun said, repressing a smile and speaking with a restraint which vaguely suggested an inner tension.

"What's your daddy's name?" the child asked the beautiful nun.

"The same."

"No, it isn't. Why do you wear that?" the girl asked, pointing to the starched white headpiece.

"We wear it," the plain nun said after a moment of hesitation.

"It's funny. Don't you have any hair?"

"Yes, we have hair."

"Where is it? I don't see your hair. See my hair," the girl said, pointing to her own hair.

Neither of the nuns spoke, and the plain one was visibly embarrassed.

The child moved off, turned around and faced the nuns again, and then came a little closer to them.

"Why do you wear black?" she asked.

"It's our dress."

"It's a funny dress. Why don't you dress like my mommy?"

"We dress this way."

"Why?"

"Because we dress this way."

"Why?"

"We do."

"Don't you take that black off?"

"Yes, we do."

"When?"

The nuns didn't answer. The plain one looked away from the girl.

"Is that cloth?" she asked, pointing at the headpiece.

"Yes," the nun said, embarrassed. The beautiful nun blushed.

"I don't like your clothes," the child said.

"Why?"

"I like my clothes. My clothes aren't black. See my dress. Why do you dress like that? I never saw anybody dress like you."

"Oh, you must have," the plain nun said.

"No, I never saw anybody dress like you. I never saw anyone. Why?"

"Because you didn't see them."

"Why?"

The plain nun didn't answer. The little girl turned to the beautiful nun and said:

"Why don't you talk more?"

"I talk," the nun said, her rosy cheeks still flushed.

"I don't hear you."

"I talk."

"Why?"

"How old are you?" the plain nun asked.

"How old are you?"

"I asked you first," the plain nun said.

"How old are you?" the child again asked.

"I don't know."

"Do you like the clothes you wear?"

"Oh, yes," the plain nun said.

"Do you?" the little girl asked the beautiful nun.

"Yes."

"I don't."

"Why?" asked the beautiful nun.

"I can't see your legs. Do you have legs?"

"Yes, of course," the plain nun said, again embarrassed.

"Where are your legs?" the girl asked.

The nuns didn't answer.

"Do you wear pants?"

The plain nun nodded, but didn't answer.

"Look," the little girl said, lifting her dress. "See my pants? I wear pants. I can't see your pants."

The nun gently put down the girl's dress.

"Don't do that. I want to show you my pants. Where **are** your pants?"

"We have them."

"I want to see them."

The nuns didn't answer.

"Can't you take that black off? I don't think you have pants. I have pants."

The girl lifted up her dress again.

"There, see, I have pants."

"Do you go to school?" the plain nun asked.

"Where are your pants?"

The beautiful nun smiled.

"What's your name?" the plain nun asked.

"I have no name. Why do you wear that? I can't see your pants," the little girl said.

The nuns looked off in different directions. Then the girl's mother came out. The girl said:

"Mommy, I don't see their pants."

"Shhh," the mother said, embarrassed, as she took the girl's hand.

The nuns smiled weakly. The girl and her mother left the office, and the girl was heard saying:

"I told the funny women that I have no name, Mommy."

The plain-faced nun went into the dentist's office. The beautiful one sat alone. She was visibly agitated, and nervously fingered her beads. When the plain nun had been treated, they left.

The two nuns walked along Fifth Avenue. It was crowded. The spring day was balmy. The beautiful nun looked at the people passing, and then down at the sidewalk. She was visibly agitated. The nuns didn't speak. The beautiful nun bit her lip, blushed, and looked at the well-dressed, chic women moving past her on Fifth Avenue.

Quest

ARTHUR, vice-president of a small but enterprising book-publishing firm, began to lose his hair at thirty-five. This was disturbing to him. Every morning he would look at himself in the mirror, hoping against hope that he would see no further signs of thinning hair. He had himself treated to a variety of oils, massages, and tonics by various barbers. These efforts were of no avail. He went to several doctors, also, but he got no help from them. He gorged on vitamin tablets, took quack medicines, tried a sundry assortment of hair oils and hair tonics advertised in newspapers and magazines, but all of this produced no results. He was losing his hair and began to grow very anxious.

Arthur had gone into the publishing business shortly after he had quit college in his senior year. His father, an oil man from California, did not know what to do with him and, above all, did not want him to go into the oil business. He considered Arthur the most stupid of his seven children and finally decided that he might as well become a book publisher. Arthur's main value to his firm was the money he brought it at a moment when the firm was on the brink of bankruptcy. Arthur considered the publishing business great fun. It gave him prestige. His name often appeared in the gossip columns and other sections of the newspapers. He went to many parties and met a number of seductive women. He married a girl with ravishing looks. She wrote graceful minor verse and was also the author of two novels, one a romantic tale of love on the island of Capri and the other an equally romantic story of Italy and the Blessed Virgin Mary. Her name was Marie. Pretending to an esthetic interest in Catholicism, she was, in her personal life, pagan and sensuous. Many men envied Arthur because of his wife. Time had passed swiftly and pleasantly for Arthur. Now, at thirty-five, his thinning hair became an ominous warning.

It led to a whole series of seemingly minor changes in his life. He developed the habit of reading the obituary notices in the morning newspapers even before he turned to the book review or to the theatrical and motion picture page. He continually speculated as to how much space he would receive in his own obituary notice. He wondered what would be said of him and again and again, in fantasies, he wrote his own obituary. He began to look at men differently, to observe their hair and note whether or not they were growing bald or getting gray. He gazed at their faces like a conspirator in order to observe signs of aging, wrinkles and changes around the eyes. He looked at their abdomens, eager to see signs of paunches. He found comfort in the presence of older men, because he could feel much younger in their presence. But even while he gained comfort and security with older men, he was frightened. He would speculate as to how they were meeting the passage of the years. Were they unhappy? Sad? Disturbed? Frightened? And then he began to have stomach troubles and feared he had ulcers. Every morning he examined his stool for blood. Whenever he suffered from indigestion, he was stricken with terror. He became an insomniac and began taking sleeping pills. These made him drowsy in the daytime. Every day around five he would be heavy-lidded. In such a sluggish state, his expected evening of pleasure seemed burdensome. He lived for his pleasures, for parties, dates, first nights, evenings at night clubs. But, half-awake, he often did not know how he could get through his evenings. Heretofore, he had drunk moderately. Now, he began to drink heavily.

His symptoms multiplied, and his states of anxiety became more regular and more anguishing. He began to regard himself as an unhappily married man. His marriage seemed dull, excruciatingly dull. He was bored with Marie and convinced himself that she didn't understand him. And she, noticing these changes, was also growing disillusioned and cold to him. At the same time that Arthur was changing, she was becoming paralyzed at her desk. She had not written a novel for five years and feared that unless she wrote another one soon her name would be forgotten. She tried in vain to write. Angry with herself, she blamed Arthur. They quarreled with increasing frequency.

Arthur, in turn, became more resentful of his wife. His hostility to her became ever more pronounced. He feared that she was contemptuous of him because of his thinning hair and also because he did not exhibit as much sexual energy as he had when they were first married. Often he simulated desire merely because he feared that, unless he did so, she would think he was not a real man. He was suspicious of her. He was constantly on guard in order to protect himself from exposing his worries and anxieties to her. He sought to find evidence that she no longer loved him and then was sorry and condemned himself. He eyed her carefully and strangely in order to see if she were getting fat, or if signs of age were beginning to show in her face. He could no longer decide whether or not her body was beautiful. He often wondered what she would do after his death. Sometimes he imagined that she had died. He would then grow very disturbed. Neither of them had wanted children, and he secretly blamed her for their childlessness, although he was as opposed as she to the idea of having a child.

At his office, he became indecisive. He could not make up his mind, even about the smallest matters of detail. When he had read a manuscript submitted for publication, he could not make up his mind, and at editorial conferences he wasted everyone's time hemming and hawing in a way that meant neither yes he wanted the manuscript published nor no he didn't. He hesitated about making dates, delayed answering letters, lost reports, and held up the publication of books by his delays.

Although he did little work and took on few responsibilities, he convinced himself that he was overworked. He took a long vacation. When he returned, his hair was a little thinner, and he fell into the same routine of indecision, worry, delay, and evasiveness.

Finally he went to a psychiatrist, and after several visits the psychiatrist indicated that extramarital affairs might help him. On a few occasions Arthur spent passing and half-drunken nights with women, but when this had happened he was always ashamed of himself and fearful that Marie would find out. As a result he hated these women. He welcomed the idea of extramarital affairs as a means of salvation. But then he became afraid. He didn't want to tell Marie. He became non-communicative, and their domestic situation worsened. Marie was suspicious, fearing he was telling the psychiatrist about the intimacies of their relationship, and she became very sarcastic.

Then he broke two successive engagements with the psychiatrist. And he got drunker than he had ever been before. He feared he was going mad, and returned to the psychiatrist and told him he was fearful of telling his wife. The psychiatrist said he must tell her. So, after building up his courage all the way home in a cab, he burst in on her and told her the advice he had been given.

"I never heard of such a fool," she said.

They had a bitter quarrel during which Arthur defended the psychiatrist, and Marie described him as a fraud. He guessed that she loved him and he was upset. During the argument, he kept telling her,

"Marie, my health is at stake."

"If you want to, I won't and I can't stop you. But don't think that I'll want you if you go whoring all over New York."

He was in a quandary. Finally he brought Marie to see the psychiatrist, and, after a private talk with him, she assented to an arrangement whereby Arthur was free to have affairs.

Arthur went philandering, on what he accepted as medical instruction and the approval of his wife. He believed he was doing it as a duty to himself, as a means of preserving his mental health. But he didn't know what to do about managing affairs and several evenings, when he went out alone, he felt lost.

Marie never discussed his philanderings with him. She acted restrained and assumed something of the air of a martyr. She seemed to prefer not to mention the subject. Arthur went to his psychiatrist regularly and in time he found various girls with whom he had passing one-night relationships. Whenever he became nervous or disturbed, he thought of another girl. Marie was easily able to guess when he had been with a woman and when he hadn't. He was always beaming the morning after such an affair. She tried to sink herself in work but was more paralyzed than ever.

Then she decided to go to a psychiatrist herself. She found a German refugee who was highly recommended and had treated three of her friends with no tangible results. She quickly became attracted to him, and after several interviews she gathered from remarks of his that no sexual experience was completely satisfying unless, at the moment of fulfillment, one swooned into unconsciousness. She went home to her husband's arms and frantically tried to lose her consciousness. She failed. Nor did he become unconscious during these intimacies.

She now believed she had never had a satisfactory sexual experience in her entire life. She considered herself to be frustrated. That explained why she couldn't write. And Arthur was frustrated. She had a frank talk with him.

"Arthur, with any of the girls you've had—have you become unconscious?" she asked him in a strained and embarrassed tone of voice.

He hadn't. He wasn't sure she was right and planned to bring it up in his next interview with his own psychiatrist. But that very night the doctor was knocked unconscious by an automobile and died. Arthur felt lost. With his psychiatrist dead, he feared he would lose his sanity. Marie brought him to her doctor. After they had got together, Marie's doctor, who charged higher fees than had Arthur's, helped them to work out a schedule. On certain nights Arthur was to have the home for women, and on others, Marie, for men.

They worked on this schedule for several months, each of them seeking a succession of lovers who would help them to pass out. After each experience they would have breakfast the next morning and discuss the details. They enjoyed these discussions as much as they had the experiences and, whenever they had lovers, they always thought of each other and of how they would describe the affair over coffee, ham, and eggs the next morning.

But Marie was still unable to write. And Arthur's hair did not come back to him.

At the end of a year, they were divorced.

They agreed amicably on the divorce, and it was decided that Marie should go to Reno. But then they consulted the lawyers and a series of difficulties arose concerning the division of their personal property. Arthur wanted the bedroom set, and Marie wanted the living-room furniture. Arthur did not want to give her as much money as she suddenly demanded. When they discussed their library, which contained many books neither had ever read, their antagonism became really exacerbated. They had been living apart and had closed up their home pending the property settlement. They met one evening to settle who was to get what books.

"You never read a lot, Marie. Why not be sensible and not make such a fuss about the books?" Arthur urged.

"I like that. You didn't read—you merely published books on oil money."

"Is that so? If I couldn't read, would my firm be as successful as it is?"

"Because of your father's money."

"That's a fine statement to make after all these years," he said.

"Well, then, give me Proust."

"But I really think you ought to let me have Proust."

Thus the argument began, and from Proust it went to other matters. And they exhibited the bitterness they both felt. Each of them had passed from one bed to another. They were saturated with ennui. Marie had sought out males of all colors,

Negroes, Chinese, Italians, and even one Mohammedan, and still she had not been able to pass out in bed. Arthur had become a joke in the circles in which he traveled. His passes at girls, his efforts to seduce his telephone operator, his secretary, the bookkeeper, his flirtations with cigarette girls and hat-check girls in night clubs, all this had set going a whole stream of anecdotes.

They were both very unhappy. Neither could bear to be alone. When Marie was alone, she was in agony, and she smoked, drank, paced the floor, and became highly irritable. Night after night she went out, and she took benzedrine in order to keep awake, and then, when she came home, she took sedatives to put herself to sleep. Arthur was always jittery, always nervous, and his partners were discussing plans as to how they might tactfully eliminate him from the firm.

Now, they poured out on one another all of their bitterness, all of the saddening and terrifying unconscious shame which they felt. They raved and shouted.

"I was a goddamned fool to marry you," she screamed at him.

"You don't assume that I was a mountain of intelligence when I married a tramp like you?"

"So, I'm a tramp now?"

"I've heard stories about you. You've been chasing everything in pants all over town. Why don't you fornicate in Times Square with some newspaper photographers around?" he said with a sneer.

"What about you?"

"Have you had a lay that put you out yet?"

"You've got a filthy mind. You're a neurotic, and you always were, and you've almost put me in a madhouse."

"I wasted the best years of my manhood on you."

On and on, they talked and ranted. They said the most cruel and personal things about each other. Marie sobbed, and Arthur looked at her unmoved. Then she told him how bald he was getting. He retaliated by talking of her weight and her age, and remarking on how she had to wear a corset, wasted time in beauty parlors, and was fighting a ridiculous fight with old age. He told her she would one day be old and gray and wrinkled. And then he added:

"If you live that long."

"You'd be glad if I were dead."

"I don't wish you bad luck. I just hate you."

"And I detest you, you cad."

Finally they had said and repeated all they could say to each other, and they sat exhausted. His tie was loose, and he looked weary. Her hair was uncombed, and her nose was shiny. They looked like two tired people, approaching middle age. Around them were all the things they had accumulated, a large, unread, and expensive library, chromium lamps, modernistic furniture, an unplayed Baby Grand piano, pictures by Georgia O'Keefe for which they had paid heavily, an expensive radio, and shelves full of the kind of expensive and glittering junk that one picks up on tourist trips to Europe and Mexico. He was close to forty, and she was thirty-six. They said nothing now; they could no longer look each other in the eye.

Arthur thought of how he had once loved this woman, of how he had been so happy when they had first married. He remembered rather vaguely how they had been so inseparable, how they had held hands in corners like school children, remembered how shyly she had first given herself to him, how she had dressed and perfumed herself for him, waited in an agony of trembling excitement each day for him to come home from the office, and then flung herself wildly and ecstatically into his arms.

All this was past. Their memories were sour, curdled. They sat there for a short period amid their junk, their furniture, their meaningless and expensive collection of things, the distribution of which had led to the onset of these bitter recriminations. And these few minutes in which they sat silent, no longer daring to look each other in the eye, these minutes seemed to be very long.

"Well, you can see my lawyer," he said, rising wearily.

"I never want to see you as long as I live," she said.

He shrugged his shoulders and left the room, adjusting his tie. She ran to a mirror and looked at herself. She burst into tears. She could not believe that the face she saw was her own. It was puffed. Her eyes were swollen. There were circles under them. Her nose was shiny, and it seemed too long. She felt she was looking at a stranger. She turned away.

He returned, ready to leave.

"Take any goddamn thing you want. You need it. You can have it to comfort yourself in your old age," he said.

He walked out of the room. He slammed the front door.

Exhausted Marie sat down on a love seat. Again she looked around, remembering her life here. Then, in an agony of anger, she went through the house, breaking furniture, tearing books and throwing them on the floor, overturning furniture. As a final act, she smashed the set of Wedgwood which her mother, now dead, had given her as a wedding present. Then she powdered her face and left. In Washington Square she got a cab and had it take her quickly to a dinner engagement for which she was late. Riding up Fifth Avenue, she looked out at people passing on the street. Did they feel as she did? Did they surge with such bitterness? Were their lives ruined?

At the dinner, she got drunk and threw everyone into stitches telling them of her scene with Arthur.

In the meantime, Arthur had gone to his hotel, then to dinner, and then to a theater. Afterward he went to a night club and sat there with some newly found friends, sipping drinks until it closed. He went back to his hotel, feeling dreary.

Arthur and Marie did not see each other for five years. And then one day they passed each other in front of Saint Patrick's Cathedral. He was fat and bald now and he waddled along. She was overdressed and looked dissipated. She, too, had taken on weight, and her cheeks were puffy. There were rings under her eyes. They looked at each other, said hello, and passed on. Shortly after, he died of pneumonia. Marie, his divorced wife, went to court and gained control of the body, arranged the funeral, and got her picture into the papers. It was a big funeral. Many figures in the book world turned out for it. When Arthur's will was read, it was learned he had left his money to Marie. The will spoke for him beyond the grave, confessing his shame and humbly asking her forgiveness. Marie squandered most of the money in one, last, wild dipsomaniacal fling before middle age crushed her with corpulence and ultimately destroyed her looks. Night after night she was to be seen in taverns and night clubs, drunk. After one such night, she was knocked down by an automobile and killed. Her body lay in the morgue for three days before it was identified. She died without heirs, and what remained of the money she had inherited from Arthur went to the state.

Boyhood

I

STEPPING ON THE CRACKS IN THE SIDEWALK, Jim English asked Danny O'Neill when there was going to be a party. Danny, busy thinking his own thoughts and also stepping on sidewalk cracks, didn't hear Jim. He liked Jim, but felt sorry for him. Jim was poor, and everybody in the seventh-grade class thought he was goofy. Danny was sometimes treated badly by the other kids, but Jim was in a worse pickle then he. His father had run away and left him and his mother alone, and she did housework. The other kids all looked down on Jim, and Jim wasn't bright in classes. Sometimes, all you had to do to get a laugh was to use Jim's words. But Danny really liked him and felt sorry for him.

They walked along Indiana Avenue. Danny booted a tin can off the sidewalk into the withered, unkempt grass. Jim gave it a kick. They went out into the street and had a contest to see who could kick the can the farthest. Danny won. He was pleased. But then, it was easy to kick a tin can farther than poor Jim, just as it was easy to be less of a goof than Jim.

Danny kept kicking the tin can. He adjusted his gold-rimmed glasses.

Jim interrupted their silence by asking when there was going to be another party.

"I don't know. I don't *like* parties," Danny answered casually between swipes at the tin can.

"Why? You go to them, don't you?"

"Sometimes," Danny said noncommittally.

Jim looked at him, skeptical. "I don't believe you," he said, shaking his head sidewise.

"I'm not kiddin'. I really don't."

Jim laughed with friendly doubt.

"I don't believe it," he repeated, laughing a second time.

"I don't care if you do or if you don't. I know if I care a whole lot for parties or if I don't."

"No, but I think you're foolin'. I really think you're foolin' me. What about all those parties you used to give?"

"There wasn't so many of them. Once in a while I like a party. Once in a while. And anyway I only gave one."

"I think you're kiddin' me."

"I'm not kiddin' you, English. I only care about parties once in a while. I don't care so much about parties. I only like them now and then."

Danny started stepping on cracks again. He took three steps to a square, but it was difficult. Jim was silent at his side. Danny kept watching how vacant Jim's face was, and he missed several cracks. "Goofy," he muttered to himself.

Jim asked Danny if he didn't honestly know when there was going to be another party.

"Don't know."

Jim seemed hurt.

"You're not gonna get sore because I didn't believe you, are ya?" Jim said conciliatingly.

"Oh, no."

Danny lost interest in stepping on squares. He began touching the railings that enclosed the plots of dried grass in front of the buildings.

"Say, Roslyn Hayes is sort of a nice girl, isn't she?" Jim casually remarked.

"Hm . . . Yes."

Danny caught Jim suddenly dropping his face in confusion.

"Well, there ain't no more baseball games until the war's over," Jim said hurriedly.

"No, there ain't," Danny said, smiling to himself.

"Maybe not for years."

"But, Jim, what makes you so interested in Roslyn Hayes?" Danny asked, thrilled to mention her name, happy to be able to talk about her without giving away how much he loved her.

"I ain't. I just wondered about her. Do you think I'm interested?"

"I dunno. You asked me a lot of questions, and I wondered."

"I'm not. I'm not interested in girls."

"I just sort of wondered," Danny said.

"Rube Waddell's one of my favorite ball players of all times," Danny said.

"I never heard of him."

"Ain't you never heard of Rube Waddell? Honest?"

"No, who was he?"

"Rube Waddell was the world's greatest southpaw, except maybe for Eddie Plank."

"Who did he pitch for, Danny?"

"Philadelphia, the Browns, Minneapolis in the American Association. And I think he pitched in the National League before 1900, but he jumped when they started the American League."

"Why's he your favorite?" Jim asked.

"He's dead," Danny answered.

"Is that why he's your favorite?"

"No. He did anything he felt like doing. That's the way he was."

"Is he really dead?"

"Yes, Jim. I guess he drank himself to death."

"Was he really good?"

"He still holds the strike-out record in the American League."

"Honest?"

"Yeah. Haven't you ever heard about some of the things he used to do?"

"No. What?"

"Go off in the middle of the season without telling Connie Mack. He might even be pitching, and walk off in the fifth or sixth inning, and then maybe some scout or newspaperman would find him a week later, fishing by a country stream, or even pitching for some scrub team in a hick burg. When he was feeling right, he would sometimes walk three men, and then call the side in to sit around the pitching box while he whiffed the next three batters. He could almost make a baseball talk."

Jim didn't know whether or not he should believe Danny.

"Honestly, did they have a pitcher like that?"

"Yes."

Jim gaped, dubious.

"They're always remembering things like that about Rube and writing them up."

Jim was still doubtful, wondering.

"Did you ever see a big-league game?" Danny asked.

Jim looked away, ashamed. Danny saw the queer, sad look in Jim's eyes. He liked Jim. He wished he could make him become something else besides the class goof.

"I seen enough," Jim said.

They came to Jim's home. It was a disheveled, unpainted, slatternly wooden affair between Fifty-eighth and Fifty-ninth on Indiana Avenue. They stood in front of it and didn't say anything for a while.

"Listen, do you want to wait and go to the store with me? It won't take me long, and then we can take a walk," Jim asked.

"No, I gotta hurry."

Jim looked disappointed.

"So long."

"So long."

Danny wandered on.

"Listen, Dan. . . ." Jim called after him.

"Yeah," unenthusiastically.

"Wanna go to a show on Hallowe'en night?"

"No, I can't get out."

Jim looked more disappointed.

II

Danny walked along. Jim didn't even know about Rube Waddell. Nobody liked Jim. He was too big a goof, and he was a string bean. He was sissified and threw a baseball and batted like a girl. He would get killed in a football game. But he felt sorry for Jim. He got a funny kind of feeling being sorry for Jim, as if it were his fault Jim was like he was.

Danny picked up a broken twig and swished it as he walked along. He remembered Jim's questions about Roslyn. Jim would like to go to the parties the kids had, and he would like to have Roslyn for his girl. He was an awful pest with his questions about Roslyn. Jim liked Roslyn. That was funny. A goof like Jim liking a girl like Roslyn. Danny had to laugh. He swished the twig and laughed again. Jim would give a whole lot to know the truth, to know that Roslyn liked Danny O'Neill. She did like him. She liked him, even if she did snub him sometimes. Glenn had said that she liked him.

Danny was very sorry about Jim. He knew that Jim was poor, and he felt sorry he had asked Jim how many big-league games he had ever seen. Yes, he felt sorry for Jim, but, then, Jim was an awful pest and was always asking the goofiest questions and expressing the battiest opinions. He was always saying crazy things about baseball and girls and everything. And he got poor marks in school. What could be battier than to want to go to a show on Hallowe'en?

Danny kept on walking, swishing the piece of dead branch.

III

There was going to be a Hallowe'en surprise party for Billy Morris. Billy was out with the kids—Danny, Dick Buckford, Ralph Borax, Glenn, Tommy O'Connor, Walter Regan, and Andy Houlihan. They had brought Fat Mulloy along, so he could be used as a pretext for running away and going up to

Billy's. They told Billy they'd ditch Fat and hide up at his house and have his mother make some hot chocolate, like she did on Hallowe'en last year. Then they said they would go out again and raise some more Cain.

They were straggling along a street. Danny felt creepy. He imagined he saw strange, funny things, witches the size of the Teenie Weenies in the Sunday *Clarion*, riding around the air on toothpick brooms, monstrous owls with fierce satanic eyes gleaming out of mysterious skies, demons from Hell dancing about fires like Indians on the warpath.

"You're a little goofy, aren't you, O'Neill?" Billy said.

He spoiled Danny's strange fancies.

"Not like you are, singing like a nut all day in school."

"Don't you wish you were able to?"

"Say, you guys, can that and let's do something," Fat Mulloy said.

"Let's kick in a window on George," Dick Buckford said.

"Let's not and say we did," Andy Houlihan said.

"Let's," several others said.

"But listen, you guys, we're liable to get in trouble doing that," Tom O'Connor said.

"Say, O'Connor, will you kindly go home and soak your head," Fat Mulloy bullied.

"Well, I don't wanna start out and land in jail," Tom said.

"You can't kick a window in on George. He's our janitor. We'll have to go someplace else," Ralph Borax said.

"What do you say about gettin' some rotten eggs or old tomatoes an' throwin' 'em in at the Chinks' laundry?" Billy Morris said.

"The Chinks are too mean and dangerous. They'll burn you with hot irons," Glenn said.

"What? Are all you guys yellow?" Fat asked.

No, they weren't yellow, they said, but—

"Well, then, let's do something," Fat said.

Everybody agreed with Fat. They straggled along.

"Wallio. . . . Walliwalli. . . . Wallioooooooooooooooooo," Billy sang monotonously.

"Morris, you better have your head examined," Danny said.

"All right, I'll do that. I sort of like your company anyway. We'll have a lot of fun at Kankakee."

"Let's do something," Fat said.

"Diz is Diz O'Neill is Diz O'Neill is Diz O'Neill is Diz O'Neill is Diz O'Neill is Diz O'Neill is Diz O'Neill," Billy droned in sing-song.

"Yeah, he is that way," Walter Regan said.

Danny ignored them, but he was disturbed.

Dick Buckford joined their chorus of raillery, saying that Goofy O'Neill's suit was a monkey suit because the coat didn't have any belt.

"Any of your business what kind of a suit I wear? Why don't you change your head? It's three times too big for you anyway," Danny said.

Several of the kids laughed at Dick.

"It's brains. You couldn't have a head this big," Dick said, and he laughed in that goofy way of his.

"Brains, hell. Your brains are in your slats," Danny said.

"You haven't even got any brains in your can," Dick said, grinning sheepishly.

"Damn it, let's quit goofing and do something. You guys are worse than my grandmother," Fat said.

"O'Neill is as dizzy as Jim English," Walter Regan said.

"I'm gonna paste somebody in the mouth tonight," Danny said.

"Diz O'Neill is as goofy as goofy as goofy as goofy as Jim English is as goofy as goofy as goofy as goofy as goofy as Diz O'Neill is," Billy sang drily.

"Goofier than English," Dick said.

Danny was hurt and angry. He wanted to be one of the kids like the rest of them, and not the goof of the gang. He did not know why they teased him so much. If he could ignore them, they would stop. But he couldn't. He always lost his temper and wanted to paste somebody. He was going off the handle now. He stepped forward, sneering.

"Damn you fellows."

"O'Neill is a crazy hot-headed Irishman, who is even goofier than Jim English," Billy Morris said.

Danny went for Billy, but Billy was too swift for him. He darted away, chased by leaden-footed Danny. Billy stood across the street, taunting Danny, who had stopped the chase. Dick joined Billy. They shouted at Danny, until he rushed toward them. They waited. Danny went at Dick and Billy with swinging fists, but he succeeded only in catching Billy with a glancing blow on the shoulder before they clinched. They tumbled; Billy was on the bottom and Dick on top. Billy kicked and squirmed and shouted and cursed, but all this effort failed to prevent Danny from rubbing Billy's face against the hard ground. Dick tugged at Danny, slowly dragging him off Billy. The rest of the kids, headed by Walter Regan, rushed across the street, shouting "Pile on." They all yelled, "Get off," "Le-go," "Le-go my ear." "Take your finger outta my eye," "Quit sockin'." Then the scramble quieted down as quickly as it started. They moved on aimlessly, and Billy started kidding Fat Mulloy.

Danny lost his resentment following the free-for-all and the shifting of Billy's attack to Mulloy. He thought of himself as one of the gang and of Fat Mulloy as an outsider. He was going to the party and decided that spoiling the night by his hot-headedness was silly. He was going to the party—and Roslyn would be there.

"Hello, fellows," Jim English said, approaching them from the rear.

They greeted him coldly.

"Where you all goin'?" Jim asked.

"Don't know," Billy said.

"We're going no place," Dick said.

"We're goin' to hell. You wanna come along?" Fat said.

"Say, all foolin' aside, can I go along with you fellahs?" Jim asked.

"We're gonna smash windows and set fires to gates and barns," Dick said.

"Are you really?"

"Yeah."

"An' we're gonna tear down fences," Billy said.

Jim gaped.

"Yeah, and we're gonna throw rotten eggs and tomatoes in at the Chinks in the laundry at Fifty-eight Street," Billy said.

"You better not come along. Soapin' windows is your speed, English," Walter said.

"Can't I come? But are you fellahs really gonna do all those things?"

"Yeah, you better not come along," Danny said.

"We don't want you," Walter Regan said.

"You can't come along. You're nothing but a big string bean," Dick said.

They were in front of the Episcopal Church. They left Jim there, speechless, telling him he would be safe in church. Danny thought he had seen a tear sliding down Jim's cheek. As he walked on, he felt sorry for Jim. But he couldn't do anything. Jim was a string bean and a goof, and they couldn't bring him along on Hallowe'en night. He didn't belong with the gang. Danny didn't know what he could do about Jim, because Jim didn't belong.

"We can't be letting fellows like English come along. We just can't," Danny said.

"No, we can't," Walter said.

We. That meant the bunch, Danny and the others. He was one of We. They only kidded him good-naturedly. We included him, soothed his bruised vanity.

They walked on, and they met a tough bunch of kids from another neighborhood.

"Don't nobody say anything to this bunch. We don't want any trouble with 'em," Walter said.

Tom O'Connor and Glenn said the same thing. Danny sensed what would happen quickly. In a fight, they would lose, and he didn't want to fight. But he knew that this tough gang would crack wise, and, if he didn't call them, he would feel that he was yellow like Dick. If they cracked wise, he would have to call them. Anyway, tough gangs weren't always so tough when you

called their bluff. They might trim this gang in a free-for-all.
Fat would fight. Billy and Ralph would stick. Walter was big
but yellow, and in a tight place he might fight like a cornered
rat. No matter what happened, Danny would be the hero.
He would bear the brunt of the fighting, and, when they got to
the party, Roslyn would hear of his bravery. That was worth
several socks in the jaw. But he didn't want to fight unless—
well, it would make things easier with Roslyn. She would see
that he was something more than the rest of them.

"Hey, you guys tough?" one fellow shouted at them.

"Any of you guys lookin' fer a fight?" a second yelled.

"We eat guys what are tough," a third hollered.

They bragged and cursed among themselves.

Danny's breath came jerkily. He was afraid. He didn't want
to call their bluff. If he didn't, none of the other fellows would.
He was afraid. But if he kept still, he would be—yellow—and
Roslyn at the party would like him better if he was brave—
and sometimes a good fight was a lot of fun. He was afraid,
and his breath came in jerks.

"Hey, any of youse guys tough?"

"Yes," Danny said loudly.

"What?" from several of the other gang.

Three of them rushed across the street. They looked very
tough. One of them, the smallest and most cartoon-like in appearance, was chewing a huge wad of tobacco.

"Where's de guy what sez he's tough?" from the tobacco-
chewer.

"Lemme getta poke at 'im," a second said.

"Listen, fellows, we're not looking for trouble or for any
fight. We didn't do anything to you fellows and we're perfectly
willing to mind our own business," Tom conciliated.

"Yah better not."

"We like 'em tough. Where's de guy what's tough? De
tougher dey are, de harder dey fall."

"Yeah, and we're pretty tough. We're so tough dat when
we spit, rivers overflow," the tobacco-chewer said, plopping a
silver dollar's weight of tobacco juice onto the sidewalk.

There was a brief, tenuous silence. Then the tobacco-chewer repeated his question and clenched his fist. The rest of his gang, noisy, motley, profane, joined him. They outnumbered Danny and the kids, two to one. Several of them poised soot bags.

"Where's the guy?"

"Lemme at him."

"You the guy what spoke?"

"Here I am," Danny said with forced dignity.

He faced them with a scowl that he felt was like Jack Dempsey's scowl when he kayoed Fred Fulton. The tobacco-chewer stepped closer, and his gang crowded in.

"Who are yah? What makes yah think you're tough?"

Danny clenched his fists tightly.

"What's your name?"

"You might tell me yours first—Pug Nose," Danny said.

Fists were clenched and teeth gritted. Five of them surrounded Danny. The others picked men.

"Wait a minute, Spud! . . . wait . . . WAIT!" a tall kid said, stepping in front of Danny.

It was Tim Cleary, who used to sit in front of Danny in school but had moved away.

"I know these guys. They're all right. Friends of mine," Tim said.

"Well, dis wise guy says he's tough."

"He is," Tim said.

"Well, I chew nails."

"Forget it, Spud. These guys are all right."

"Well, if they're friends of yours—but I like 'em tough."

The tobacco-chewer spit again.

"I'm always ready to 'commodate guys what are tough," he said.

"Forget it, Spud. They're a good bunch."

"All right, Tim, but—"

"And what do you say, Dan?"

"It's all right, then, with me, Tim."

The two groups became vaguely friendly. They talked of their evening's braveries, real and imaginary.

"We put an old tree through a window," Dick said.

"We got shagged by de dicks. One of 'em shot at us. We were knockin' fences down," a member of the Cleary bunch said.

"We were almost made into chop suey by the Chinks. Threw tomatoes at 'em. One Chink got plumped in the face. Gee, it was funny. Dick here threw the tomato, an' it hit him in the face," Walter said.

"Yeah, it was a lucky shot," Dick said.

"We caused a blockade by piling boxes on de cartracks over our way on State Street. Cars were stretched along the whole block," Spud said.

Then they separated, mutually refusing offers of uniting.

"Gee, you're crazy," Billy said to Danny.

"Listen, Dizzy, you can't be pulling that stuff with us. Only for Cleary, we'd of had our blocks knocked off," Walter said.

"O'Neill's goofy. Just because he's gotta hard head, and you can't hurt him, he thinks everybody's like that," Billy said.

"Well, anyway, I was all ready to lam the guy that was chewing tobacco," Dick said.

Walter and Glenn also said that if it had come to a fight, they, too, would have done some lamming.

Danny defended himself by declaring that he would have been yellow if he hadn't called them, and that he wasn't yellow, like some guys.

They fooled away an hour, going up one street and down another, placing a few ticktocks on windows, ringing doorbells, planning adventurous ravages. At about nine o'clock they decided it was time to ditch Fat Mulloy. Walter whispered to Billy. The plan was to have Fat break a window, and then in the shag to outrun him. Tom O'Connor and Andy Houlihan, who were slower than Fat, said they were going home and left the bunch. Fat said it was good riddance.

Danny was pleased with himself, planning to cop all the honors at the party. He knew Roslyn would hear of his courage and admire him. She was going to like him. He was going to kiss Roslyn.

Danny knew he was going to kiss Roslyn, and that it would be different from all the other kisses he had ever had at parties.

"Fat, you're afraid to kick in one of the Hunky's windows," Billy said.

"No, I'm not."

"Yes, you are. You're afraid. You're yellow."

"Why don't one of you brave guys do it?"

"We will, but you're afraid to do it."

The others joined Billy in questioning Fat's courage, even Danny. He was one of the bunch and not a Fat Mulloy or— a Jim English.

"I'm gonna punch one of you guys in the snoot," Fat said.

They looked at Danny. He said nothing, walking along casually. Fat looked at Billy and stepped closer to him. Billy retreated.

"I'll sock you in the jaw," Fat bellowed.

"Yes, you might do that, but you're yellow when it comes to kickin' in one of the Hunky's windows," Billy answered.

"Am I?"

"Yes."

"Well, come on. Then I'm gonna lay one on you."

They went to the corner building at Sixtieth and Indiana. Fat walked up to one of the basement windows, and the others ranged themselves close by, ready to run. They were breathless. Fat looked at the window and then glared at Billy. Fat retreated but returned when Billy laughed at him. He kicked viciously, and the glass hit the basement floor with a metallic ring. They fled, soon followed by the Hunky, a swarthy man, who yelled after them in angry foreign accents. They turned corners, dashed up and down alleys, climbed fences, cut through dark gangways, flashed in and out of secret courtways. Danny fell and ripped his stockings. Billy tore his trousers. Ralph was almost hit by an automobile. And Fat lumbered at the rear, puffing, after the Hunky had given up the pursuit, yelling for them to wait. They ran on wildly. Danny lost the others

in an alley. But he was happy. He knew the party would be
lots of fun. He thought how Roslyn would kiss him and admire him for his courage. He was going to have a good
time at the party. Everybody would have some fun. They
were all a good bunch of kids. They didn't mean anything by
teasing each other. And he was one of the bunch, and not a Fat
Mulloy or a Jim English. He was going to the party, a conquering hero. He was going to the party—going—to—kiss—
Roslyn.

IV

Danny arrived at the party. The others were playing tin-tin
and paid no attention to him. He found a seat in a Morris chair
over in a corner and sat there, alone and awkward. He looked
at Roslyn. She sat on the piano stool at the other side of the
parlor, dressed in a worn gray suit of Glenn's. Natalie O'Reedy
sat next to Roslyn. Natalie was the prettiest girl at school.
But Danny watched Roslyn. He gazed around at the other
girls, Helen Scanlan, Loretta Lonigan, Cabby Devlin, and fat
Marion Troy. His eyes turned back to Roslyn.

The tin-tin game grew dull, and they talked. But Danny had
little to say. He was an utter failure at thinking up things to
say when there were girls around, particularly Roslyn. He
watched Roslyn, and slouched further down in the Morris chair.
He wished they would talk of the meeting with Tim Cleary's
bunch. Several times he hinted at it, but no one followed up
his hints. He kept watching Roslyn, until she caught him and
squelched his spirit with a glance. He sat slouched and miserable,
losing the last tatters of the feeling he had had coming here.
He attempted to start conversations with several of the fellows,
baseball with Dick, grammar with Tom O'Connor, dogs with
Glenn. But they all had other people to talk to. Danny slouched
further down in the chair and felt even more miserable.

The party dragged on.

"Le's do something," Danny finally said.

Something, he hoped, would be post-office.

"What?" someone asked.

"I can't play any kissing games. My mother told me not to," Natalie O'Reedy said.

Danny was not alone in his disappointment when Natalie spoiled all hopes of post-office.

"Well, let's do something," Danny said.

"Maybe you'd like to start another fight," Walter answered.

"Listen, Regan, don't get snotty."

Billy told Danny that he couldn't allow any fighting in his house, and also that girls were present. Roslyn stared at Danny with sudden scorn. He said nothing; he couldn't think of anything to say. He slunk further down in the Morris chair.

Tom O'Connor suggested dancing. Marion Troy played the piano, and the fellows who knew how—Tom O'Connor, Glenn, Billy Morris, and Andy Houlihan—danced. The others looked on.

After about six dances, Roslyn said, "Let's sing."

She took Marion's place at the piano, and they all gathered around. Danny stood directly in back of her, with his arms around the shoulders of Dick and Ralph. He felt like one of the bunch again, as he stood looking at her in front of him. She was not only good and sweet and pretty, but also talented, and she could dance and recite and play at a party.

He watched her playing, her small slender hands sliding from key to key with a soft grace. Somehow it made him think of the seagulls flying over Lake Michigan off Jackson Park. Her hands impressed him that way.

They sang *Mickey* several times. Everybody liked it.

> "*Mickey, lovely Mickey,*
> *With your hair of raven hue,*
> *And your smilin' so beguilin',*
> *There's a bit of Killarney bit of the Blarney, too.*
> *Childhood in the wildwood,*
> *Like a wild sunflower you grew.*
> *Mickey, lovely Mickey,*
> *Can you blame anyone for falling in love with you?*"

They sang other songs: *Just a Baby's Prayer at Twilight, Over There, America, Here's My Boy, We'll Knock the 'Ell Out of Kelly.*

Danny sang throatily, unable to carry a tune. He thought that now his dreams would begin to come true. For a moment, it seemed as though Dick and Ralph next to him were not real any more. Everything seemed shadowy, except Roslyn's white hands. He kept watching her hands. They were so vivid, white, beautiful. Then he daydreamed. He thought of wartorn French roads and towns, of airplane fights, sea battles in uncharted waters. And through all these came Roslyn, the girl with the white hands, to kiss him. He watched those hands, the hands of a wisp of a wonderful girl in a boy's suit, sliding from key to key and making him think of the seagulls over Lake Michigan. Roslyn.

Suddenly he grew intensely lonely. He felt out of place at the party, a misfit. The girl before him, with the beautiful white hands, was a stranger. She was worse than a stranger. She was an enemy, ready to hurt him every time she could. And no one could hurt Danny O'Neill as much as Roslyn. The whole room was full of strangers, half-sneering strangers who were jealous of him, afraid of him, hating him. They were all friends, but he remained on the outside. He had to fight against them all the time, and he was tired of it. He wished his folks would move to a new neighborhood, where he could start all over again. He looked around from face to face. He wanted to punch them all, to go from person to person and bust each one—except Roslyn. He was lonely, and he didn't belong at parties where there were a lot of girls. He belonged on a baseball field or in a fight. He was lonely.

> *"Just a baby's prayer at twilight*
> *For his daddy over there."*

V

Mrs. Morris called them into the dining room for sandwiches and hot chocolate. Danny thought she was very gracious.

"Eats, eats, everybody," Billy said.

"Tie Buckford up so the rest of us'll get a chance," Andy Houlihan said.

"Yes, we better tie him up," Danny said.

He didn't feel so lonely now. The whole bunch was so good-natured. He liked them all.

"Go on, O'Neill! At my party you ate six sandwiches," Dick said.

Roslyn gave Danny a sudden, darting look.

"Now, line up, and each boy select his partner," Mrs. Morris said.

Danny wanted to walk across the room and take Roslyn's arm, but he couldn't. He stood in a corner and looked at the geranium-patterned wallpaper. Tommy O'Connor was near him, and Danny felt awkward, and so he started talking with Tommy about diagramming sentences. Tommy wasn't interested. He went over to where Dick was standing and asked Dick about his uncle, a minor-league ball player. Dick was busy talking with Helen Scanlan. Danny had been in love with her until he began to love Roslyn in the sixth grade. He looked around the room, shifted his weight from foot to foot, and felt completely miserable and unnecessary. He wished Roslyn would come over and stand next to him. He glanced at her, and she glanced the other way. He watched her, standing demure and possessed. He wanted her for a partner, and he was afraid to ask her. The other fellows seemed equally hesitant about selecting a partner. They stood about the room and waited.

"Come on now, boys. Line up with your partners," Mrs. Morris said.

Finally Billy Morris lined up beside Natalie. Glenn pulled Roslyn by the elbow, next to him, behind Billy and Natalie. The others rapidly found partners, except Danny. He marched into the dining room at the end of the procession, feeling like a goof and a dunce and wishing he hadn't come.

The table was set with small, yellow-ribboned baskets at each plate, while orange streamers were draped from a pie in the center. More orange streamers hung down from the chandelier. Under each yellow paper napkin there was a favor.

They sat down and immediately began talking loudly. Everyone was curious about everyone else's favor, except Danny's. Glenn pulled out a small whistle, which he futilely attempted to blow, and they all laughed. Roslyn displayed a tiny automobile, which she rolled around her plate, and there was more laughing. Billy held up a miniature washing board and set the party into spasms when he rubbed on it with mock vigor.

"Washing, washing today. I'm forced to take in washing by my wife, Natalie." They all screamed with laughter. "She makes me work, washing for a living. Washing. Washing," he said.

Danny's favor was a dunce cap of reduced size. He put it on and grimaced awkwardly. No one noticed him. They continued to look at Billy, who was pretending to tear Dick's shirt in the washing.

"Gotta go faster and faster. Life beats me when I loaf," Billy said, rubbing vigorously, utilizing his entire body in movement.

They roared.

Danny envied Billy. He wished he could think of funny things to say, like Billy did. He wished he could make people laugh and like him, as Billy did. He wished he wasn't something of a dunce. He never could think of anything to say. He sat and played with his dunce cap and tried to think of something funny, but couldn't. He played with his dunce cap and made funny motions with his arms.

"Look-it," Marion Troy said, noticing him and causing everyone to give him a passing glance of attention.

They all seemed to be having a good time except Danny. No one laughed at his jokes. The other fellows, particularly Billy, could have said the same things and made everybody laugh. Billy's description of how he brought Chinese laundry checks to school was a scream. Danny tried to have a good time, and he laughed with all the effort of a man laboring. But he kept telling himself that he didn't belong at parties.

Several times, as Danny tried to repeat how goofy Jim English was, he was hit in the eye with a peanut. The fourth time he was hit, he started shooting peanuts back.

"Cut out slingin' peanuts, O'Neill. You're not home now," Billy said.

"Yes, this isn't a barn," Dick said.

Dick had started the peanut throwing.

Danny blushed. He imagined Roslyn staring at him, with eyes that bored into his soul. He was afraid to face her. His cheeks grew redder and redder. He wished he had never come to the party and vowed that next week at school he would paste every fellow present in the snoot.

VI

As the party was breaking up, Tom O'Connor, Walter Regan, Dick Buckford, and Glenn commenced fooling around and wrestling in the parlor. Danny was caught in between them. They were shoving and pushing, and he stepped aside. He didn't want to fool around. He stood aside, with his back to the four of them. Suddenly he was shoved violently from the rear and pitched forward. Everyone laughed, laughter that burned like streaks of flame. He got up, angry. His glasses fell off. He picked them up bent. When he tried to straighten them, they split in two. He was angry. He was sure that Wallie Regan had pushed him, but he couldn't prove it. He put his broken glasses into his pocket.

"Who pushed me?" he growled at Walter.

No one answered. Glenn and Walter snickered.

"If I find out who pushed me and broke my glasses, I'll kill him," he said to Walter.

"What are you lookin' at me for?" Walter asked blandly.

"Because you did it."

"I did not."

"You did, too."

"You're a liar."

"Who's a liar?"

"You are if you say I did it."

Danny stepped forward, and Walter retreated. Billy Morris moved between the two of them and said that they were in his house. He looked scornfully at Danny. Billy's mother was disturbed, and asked the boys please not to start a fight and break any of her furniture.

Outside, the kids would not allow them to fight. They haggled and argued.

"Regan'll kill you," Dick said.

"Come on an' let him try."

"Why, you're goofy. Look at how much bigger than you Regan is," Ralph said.

"Listen, he's goofy. You can't hurt him. What's the use of fighting with a guy like that?" Andy Houlihan said.

Danny closed in towards Andy.

"You little shrimp."

Ralph, Walter, and Dick crowded in between Danny and the cowering Andy Houlihan.

"Come on, Regan. I'll take you an' Houlihan."

"I gotta go home. I can't be hanging around fighting somebody who's as goofy as you."

Danny clenched his fists and went for Walter, but he was caught from behind by Ralph and Dick.

"Come on, Glenn, I can't be staying out all night to watch that roughneck start a fight. Take me home," Roslyn said.

Glenn and Roslyn started to leave. Walter and Andy joined them. Danny was crying as he shouted after them. He cursed Ralph and Dick, too. He crossed the street and went home alone.

He walked home slowly. The night was shivery and silent on Fifty-eighth Street. The moon was weird, like a witch. Danny cried and cursed.

VII

On the following Sunday, Danny went to a movie at the Prairie Theater at Fifty-eighth and Prairie Avenue with Fat Mulloy. Danny still felt humiliated about Billy's party. At school they had laughed at him.

After the show Danny and Fat stopped at a soda fountain next door to the show.

"Fat, do you like Regan?"

"No."

"I was wonderin'. I'm gonna get him."

Fat doubted Danny's ability to get Regan. Danny repeated that he would, and could, get Regan. He knew he could knock the hell out of Regan, but he was anxious. The bunch would all be with Regan. He was rich and could buy them sodas and candy. Sometimes he took them riding in his father's automobile. It was a big limousine with his father's initials on the door. Danny knew he would be out of the bunch if he fought with Regan. He knew he would lose any friendship that Glenn might have for him. Glenn was only a runt and even a sissy, but he was Roslyn's cousin. He loved Roslyn and thought he should remain friendly with Glenn. If he beat up Regan, he would be left out of parties, too. He would be lonely. But he had to get Regan. And he would.

Fat and Danny talked over their sodas. Suddenly Fat pointed out of the window and said, "There's Regan."

Danny turned to see Regan pass by. Danny was afraid.

"Here's your chance," Fat said.

Danny rushed out of the soda parlor and called after Regan in a mood of desperation.

"Listen, Regan, I want to see you."

"What for? I'm in a hurry."

Regan walked back slowly.

"What do you wanna see me for? I'm in a hurry."

"Commere an' I'll tell you."

Danny found himself calm now. He was calm and he hated

Regan. He hated Regan so much that he wanted to keep punching him and watch his face bleed.

"You shoved me."

"I didn't."

"You're a liar."

"I'm not a liar."

"You are. Now, listen. Will you fight?"

"I'm in a hurry. Anyway, I could lick you."

"Are you yellow or will you fight?"

"I'm in a hurry, and I can't now. Anyway, I could lick you."

"You *can*?"

"Can't I, Fat?"

Slap! The back of Danny's right hand snapped against Regan's lip, causing a thick trickle of blood. Danny was thrilled by the sight of Regan's blood.

"Damn you, will you fight now?"

"I can't now. I haven't the time, I tell you. But I'll get even with you for this. I'll settle with you."

Regan walked away.

"Yellow," Danny shouted after him.

"Yellow belly," Fat yelled.

VIII

"Are you going to Roslyn's party tonight?" Ralph asked Danny.

It was an autumn-weary day in the middle of November. Ralph and Danny were walking together on Indiana Avenue.

"No. I'm not invited."

"I don't think anyone was especially invited. She saw Billy and all of us the other day and asked us to come. Said she couldn't go up to everyone separately and ask them. She said she'd feel kind of funny if she did."

"Well, she never invited me. I saw her a couple of times last week, and she never invited me."

"Well, I know she meant that everybody should come."

"No, she never invited me."

"Well, I think she meant everybody. I know I'm goin', and I'm gonna have a good time."

"Hooray—Hooray—Giddap—Giddap—Bang, Bang, Bang —Look out, here I come on Pinto, chased by the sheriff, Fat Mulloy. Bang, Bang, Bang."

It was Billy Morris. He galloped past them, turned around, galloped back, and walked along at their side.

"Billy, in a way you're goofy," Ralph said.

Billy didn't say anything. They stopped in front of his home, a three-story, gray brick building.

"Where you going, Ralph?"

"Nowheres."

"And you?"

"Same place."

"Let's all go together. Or let's just sit here and talk for a while."

They sat down on Billy's front steps.

"I gotta go upstairs and take a bath for the party in a little while," Billy said.

Danny didn't want to sit, talking with them. It was one of those days when he wanted to be alone. But he thought that he might get them to go over to Roslyn's home and take a walk down around that neighborhood. Then maybe they would meet Roslyn, and she might invite him to her party. He knew Roslyn liked him despite everything. It was just pride that made her act like she did. Glenn once told him that she cared for him.

"Let's go up and see Glenn," Danny said.

"Glenn's gone downtown to get some favors for the party," Billy answered.

"We ought to have a good time tonight," Ralph said.

"Yeah, I always have a good time if Natalie is around. Gee, but she's a pip. She's got wonderful legs, too," Billy said.

"Yeah, she has, all right," Ralph said.

"She's more than all right. She's a pip," Billy said.

Danny envied Ralph and Billy. He was jealous of the easy

way in which they talked of girls, of their popularity, and of their invitations to Roslyn's party. He wished he could talk of, and to, girls as naturally, and that he could get along with them as well as Billy or Ralph did.

"Let's take a walk down and see Andy Houlihan. Maybe he'll have a good bonfire going in the prairie next to his house," Danny said.

Andy lived one block away from Roslyn. Maybe they would see her if they went around that neighborhood.

"It's too far. I gotta get ready for the party," Billy said.

"So do I," from Ralph.

"We don't have to stay long," Danny said.

"Helen Scanlan's going to be at the party tonight, isn't she?" Ralph asked.

"Yeah. Say, you kind of like her, don't you?" Billy asked.

"Yes, she's a nice kid," Ralph said.

"She's another pip, all right. She's got legs almost as good as Natalie's," Billy said, getting enthusiastic.

"Yes, she has."

"I wouldn't mind playing post-office tonight. Oh, boy! . . . with Natalie tonight. With some girls, too, but not Natalie, you can get 'em in the dark and cop a couple of feels," Billy said.

"Well, I wouldn't mind, either."

Danny wanted to protest against something, but he couldn't find any word that would tell him what that something was. He wanted to protest, because somewhere there was unfairness. He wanted to know why Ralph and Billy got along so much better than he did, and why people liked them better. He wanted to know why they should be invited to the party and not he. He could do almost everything better than either of them. He could fight, wrestle, play football better than they. They didn't even know the first thing about basketball. He got better marks in school, too. All Billy could do better than Danny was dance and make wisecracks. There was something unfair in the world somewhere, and he wanted to protest about it.

"Natalie and Helen are the best lookers in school," Billy

said, and Danny but half heard the remark. He sat pitying himself. There was something unfair, and he was being hurt because of unfairness and he wanted to fight, even though he was afraid of fighting.

"Yeah," Ralph said.

"Roslyn used to be, but she fixes her hair up funny now, and she's got skinny legs," Billy said.

Danny hated Billy for this remark. He looked at Billy, thinking of Billy's own toothpick legs, his ugly peanut of a head, his dirty brown skin. He hated Billy, and told himself that Roslyn was an angel.

"Billy, didn't Roslyn mean for everyone to come to her party?" Ralph asked.

"I guess so. Why?"

"I was telling Danny that, and he said it didn't mean him."

"She said she wanted everyone, but, then, she doesn't like him."

"Who wants to go to her damn party?" Danny said.

"I do. I expect to have some fun," Billy said.

A few minutes later Danny left, determined that Ralph, Billy, and Roslyn, too, could all roast in the hottest part of Hell. But he was glad the kids didn't know that he was so much in love with Roslyn. If they did, they'd never stop ragging him.

He had intended to go home. He walked down to Sixty-first and South Park and proceeded to go around the block several times. Each time he passed a lace-curtained window on the second floor of an ornate building in the middle of the block, he stopped and gazed up, as if interested in the stars that were just coming out.

A passer-by might have noticed that he was wistful as he gazed up past the lace curtains.

IX

Danny heard all about Roslyn's party. He was told that it was the best party ever given. They had played spin-

the-bottle, post-office, wink, and tin-tin. Roslyn's father had
played with them, and the kids said he was a regular fellow.
And there had been all kinds of eats, too. Roslyn had called
Andy Houlihan to the post-office a number of times, and Helen
Scanlan had been sweet to Ralph. Glenn had copped off Natalie. He was a devil with the women. Billy Morris had been
a scream. Every time he talked, he had made the whole party
laugh. It had been a scream when he plopped the peanut into
Dick's coffee.

And there were half-whispered conversations of what had
been said and done in the post-office.

X

Danny met Ralph one afternoon about a week after Roslyn's party. He hadn't been playing with the bunch of late and
was lonesome. He was glad to see Ralph and wanted to talk
to him about a lot of things, particularly about Roslyn and
her party. She had spoken to him, asking him why he hadn't
come. He knew she liked him. He was glad to see Ralph, too,
and wanted to talk about Roslyn.

"Hello, Ralph, how are you?"

"All right," Ralph answered with self-conscious casualness.

"Where you going?"

"No place."

"Let's go together," Danny said.

Ralph didn't answer. They walked slowly.

"You're kind of droopy. Do you know it?" Ralph said suddenly, following his remark with a scornful laugh.

Danny looked at Ralph.

"Yes, you're dizzy."

"How do you get that way?" Ralph asked, muffling his anger.

"Yes, you're dizzy."

"Well, what if I am?"

"Nothing. Only you're dizzy and a droopy drawers."

"Supposing I am?"

"Nothing."

Ralph laughed again.

"Yes, you're an old droop. Look at the way you walk."

"No, I'm not. I just walk—slow."

Ralph laughed again.

"You're not any too fast or straight when you walk," Danny said.

"I'm not a droopy drawers," Ralph said.

He laughed again.

"You're worse."

"I am?" Ralph asked. He was angry, and his voice throbbed.

"Yes, what are you gonna do about it?" Danny asked, arrogant.

"I am worse than a droopy drawers?"

"Yes."

"Well, what am I?" Ralph asked menacingly.

Danny couldn't think of anything more to say. He answered that Ralph was—just worse than a droopy drawers. That was all. He was worse.

They glowered, and Ralph cried slightly, from anger.

"Take that back," he demanded.

"Not unless you do."

"Take it back."

"No."

"I beat you once."

"That was in the fifth grade. But you can't do it again," Danny taunted.

"I beat you once. I punched the crap out of you. I can do it again if I want to."

"You're afraid to try it again."

"Remember that time you socked Billy Morris? Well, I licked you, didn't I?"

"Yes, but you can't now. Go get Morris, and I'll take the two of you."

"You know I can lick you if I want to."

"Wanna fight?" Danny asked.

"I licked you once. You just be careful about saying that I'm worse than an old droopy drawers."

"Then you watch what you say."

"Suppose I don't?"

"Then I won't."

"Don't forget that I beat you once."

"I can take you and Billy together now."

"You think you're tough, don't you?"

"No, but I'm tougher than you are," Danny said.

They walked for a block, silent. Then Ralph repeated that he once licked Danny, and Danny repeated that he could lick Ralph. Ralph repeated and Danny repeated.

"I can't play with you any more," Ralph suddenly said.

Danny ignored Ralph.

"I can't play with you any more, because my mother knows there's swearing in your house, and your aunt gets drunk."

"It isn't so," Danny said hotly.

"It is," Ralph said. "I don't care. My mother told me not to play with you any more. She says you'll grow up to be a bad influence."

"Well, don't walk with me," Danny said.

"You started walking with me," Ralph said.

"I'm walking this way, and I'm gonna keep walking," Danny said.

"So am I."

They strolled on side by side, without any further conversation.

XI

Walter Regan, Ralph, Billy, Dick, Glenn, Andy Houlihan, Fat Mulloy, a kid nicknamed Blackie, new at St. Patrick's, and Danny were all standing in front of school.

"Diz here is goofy," Dick said.

"He's crazy. Crazy people always have dreamy eyes like he got. You know, eyes that are always asleep," Billy said.

"What if I am?" Danny answered.

"No if about it," Dick said.

"Shut up, Buckford!"

Dick grinned foolishly.

"Gee, you're a hot-headed Irishman all right," Billy said.

"Well, Dick gives me a pain. If he wasn't yellow, I'd bust his mush for him."

"He's goofy with an ivory head. He's the kind of a guy you can't hurt. You keep hitting him until you get tired. He's got an ivory head," Dick said.

Glenn and Billy started poking each other in the ribs and wrestling. Then they ran around in circles, chasing each other, and shouting. Soon they were on the ground, wrestling. Walter Regan and Dick joined in with a whoop. Danny moved to do likewise.

"Who asked you in?" Walter asked.

"None of your damn business."

"It is, too, my business who I play with."

"And mine, too," Glenn said, getting up.

"And I don't wanna play with a roughneck Irishman who is always lookin' for a fight. Why, you're worse than the Germans," Walter said.

"Yes, and my mother told me to have nothing to do with him because there's always a lot of swearin' and cursin' goin' on at his house," Ralph said.

"Yes, and he hasn't any breeding. He's like a Hun, throwing peanuts at parties and starting fights in other people's houses," Billy said.

"He's goofy about my cousin, and she hates him," Glenn said.

They laughed at him.

The remarks had come so swiftly that Danny was without a reply. He stuttered in anger. Walter Regan invited the bunch to go with him, and they all accepted.

"You can't come," he said to Danny.

"Who wants to play with a yellow belly?"

"You can't."

They all left, laughing back at Danny, who stood, tearful and defiant, shaking his fists at them.

XII

Danny remained in front of the school for about five minutes. He was hurt and angry. Then he headed east along Sixty-first Street, planning to go for a walk all the way to Jackson Park. He was lonely and, whenever he felt that way, he took a long walk. He usually walked in Washington Park, but today he'd walk in Jackson Park. As he drooped along, he planned scenes bloody with the revenge he would wreak. When he grew up and became a great basketball player and a greater fighter than Benny Leonard, he would snub them. And the next time they needed him in a scrap, he wouldn't stick with them. He was through with them, and he could wait for his revenge until he became great. He was through with them, and all winter he would remain at home, reading.

He thought of Roslyn. He wondered if Glenn had told the truth. Did she hate him? If she did, well, the hell with her, too. Some day she, all of them, would feel sorry. If he met her he would snub her. He did meet her. She opened her mouth to speak. Danny didn't look at her. In fact, he didn't see her. After she passed, she turned around and yelled, "Funny face."

He came to his senses with a start and turned around.

"Funny face," she repeated.

"If I'm a Funny Face, you're one, too," he said.

She stuck up her small nose, turned her head pertly, and walked away.

He felt like a fool. He was sorry, and angry. He told himself that she could go to the devil, and for an entire block he imagined her burning in Hell.

When he came to Jackson Park, his mood changed. He became moody and lost in a vaporous sadness. There was a sadness about the park, half mellow with autumn, half bare with the wounds of the early winter winds. The park seemed to console him. He forgot all about the raggings he received from the bunch. He imagined himself alone, away from the world, a Robinson Crusoe on some distant sphere. Things seemed strange to him. He imagined that he was a soul in Purgatory, a soul cast there willy-nilly.

He walked. The park seemed bare, cold, strange, lonely; dusk covered it like a robe. Overhead, a frosty moon had blown the sun out of the sky, sinking it in the oblivion of another day. He saw etched against the distant sky the vague outlines of a human figure. He watched it approach slowly. It was bent and familiar. He looked at it, and then at the moon, alone and companionless in a sky empty of stars. He remembered all that had hurt him in the past weeks. He was lonely. The figure was upon him.

"Hello, Danny," it said.

"Hello, Jim."

"What are you doing here?" Danny asked.

"Oh, taking a walk," Jim said.

"So am I. I like Jackson Park better than Washington Park," Danny said.

"So do I," Jim said.

Danny wished he lived in the Jackson Park neighborhood and knew a new bunch of kids.

"Goin' home? It's late and it'll be a long walk."

"We can get a hitch on a truck," Danny said.

"Where were you going?" Jim said.

"Over to the lake."

Jim seemed moody, too. They walked on to the lake in silence and looked at it.

"Looks rough today," Jim said.

"It's always rough at this time of year. It's kind of cold, and the wind is coming up," Danny said.

"Yes, it is," Jim said.

"It's gray and kind of dirty," Danny said.

"Oh, boy, what whitecaps," Jim said.

"I like the noise it makes. I like it kind of wild," Danny said.

"I don't. You couldn't swim in it this way," Jim said.

"I'd like to. I'm going to try and swim in it against those waves some time."

"I don't believe you."

"I will some day," Danny said.

The two boys stood before the lake in the gathering darkness, looking at it, listening to the wild monotony of its slashing waves. Danny looked far, far out and saw the dark horizon. He looked and looked. He wanted to see the seagulls today, flying and crying in the darkness over the rough lake. He thought of Roslyn as a seagull. But he saw none. There was nothing but gray water, gray water and waves and foaming whitecaps on the lake. And there was no one around, no one in sight, only himself and Jim. They stood looking at the lake.

"Yes, it's better this way than when it's calm," Danny said. They turned and walked back.

"Yes."

They walked along together.

"Where were the kids today?" Jim asked.

"I had a quarrel with 'em. They give me a pain, and none of them would fight."

"I don't like them either," Jim said.

Danny didn't answer.

"Was Glenn with 'em?" Jim asked.

"Yeah."

"Does he still tease his cousin?"

"He ought to. She's an old Funny Face. Worse than he is."

"I thought she was a nice girl."

"She gives me a pain."

"I kinda think she's all right," Jim said.

Danny changed the subject to baseball. And he had enough money to pay for both their carfares. They talked baseball all the way home on the car. They got off at Sixty-first and South Park. Danny looked up at Roslyn's window. It was lit up. He wished she'd look out and see him. They walked on.

Just as they were parting at Fifty-first and South Park, Danny said, "Listen, Jim, you come over to my house after school tomorrow?"

"Sure," Jim said.

"Danny, was that true what you told me about Rube Waddell?" Jim called after him.

"Yeah. I'll show you his records in the Spaulding and Reich guides tomorrow. I like a guy like him."

"So long, Danny."

"So long, Jim."